Danica Winters is a multiple-award-winning, bestselling author who writes books that grip readers with their ability to drive emotion through suspense and occasionally a touch of magic. When she's not working, she can be found in the wilds of Montana, testing her patience while she tries to hone her skills at various crafts—quilting, pottery and painting are not her areas of expertise. She believes the cup is neither half-full nor half-empty, but it better be filled with wine. Visit her website at danicawinters.net

Two-time RITA® Award nominee and Golden Quill award winner **Jennifer Morey** writes single-title contemporary romance and page-turning romantic suspense. She has a geology degree and has managed export programs in compliance with the International Traffic in Arms Regulations (ITAR) for the aerospace industry. She lives at the foot of the Rocky Mountains in Denver, Colorado, and loves to hear from readers through her website, jennifermorey.com, or Facebook.

HER ASSASSIN
FOR HIRE

DANICA WINTERS

COLTON FAMILY
BODYGUARD

JENNIFER MOREY

MIX

Paper from
responsible sources

FSC   FSC C007464

This book is produced from independently certified FSC™
paper to ensure responsible forest management.

For more information visit www.harpercollins.co.uk/green

Printed and bound in Spain
by CPI, Barcelona

MILLS & BOON

First Published in Great Britain 2020
by Mills & Boon, an imprint of HarperCollins*Publishers*
1 London Bridge Street, London, SE1 9GF

Her Assassin For Hire © 2020 Danica Winters
Colton Family Bodyguard © 2020 Harlequin Books S.A.

Special thanks and acknowledgement are given to Jennifer Morey for her contribution to *The Coltons of Mustang Valley* series.

ISBN: 978-0-263-28019-7

0220

HER ASSASSIN
FOR HIRE

DANICA WINTERS

To Mac, don't worry, I'll keep bringing the cheese.

This series wouldn't have been possible without a great team of people, including Melanie Calahan and Clare Wood, my #1k1hr friends, Jill Marsal and the editors at Mills & Boon—thank you for all your hard work.

Also, thank you to my readers. You keep me writing.

Chapter One

In life, there comes a point when all people are forced to pick a side and show who they really are. In the stories, it was always good versus evil—and those with the purest hearts won. However, in reality, nothing was ever that simple.

As a child, Zoey Martin had a favorite maple tree. It stood proud and unyielding in her family's front yard, a symbol of strength and longevity. She would spend hours climbing around, whispering her secrets into its bark and imagining her future…a future that would bring only happiness and success. Each dream was a bit different, but there was always the same ending— her, standing in front of a crowd of cheering fans, wearing the shining armor of a knight who had once again saved the innocent.

She had relied on the strength of the maple tree and over the years had almost come to take it for granted. It was always there, always shielding her as she hoped to shield others someday. In a way it was her hero.

One day, when she was nearly ten years old, the seemingly healthy limb she had been sitting on snapped beneath her. She had tumbled to the ground. Even now, so many years later, if she closed her eyes and concentrated, she could still hear her leg snapping as she struck the unyielding roots of the behemoth she had loved.

Over the years, when her first boyfriend cheated on her with her best friend, and later when her college boyfriend ghosted her, she thought back to her tree. It was her first hard-learned lesson in the wicked truths of trust—just because everything looked good from the outside, healthy even, it didn't mean its heart wasn't rotten.

Since then, Zoey Martin had been happy giving her trust to a few within her family. Her only heroes were their STEALTH team and their teams of courageous contractors.

Even limiting who she loved and trusted, ever since her sister's death, she felt herself tumbling to the ground. Her family's work in STEALTH, something she believed in so strongly, had pulled the stable branch out from under her family.

She'd had to move forward in the faith that she was sure she was bringing something positive to the world.

She tugged down the edge of her hot pink dress as she sauntered to the front of the tent. Her high heels clicked on the hardwood floor she had her staff put down just so her shoes wouldn't stick in the grass. Today everything had to be perfect...especially her appearance.

Rubbing her lips together, ensuring her specially blended-to-match lipstick was in place, she turned to face her audience.

They looked bored, most checking their phones or staring longingly at the bar in the corner of the room. No doubt, the crowd was made up of gold-laden investors, soggy board members and straight-backed rivals.

They all held their pints of beer or flutes of champagne like lifelines.

She couldn't wait to see their faces when the fun started.

So far, it had been two days of looking over the next year's models of top-of-the-line weaponry and tactical gear, speeches on the merits of self-protection and gun advocacy, and the late-night bar meetings that led to the next morning's multimillion-dollar deals. And she had one hell of a hangover.

Though their new line of tac-gear wasn't through the final phases of testing, they were taking orders. And after today, they were going to come flooding in.

There was a smattering of polite but unenthusiastic applause as she took out her prepared speech. She couldn't blame those in attendance for their lackluster response. Zoey wasn't one of her brothers. Until recently, it had always been Jarrod who had been the face of their private government contracting company, STEALTH, and no matter where Jarrod went, with his wide jaw and Dwayne "The Rock" Johnson brooding but sexy scowl, women and money followed. Thankfully her new friend and her brother's fiancée, Mindy Kohl, had put a stop to that party and Jarrod had settled down.

As Zoey cleared her throat, she checked to make sure her team was in place. The two men stood at each of the front corners of the tent in ready position, looking more like her private security team in their black suits and earpieces than what she had actually brought them here for.

She looked toward the waitstaff who were lowering the lights and closing the flaps to shut out the bright, midevening sun. The lights on the catwalk came to life, readying for the show.

A smile played at the corner of her lips as she adjusted her formfitting little hot pink dress one more time.

She didn't want to die...but if this was how she went out, at least she'd go out with one hell of a bang.

Either way, she was about to become infamous.

"Good afternoon, ladies and gentlemen," she started, looking out over the crowd as they found their seats. Most took out their phones like they were going to take notes, but in reality, were probably checking their backlog of emails from their days away from the office. "I appreciate you coming to the Heinrich and Kohl Alliance demonstration today."

It felt strange to have their new venture into tactical gear manufacturing umbrellaed under Mindy's company. But it was best to stay shielded from the public... especially when it came to her family and the worldwide manhunt that centered on them. Anonymity was their only saving grace.

"As some of you may know, our team has been working diligently over the last few months to bring you a new and innovative line of tactical gear and body armor." A man slipped into the tent and into one of the many open seats at the back of the room, carefully keeping to the shadows.

"Our decision," she said, thinking of Mindy, "to expand our manufacturing businesses to include self-protection and advocacy, came from a very honest place." And she honestly couldn't help but feel like she was using her sister Trish's death to profit—and she hated herself for it.

She cleared her throat as a few people turned off their phones and glanced up at her. "Last fall, my sister was shot and killed in the streets of Turkey." The last few voices in the crowd were silenced. "She had been there on a mission of her choosing. She was wearing body armor and was well equipped for the fight she knew she would face. But when the mission played out, her tac-gear and armor weren't enough to save her."

A woman near the catwalk shifted in her seat like talk of such a death at an arms show and convention was strictly taboo. Regardless of social mores, it was the truth. These people had to know death, and fear it, as they were the only constants in their line of work.

"Her death was a major blow not only to our family but to our business, as well. She was our linchpin, the one who always brought us together even in the hardest of times. She was our rock. And now she is gone." A lump rose in her throat, but she forced the emotional traitor to submit as she swallowed it away. "As you can imagine, thoughts of vengeance led to plans of retaliation against the group responsible. However, these thoughts were soon checked. Logic must reign when emotions threaten to rebel."

There were a few ill-timed chuckles, but she appreciated them.

"After careful planning, we chose to use her legacy to advocate for positive change, and this new line of tactical gear was designed in her honor. Through our work, we hope that no one else will ever have to endure such a tragedy."

She paused. There were no longer any dim lights from people playing on their cell phones in the crowd. Finally, she had everyone's rapt attention. *Perfect*.

"At H&K, we are in the final stages of testing our new lightweight phase armor we have affectionately dubbed Monster Wear. Today we will be taking pre-orders for our designs. Please feel free to see any one of our representatives, those with the white name tags, throughout the rest of the conference." She waved at two women who were staged beside the main entrance. "Without further ado, we are excited to unveil our full line of Monster Tactical Gear and Specialty Fashion for you today."

She gave a small clap, and the curtains opened from the side of the tent and their first model came out and strutted down the runway. He had on their line of UV protection sunglasses, their shellback tactical Cyclops plate carrier, tac pants and full duty gear. With his well-toned arms and buttery tan, the man looked like he'd just walked off the battlefield. *Perfect.*

Several more men and women followed, each wearing gear from the new line, but none wearing the best-of-the-best—at least not yet.

Zoey scanned the crowd. They seemed interested, but underwhelmed by the nearly generic gear on display. Which was, for now, just fine by her.

The man who had come in late stood up and moved closer to the catwalk. Zoey couldn't see his face, but something about his dark brown hair and V-shaped body seemed all too familiar. Maybe it was the way he roll-walked through the crowd, or how he seemed to be most comfortable in the shadows, but she was intrigued.

Her thoughts moved to Eli Wayne, her ex-boyfriend and STEALTH's former ghostlike point man. From the back, the man looked just like him.

The lump in her throat returned.

It was more than possible he would be here, sniffing around her demonstration in hopes of making contact with her. He'd always been like that, lurking in the darkness and waiting to sweep her off her feet just when she was at her most vulnerable—it was also one of the things that had made her fall for him in the first place.

In many ways, she missed him. And she hated him for breaking her heart. And… *Ugh… No.* She couldn't let thoughts of Eli mess with her head. She was here to do her job. To make her family proud, and to put him and their cursed past even further behind her.

She had to focus.

Ten different models moved through their line of gear, each doing quick changes in the back, before reappearing on the catwalk. A few in the crowd oohed and ahhed as the models rolled out.

As the time grew nearer to unveil their greatest achievements, the nervousness swelled within her. She took a series of deep breaths as she tried to control herself. This was just a simple event—a sales pitch. It was nothing in comparison to sitting behind the screen and running IT for her family as they infiltrated and took down an enemy encampment. Now, that was something to be nervous about. One poorly timed click of the button, one little sneeze, and she could blow away an entire village—or hurt one of her own.

And yet there she was, getting butterflies at a fashion show. Maybe she was more of a girlie girl than she had realized. Or maybe it was the thought of Eli being in the room that was really getting to her.

She ran her hands down her dress, trying to dry her palms.

Feeling this way was simply ridiculous. He wasn't

here. He didn't care about her anymore. Even if he was here, he wouldn't waste his time by checking in on her.

"And finally," she said, as the last model slipped behind the curtain, "I'm proud to announce the arrival of our new and groundbreaking line of fashion... Please give a round of applause for our models wearing our new Level III ballistic protection Monster Wear."

The curtain opened and a man came out in a well-fitted black suit nearly identical to the Armani her men at the side doors wore.

She walked over to the model and gave him a smile. "If you note—" she lifted the fabric of the jacket and twisted it in her fingers "—the cloth moves and breathes just like regular cotton. It is thin, light and available in a variety of colors. No more need for steel plates and heavy, movement-restricting armor."

A few in the audience caught their breath.

Zoey waved the model on. He took off his jacket, revealing his white dress shirt. He glanced back at her and gave her a sly smile as he dropped his jacket to the ground. He leaped forward, his hands raised in the air, and he did a tight spiral backflip onto the ground, landing just in front of the woman seated in the front row.

There was a roar of applause.

Yes.

Money would be flowing in no time.

If they could sell just ten thousand button-up shirts, they would recoup their entire investment, and anything beyond would be gravy.

She sent a silent prayer up to Trish, one begging for her forgiveness.

As the model weaved through the crowd, letting the

audience touch and feel the Lycra-like cloth, the next model entered from the side. She wore a black pair of yoga pants and a white T-shirt. Nothing fancy, and nothing to indicate she was prepped for a firefight.

"We are proud at H&K to design clothing that meets everyday needs for all. We don't simply create clothing for high-profile events and celebrities, but we also want to protect those who are just like us—those out there risking their lives for the greater good."

Several models followed the woman as the crowd jostled in their seats for a better view. People were slipping in from the back entrance and, as there were no longer any seats available, standing room became a premium.

As the last model disappeared, the crowd moved to their feet with applause.

"Thank you," Zoey said, glancing over to her guards, who now looked more nervous than ever. "We appreciate your support in our continuing effort to bring safety to those who most need it."

A woman's scream pierced through the air.

Zoey turned to her right. There, just a few yards away, one of her guards raised his gun. He didn't hesitate as he pointed it straight at her center mass and pulled the trigger.

The bullet struck true.

She crumpled to the ground as pain flooded her senses. "It's okay, everyone. He works for me." She struggled to catch her breath.

Her hands moved to her chest. A trickle of blood seeped between her fingers.

We should have done more testing.

Or maybe Trish is calling me out for using her death

*to profit. If she was still here, I would tell her this was
for her...all for her...*

The world spun as Zoey tumbled downward and
darkness swallowed her whole.

Chapter Two

What in the hell was that woman thinking, having her man shoot her to demonstrate one of her products?

Eli raced to the front of the tent and elbowed his way through the throngs of people who had rushed to help Zoey Martin.

Damn that woman.

He couldn't believe she would ever do something so foolish, so brash. Then again, should he really be surprised? All she ever cared about was being at the center of everything—attention, plans, a firefight—it didn't matter. It was Zoey Martin's way or no way at all.

Damn her.

And damn himself for thinking he could come here and walk away from her unscathed. Whenever he was near Zoey, he should know something bad was bound to happen.

If she was dead…he'd kill the man who'd pulled the trigger.

Who would have ever gone through with such a stupid publicity stunt?

Zoey lay in a fetal position as he got to her, her pink dress pulled up high on her thigh and exposing a little pair of black shorts. Her side rose and fell as she breathed, and aside from her lying there, and him having watched her being shot, she didn't look too much the worse for wear.

He pushed the crowd back from her, yelling at them to give her some space. He knelt down in front of her. "Zoey?"

Her eyes were closed and her lips were pursed as though she were trying to Lamaze her way through the pain. Even doing that, he'd be damned if she still wasn't one of the most beautiful women he'd ever seen. And *that* dress…

He held his chuckle as he realized once again he had found himself in trouble because of the perfect dress… and once again it was on Zoey, the woman his world had revolved around just two years ago.

Oh, how the mighty fall.

Zoey's eyes fluttered open, revealing her caramel-colored eyes. If only she were half as sweet as those eyes looked.

"Eli?" she said, her voice ragged with pain. As she moved to sit up he could see the blood on her fingers.

His heart dropped. She was really actually hurt.

His anger morphed into panic. "Zoey, we need to get you out of here and to the hospital. Do you think I can move you?" He leaned in and moved her hand.

There was a crushed slug embedded into the fabric of her dress.

Though he had heard rumors about the bulletproof capabilities of her new clothing line, he hadn't truly believed it until now. It seemed unfathomable that something like this was possible.

"Holy crap, Zoe…" he said. His breath escaped him as he reached down and pulled the slug from her dress.

The pink fabric was still in place, with not even a single tear. Where the bullet had impacted, there was a bit of blood seeping up and through the fabric. How could something stop a bullet, but then let blood through?

He stared as he tried to make sense of it until he finally pulled himself back to the task at hand.

"Zoey, are you okay? Can you move?" he asked.

She stared at him. "Eli, what in the hell are you doing here?" She moved to sit up. "You… You shouldn't have come."

"And you shouldn't have done what you just did." He gave her a hand and she pulled herself to standing. As their fingers touched, he couldn't help but be a little surprised that she had taken him up on his offer of help. She must have been hurting.

She pulled her hand from his. With a nod of acknowledgment, she made her way back up to the podium.

"Everyone," she said, clearing her throat and forcing herself to stand straight. "Everyone, please quiet down," she said over the manic cacophony of sound. "Excuse me."

The room silenced.

"As you can see, our new Monster Wear has the capability to stop a bullet at close range, all while being cool, comfortable and stylish," she said, stepping out just slightly so all could see her dress. "I am fine."

"You're bleeding!" someone in the crowd yelled.

"I said our clothing was bulletproof, I didn't say being shot would be pain-free." Zoey laughed, the sound tight and high like it hurt for her to breathe. "Like I always say, if you can't handle a bee sting then you need to stay out of the nest."

Eli shook his head.

Once again, he felt as if she had played him for a fool. Why did he have to be so stupid when it came to Zoey Martin?

He turned, about to walk out.

"Can we all give my assistant who was willing to pull the trigger, at my request, a big round of applause? And can we also please do the same for Mr. Eli Wayne for coming to the rescue of a lady?" She motioned in his direction and gave him her perfect, sexy smile…the one that always drew him back into her nest.

Applause filled the tent. Heat rose in his cheeks as men came up and patted him on the shoulder. He wasn't a hero. And though Zoey put on one hell of an act, she definitely wasn't a lady…at least not in the bedroom.

Almost as if she could read his mind, Zoey reached up and unzipped her dress. The fabric gripped her body and she had to roll it down in order to get it off her. Beneath the dress were those little black shorts and a black sports bra and nothing else.

His mind went to the last night they had spent together. What had it been, two years ago now? Sometimes their breakup seemed like a lifetime ago and then on days like this, it seemed like only yesterday.

He could still recall the way she smelled after her runs, a mixture of fresh air, sweat and strength. And when she was happy, her voice always took on a special lilt as though whatever she was saying was just for him. That was one thing he missed the most, the way she had always made him feel like he was the only man she had ever loved. And yet, he was left with nothing but a broken heart and fantasies of what could have been.

Oh, Zoey… Why did she do this to him?

She turned and smiled at him as her hand moved down her waist and rested gently on her hip.

His body disobeyed his mind and he could feel himself stirring to life in all the wrong places at the sight of her half-naked body.

The last time he had seen her this unclothed, it hadn't taken but a matter of seconds to get her into nothing at all. He could still remember the way she had tasted of salt and sweat on his lips as they made love. They had been on a takedown outside Tikrit, working a small village where a group of high-grade mercenaries, or mercs, had been holed up.

As he closed his eyes, he could almost feel the sand that had stuck to her skin as he worked his fingers down to her navel.

He stiffened further.

No.

He couldn't think of anything sultry about Zoey. No. She had watched his heart break and left him standing alone, without a job, without a home, without a family and completely adrift.

No matter what, he couldn't forgive her for all she had done to him and the wreckage she had left in his life.

"If you look," she said, motioning to her midsection, "the bullet left a bruise and an abrasion, but nothing more." She wiped her hands together in a feeble attempt to hide the blood that stained them.

She was swarmed by questions and she took her time answering each one.

He was relieved as a guard brought her a robe and she pulled it on over her body.

She was fine. She would always be just fine. She was the epitome of resilience.

He turned to leave, but Zoey waved to him as she ended the questions and bid goodbye to the crowd. He turned away, not wanting to once again do her bidding, but his resolve weakened. At the very least, before he left, he could make sure that she really was okay.

She could get up there and say she wasn't hurt all she wanted, but that didn't mean there wasn't some kind of internal damage from taking a hit like that. She was all show.

And he had always been the one to make sure that she wasn't faking things so much that she couldn't find her way back to reality.

Which made him wonder if that was part of the reason she had chosen this conference to unveil her new gear. She had to have known he would be here, hoping to catch sight of her. She had probably even known he would come to her rescue.

Maybe she missed him just as much as he missed her.

Wait. No. He didn't miss her or her stupid pink hair, or her wide-set dark-lined eyes, or her watermelon-colored lips that usually tasted of her mint sugar-free gum. And he definitely didn't miss the way she had loved to fall asleep in the crook of his arm, making his arm go to sleep and then later throb with pain when she finally rolled to her side in their bed.

Yep. He didn't miss her at all.

Damn it.

As the crowd started to dissipate, she made her way over to where he stood at the back of the tent.

She tugged her robe tighter around her body, like she was suddenly self-conscious in his presence.

"You're welcome," he said, fully aware from the slightly pursed look on her face that the last thing she wanted to say to him was thank you.

"I didn't tell you to come here." She brushed her pink hair out of her face. Up close, he couldn't help but notice it was dyed the same shade of Barbie pink as her dress.

"Uh-huh," he grumbled. "You and I both know Billings is my territory."

"I thought you were out working for a new crew. I don't keep tabs on you, Eli." She crossed her arms over her chest, but as she moved her arm over the place she'd taken the hit, she winced with pain and lowered her arms.

"Why did you do such a stupid thing? What would have happened if your guy had missed? What if he'd shot you in the neck?" He reached over and put his finger against the place that the bullet had struck. "You could have died, Zoey."

She moved away from his touch. "This was hardly the first time, or the last, that I stood at the edge of death, Eli. This is our life—dealing with pain. And you know it just as well as I do."

And perhaps that was one of the main reasons he was glad they really were no longer together.

"It doesn't mean it's okay to make stupid choices."

"Doing my job isn't making a stupid choice." She leaned against the back of a chair. "I believe in the H&K products and its people." Her tone made it clear he didn't make her short list.

"Why did you want me to stay, Zoey?" He wasn't about to stand there and continue to be her whipping boy. "Is it just so you can tell me all the reasons we don't work anymore?"

Some of her antagonism seemed to seep out as she dropped her shoulders and sighed. "I…" she began. "Actually, I was hoping you would give me the slug. You know. For marketing and such." She stuck out her hand like a child asking for a quarter.

"Yeah, right." He reached into his pocket where he had dropped the spent bullet. With it came his business card.

He stared at the card in his fingers, but before he could think about tucking it back into his pocket, Zoey reached out and took them both.

"I… Uh…" She paused, collecting herself. She pulled out her phone. "I guess I should thank you properly for what you did back there."

She opened up her phone and punched in his number, then moved to her calendar like she was thinking about finding a time that would work for them to go out. On her schedule he could make out the words *Therapy appointment* set for tomorrow, and beneath was an address.

He looked up at her as she tapped through her schedule.

Was she really interested in going out with him? And was she really going to a therapist?

Did it have something to do with what had happened to them?

He was glad she was seeing someone, but Zoey had never been the kind to open up. Maybe she had changed since she had left him.

"Hey," he said. "By the way, I'm sorry to hear about your sister. She was always wonderful to me. If I had it to do all over again, I would happily work by her side."

Zoey stopped with her phone and looked up at him, staring at him like she was looking for some kind of meaning to what he'd just said. "Are you saying you want to come back to STEALTH?" Her voice was choked.

"No. It's just… I meant…" Now, he was the one stammering. It wasn't that he hadn't missed his old job and the STEALTH family, but she didn't want him there and they both knew it.

Why was any interaction between them so awkward?

"I meant that I just wish nothing had happened to Trish. We lost a good one with her."

She nodded, but her gaze stayed locked on his face.

A blonde woman wove through the chairs over toward them, and Zoey finally looked away.

"I have to go, Eli." She handed him back his card. "But maybe…someday, we could catch up."

Catching up? Was she for real? They both knew after this moment it was unlikely they would ever see one another again.

And the thought, just like the woman who was walking away from him, threatened to rip out his heart.

Chapter Three

The ride back to the Widow Maker Ranch seemed even longer than she had remembered. She had driven through entire countries faster than she had driven across the state of Montana. The conference had gone well, and she was getting texts and alerts about new orders that were coming through the doors, but her mind kept circling back to Eli. Maybe it was his fault that the drive had seemed to take so long.

He had a way of making everything in her life more complicated. It was a good thing that she was putting hundreds of miles between them.

But it had been stupid of her to take his phone number. She had excised him ever so precisely from her life already, and now she had allowed him to slip back in. What was wrong with her?

She'd always stuck to the Band-Aid breakup model—one quick rip and throw it away. She was too old to make such a stupid mistake and let him reappear. His coming back would only open up all those old wounds. Not that everything had been bad between them. Some days had been incredible, while others—especially at the end—had been pure hell.

One time, when they had been in the belly of Italy,

they had taken a contract on a set of twins. The brothers they had been hired to kill had been members of a notorious terrorist organization, in so deep that they had helped establish the group's core documents and constitution. Thanks to their work, the group had grown to over five thousand international members and was responsible for the deaths of over two hundred civilians—men, women and one child.

During the strike, she and Eli had been forced to camp out under the stars while they waited for the brothers to return to their compound. While she had tracked the brothers' phones, she and Eli had started out talking about throwaway things—the weather, locations and food preferences. After a few hours, however, something changed and they began talking about those things in life that make a person unique—family, beliefs, culture. He had even told her about growing up in rural Idaho, near Boise, where he had learned to shoot a BB gun and take care of his family's bevy of animals.

The number one rule of their occupation as hit men was that everything was a secret. To open up, even the tiniest bit meant death.

But as they had talked, she forgot that rule. She was surprised to learn that he was such a sucker for animals. Maybe it was the thought of him holding a puppy, but whatever reservations she had about their growing intimacy quickly disappeared.

Everything between them changed. They became a team. And then that team mentality had taken another turn, and taking aim at killers and thieves had turned into taking aim at each other's hearts.

She had been a fool to get involved with him. When she kissed him she had stripped her life of one of her best friends and one of just a select few that she had trusted.

The only other person she had trusted in the same way had been her sister. When Trish had been alive, Zoey had been able to turn to her, to talk to her a bit about the things that were going on in her life. Their lives were so unique and challenging that it took someone who had the same lifestyle—one of long nights in bunkers and days spent in the mud—to completely understand what it meant to fall in love.

As she pulled down the road that led to the ranch, her headlights bounced as she hit the obstacle course that had been carved into the dirt by the summer winds and fall freezes. The rhythmic back and forth motion of the car comforted her, knowing that the Widow Maker Ranch was protected by the grounds around it. With potholes and ruts this deep, few would venture down their road; the fewer the people, the better.

After Jarrod and Mindy's run-in with the Gray Wolves's—and their leader Bayural's—hit man, they had been trying to stay out of the public eye. That was, until her reentry into society at the trade show. When it came to protecting the innocent, even if it meant coming out of hiding and putting herself in danger, Zoey had been willing to personally take the risk. Their clothing line would make the world a better, safer place. Women like Trish could use their tac line every day and just maybe Zoey could keep someone else from losing a sister.

She checked her rearview mirror one more time. There was a set of headlights behind her, and in the rural Montana countryside they made her nervous. Though she was sure she was overreacting, she pulled her car to the side of the road and let the person behind her pass by. The sedan was blue and had local plates, but she didn't get a good look at the driver.

Not for the first time during the drive, she wished she hadn't gone alone. Mindy had offered to come with her by flying over from Sweden, but Anya—Mindy and Jarrod's adopted daughter—had come down with a cold and it hadn't seemed right for her to leave the girl's side.

Zoey picked up her phone, checking it one more time before she started driving again. As she clicked around her emails and screens, her contacts popped up and front and center was Eli's information.

Was it a sign that she should call him?

It would be nice to hear his voice one more time— maybe it could provide even more closure and she could put her memories back in the past. She stared at the number and her finger trembled over the green phone icon.

If she called him, for a few moments, it could seem like she wasn't completely alone. For those few precious minutes, it would be like she could go back in time and fall into the sweet world of flirty banter and the flutter of excitement that always came with hearing his voice.

No. There was no going back in time, no making things right, and no amount of forgiveness that could right her wrongs.

She clicked off her phone and turned back onto the road. She had to be careful not to lead an attacker back to their hideout.

As she slowed down to avoid another rut in the road, a deer careened out of the darkness, sprinting through her headlights and forcing her to slam on her brakes. The phone went flying in the darkness, flipping to the passenger's side floorboard with a crunching sound. The screen flashed a rainbow shard of colors from the broken screen and died.

The deer stopped on the other side of the road and looked back at her, like it was some messenger of the fates. Bambi killing her phone was one hell of a sign that she was never supposed to get in touch with Eli.

About a half mile from the ranch, the car that had passed her was parked on the side of the road. It looked to be last year's Chevy sedan. As she slowed down to look inside, she noticed that the driver was gone.

There wasn't anything near the car, just pastures that led up to the ranch house. Beyond that was public forest. So why would they have pulled over here and gotten out of their car? She glanced around, but the light of her headlights illuminated only a few yards of grass peeking out from under their blanket of heavy snow.

Maybe the driver had to relieve themselves, or it was possible that they were getting high.

No one knew where her family was hiding. Her paranoia was nothing more than her guilt rearing its ugly head. It had been a risk by coming out of hiding for the trade show, but it wasn't like she had announced to the world that she was going to be there. It had been quick, and she had tried to fly under the radar before the unveiling.

She couldn't let her anxiety get out of control.

The car was just a car. Besides, her enemies wouldn't be stupid enough to even give her a clue that they were coming.

She took one more look at the Chevy. Her brother's favorite joke came to mind. "How do you find a Chevy owner? They're always sitting in the repair shop."

It was stupid and not really true, but it made her chuckle. More importantly, it relaxed her nerves.

Jarrod and Trevor were already at the main house, but Chad had gone to Sweden to iron things out with the members of the parliament who had finally come around and allowed them to start work at their manufacturing plants. Only a handful of people knew about Chad's whereabouts. She hoped that their being split up would make it harder for any one of them to be located by the people who wanted them all dead. They had been smart and prudent.

We are safe, she told herself.

She peeked back at the car. Still empty.

It's okay. It's human nature to feed into fear-based paranoia, she thought, trying to put a name to her feelings in an attempt to get them under control.

There was a long-standing conversation that circulated throughout law enforcement and military personnel about the differences between paranoia and preparedness. It wasn't crazy or over-the-top to think about the "what ifs" and to take steps to mitigate any dangers. What was crazy was believing that all the "what ifs" were real and out to destroy her.

She considered pulling over and running a scan for any unusual cell phone signals that could be found nearby. But she shrugged off the paranoia and just kept driving.

She sighed, finding more comfort in the vast control that was at her fingertips thanks to technology—her bread and butter.

When it came to tech, she was a badass.

Sitting up a little bit in her seat, she blew off the

last bits of fear that wafted through her. The car was nothing.

As she pulled through the gates of the ranch, their newest acquisition, Sir Galahad of Lucktown also known as Sarge, their black gelding, stuck his head over the front fence. He whinnied in greeting as she got out of her car. He threw his head has he pranced around near the fence line.

"Heya, Sarge. Hoping for a cookie, are we?" she said to the horse.

He threw his head again and picked up his pace like he knew exactly what she had said.

"You are spoiled rotten." She chuckled as she walked over to him and ran her hand down the blaze on his forehead. He relaxed under her hand, moving into her touch.

For a new horse, she and the animal had a surprisingly instant bond. It was as if the horse could pick up on the sadness of her losses and the pressure she felt in keeping the family safe.

The house seemed buttoned up and quiet, with the front curtains drawn and the living room light showing through. Everything seemed fine.

It was good to be back at the ranch.

She paused in front of the barn doors and stared up at the chipping white paint of the doorjambs and the hayloft door. The Widow Maker brand was emblazoned above the hayloft door, a broken heart and crooked slash. Oh, the irony. She had come here to move forward, to find safety and to be with the people she loved, but she was constantly reminded of the heartbreak she had suffered with Eli Wayne.

Sarge huffed from the pasture, reminding her that

there was no time to waste when it came to getting him his nightly treats.

The barn door squeaked as she slid it partially open and stepped inside. The place smelled of earth, horse manure and hay. And, as odd at it may have seemed, she loved the scent. It was the aroma of a life well spent, but she wasn't sure if it or the smell of gunpowder brought her more satisfaction.

When they had been young, she and her brothers had come to the Widow Maker to visit their cousin and her family until Gwen's father had died in a haying accident. After that, everything at the ranch and in her cousin's family had seemed to fall into disrepair until Gwen and her mother had finally decided to sell the ranch to Zoey and her brothers. The sale had been somewhat fortuitous. The opportunity had fallen into their laps at the right moment, just when they needed to get their heads down.

Though she had spent time there, it still felt like they were guests. She had hoped that by getting Sarge, it would help with some of that. If nothing else, she could have something that concretely tied her to the place by needing her almost as much as she needed it.

The lights were off in the barn, and she searched around in the dark for the light switch, wishing she had her cell phone to light it up.

It was childish, but one of the things she feared the most was darkness. Perhaps it reminded her too much of death, or perhaps it was just that illogical, primal instinct that evil hid there. There was no way that she would have been out here in the middle of the night looking for food if she hadn't loved Sarge with all of her heart. Evil probably wasn't lurking in the dark, but bears certainly could be.

The horse called to her from the pasture, making her chuckle. "I'm coming, I'm coming… Jeez, you're such a typical dude, always wanting what you want when you want it."

As she groped for the light switch one more time and missed, she gave up hopes of finding it. With the days getting shorter she was going to have to figure out a better system if she was going to be spending any amount of time out here in the barn.

Making her way to the corner of the bench by feel, she came to the end and reached down into what she knew was a bag of horse biscuits. She rolled a few around in her hands and stood up.

Her skin crawled as she stared out into the darkness. "So dark that you couldn't even see your hand in front of your face" wasn't just an adage.

It's nothing. I'm fine. I'm fine.

When was she ever going to get over this fear?

As she moved in the direction of the door, a draft brushed against her cheek.

It's just the wind. Don't be a chicken.

She clenched her eyes shut as her fingers trailed along the rough, splintered edge of the plywood top of the tool bench. She could feel every crack and split in the wood, every sense heightened by her blindness.

Unfortunately, they weren't heightened enough.

A hand wrapped around her mouth from behind. Before she could even realize what was happening, her body hit the ground. She opened her mouth to speak, but only tasted oats and mud as her assailant pressed her face into the dirt floor.

The Gray Wolves had found them.

They were all going to die.

Grabbing her hands, they wrapped them behind her back high and tight, and drove their knee into her back, pinning her in place. She writhed, hoping to break their grip on her hands, but their grip only tightened—the human equivalent of quicksand.

"Where's Chad?" The voice was tinny and robotic, as though the sound was being emitted from some type of voice-changing tech.

"Get off me," she said, spitting out the debris from her mouth as she spoke.

The knee in her back drove deeper, making pain shoot down her legs. But her assailant said nothing.

She tried to look over her shoulder, hoping to catch a glimpse of something that could help her identify the person on top of her. However, as she moved, a hand grabbed and rolled her face downward. Their touch was rough, likely a man's hand. But from his clean take-down, she doubted that he actually wanted to hurt her.

In this barn, without anyone knowing that she was home, this person could kill her and no one would be the wiser until tomorrow morning. But they were choosing to keep her alive. There was some hope to be found there, but minimal.

Perhaps they were only keeping her alive to question her.

"Where's Chad?" the same robotic voice asked—definitely a phone app.

Why hadn't she run her detection device? She was so stupid sometimes.

Why was it when it came to protecting the ones around her that she was so much more on the ball?

When was she going to learn that the trap of "it won't happen to me" would get her every freaking time?

She squirmed under the person pinning her to the ground. They drove down their knee, making it hard for her to breathe. As she struggled, her body fought for sweet, sweet air. Her squirming turned to thrashing.

She had to fight. There was no way she could surrender. Not just her life was at stake. Her brothers, their fiancées and Anya…they all depended on her.

For a split second, her thoughts moved to Trish's last moments. Had this been what she had been feeling? Incapacitated? Unable to save her own life?

The person holding her down grumbled, and the sound was deep and heavy…that of a man.

"Stop moving," the man said, using the robotic voice app.

It was soul-wrenching that he had taken enough time to type his words out when she had been putting all of her strength into an attempt to break free. It was like she was a grasshopper in the hands of a sadistic boy, a boy holding her down and just watching in sick glee until he was ready to rip off her legs.

She was nothing to this person.

She was powerless.

Chapter Four

Tracking a phone wasn't as hard as a person thought. Zoey knew that just as well as he did, which was probably why she'd turned off her phone. Eli parked his car in the last spot he had gotten her signal. Just down the road was an abandoned car. Had someone picked her up? Was this the car she had been riding in? Had the car been dropped here in a nearly abandoned location in Nowhere, Montana, to mask her real location?

She was smart. No doubt about it.

With the hit out on Chad, it was no wonder that she was taking extreme measures to protect herself and her family.

At the same time, though, did she even know about the hit? It had only come down from the top a matter of hours earlier. He had refused to take the contract, but that didn't mean that other independent operatives hadn't taken on the job.

He should have told her about the contract. He should have gone out of his way to help her. But at the same time, their relationship had been the reason he had been forced to leave his last posting. He couldn't get wrapped up with her again.

Yet, here he was…parked on a nearly deserted country road trying to jump headfirst back into her life.

The mind and the heart were truly different beasts.

If he did find her, he would tell her. He *had* to tell her about the hit on Chad. He didn't know who had taken out the contract on her brother, but from the word on the street, it sounded like they were at odds with a Turkish crime syndicate called the Gray Wolves. The Gray Wolves were responsible for the death of Trish, but why they had continued to come after the Martins was something only Zoey could answer for him.

He looked around for any obvious place she might have gone, but aside from the abandoned car, there was little to go on. He'd made a series of phone calls to friends of his in the FBI and CIA. No one had any knowledge about where Zoey or the rest of the Martins were. One of his friends said that the last known location for Chad had been somewhere in Cairo. However, that had been nearly three months ago and made that information about as useful as an umbrella in a hurricane. He'd thanked them, but he couldn't help feeling that he was wasting time.

He found himself drawn to her. It was inexplicable, but from the moment they had met, they had had this intrinsic bond. Sometimes it was almost as if they were twin flames, one being able to read the mind of the other, and often that meant that they could also feel for what the other was feeling… And right now, that was terror.

He had to find her. He had to get to her. Even if she never knew that he was there, he had to make sure that she was okay.

Parking his truck, he made his way over to the abandoned car and peered into the window. Inside, mounted on the dashboard, was a detection device. Over the last decade, these devices had become more and more accurate, even to the point where they could pick up exact locations, and pretty much anything tech based. They were a hit man's best friend.

It was odd how many people felt safe behind the anonymity provided by their cell phones. The general public didn't realize how easy it was to hack into any phone call, any phone, any tablet or computer. Anything that put off a signal could be used against them. In many ways, this new generation of tech defense was part of the reason that crimes had started to go down on a national level. For most criminals, technology was above them. Now, it was only highly educated, highly trained tech wizards who could get away with high-level crimes.

Gone were the days of the old-time bank robberies that involved nothing more than a gun and a face mask. Sure, a person could still do it, but the chances were that by the time the perpetrators made it back to their house, the police would already be there waiting for them.

That wasn't to say there weren't petty crimes that went unprosecuted. Hardly, but it wasn't because of law enforcement's inability to get information, rather, it was often that the local officers couldn't afford to handle crimes that didn't warrant it. For example, why spend work hours on a car break-in if an insurance company would pay out for the damage and loss, especially when there was someone else being stabbed three blocks away? Life was irreplaceable, and insurance was there for a reason.

It was part of the reason that, in most large cities, officers didn't even bother responding to misdemeanors. As it stood, the last figure he had heard was that eighty-six percent of robberies went unsolved—and that figure was of those that were reported. He shook his head.

It was no wonder that he had a job. People needed men like him, men who would take a stand against the worst of the worst…a man who was sworn to protect, albeit privately funded by those willing to hire him.

Then again, it wasn't all about the money or he wouldn't have been standing out here in the dark looking for a woman he had sworn to write off again and again.

He stepped back and took a look over the Chevy Malibu. It appeared to be a new car, maybe last year's model. He didn't really track cars; he was more of a truck kind of guy. That was, all except the new Charger Hellcats. Damn, he could really go for one of those. Zero to sixty in 3.4 seconds. In all the right ways, it reminded him of Zoey. Power and strength under the hood, and a body to match, but danger and mayhem was quick on its heels.

He patted his stomach. If he wanted to have even half a chance with her, now or ever, he was going to have to do even more sit-ups.

For her, he wanted to be perfect. Everything she could possibly want and need in a man—at least the man she had said she wanted in the days and nights they had spent together in the field.

He thought about the last time he had seen her. It had been the night everything between them changed… A night from which there may well be no coming back, but damn it…after seeing her in Billings, and seeing her face every time he closed his damn eyes, maybe he had to try. Perhaps they couldn't or wouldn't end up together. His life hadn't been anything like some well-scripted romance, but maybe he could set things right and make sure that everything in her life was okay and she had started to heal—especially since she'd once again lost someone she loved when Trish had died.

He knew how close she had been with Trish. She was the only person that Zoey had ever seemed herself with—besides him. With her sister, she opened up and laughed…really laughed…the kind that made stars dance in her eyes and her cheeks redden.

Zoey was always beautiful, but when she really let herself go and laughed…damn, she was like a sunbeam that could burn away the clouds of anger and loneliness that settled into the valley of his soul.

He found himself staring at the red flickering bar on the Protection 1207i device mounted on the dashboard.

It was possible that she had been tracking him as he was tracking her. He certainly wouldn't have put it outside the range of possibility. And maybe once he had gotten close, she had called "No joy" and bugged out. She was and had always been clever like that, capable of keeping him just close enough and yet just far enough away to keep herself safe.

He peered into the back seat, hoping to see anything that would definitely tie the car to her. There was no hot pink bulletproof dress, no luggage or bags of freebies from a weekend spent at a conference. Hell, there wasn't even a stray straw wrapper.

He pulled the plate number on his phone. It was registered to a shell company out of the Caymans.

Just as he thought. This was the car of someone who

knew it was going to be dumped—someone who didn't want the car to be tied to them in any way.

But when he'd worked for STEALTH, they didn't use the Caymans—or Chevys. Either things were changing, or this wasn't actually Zoey's drop car.

His stomach clenched. If it wasn't Zoey's car, then it had to be someone else's…someone who was also tracking her…and it wasn't a wet-behind-the-ears mercenary. They weren't great, leaving the car here and all, but they at least knew the right end of the gun. Which meant that his longtime friends were being hunted, and they were in trouble.

He had heard word of their comings and goings with the Gray Wolves in Turkey, and Trish, but he didn't know the ins and outs of what exactly had happened. Operations like theirs were always kept pretty close to the vest. But, given the fallout, they had to have known that hell was coming in a wave of highly paid killers. Killers without honor—killers that were nothing like him.

He shone his flashlight at the tracks on the dirt road. There were only tire tracks heading down the road and away from the highway. If he acted fast, maybe he could still find whoever had dumped the car.

Hopefully Zoey's phone going black had nothing to do with whoever had left this car.

His mind raced with all the things that could be happening to Zoey right now, ranging from kicking the merc's ass all the way to her tied up and moments away from death somewhere.

He ran back to his truck and, with a spray of gravel, raced off in the direction the tracks were going. Though he had no idea where the road led, or who it would lead to, he had to move. He had to save Zoey. He had to keep her safe.

Using Google Maps, he pulled up a street image of the area around him as he tried, and failed, to weave around the ruts and potholes that littered the dirt road. As he drove, a thin dusting of white snow skittered down from the sky, forcing him to slow down. It was almost as if there were some higher power that wanted to stand in his way, making what he hoped wasn't a life and death situation that much more perilous.

The maps showed a private ranch less than a mile up on his left. Beyond was US Forest Service— public lands.

Crap.

If someone had kidnapped her, or taken her hostage, they very well may have taken her up into the mountains that hugged the valley. If they were up there, and it was starting to snow, it was more than possible he would lose track of them. A matter of a few minutes and a hard snowfall could cover any evidence of her location.

He tried to talk himself down off the ledge of panic. She always complained that he had a way of blowing things out of proportion and being overly dramatic. He could have almost sworn that her favorite thing to say to him had been, "The sky isn't always falling, Eli."

And oh, the look she always gave him when she said it.

He had to see that look again. He had to see *her* again.

The snowfall quickened, coming down in a blizzard of early season white, nearly blinding him thanks to his headlights. As he ascended a hill, his tire connected with a rut, sending his truck to the right and nearly striking the wooden fence post next to the road. He slowed down even though all he wanted to do was hit the gas and not stop until he saw Zoey. Ahead, not too far, was a streetlamp set in the center of a parking lot. It seemed out of place, like a stoic sentinel bravely holding a beacon for weary travelers.

Huddled around the parking area was a barn and, tucked in closer to the mountain, a ranch-style house. This must have been the ranch he had seen on the map. The place was buttoned up; the only sign of life was a deserted pickup parked haphazardly at the edge of the drive, a car behind it and a horse that was skittering back and forth at the fence line.

Zoey had always loved horses. But it seemed like a far stretch that the woman he had known would be settled down enough to buy a horse, live on a ranch and still have time to work with a military-grade weapons manufacturer with worldwide ties to create a line of ballistics gear—and to top it all off, combat Turkish terrorists. Damn, if she was living here, she had one hell of a life.

Unsure whether he should stop or not, he pulled under the light and shut off the engine. Snow landed on his windshield and melted, leaving a smattering of droplets of water as the only reminders of the unique beauty that had fallen from the heavens. It struck him how, in a single instant, something so special could simply be struck from existence.

He tried not to see it as a sign of anything that had to do with Zoey. She was fine. She was going to be all right. He was making something out of nothing.

She was probably inside the ranch house, having a cup of coffee and making plans for her next mission. That was it. He tried to control his thoughts as he stepped outside. The cold bit at his skin and burned his lungs as he drew in a long breath.

There was a rattle of metal on metal and a thud coming from inside the barn. He moved toward the noise. The barn's door was open, but the lamp overhead made the darkness inside the barn even more abyssal.

As he grew near, there was the unmistakable sound of a round being jacked into a gun's chamber.

He rushed toward the sound, pulling his Glock and flicking on his weapon's light, being careful to keep out of sight. He took a moment, scanning the grounds in an attempt to secure the outer perimeter. His only witness was the horse.

Fear threatened to creep in on him as he moved behind the door. He channeled it, forcing it to submit into aggression. Whoever was inside this barn, whatever they were doing, it was going to come down to him or them. Kill or be killed.

His finger moved on the trigger guard, ready. The cool steel against his finger calmed him, centering his focus back to his objective.

He moved around the side of the barn, clicking off his light to stay undetected as he carefully slipped under the pasture fence. Most barns had a Dutch-style door in the back for horses and livestock to come and go. From that vantage, he could enter the scene undetected. As he hustled, the door came into view. Though it was cold, the top of the back door was open. The closed bottom wouldn't provide a great deal of protection in the event of a firefight, but if he played his cards right, things wouldn't go that far. If he was called upon to use deadly force, he felt confident that it would be one and done.

From inside, he heard a woman's muffled groan. "Why?"

He slid open the lock on the bottom of the back door and wound his way inside. The sliding front door let in just enough of the streetlight so that he could see the edge of a silhouette ahead, but remain unseen in the back. He did a quick scan of the stalls as he moved silently to get out of the fatal tunnel created by the barn. The stall just behind the silhouetted man was open, creating the perfect place to hide. He rushed forward, hoping to remain in control and undetected.

As he stepped into the stall, the man in front of him kicked, his foot striking a body that lay on the floor. The woman moaned, the sound wet and gurgling, but muffled by the ground.

He prayed the woman wasn't Zoey—that somehow, he had just come upon a random attack.

"Who sent you?" she asked.

This time, he recognized that voice, *her* voice.

He pointed his gun at the objective's center mass. A light clicked on in the objective's hands. A cell phone. He clicked away, typing something. His face was lit up by the blue light. From where Eli stood, he could make out the dark complexion of the man. He had a tribal-style tattoo that wrapped around his neck and disappeared beneath the dark shirt he wore.

"Where's Chad?" a robotic voice sounded from the man's phone.

It was all the confirmation that Eli needed.

As he pulled the trigger, the bullet ripped from his barrel.

The man didn't even know what hit him.

Chapter Five

Zoey had never been the kind of woman who had hoped for a man to save her, but right now, staring up at Eli's face in the dim light of her attacker's cell phone, she could have kissed him.

It was crazy how one little decision had nearly gotten her killed. That was the last time she would go into a barn without using a light switch.

"Eli," she said, his name dripping from her lips like nectar.

"Is there anyone else?" he asked, moving to clear the rest of the barn. He walked to the front of the barn and flicked on the lights that she had struggled to find.

"I don't think so," she said, lifting her head up from the mud of the ground and glancing around. She moved her hands, which were zipped to her feet behind her back. "Hey." She motioned toward them with her chin.

Taking her unspoken direction, Eli pulled a knife and cut her free.

"Thanks." She sat up, rubbing her wrists where the clear plastic had cut into her flesh. She wiped the dirt from her lips, spitting the remnants of mud and guck from her mouth.

"You okay?" he asked, walking over to her as he holstered his weapon.

She thought about standing to make a point of how strong and unaffected she was by the attack, but her body refused to comply. As she breathed, her ribs ached and her head felt as if it were about to explode. The best she could do was lie. "I'm fine."

Or, at least she would be in a day or two.

He knelt down, coming face-to-face with her as he assessed her well-being.

"Seriously, I'll be okay."

He reached up and his fingers grazed against her cheek where she could feel a lump swelling on her skin. "Your eyes are bloodshot." He looked down to her neck. "You're lucky you broke free of his grasp."

If she was feeling a bit better, she was sure she would have said something about him stating the obvious, but as it was, she could only agree with him. The man's body lay at her feet and, as she glanced in his direction, his body twitched. His head rested on the ground, just feet from where hers had been only moments before. There was a red hole at the center of his forehead and blood was dripping out, twisting down his temple and oozing to the floor where it nearly disappeared in the black dirt and spent hay.

She touched her neck, feeling the hot bruises where the man's hands had wrapped around her neck and nearly ended her.

"Where're your brothers?" Eli asked, pulling her back to the reality that waited just outside the barn.

His question put her on alert. It was too similar to her attacker's robotic "Where's Chad?"

"What do you mean?" she asked, trying not to sound suspicious.

"Are they inside?" He motioned toward the house.

She shook her head and felt some of the tightness recede from her body as she slipped her hand into Eli's. Squeezing his warm fingers, she tried to force a smile. "I just got here. I don't know about Jarrod and Trevor." She slowly moved to standing with Eli's help.

He brushed her hair out of her face for her. The action was intimate—he was far too close. She let go of his hand and stepped back from him. As much as she loved his touch, it had no place in her life.

"Wait," she said. "What are you doing here?"

He glanced away. "That's not important. What are we going to do with this bastard's body?"

He wasn't getting away from her question that easily, but they did need to focus. The only good news was that, out here in the middle of Mystery, Montana, gunfire wasn't something that was feared. The ranch was close enough to public hunting lands that if anyone heard it, they would write it off as a successful hunter.

Her thoughts turned to the dead guys in the shanty her brother had found and she grimaced, thinking about how often her family found themselves in need of body removal.

"I would say he could stay in here, but I don't want my horse to spook at the smell." She nudged the body with the toe of her boot.

Eli patted the body down, pulling a wallet from the guy's back pocket. Opening it up, he pulled out a military ID card. "Smitty Foster. Know him?"

She shook her head.

"Is he one of your brothers' friends?"

There was little chance that this bastard wasn't connected with the Gray Wolves—not that they didn't have other enemies. But she wasn't sure she wanted to open up to Eli about everything that was happening in their lives right now. However, the hit man market was a small world. He had known about Trish, which meant it was likely he knew about the Gray Wolves.

"Are you just fishing for information? Or do you really not know what's going on here?" she asked, trying to sound as nonconfrontational as possible. She didn't want to push him away, just get an idea of what they were working with.

He gave her a guilty smile.

"That's what I thought." She wiped off the front of her shirt. "How much do you know?"

He stared at her for a long moment, almost as if he were trying to decide how much information he wanted to give her. His silence ticked her off, but it also drew in memories of what it had been like to be with him day in and day out.

Spontaneity was something she couldn't live without.

"You know about Bayural? About what exactly happened with Trish?" she said, not waiting another second for him to answer.

He nodded. "I got the highlights through the grapevine."

"Uh-huh," she said, holding out her hand and motioning for the guy's wallet so she could give it a quick once-over.

He handed it to her. "Sounds like you ticked off the wrong people."

"You can say that again." She flipped open the wallet. It was definitely bare bones. ID—probably fake—

one credit card with the same name as ID, and two hundred dollars in cash. "But we were just doing our jobs."

"When you take out the CIA's trash, you're bound to get your hands dirty."

She closed the wallet and stuffed it into the back pocket of her jeans. "Getting elbow deep in the muck is fine, but it's an entirely different thing when I'm face-down in the crap in my own home."

He stepped closer to her and wiped a bit of mud off her cheek. "If you want, you don't have to face these bastards alone."

"I..." she began, not sure exactly what to say. It was a generous offer and she wanted him to stay, but he had a life of his own, a job that required him, probably a girlfriend everywhere he went, and that was to say nothing of her own life and roadblocks she had carefully put in place when it came to him. "I'm honored that you would offer, but—"

"Stop, Zoey." He put his hands up like he was a street cop controlling traffic—but this was one wreck he couldn't avoid.

"I know what you're going to say," he continued, talking over her feeble attempt to mutter her protests. "I know you. I know what you're thinking. I know that you think my being here is a bad idea. And I agree."

She wasn't sure what hurt worse—the fact that he thought he knew her mind but wasn't trying to make a move on her, or that he agreed it was a bad idea they spend any time together.

"You can't possibly know what I'm thinking." If he could, he would have been running for the hills.

"I think I get the gist. Regardless, though, you need me here."

"I have my brothers," she argued.

"If that's true, where are they now?" He waved around the barn and to the dead man on the floor. "I know you love them, and they love you, but didn't Trish's death show you the limits of what family can *actually* do?"

"How dare you come after my brothers? My team? My sister?" She threw her arms over her chest to keep her hands from striking him. He had no business calling out her family, or what he perceived as their mistakes. Trish's death was a tragedy, and sure, mistakes had been made, but it was none of his business.

He sighed. "I didn't mean it like that. At all. I'm just worried about you." He gave her a cute contrite look that was in direct contradiction to the anger that roiled in her gut. "I just mean that you need protection, someone who is with you through thick or thin. I can do that."

There was no way he was going to take no for an answer, and she wasn't sure that she could even get the word past her lips—not when he had just saved her life.

"Let's just take one day at a time."

A huge smile spread across his wide face, accentuating his chiseled jaw and piercing green eyes. There was a quickening inside of her, as though her body was springing back to life after being so close to death.

"I'll take a day," he said. He crouched down and grabbed the dead guy under the arms.

Unwilling to stand idly by and simply watch as he did the heavy lifting, she took hold of the man's feet and lifted him up. "Where do you think we should put this trash?"

He grunted as he shifted the dead weight in his arms and walked backward toward the open barn door. "Your trunk empty?" he asked, motioning toward her car with his chin.

"It can be." They lugged the body over and dropped him on the ground. The body wheezed as it deflated.

"Huh," Eli said, looking down at the guy. "That's a new one. You ever hear that sound before?"

Though she'd never pulled the trigger and killed a man, thanks to STEALTH she'd heard more than her fair share of dying breaths—just never one postmortem. Bodies did strange things after the soul left them.

"No," she said, opening up the trunk, unloading the boxes from the conference and putting them on the ground next to the body. "What's the weirdest thing you've ever seen with a body?"

He grabbed a box out of the trunk and set it on the ground, taking a moment. "Postmortem hyperthermia. Hands down." He nodded, grabbing a box from her hands. "I was on assignment in Guatemala and came across a woman who had just died of what I think was a drug-induced heart attack. Her daughter had tried to resuscitate her before I arrived on scene. By the time I got there, she'd been down about forty minutes, but she was hot to the touch—hotter than a fever. Like, *crazy* hot."

"Okay, that's weird." She took hold of the dead guy's feet and they flung him into the back of the car. As he landed, the car bounced.

"Yeah, but it got better. The daughter swore that her mother's body had been taken over by a demon. Went into a full panic. I tried to calm her down, but she ended up setting the entire house on fire—mother's body and all."

"Can't say I blame her." She wiped her hands on her dirty jeans, aware that they were precariously close to slipping back into their old ways—bantering with one another, having strange conversations in even stranger circumstances and at the same time enjoying each other's company.

She needed to go back to being pissed off at him. It would make it easier to push him away.

One day at a time.

"I need a shower," she said, trying to avoid spending another second with the man who drew so many feelings and questions. She walked to the barn to make sure there were no obvious signs of a struggle in case anyone stopped by. Thankfully, she appeared to have taken all the damage. She ran her fingers over the spot in her gut where the bullet had struck her only hours before.

Bullet to the chest, nearly strangled to death, beaten and now dealing with her ex—it had been one hell of a day.

Clicking off the barn's light, she walked back to the house with Eli at her side. They were in step with each other as they made their way up onto the porch. It struck her as she grabbed her keys and unlocked the front door that there was no way to hide Eli from her brothers in the light of morning.

They were going to rib her something fierce.

She stopped herself before she opened the door and turned to him. "It may be best if you sleep—"

"In the barn? No. And it's too cold to sleep out in my truck," he said, cutting her off as though he could really read her mind. "I'll take post outside your bedroom."

"So you can listen to me snore?" she said, opening

the front door. He pushed past her, taking point as they entered the house.

"Snore, chat, whatever…" His mischievous grin returned.

She looked away in an attempt to hide her own grin. He couldn't know that he still flustered her. "Don't you have to go to work? Make those bosses happy?"

She could almost hear his grin fade as she brought up one of the many things that could drive them apart, though none were greater than the old hurts that lay between them. "As far as they're concerned, I'm still in Billings at the conference, at least for the next few days."

"And what happens when those few days are over?" She closed and locked the door behind them, then threw her keys into the bowl that sat next to the door.

"Like we said, one day at a time." He walked toward the kitchen like he knew the place. "Besides, I make my own hours."

She raised a brow. When he had worked for them, he was on salary and worked at her side constantly. There was none of the "we'll call you when we need you" freelancer thing. He had been a major part of their team and their lives. It was because of him that they had been forced to change the way they worked. When he left, it became abundantly clear that it was a liability to let anyone outside the family inside their circle at that level…security could be breached best by trust.

There was the sound of him putting water in a teakettle as she walked into the kitchen.

"London fog?" he asked, holding up a box of decaf Earl Grey.

"Sure."

"You're still drinking it every night before you go to bed?" he asked, his back turned to her as he set about working.

It made her squirm that he knew her that intimately. "Um, yeah. Most of the time."

She wasn't sure she should admit it or not. It would have made her feel better to lie and tell him she had changed, that she wasn't the woman he had once known, but aside from making her feel better, it wouldn't have served any purpose. The only thing that had really changed—besides her location—was the need to keep people, and love, at arm's length.

If she could just figure out how to keep Eli close enough to ensure her safety, but far enough away from the danger of falling in love with him all over again.

Chapter Six

Aside from the dead body in the trunk of Zoey's car, things had gone better than he had expected—and he hadn't been forced to tell her anything about what he knew about the situation with Chad. But as he stared at the wall across from her bedroom door, he couldn't help but feel like he had made a mistake in not coming clean.

She needed to know about the contract out on Chad's head.

There was the creaking sound of the floor as she paced around her bedroom. Either she was trying to calm down after the attack or she was working away. Knowing her, it was probably a little bit of both.

It was a relief he had gotten to her in time. A couple of minutes later and who the hell knew what kind of condition she would have been in. She had seemed to think the man only wanted information about her brother, but if that was true, why had he used a voice-cloaking device and attacked her in the dark?

Eli couldn't make sense of why the man had gone about the attack as he had. If Eli had taken the contract on Chad's head, he wouldn't have dinked around going after his sister in the night; he would have waited, watched and calculated before making any sort of move. The man had been reckless.

By coming here and following Zoey, the man must have been desperate. Perhaps the clock was ticking.

He hadn't gotten the specs on the hit, just that there was a job up for grabs. However, some employers loved to give little bonuses for quick and "accidental" deaths. But it didn't seem like the kind of thing a group like the Gray Wolves would do when ordering such a hit.

But there were a million different conditions and factors he didn't know. Maybe it would have been better if he had taken the contract. At least that way he would know more about the job and what he and Zoey's family could expect. If nothing else, when he decided to tell Zoey the truth, he wouldn't be going to her empty-handed and clueless about what the future was going to bring—other than madness.

He clicked on his phone and contacted his boss, James, at Watch Dog.

ON RECON. SEND ENCRYPTED FILE ON CASE #19807—M8.

In a matter of just a few seconds his boss emailed him the posting. It was the basic details. Chad Martin, date of birth, last known location and a picture. The photo was grainy and looked like the kind that had been pulled off a surveillance camera. There was a black star at the corner of the picture.

He texted James back:

BLACK STAR =?

This time he waited for James's response, almost as if James had to look it up. After ten minutes he got a text back:

Foreign GOVT assigned

If that were the case, it couldn't have been the Gray Wolves that had put out the contract. Or could it have been? There were several known persons within foreign governments who were also members of militant groups, or funded by them. Perhaps Bayural had paid someone within the Turkish government to put out a hit on Chad. Or, for all he knew, Bayural held a seat in the government.

WHICH ONE? he texted back.

UNKNOWN. MORE INFO ON HIRE.

If he took this job, his employers would expect him to get the kill. They weren't in this business for the familial honor, not like the Martins were. The only thing that mattered to the Watch Dogs was their bottom line. Which meant there was no room for failure if he accepted this contract—if he failed or let his feelings get in the way of finding and killing Chad, they may well put a bead on him. His bosses loved to reiterate that they were only as strong as their weakest link, and they would stop at nothing to be the strongest chain of contractors in the world.

He couldn't rush this decision. But there were no other options to get the information he desperately needed to figure out who had taken out the hit.

He did a quick search on the Gray Wolves and their

leader. The public information on the group was sparse: just a few mentions in Turkish papers, Al Jazeera and the BBC. No information on Bayural, or any ties he held in the government or to the prime minister.

Eli didn't know how he would come out of this without hurting himself or someone he loved, but his options were limited. He had to do what he felt was right.

I'LL TAKE THE JOB.

DONE. STANDARD RATES.

He had no problem giving the Watch Dogs their cut so long as he could do what he was really trying to do by taking this job.

Before he clicked off the screen, an email from James landed in his encrypted in-box.

Glancing back at the closed door beside him, he could make out the sounds of Zoey's pacing. She had to be upset—she was just dealing with it in a different way than he was.

He clicked on the email and took a look at the details spread out before him. Whoever was picking up the tab was serious. As he had assumed, there was a bonus of one million dollars if someone could get the job done within seven days of the posting. According to the date, that was three days ago.

Based on the craziness of the man in her trunk, there was no way they were done dealing with mercenaries who were hungry for a profit.

In addition to the bonus, it looked as though there was a four million flat on taking him down. Five million dollars was a lot of money—his normal jobs paid only low five figures—and then cut the company's commission. Even in his own life that kind of money would make a huge difference. He would never have to raise a gun again. He could retire anywhere. No wonder even the poorly skilled sewer rats had come out to take on the job.

He could see snow still coming down through the window at the end of the hall. Winter was crashing in upon them.

If he did kill Chad, he would probably walk away with more than enough money to buy a place just like this ranch. It was just too bad he knew and liked the man he had just agreed to take out—only time would tell if he would have to pull the trigger or not. The only person he truly wanted to take aim at was the person responsible for putting his friend in the sights.

Though he was paid to think about the "what ifs" in any situation, this time he focused on putting those kinds of thoughts to the back of his mind. For so many years, working with STEALTH, they had always had a focus on the family sticking together. At one point, before things had blown up in his face, he had definitely been part of that family.

Nostalgia beckoned him, but the door to the room beside him opened, and Zoey stuck her head out. "You can't sleep, either?" Her hair was ruffled, as though she had tried to sleep and had wrestled with her pillow. He savored the opportunity to see Zoey in her natural, beautiful state. It reminded him of waking up with her at his side every morning.

"Have a job to do." He slipped his phone into his pocket as his words echoed in the night.

It is just a question of which job, and where my loyalties will stand or fall.

He could feel her gaze upon him, as though she was trying to read between the lines.

"I can leave you alone then," she said, moving to close the bedroom door.

"No," he said with an adamant shake of his head. The last thing he wanted to do was sit out here any longer by himself—especially if she was offering some kind of olive branch. "I was just filling my time while I waited for your bogeyman."

"So, you've come to believe that the man was here for me, not Chad?"

He stood up, his knee popping as he moved.

"Ha," she said, glancing down to his offending appendage and not waiting for him to answer. "Getting older, are we?"

He chuckled. Zoey always had a way of finding his vulnerable spots—and aging, especially in this business, was one of them. Killing for a living was a young man's business, and not for someone in their midthirties with a repaired rotator cuff and pins in his ankles that required him to announce their presence anytime he wanted to catch a flight.

"Hey now, I'm not old. I'm just getting more refined," he said, giving her the grin that used to beckon her into his arms.

This time, it didn't work. Instead, she stepped inside the bedroom door. But then she waved for him to follow.

There wasn't much in the way of furniture in her room, just a bed, a dresser and a love seat tucked in the corner. She nodded toward the couch as she walked over to the bed and sat down on the edge on top of a sleeping bag she had unzipped and smoothed into a bedspread—as much as a blue-and-red flannel mummy bag could.

Nervous energy. She'd never been one for caring about the state of her dwelling. They were never in one place long enough to unpack—at least, usually. He remained standing.

"How long have you been here?" he asked.

She cringed as she ran her finger over the zipper of the bag. "Uh, a month or two."

"Going stir-crazy yet?" he asked.

"You have no idea." She pursed her lips, nodding. "Jarrod tried to convince me to stay home, to stay away from the show in Billings, but I couldn't stand staring at these four walls for another second."

"I thought you were working with Mindy on H&K's new line?" he asked.

"Remotely, I'm still working tech with STEALTH. But ever since…well, you know…we've been keeping a low profile." She sucked in a breath. "Which for some, has been easy. Chad has really liked catching up on old basketball highlights." She cocked her eyebrows in feigned annoyance, but he could see the glimmer of love for her brother and his quirks in her eyes.

"He's here, then?" he asked, motioning toward the bedrooms down the hall.

"No," she said. "I'm not sure where he is now, but he was supposed to be coming home from Sweden this week. He had been checking on our manufacturing plant, the one Mindy's father had built near Stockholm." She glanced over at her phone and its broken screen. "I tried to call him when I was driving back from Billings, but it went straight to voice mail. I pulled the info on his phone, but the last data usage was from Sweden two days ago."

Damn, he forgot how good Zoey was to have around when it came to tech. His new team didn't have anyone that could even compare. She could pinpoint just about anyone on a map at any time, using anything with a digital footprint.

Which reminded him of his phone. All of a sudden it—and the secrets it held—weighed even heavier in his back pocket.

If, even for a moment, she considered him anything less than one hundred percent trustworthy she could probably hack into every device he owned within a matter of hours.

The thought provided him with a new and deeper sense of foreboding.

But if he opened up to her now and told her what he had done, she would probably be forced to turn him out. How could she possibly trust him when five million dollars sat on the table? Zoey would undoubtedly think he was just using her to get close—and he couldn't risk having her flee. If she disappeared, the only time he would likely ever see her again was when her face flashed across the news as a missing person—or worse.

She could glean far more information from the actual post than he could. With all of her skills, she could probably pull everything from the post's initial location and time stamp all the way down to the author's eye color and their DNA sequence.

He *had* to tell her. The chances were okay that he would be able to make her understand why he had taken the job if he told her now, but if he waited…well, those minimal chances decreased by each passing nanosecond.

He was torn between his promises to his employers and the girl who had broken his heart.

Damn his heart.

"Zoe…" he said with a sigh.

She stopped pacing and looked at him. As though she could read that there was something up on his face, she moved closer. Her scent wafted toward him carrying the floral notes of Marc Jacobs Daisy…her signature scent.

He could feel his pupils dilate as he took her perfume deep into his lungs.

"What's wrong, Eli?" she said, touching his shoulder.

Her fingers were barely touching him, but he could feel them burn into him like they were sparking against his skin. She was the only woman who had ever had that effect on him, but no matter how much he cared for her, he couldn't be sure if those sparks were the kind brought on by lust, love or the magnetism of the forbidden. Knowing his luck, it was probably a combination of them all—but none more than the latter.

"Nothing," he said, drawing himself back as he looked at the hard pink lines of her lips. Damn, what he would give to kiss those lips and to have them both make promises of a future, a future without the pain that no amount of "I'm sorry" could make them forget.

"I know you better than that. Don't lie to me." She stepped even closer, like she was feeling the same pull he was. "If there is anyone in the world that you can be honest with, you know it's me."

Nothing could be further from the truth—but it wasn't because he didn't want to tell her everything. It was just…well, *time* had proven that trusting Zoey Martin with his heart wasn't wise.

He reached up and cupped her cheek in his hand. She

drew in a long breath, as though his touch had surprised her. The sound made him drop his fingers from her face and, as they lowered, he grazed his fingertips down the front of her T-shirt, slipping over the hardened surface of her nipple that pressed against the cotton. His body quivered to life as his mind drifted to all the times he had touched that exact place in the past—times he had taken for granted.

"I thought you were here to protect me," she said, her tone as much a question as it was a warning.

They were too close to the past, the future and a place where both of their hearts were threatened. And as she was so kind to remind him, he was there to alleviate the threats to Zoey, not to create more.

He took a step back.

They both needed to sleep. With fresh minds, they could make better decisions. Nighttime was fodder for wicked thoughts and even darker deeds.

"I am." He moved toward the bed, looking back over his shoulder. "You need to get some rest." He pulled back the sheets, fluffed her pillow and motioned for her to get into bed.

"You aren't trying to tell me what to do, are you?" She sounded annoyed, but at the same time there was a lightness to her tone like she found his actions charming.

"Never. I'm smarter than that." He gave her a wicked grin as she walked toward the bed and took off her slippers.

He turned away before she moved between the sheets.

"I'll be just outside your door." He motioned to the hall. As smart as he thought he was, he would never be gifted enough to see the future—or to know the right answers. For now, the only thing he knew with any certainty was that he was playing with fire.

Chapter Seven

It had been a hell of a long night and she had spent most of it setting up her new burner phone's security until she finally slipped into bed. The little dreaming that she did and that she could remember was all about Eli and being wrapped in his arms. The dreams were just as disconcerting as the reality that he sat just outside of her bedroom door.

They had been close—too close—last night. If he hadn't backed off after he had cupped her cheek, she was sure she would have been putty in his hands.

Her body ached from the refusal of the desires that had pulsed through it like poorly timed techno beats.

She was too old for this kind of feeling. It wasn't like she was eighteen years old and new to fluctuating emotions, no. And it wasn't that she had expected the longing she held for Eli to go away over time, but since they had lost their baby and she had left, she had thought them greatly tempered. How could she want someone so much when there were so many heartbreaking memories that came to mind every time she heard his name?

After getting dressed and checking to make sure that not even a strand of her Barbie-pink hair was out of place, she went to the door. It was no big deal to see him again this morning. He probably hadn't been feeling anything even remotely close to what she had. And, as such, there didn't have to be any awkwardness between them—at least nothing outside of her own head.

She trailed her fingers down the door to the handle just as he had trailed his fingers down her chest last night. Maybe there was something more to his feelings.

She pushed the thoughts away.

Even if there were, it couldn't matter. They had already loved and lost. They had been broken.

The doorknob twisted in her hand as he opened it from the other side.

She cleared her throat and took a step back as the door swung open.

"You don't knock now?" she asked, trying to sound annoyed.

Eli's hair, what little there was of it thanks to his high-and-tight haircut, was ruffled from a night spent pressing his head against the wall. His eyes were bloodshot and there was the scent of morning on him.

"I have to talk to you." His voice was hoarse, as though he hadn't slept at all.

Apparently, her night of tossing and turning was nothing compared to his.

"What?" If he said anything about what had transpired between them last night or in the past, she wasn't sure exactly what she would do. She had to head it off at the pass. "You don't have to worry about last—"

He stopped her with a shake of his head and she couldn't have been more grateful.

"It's about Chad." His words came so fast that they bordered on frenetic.

Her breath caught in her throat. "Did you find him?"

"No." Eli slipped his hand into hers and led her downstairs and to the dining room, away from Jarrod's and Trevor's bedrooms.

He sat her down at the table and brought them each a cup of coffee, but she didn't touch it.

"What's going on, Eli?" She couldn't handle the suspense.

He moved the chair like he was going to sit down beside her, but then he stopped and started pacing. He took a long drink of his coffee as though it could steel his resolve to say whatever it was that he was trying to hold back from her.

"There's a hit out on Chad." His words came out unexpectedly and at a clip.

Numbed by his news, she stared down at the table. She wasn't surprised, but the words sounded hollow, meaningless…as though, if she refused to internalize them, they wouldn't be true.

She took her new burner phone out of her pocket and turned it on. She dialed Chad's number and put it on speakerphone as she waited for it to ring. The call went straight to voice mail. She was going to tell him to call her, but his mailbox was full.

That wasn't like Chad. Sure, he was busy once in a while and unable to get to his phone, and some people would even call him a bit of a pain in the ass when it came to getting back to them, but he never ignored his work long enough for the mail to be full.

Something was wrong…very wrong.

She closed her eyes and tried to feel Chad, like she had some kind of internal barometer that could read if another of her siblings was alive or dead. No matter how hard she tried, she couldn't feel anything.

Not for the first time in her life, she wished that she had just a little bit of a sixth sense, something like the twin bond that Chad and Trish had sometimes seemed to have...nothing crazy, just enough magic to calm her nerves.

"It's going to be okay, Zoe."

Eli could try to calm her, but he wasn't magic, either. She couldn't lose another sibling. She couldn't lose her brother.

There was only one thing she could do—she had to kill whoever took out the hit on him.

"Who took the job?" she asked.

She wasn't sure, but she could have sworn Eli's face paled.

"It's an open contract." He paused. "Five million."

That was a lot of money—killing a diplomat kind of money. Not the kind of money that was normally put out on a man like Chad. And an open contract?

Her stomach churned. With an open contract it meant that every jerk and his father would be on the hunt for her brother.

She would have to take down any possible mercenaries one at a time.

Before Eli could say another word, she rushed from the table and sprinted upstairs. She pounded on Trevor's and Jarrod's doors. She couldn't handle this news alone. Not now.

Trevor wasn't going to take this well—he was still having guilt over the loss of Trish. He thought her death was his fault. Though he was taking steps toward forgiving himself, there was no changing the fact that he had watched her die.

Zoey couldn't imagine the state Trevor would be in if they lost Chad, too.

Some losses were too great even for the toughest of men and women.

"Meet me downstairs," she said, calling out to them through their doors.

She hurried back down. Eli was staring into his cup like it could give him a readout on Chad's whereabouts.

"That's not all," he whispered.

"What? What do you mean? Did someone already get to him?" Zoey stopped moving, but her blood pounded in her veins.

"Watch Dog took the contract."

She was breathless. "The company you work for?" she asked, though she knew the answer.

He nodded.

"Which operative is working the hit?" she asked, afraid she already knew.

He looked up at her, pain in his eyes. "I am."

What little was still together inside her shattered. "Get out. Get out of my house."

Eli's face pinched, and he shrank back as though she had punched him in the gut and not the other way around. What in the hell was he thinking?

She had been wrong to think that she could bring Eli back into her life. She should have known that when it came to him, the only thing they were good at was bringing the other to their knees. She had been stupid to think this time would be any different.

He stood before her, unmoving. He had to have heard her tell him to get out. He had to have heard the pain in her voice and the anger that leached through the cracks he'd just reopened in her soul.

Well, if he wasn't going to get the hell out, that didn't mean she couldn't.

She turned to walk out of the room.

Screw him and the horse he rode in on.

She had been his fool too many times.

As she started to leave, Trevor and Jarrod strode into the room. Jarrod's hair was disheveled and matted against the side of his head, uncharacteristic for the stoic and typically well-groomed man it belonged to.

"What's up?" Jarrod asked as Trevor yawned and wiped the sleep from his eyes. "Wait, Eli? What in the hell are you doing here?" Jarrod shot her a look.

"You talk to him," she said, jabbing a finger at him. "I wash my hands of his nonsense."

She ran upstairs to her room, shoved some toiletries into her purse and grabbed her passport. Though she didn't have a clue where Chad was, it didn't matter. All that was important was getting the hell out of Dodge. If her ex and a hit man had tracked her down and suckered her in, who knew who else was on their way here.

For safe measure, she went to her closet and unlocked her gun safe and pulled out a box of rounds and the M4 she kept there for emergencies.

It had been at least a year since she had actually fired a gun, but she had no doubts about her capabilities as a marksman.

Though her brothers were always the men who pulled the trigger, keeping her at the keyboard, the reality was that she had always been the best shot.

When they had been young, their father had taken them out to the range and soon had them honing their skills at five hundred yards. It had taken her only a day or two at that range before she had dialed her aim into a grouping the size of a nickel.

Yet no matter how accurate her shot, it was another story when it came to taking aim at a man and pulling the trigger. To her, being a woman meant only one less dangling appendage. She was capable of almost anything they could do, except when it came to delivering death. There, she was a world removed from her brothers. They could share a sandwich with a man and then draw and fire upon him with their next breath.

She set the M4 back in the case, and the metal safe made a hollow ring as the gun's butt came down on the cold steel.

It was one thing to order a drone strike on a faceless enemy, but something entirely different when she could look into the eyes of her target.

If only she could order a drone strike on the Gray Wolves.

Her bedroom door swung open and Jarrod walked inside. "Did you actually talk to Eli, or did you just go shooting off at the mouth like you normally do?" Jarrod asked.

Oh, no, he didn't.

She closed the gun safe, rolling the combo wheel to lock it, each action deliberate and slowed by fury.

"You really want to talk to me about going off half-cocked?" She could feel her neck bulge as she seethed. "What, were you down there a full five minutes? I'm sure, in that epic amount of time, Eli could tell you everything… How he just randomly happened to see me in Billings, how he saved me from a killer in the barn and how he was forced into taking a five-million-dollar contract someone put out on Chad? Isn't he just a freaking hero."

"You dropped him, not the other way around. You don't get to be angry with him about everything that happened."

"This…" she spat, motioning to her face like it was a flashing danger sign. "This has nothing to do with that. This has to do with the fact that he just agreed to kill our brother…and his former friend."

Jarrod laughed, causing another rise in her nearly stroking-out-level blood pressure.

How could Jarrod possibly laugh at a moment like this?

He must have finally noticed how angry he was making her. He stopped laughing. "Dude, Zoey…"

"Don't *dude* me. You are the one being ridiculous right now. It's obvious that Eli is here to manipulate us and get as close to Chad as possible in order to take him out."

Jarrod walked over to her bed and sat down on the edge, just like he had done when she was a child. "I'm not saying that you're not right to be concerned. However, if I were in Eli's shoes, and I needed more information about the contract and how best to close it out, I would have done the same thing. It was smart to agree to the hit." Jarrod rested his hands between his knees. "If he really wanted to kill Chad for the money, do you really think he would have told you about the hit? Eli could have kept it a secret until he had pulled the trigger."

Or he was lulling them with a false sense of safety.

It was smarter that way, keep them in the loop about the hit, make her and her brothers work to keep any other hit man from getting close, while getting closer himself.

There was a whisper from just outside the bedroom door. "Trevor, Eli, if you are going to stand out there eavesdropping you may as well come in and join the damned conversation."

Eli stepped in, but his gaze was firmly planted on the floor. Trevor was close at his heels. They looked like little boys who had been caught with their hands in the cookie jar, but this wasn't some misdeed that she could just shrug off. They were talking about murder.

"Zoey, I promise you that I took the gig with the purest of intentions." Eli finally glanced up at her as he gave her a placating look.

She said nothing.

Trevor stepped beside Jarrod. "I for one think Eli is telling the truth. Now, he could be our greatest source of information. We can watch the posts coming through, maybe even be able to get to Bayural by pinpointing the IP address."

That wasn't exactly how IPs worked, but she didn't bother explaining it to Trevor.

"Actually," Eli started, "I don't think that this job was posted by a Gray Wolf. According to my info, the contract was put out by a foreign government, not an individual."

She huffed. "Turkey, I am sure. Bayural has his hands in every diplomat's pockets."

Eli shook his head and sent her an apologetic glance. "No… I just got word that it was put out by someone in Algeria."

"Algeria?" she asked, surprised. There was a collection of countries that Bayural and the Gray Wolves could have maybe been working with, but Algeria didn't seem like the kind of country that would be on that list. They had nothing, at least that she could think of, that would be gained by allying themselves with a terrorist group and then doing their dirty work.

"From the way I see it, it doesn't make a whole hell of a lot of sense, but at least we have a bit of information to start working off. It's better than nothing." Eli gave her self-effacing smile.

Though she was still miffed, Eli was proving to be more helpful than she cared to admit. Without him, they'd have no knowledge of what was coming down from behind the enemy's lines.

"Eli has a point. Good work, man," Jarrod said with a slap to his back, as though he was just another of her brothers. He turned to Eli. "But what was that talk about a dead body?"

Chapter Eight

He wasn't even close to being out of the woods when it came to getting back into Zoey's good graces. Though Jarrod had managed to get a pass from Zoey, from the way she looked at him, she still clearly thought he was trying to make a move against the family.

He was going to have to prove that he was someone she could trust. Even if it took him his whole life, he would prove to her that he wasn't the man she thought she knew.

Jarrod looked at him, waiting for him to answer for the dead man in Zoey's trunk.

"What can I say, the dude picked the wrong woman to come after." Eli smirked as he gave an appreciative nod in Zoey's direction.

"Do you think this is going to be a continuing problem?" Jarrod asked. He was always the one taking charge.

Eli nodded. "Unfortunately, I think it's possible. I believe he was working some of the same angles as I was, scoping out places your family would be tempted to go. After hearing whispers about you guys getting into large-scale gun manufacturing in Sweden, I narrowed it down to just a few places you would likely make a public appearance."

Zoey opened her mouth like she was going to speak, but quickly closed it.

"If I can figure out your family's possible movements, then others will, as well."

Zoey stormed off toward the door, grabbing her purse. "We have to get out of here." She looked to Trevor and Jarrod. "Where are Mindy and Sabrina?"

"They haven't gotten back from their trip to H&K. And they have Anya with them." Trevor took out his phone and tapped on the screen like he was hoping to hear from his fiancée at any moment.

"When do they touch down?" Eli asked.

Trevor looked up from his phone. "They're supposed to be arriving into Missoula at about five thirty tomorrow. They are leaving Stockholm this afternoon. Coming through London."

Eli nodded. "Tell them to stay in place."

"Have they seen Chad?" Zoey sounded like a frantic mother.

Jarrod scowled. The unspoken tension between Jarrod and his sister was nearly palpable.

Eli wasn't sure what the source of mixed feelings was between them, but he knew well enough to let it alone. The Martin crew was a special breed—loyal to the death, but often found nipping at each other's ankles.

On more than one occasion, when he had first taken the job with their team, he had found himself at the center of one of their feuds. Zoey and Jarrod had been discussing which scope covers to buy and use for their growing team. Their discussion had quickly turned into a near yelling match. The only reason it hadn't was that Trish had stepped in and acted as their ballast.

It struck him that perhaps that was what was going on; the Martin equilibrium was thrown off due to Trish's death.

"No one has spoken to Chad in three days." Trevor's face pinched.

Even for a Martin outsider that was concerning. "That was when the contract went live," Eli said. "The good news is that the contract is still active. As of now, he is still considered to be alive." He tried to sound hopeful though everyone in that room knew just as well as he did that sometimes it took several weeks for a contract to be taken down after being completed.

"We need to find him," Jarrod said.

Zoey gave him an irritated look. "Thanks for joining the party."

Jarrod ignored her. "Did you check his credit card activity yet?"

Zoey opened and then closed her mouth. She shook her head. "I was hoping to hear that one of you had spoken to him."

She looked a bit crestfallen that Jarrod had gotten the better of her.

"You take care of looking into his paper trail and Trevor and I will take care of your friend out in the trunk and his Chevy." Jarrod strode to the door as he worked away on his phone, likely calling in their disposal team. "We'll take your car. If you need to go anywhere you'll have to make amends with Eli." Jarrod gave him a sly grin.

He had always gotten along well with Jarrod, which had sometimes irritated Zoey when they didn't see eye to eye, but the brother's attempt to help further their reconciliation surprised him. It made him wonder if Jarrod knew something he didn't. Perhaps he advocated their getting back together…or perhaps he just liked having an extra set of hands around in this emergency.

Or maybe he didn't trust him and the best way to keep tabs on him was by keeping him at heel.

He liked his first thought the best.

As the brothers left him alone with Zoey, there was a long moment before either of them spoke. When she sighed, he was afraid she was about to let him have it. He certainly deserved it. Instead, she surprised him. "Sorry about that display with Jarrod. Some things never change."

And from what he saw, things had only gotten worse.

"You're fine. You know how things are with my family. I'm in no place to judge."

"You still don't speak to them?" The look in her eyes moved a click closer to pity.

"No." He shouldn't have brought his family up. They, and the nonsense they brought with them, was one topic he would rather leave buried in the past. "And what Jarrod said about amends, don't worry about it. Whatever you're feeling toward me, it's justified. I should've let you in on the truth from the very beginning, I just didn't know how to go about it. With everything that happened between us, I just wanted to get everything right."

She dropped her purse to the floor and walked over to him. Putting her hands on his face, she looked him in the eyes. "I'm the one who should say sorry. I know I can be hard to put up with, and I can get things so wrong sometimes—especially when it comes to relationships."

Her fingers were warm on his cheeks, and she ran

her thumbs over the stubble that had accumulated over the last day.

"I shouldn't have just left you," she said. "I just didn't know where I wanted things to go with us. We were getting so close to having our own family. I guess it scared me. And then when…"

"We lost the baby…" The words threatened to choke him as he finished her sentence. "It hurt me just as much as it hurt you. I hope you know that I've thought of you every day we were apart. And I don't expect us to get to the place we were ever again, but I'm hoping we can be friends."

"Is that why you're *really* here?" Her hands moved to his shoulders and then drifted down his arms.

It was one of the many reasons, and though he wanted to tell her he had spent almost every waking hour dreaming of her and what the future could have been, he said nothing. It took Zoey so much to open up to him that he didn't want to make this about himself. She was the one who really mattered.

He leaned in to kiss her, the movement instinctual. Just before their lips met, he realized what he was doing, and turned his face so his lips brushed against her cheek. He let them rest there for a second too long, as he took in a long breath of her.

She stepped back, but her hand drifted into his and she squeezed his fingers. "I'm glad you're back, Eli. And I think you're right… I don't think we're ever going to get to the same place again. I was never meant to have children."

There was a finality in her words, and they tore at his heart.

She let go of his hand, moved across the room and grabbed her computer out of her bag. She clicked it on.

After about an hour of them working side-by-side, he excused himself and went to get two fresh cups of coffee as she continued to work. Her brothers, and the car in the driveway, were gone.

As he moved around the house, he couldn't deny that this place somehow felt like home, though he had never been here before. Perhaps it was just that she was here.

He took a sip of his coffee as he stood in front of the bay windows and stared outside. He could live here, surrounded by the wilderness and watching the snow as it drifted down from the sky. There was no traffic, no crowds, no dust storms on the horizon, and no sand wedged into every crevice of his body. If there had been a crackling fire in the fireplace, it could've been the quintessential Montana dream.

There was a creak in the floorboard behind him, and as he turned there was the blur of an object coming at his head. He dropped down, dodging the impact. The coffee cups he had been holding shattered as he let them fall from his grip. Hot coffee spread across the floor and splattered upon his hands, but he didn't feel any pain.

A man lunged toward him, a shotgun in his hands. He racked a shell into the gun's chamber with a loud metallic crack. Eli couldn't make out the man's features, but he looked to be about six foot five and pushing three bills.

It was a wonder the man had tried to be stealthy by swinging the gun instead of shooting him. Eli had been lucky.

The giant aimed from his hip as his finger moved to the trigger. Eli threw himself toward the couch. He rolled behind it as the gun boomed and a spray of BBs hit the corner where he had just been. Tufts of the cushions flew up into the air, making it look as though snow was falling inside of the room.

Eli reached behind his back, looking for his Glock. His fingers wrapped around the gun's handle and he pulled it from his holster. There was already a round in the chamber. All he had to do was get a bead on this dude without getting hit.

He thought of Zoey upstairs. What if there were more than one hit man this time? Even if not, Zoey would be rushing down here at the sound of the gun's blast. He needed to make quick work of this guy to make sure she didn't find herself in harm's way. He had to protect her.

He belly crawled to the edge of the couch where a round had just struck. The man's footsteps pounded against the wood floor as he rushed toward him and racked another round into the chamber. The giant had only two more shots before the magazine was empty.

Eli took a breath as he rolled around the corner and took aim at the man's center mass. He pulled the trigger. The shot rang out and struck true. The giant stepped back, shock on his face as his left hand dropped from his shotgun and he looked down at his chest. Blood seeped through his gray T-shirt.

"What in the hell?" the man said, like he was surprised any bullet had ever found him.

Eli fired again, hoping this time to bring the man to the ground and eliminate the threat. The bullet struck millimeters to the left of his original shot.

The giant took another step, obscenities streaming from his mouth like a spray of spittle.

He still didn't fall to his knees. The man raised his

shotgun. Eli dodged behind the couch again, hoping this time he would still have enough cushion to provide cover. The giant fired off another shot in Eli's direction. A BB struck Eli's shoulder, embedding in his skin. He touched the spot—it was already bleeding.

The couch was one piss-poor excuse for a barricade, and it wouldn't withstand another shot. He held no doubt that the man had another firearm with him, probably something very similar to his own.

He crawled toward the other corner, hoping against all hope that he would get there in time enough to surprise his attacker and go for the one shot he knew would take the man down.

As he neared the far corner of the couch, he moved to round it as he was met with the sound of the man racking a round into the chamber. It was now or never—he lunged his body around the corner and took aim, the motion instinctual.

The giant pulled the trigger of the shotgun as Eli's round ripped through him. The shotgun's recoil went unchecked by the man's strength, sending the BBs astray and just above Eli's head, barely missing him and striking the wall behind him with a cascade of dull thuds.

The man crumpled and collapsed onto the ground.

Eli got up. Standing at the top of the stairs, looking down at them with a gun in her shaking hands, was Zoey.

He motioned for her to stay put as he moved closer to the man, keeping a bead on him in case he wasn't dead. Yet, as he drew nearer, he could make out the round edge of a bullet wound between the guy's eyes.

There was the sound of a gun hitting the floor as

Zoey rushed down the stairs, straight to him. "Are you okay?" she asked, looking him over. "You're bleeding. Do you need to go to the hospital?"

He glanced down to the blood spot at his shoulder. "It's nothing. I'll be fine."

He shoved his gun back into its holster. Zoey stepped over and looked at the dead man lying in the middle of her family's living room.

She was the one who wasn't okay. None of her family was going to be okay. They had to act. Fast.

This was no longer a game of rekindling old flames; it had swiftly become a battle of kill or be killed.

Chapter Nine

Zoey's hands trembled as the adrenaline worked its way out of her system. The residue of fear mixed with the elixir of relief made a sickening sense of nausea rise up from her core. She had nearly pulled the trigger. In fact, it could have been her bullet that had ripped through his skull.

Blood pooled on her mother and father's Oriental rug. It had been in the family for years and now it was destroyed. The cranberry-colored liquid seeped into the ochre strands as the reality of what she had almost done crept deeper into her core.

She could have been a murderer.

"We have to get out of here," Eli said. "My truck is just down the road. We can go anywhere you want, but you can't stay in this house until this thing with Chad is under control."

Though she heard the words coming out of Eli's mouth, she couldn't process them. It was as if he was talking to her through a tin can, the sound ringing and otherworldly.

Her finger twitched as she stared at the man on the floor.

All she had thought about was that if she didn't pull

the trigger Eli was going to die and he would be gone from her life forever.

And yet, she had failed to be brave enough to take the shot. The world started to spin.

Eli moved closer to her, wrapping her in his arms as though he could sense she was about to go down.

"You're okay. It's going to be okay," he said, moving her toward the nearly destroyed couch and making her sit down.

This couch had been all that stood between him and death.

What if she had come downstairs instead of Eli? In the barn, Eli was the only reason that she had even survived. In a sense, he had saved her twice.

It was like they were back in a war zone, except this was the place her family had intended on making their home. Now, BBs were lodged in the couch and there was blood spatter on the wall behind the attacker. Her home had become a death zone.

"Just breathe," Eli said as another wave of light-headedness came over her.

Her hands were still trembling in her lap and she was shaking her legs, restless.

It was okay. Everything was going to be fine.

Eli was right. She couldn't deal with the emotions that came with what had just happened. She had to keep moving. If they fell under attack once again, the odds might not play out in their favor.

They had to get the hell out of this shooting gallery.

She stood up. Her knees were weak and threatened to buckle beneath her, but she summoned as much strength as she could to take a step. As she moved, it reminded her of the day she lost the baby, leaving them alone in the world. Here she was again, her world threatening to collapse. The only thing she could do was find the courage to keep moving forward, just as she had done before.

Thankfully, Eli was here. This time, she had to stay. She couldn't just walk out and deal with this on her own as she had done before. Though things would be different between them, and they weren't likely to find their way back into a serious relationship, that didn't mean they couldn't be each other's greatest ally.

It took them only a few minutes for her to grab her go-bag and bug out, leaving the dead guy on the floor. No one would find him. She called her brothers as they walked down the road to Eli's truck. Being in killers' crosshairs was proving to be much harder than she had ever assumed. If things ever got back to normal, she would never complain about sitting behind a computer again. She would take carpal tunnel over a bullet any day.

Trevor answered his phone on the second ring. "It's done," he said, not waiting for her to speak.

"There's more trash to take out. I left it in the living room for you." Her footsteps crunched in the fresh snow as she walked to the passenger side of Eli's Dodge pickup. "I recommend leaving it there for now. It's too hot in the house for any of us."

There was a long pause on the other end of the line as Trevor must have been deciphering her code. Now more than ever, it seemed that everything in their lives was coming under scrutiny. Nothing they did or said over open communication lines was safe. They were being monitored.

"Understood."

"We need to enact COBRA," she said, using the code word for going underground. All their cell phones would be destroyed, along with any other forms of communication technology that could be tracked back to them.

In a sense, they would all be going dark. It was likely what Chad had done and why he had been so impossible to pin down—if he were still alive.

It was what they had all been trained to do in an event like this—stay low, seek shelter.

Unfortunately, with their house no longer available, there were no safe zones. Thankfully, they had protocol for this type of event. Each of them had bags stashed in various locations with devices with state-of-the-art encryption—she had taken care of all the phones and tablets herself.

She grabbed her go-bag and rifled through it. It had everything she needed to get away. As it was, however, they wouldn't have access to their regular email accounts—they were already known and the information within them lay in the hands of their hunters. And, if they accessed their accounts through their new phones, it would be only a few hours before their locations would once again be known.

They would have to be extremely careful. There were nearly a million ways they could be tracked down if any one of them accidently clicked on the wrong button.

The other end of the line was muffled as Trevor must've said something to Jarrod. After a moment, he returned to the phone. "Done."

"In the meantime, look into our new friend in the government. I will expect to hear from you soon."

Trevor grunted in acknowledgment on the other end of the line. When the line went dead, she took out the battery from her phone and snapped the SIM card, then threw them all out the window toward the pasture.

When they were well away from the ranch, she would turn on her other equipment, but not yet, not with possible enemies lurking around every corner.

Eli started the truck, letting it roar to life. He kicked up bits of snow and gravel as he took off.

She wasn't sure whether she should ask him where they were going or just let him lead the way. There was enough information out there that if someone wanted to find her, it may not have taken too much digging. But no one would guess she would leave her heart and safety in the hands of her ex—only a madwoman would do something so stupid…or someone incredibly desperate.

The midday sun bounced off the front window just as they crossed over the Montana-Idaho line. They were stuck behind a line of truckers ascending the pass. There always had to be that one driver who found fault in the others around them and decided to pass the line of cars, only to find that the left lane was snow packed and icy and far more treacherous than they had anticipated. In a way it acted like a metaphor for her life— just when she thought she was ready to take control of the world around her, her hubris caught up with her.

She should never have gone to Billings. Everyone had warned her to stay home and out of the limelight. She had been an idiot and fallen into the trap of complacency. She should've known better.

As they crested the hill and made their way deeper into the panhandle of Idaho, she turned on her phone. Eli gave her a glance, like he wasn't sure whether or not it was safe for her to be doing so.

"Even if people are tracking phones, if they find the

signal they won't think anything of it. This line is assigned to an alias. Even if they take the time to look it up, the findings won't go anywhere. We are safe, at least for now." She didn't tell him the part about how she didn't dare to delve too deep into the internet.

She wanted to reach out to her brothers to make sure they were okay, and to see where they were headed, but she didn't dare just yet.

"I'm coming to learn that safe is relative," Eli said.

"Why would you say that?" She clicked off the screen after making sure the phone was fully charged.

"I shot that man twice, center mass. Nothing happened. He wasn't wearing standard body armor, but the bullets didn't penetrate. It was like he was wearing something similar to your dress at the trade show." Eli gave her an appraising glance like he was questioning her culpability in the attack.

"If you're implying that I gave this man bulletproof clothing so he could break in, shoot up my house and try to kill us, then you are crazy." Something like that wouldn't even make sense. "I thought by now you would know you can trust me, and I thought I could trust you. Let's not take two steps back. Not now. The only way we are going to make it out of this, or at least the only way I will make it out of this, is if we stick together. Eli, I can't do this alone." She could hear the pleading edge to her voice, but as she spoke she didn't try to muffle it.

"I know." He sat in silence for a long moment, staring at the road. "I just wanted to make sure that you weren't somehow involved in this."

"I know it's been a long time since we were together, but I'd like to say that I've changed for the better." She felt exhaustion seep into her core at having to fight to prove who she was. "I'm not entirely evil."

"Well, now I know you're telling me the truth— you're still a little bit evil. If you tried to tell me you were a saint…we'd be having a very different conversation," he said with a laugh. "In fact, that bit of duality is part of the reason I have always thought of you as someone special—you're not like everyone else. You say what you mean, even if it's something you know people aren't going to want to hear, and you are unapologetically yourself."

She laughed. He hit the nail on the head with that one. Most people wouldn't consider those strengths, but rather character defects. More than one of her exes had chewed her out for embarrassing them by saying the wrong thing to the wrong person.

Luckily, she had never let the criticism of others change her. She was unstoppable. But Eli's compliments made her uncomfortable, like a jacket that brought her warmth but rested too heavy on her shoulders.

It was easier to shrug off criticism than it was to accept praise.

"You're only saying that because you saw me in that pink dress," she teased, hoping to ease some of the pressure. "I saw the way you looked at me up there."

She could have sworn that she saw a blush rise on his cheeks, but it was something so rare on him that she couldn't be sure it wasn't simply a trick of the light.

"Ha! Is that how you respond to a compliment, by searching for another?" he joked. "If that's what you want, well… I have to admit—"

"Wait," she said, interrupting him as a thought crossed her mind. "Mindy had her marketing team give samples of our new line to a select group of foreign leaders."

"Algerian leaders?"

She shrugged. "I have no idea who we ended up sending them to."

"Looks like we're going to need to give Mindy a call," he said as he took the off-ramp at the first exit in Coeur d'Alene.

She moved to make the call, but stopped herself. It was more than likely that there were people out there who were monitoring Mindy's phone calls. She had to use another number. Using an app, she grabbed a number assigned to a man out of Newark. It would do the trick. If their enemies went digging they would be looking on the other side of the country.

She dialed, hoping Mindy would pick up even though she wouldn't recognize the man's name or number.

After a couple of rounds of ring backs of "Woman Up" by Meghan Trainor, Mindy picked up the phone. "Hello, this is Mindy. How can I help you?" she asked, like she was a well-seasoned receptionist instead of the owner of a multimillion-dollar company.

"It's me," Zoey said, hoping she would recognize her voice. "Are you holed up?"

She could almost hear the relief in Mindy's sigh. "Yes, we're in—"

"Don't tell me. But you are safe?"

"Yes, I'm with Sabrina. Everything is fine. Are Trevor and Jarrod okay?"

"They're good," Zoey said, hoping that she was right. "I'm calling about the samples we sent out for the new Monster Wear. Do you have a list of people we shipped samples to?"

Mindy paused. "I think so."

"Perfect." Zoey gave Eli a thumbs-up. For once, the stars were almost aligning.

There was a moment of quiet as Mindy must have been scrolling through her phone. "Okay, it looks like we sent out samples to about thirty heads of state."

"Did you send any to Algeria?"

Mindy made a noise as though she were sucking on her teeth as she read over her list. "Yeah, looks like we sent three white T-shirts and two pairs of Monster Wear jeans to the prime minister."

There was no way that the man in the living room was the prime minister of Algeria, that much she knew for sure. "Did you send the white T-shirts to anyone else?"

"Looks like members of the Swedish parliament, but no one else. Why?"

Was someone in the Swedish government coming after them and trying to make it look like it was an Algerian hit? Zoey's thoughts moved to a few months ago and the nerve agent attack on Jarrod and Mindy.

"Do you still have enemies in Sweden?" Zoey asked.

"No, I don't think so. We've been well received after…well, everything. In fact, most have been apologetic about the whole incident."

That didn't mean they were in the clear when it came to Swedish ties, but she had to hope that this case was going to be more cut and dry than the last. "Good, but let me know if you think of anyone or anything that strikes you as odd," Zoey said, trying to make sense of all the thoughts that were flooding her mind.

"Actually, did you make a wire transfer out of our corporate expense account?" Mindy asked.

"No, why?"

"It looks as though someone transferred $500,226.23 from our account. Do I need to flag it at our bank?" Mindy sounded a bit breathless. "Do you think someone stole it?"

That was a lot of money. And an odd amount. Who transferred twenty-three cents in change? "Have you looked into it at all?"

"Looks like it was transferred to a bank just outside of Barcelona. A town called Sitges. It was processed to be taken out in cash."

"Do you know who picked it up? Their name?"

"John Smith." Mindy huffed. "I was hoping you had something to do with it."

"I'll take a look at it. For now, have the bank put a hold on all accounts not vital for handling the daily expenses. Only give access to our VP of finance and you and me. We need to stop any leaks before we lose everything."

Chapter Ten

Five hundred thousand. That was more than the average American's initial mortgage loan. For some, it would be enough to live off for the rest of their lives. And yet, H&K had enough liquid resources to transfer that kind of money without anyone panicking. Eli shook his head.

Now the five-million-dollar bounty on Chad's head made sense. Everyone around him was rolling in money.

He would never know what a life like that was like. Sure, he had enough to pay his bills and never have to worry about where his next meal would come from, but he couldn't imagine not being overly concerned about a missing five hundred grand from his bank account.

"What do you think is going on?" Eli asked.

Zoey was staring down at her phone. Maybe she wasn't taking the loss of that kind of money as flippantly as he thought she had been.

"Are you okay?" he asked, when she refused to answer.

She pointed in the direction of a Starbucks. "I'm going to need a coffee."

Yep, she wasn't taking this well. His body relaxed a little bit as she returned to the land of normal Americans who lived on a budget. He loved the idea of her being successful and doing well with her family and their businesses, but he wasn't sure that he could be with a woman who was a magnate—he would always feel completely out of her league. He wanted to be an equal partner in any relationship, and that wasn't limited to fiscal matters.

He pulled into the Starbucks and parked. "Want a caramel macchiato, two pumps of hazelnut?"

She smiled. "We can go in together. You still like your coffee so dark and bold that it can hold the spoon up, right?"

He laughed. "A lot can change, but as far as I'm concerned there is only one way to take coffee and that's it."

She rolled her eyes in feigned exasperation. Before getting out, she turned around and grabbed a tablet from out of her bag. She turned it on and connected into the Wi-Fi.

"Seriously, open Wi-Fi? You're good with that?" Eli was surprised.

"Often, it's best if we just hide in plain sight." She gave him a sly grin as she took a beanie-style hat out of her bag and slipped it over her pink hair. She handed him a baseball cap. "But I would hate to be too obvious."

He slipped on the hat, aware that it would keep him anonymous in the coffee shop's cameras.

Inside, the place smelled like pumpkin spice lattes, hopeful writers and daring entrepreneurs. He loved it.

After ordering the coffees and making their way to a private table, Zoey turned her tablet back on and set to work. He watched her as she frowned and nibbled on her lip. She had always made the same face when she was concentrating and working hard. He had nearly forgotten how beautiful it looked.

There was a strand of pink hair poking out from under her gray hat and it sat at the center of her forehead. Each time she huffed, the little hair would flutter up and down like a frustrated mother's arms.

Finally, she smiled and looked up at him with a vindicated look in her eyes. "I think I got it."

"What?"

She moved so he could see her screen. "It looks as though the money was transferred to the BBVA bank in Sitges. About six hours ago, a man came in and picked it up, one John Smith." She clicked on a few buttons and pulled up the bank's security camera feed.

"Did you seriously hack into a bank's mainframe on public Wi-Fi in a matter of minutes?" he asked, both impressed and uncomfortable. Out of some intrinsic fear, he looked over his shoulder, as if one of the other people in the shop could see what they were up to.

She put her finger to her mouth, motioning for him to be quiet. "This is the best place to do it. Now watch," she said, pointing to the screen.

The video was of the entire bank's lobby, and though the area wasn't large, the size of the room made it seem as though they were zoomed out quite a bit. A man walked in from the street wearing a dark tan jacket and a wide-brimmed hat. He made his way up to the teller. A few moments later, a woman walked into the bank and stood behind him.

Though she was never closer than five feet from him, the way she moved made Eli wonder if they were together. The teller disappeared from the screen for a moment, then returned and started talking to the man.

Though they could not hear what the people were saying, they watched as the man produced an ID. The teller nodded, seeming appeased. The teller walked out of the frame and quickly returned carrying a small stack of wrapped euros.

Perhaps there was an odd number in the transfer because of the exchange rate. And there might have been some sort of fee for sending the money, but he wasn't sure.

The manager turned toward the cash drawer and pulled out a random selection of coins. Eli shook his head. Maybe his theory was wrong. Maybe this had nothing to do with exchange rates and fees. Rather, there was something more to the odd number of transferred monies. But what?

The man in the video turned, and looked straight up at the cameras. As he moved, the woman behind him jabbed him in the ribs, forcing him to look down. They took the money and quickly left.

Zoey turned off the video. "Did you see that?"

Of course he had seen it, it was a video. But it didn't seem like the time to be a smart-ass. "Which part?"

"That." Zoey turned to her tablet and skipped back to the moment the man looked up at the camera. "There... That's Chad. He's alive." There was palpable relief in her tone.

"Good." Hopefully Chad would stay that way. Eli squinted in an attempt to make out the man's face just a little bit better. "Who's the woman?"

"I have no idea," she said, moving closer to the screen like she was trying to see some tiny detail that could possibly give away the woman's identity.

"Has Chad been dating anyone?"

"No. At least not that I know of. But who knows

what he's up to these days. When it comes to that kind of thing, he normally keeps to himself."

He and Chad had never been super close. They had never worked a job together, but it wasn't because they had a difference of opinion or didn't like one another. It was just that Chad was normally the man they sent to be a bull in a china shop and Eli was the man they sent in to make a death look natural. Needless to say, they had different methods when it came to doing their jobs.

After finishing their coffees, they made their way back out to the truck. With the door closed, he turned to her. "Let's have Mindy and Sabrina look into the Swedish and Algerian ties—maybe they can get info about the officials there and find out if anyone has a grudge or reason to want to align themselves with the Gray Wolves."

She let out a long exhale. "Do you think we should go to Spain?"

"It's as good a place as anywhere. As far as we know, no one else has spotted Chad. If we get there before anyone else does, we have a chance of getting him to safety."

"Where would *safety* be, exactly?" she asked, sounding tired.

He couldn't answer her with any level of honesty. Right now, her family's world was upside down, and tangentially his was as well since he had allied himself with them. "The Gray Wolves can't hunt you forever." Even as he spoke, he heard the lie in his words.

"I'd like to think that, but so far that has yet to be true," she said with a haggard look.

He should have stayed quiet.

Calling Mindy, Zoey told her the plan. It took only a

few minutes, and though Zoey hadn't heard from Trevor and Jarrod yet, it would be only a matter of time until she did—as long as they were safe. He had to assume they were all right. At the thought, he could feel his blood pressure rise, putting pressure on his eyes. The last thing they needed was for all of the brothers to be one step away from being murdered, but it seemed like that was exactly where they were.

He had to stop playing out the worst-case scenarios in his head. This wasn't getting them anywhere.

"You have your passport?" he asked.

"Which one?" she said, motioning toward the back.

This was going to be one hell of an adventure—hopefully, they would both make it out alive.

Chapter Eleven

There was a private jet waiting for them on the tarmac in Spokane. They drove out to the plane and made their way in with a simple nod to the pilot and the staff.

Thankfully, there had been no snow on this side of the continental divide and it appeared they would have an easy flight to Spain.

Back in the day, when they were dating, Eli would have undoubtedly made some stupid joke about joining the mile-high club. Instead, once he was settled, he sat in near silence across the aisle from her. He sipped on a tumbler of Kentucky Bourbon and flipped through a magazine. Somehow, they had gone from lovers, to enemies, to allies, to an old married couple in just a few days.

Oh, how time flew.

As the sun began to set as they headed east, it lit up the cabin and a shaft of bright pink light was reflected against his cheek, making his stubble stand out. She had always loved that look on him and it harkened to a time when they had been comfortable enough to really let the other see them—warts and all.

She thought of herself; he may have had a wart or two, but she was the one who was weighed down by them.

He flipped the page of the magazine.

"Are you going to stare at me the entire flight?" he asked, giving her a sly grin.

Without missing a beat, though she was embarrassed at being caught staring, she replied, "I was just wondering how long you were going to go before you noticed the booger hanging out of your nose." She laughed, mocking him by playfully wiping at her own.

He instinctively rubbed at his nose, finding nothing. He smirked. "You think you're cute, don't you?"

She laughed, the noise coming from deep in her belly. As the sound escaped her, she caught herself, afraid that by really truly laughing she was minimizing the situation in which they found themselves. As she thought about it, she realized this was the first time she had really laughed in months—since Trish's death.

"What are you reading?" she asked.

"You know, you didn't have to sit all the way over there." He nudged his chin toward her. "Why don't you scoot over and we can check it out together?" he said, motioning for her with the magazine. "That is, unless you want your own space."

As much as she did appreciate the extra armrest, she grabbed her Moscow mule and stepped across the aisle. As she settled in, she noticed that there was a subtle warmth that radiated from him, almost like she was sitting next to a space heater.

She had forgotten how he had always seemed to be just a few degrees hotter than her. At night, in the winter, she had loved getting into bed and setting her feet on his leg so she could get warm. He had complained about her icy toes, but at the same time he always moved closer to her when he knew she was chilly.

After she had lost their baby, all the things that had made her love him had vanished. It was as if all the little moments were erased the moment the nurse put the lifeless newborn into her arms.

She wasn't sure which one of them was no longer moving closer in bed at night after it had happened, but the days after their loss had broken them. Irreparably.

Or, at least she had thought.

She moved her foot closer to his, like she used to do when they were in bed with one another. Without seeming to realize, he bridged the distance between their feet until they were touching.

He leaned in, his shoulder brushing hers as he spoke about whatever article was on the page. It was something about a guest ranch in Wyoming, but she barely heard him. Rather, all she could think about was how his body felt against hers.

Be still her heart.

Though she should have moved away, and kept her distance from him, she found herself pulling in his scent—a mixture of his Aqua di Gio and fresh leather. She could feel her cheeks flushing as desire coursed through her.

Damn…

When they had been apart and a man had walked by wearing Eli's cologne, she had always taken notice, but none of them had ever smelled this good. Pheromones were for real.

She crossed her legs as she tried to gain control over her body. She wasn't a cavewoman who needed to cede her better judgment to her baser instincts. She was a grown-ass woman.

"Zoey?" he said like he had asked her a question and she had failed to respond.

"Yes," she said, trying to cover her lack of attention.

"You have been to a gentleman's club?" he asked, with a dumbfounded look that made it clear she had made a major error in not listening.

Crap.

"No…" she said, heat rising in her cheeks. "I mean, yes…but, no."

He folded the magazine and looked over at her. "Now I'm going to need to hear *that* story."

"Yeah, right. I already feel stupid enough without opening myself up for further scrutiny from you." She stuck out her tongue playfully.

"Oh, come on now. Did you dance on the pole?"

"Kiss my butt."

He laughed. "Just when it's getting good, you have to bring out something that much better."

The heat in her cheeks intensified. She hadn't meant it like *that*.

"You know very well that wasn't what I meant," she retorted.

He put his hands up in surrender and made an innocent face like he had no idea what she could have been referring to. "My apologies."

This was too close to flirting. Yeah, she loved the banter between them, but she had to nip it in the bud before it became more.

She caught another whiff of his cologne and he moved to put the magazine down on his table. She forced herself to check her grumble, a sound she was sure would be a mixture of desire and annoyance.

From the side of his chair, he pulled out his computer and handed it to her. "I was thinking that it would be good if you ran a scan, see if we can pick up your brother anywhere else in Sitges." There was a tightness in the way he spoke, as though he were uncomfortable with them growing emotionally closer, just as she was.

She was grateful for the change of direction. Neither of them needed to complicate their lives more than necessary.

Once this was over, and they had tracked down whoever put out the hit, she and Eli would both have to go back to their lives—lives that didn't revolve around one another.

No doubt, Eli would have to go back to Watch Dogs and begin work on another contract.

Though, maybe she could talk to her brothers about bringing him back on in STEALTH. Since she had started working mostly for their new military-grade tactical gear line, she had left a void in their company. He wasn't up to her level of tech acumen, but he could act as another hand. They needed someone they could trust.

She started running through the databases, pulling facial recognition and looking for her brother's features. There were a few vague hits, but nothing for the area and the time he would have been in Spain. Aside from his brief moment in the bank, it was as though he had disappeared.

The thoughts of all that could have happened to him crept into her consciousness, but she tried to sweep them away. It did her no good to think about whether Chad was alive or dead. As far as she was concerned, until she was one hundred percent certain of anything else, he was alive.

She grumbled.

"Finding anything?" he asked, careful to not look over her shoulder.

She had always appreciated a man who gave her space, especially when it came to her job.

"No, and it's starting to piss me off." She closed the computer and rubbed her hands over her face.

"Just because he isn't appearing anywhere right now doesn't mean we won't find signs of him tomorrow. You'll see," he said, but even she could hear the false optimism in his voice.

"You don't need to try and make me feel better— we both know that this may not turn out well. By now he may even be on the other side of the world. There's nothing to guarantee we're heading in the right direction." The thought made her stomach cramp.

"Your brothers are smart. Chad came out of hiding to appear at a bank—a place he knew he'd be on camera. He has to have known you were monitoring every eye in the sky for him. He did it on purpose."

Man, she hoped so.

"If that was the case, why didn't he give us more of an idea of what he is up to? Or where we can find him? Better yet, why not give us a sign to at least let us know he's okay?" She took a breath. "He would have sent me something to let me know he was safe—and yet…"

"Maybe he did. We could take another look at the video." He went to open the computer, but stopped as he glanced over at her.

"I have looked at that damned video at least a hundred times now. I've run every kind of test on the damn thing, and there's nothing. Nothing beyond what we already found."

"Did you pull the video of them leaving the bank?"

Eli asked gently, trying not to get her even more riled up. "Maybe we could at least see which direction they headed?"

"There's nothing." She could feel the storm clouds of a migraine rolling in. Eli was trying to help, and bless him for it, but he was crazy if he thought she hadn't exhausted every resource at her disposal to get a pinpoint on Chad's location.

She'd even looked deep into the dark web in hopes she could ID the woman at Chad's side, but it had been to no avail. The woman had been careful to not show too much of her face.

Though she loved and trusted her brothers to keep her safe and to do their best, there were only a few things in her life that she had ever trusted with every part of her soul. One was Trish, who was now gone, leaving her with her only other source of comfort—technology. It never let her down. It kept her safely tucked away from war zones but close enough that she could deal a death-blow upon faceless enemies. She could control the digital world like it was a ball of clay, only limited by her abilities—abilities that could give the world's best hackers a run for their money.

For the first time ever, she felt let down by the one thing she identified herself by. For there to be no more signs of Chad felt like there was a void in her heart, as well. But was it her abilities which failed her, or was it the machines she loved so much?

She was so very tired.

Like he could read her mind, Eli took the computer and put it away. "Let's just call it a night. When we get to Sitges, if your brother isn't there, so be it. We can call this expedition a vacation to the Med or something."

She sent him a drawn smile. "It's been a long time since I put my feet in the sand."

He cringed slightly as she spoke of sand, making her wish she had said something else instead.

"I just mean—" she started, hoping to correct her misstep.

"Do you remember that night in Tikrit?" Eli said, interrupting her.

"The night we were going to take down the leader in ISIL." She nodded as her thoughts moved to the cool night spent under the stars of the Iraqi desert. She had loved lying there, next to him, watching the darkened windows of the house for any sign of life in hopes that she and Eli could relay coordinates for the drone strike.

"Boots on the ground, baby," he said, quoting their old inside joke.

Whenever they were in a new place, a place they found they often hated either for the job or the people they were sent in to destroy, he'd always say, "Boots on the ground are worth a thousand in the office." And he'd always been right. It was part of the reason they were so highly sought after as a company. They always brought down their target.

It was his boots that were always on the ground, and the simple reminder was just his way of telling her he would catch her if she fell.

Eli glanced over his shoulder toward the rear of the plane. "There's a couch back there. I bet it folds out into a bed. Why don't you take this chance to relax? I have a feeling that when we get to Spain, the last thing on our minds is going to be sleeping.

There was a certain sadness that seeped into her as she looked over at Eli's strong green eyes, his wide-set jaw. Her gaze moved down to the muscles of his neck and the place where they gracefully melded into the burgeoning muscles of his chest. His pecs had gotten bigger since the two of them had gone their separate ways.

She gave herself a quick apprising glance. Maybe she should have put in a few more miles at the gym, but how could she have known she'd be hoping to attract a man—and not just any man, but Eli Wayne.

No, she was not trying to attract him. She couldn't be. They were friends. Only friends.

Just like before, with him so close to her, she wasn't sure that relaxation could possibly be in her future. But she was tired. And he was right; once they arrived it would be go-time.

"You don't think someone is running a decoy to flush us out of hiding, do you?" she asked. "I mean, think about it, even if the Gray Wolves have nothing to do with the hit out on Chad, they have to know of its existence. If so, they probably know we are looking for him. And what better way to have us come running than for us to spot him and fear for his safety?"

"How well do you know your enemies?"

She pursed her lips. "Well enough to know they would do anything it took to wipe us off the map."

There was a long silence between them, as he, too, must have realized the validity of her concerns. They may well have been walking into a trap—and it was quite possible that she and Eli wouldn't make it out of this one alive. One of the good things about her sending her brothers away was the fact they were unlikely to fall victim to the same fate.

At a certain level, she should have been afraid, but an odd sense of excitement filled her. It was like the threat of pending death made something click inside of her. Perhaps it was residual anger from the attacks at the ranch, or that someone was willing to use her brother to get to her, or maybe it was something else entirely, but she couldn't help feeling justified in making whoever was behind this pay.

"What are you thinking?" Eli asked.

"I'm thinking, if that's the case, and someone is setting up a trap for us, we should set it on its ear. Let's turn the hunters into the hunted."

He nodded, and his eyes brightened.

They weren't prey.

"If Chad really is behind us spotting him at the bank, then we have nothing to worry about, but if I'm right about others possibly being involved, we need to make a plan." She got up and walked back to the couch where, in front of it, was a small table with a pad of paper and a few magazines spread across the surface.

Eli followed her.

As they sat down, the flight attendant came out, refreshed their drinks and brought them each a sandwich before retiring to the front of the plane, closing the door behind her. Zoey couldn't remember the last time she'd eaten more than a few breath mints. Looking at the plate, her mouth watered. As Zoey took a bite of the pastrami sandwich, the mustard oozed out and a blob landed on the notepad on the table.

Eli laughed and she gave him the side-eye. As she did, he took a bite of his sandwich and a bit of mustard dribbled down the front of his shirt. "You know what I call that," she said with a chuckle, "*karma.* It serves you right for laughing at me." She nudged his knee as she teased him.

"For the record, I wasn't laughing at you." He dabbed at his button-up shirt with a napkin as they finished their sandwiches. "Actually, I was thinking about that little bistro where you and I went to dinner once. You know, the one where the guy played the accordion?"

She hadn't thought of that night in forever. That was when she had first told him she was expecting their child.

The little restaurant had been at the center of Avignon, an area seldom visited by tourists in one of the best eateries in the city. It was private and quiet. Their table had been just outside, set on the edge of the cobblestone street. When they had arrived, no one else was there as it was early and Eli had teased her for wanting to go to supper with blue hairs.

It had been a warm spring night, and the air was filled with the scent of lavender and the salty freshness of the sea. In many ways, the place was like the setting of a beloved rom-com in its perfection.

Was Eli bringing this up in order to talk about what had happened with their child, or was there another reason? She didn't want to ask him as she wasn't sure either of them was truly ready to confront the past.

"What about it?" she asked, hoping he would play by the unspoken rules that kept them from reopening those old wounds.

His eyes softened as he glanced at her, as he, too, must have been thinking of the news she had shared with him that night. "I think of that evening all the time. I often think about how beautiful you looked. Your hair was dyed black then—you remember?"

"I haven't dyed it black since then."

"You always look beautiful, no matter the color of

your hair. But that night, there was just the right amount of sunshine to light up the strands of your raven hair. And when you turned, your hair would shimmer and take on faint hues of copper. I didn't tell you then, but you reminded me of a butterfly."

She took in a long breath. It had been so long ago, but he seemed to remember that night with crystalline clarity. In a way, she felt guilty for not remembering it nearly as well as he did, but her guilt was quickly replaced by endearment. He had definitely loved her once.

"A butterfly?" It seemed unreal that she could ever remind someone of something so delicate.

He nodded. "You were, and have always been, breathtaking."

For the second time that night, she could feel herself melting. No one spoke to her as he did. She had forgotten how charming and special he was—and how he could make her feel.

She wished she could be as eloquent and respond in a way that would make him feel as beloved, but she could come up with nothing. There were no words that would capture the tumultuous storm that filled her when he was near.

"Do you remember the song the guy was playing on the accordion?" he continued, graciously taking the pressure off her and only further reminding her of how wonderful he was.

She shook her head. That night had been mostly a blur thanks to the nerves and anxiety that she had felt knowing that she had to tell him that their lives were about to change.

"It was 'Falling in Love Again.'" He took her hand

in his and she moved into him, putting her head on his shoulder as he lay back on the couch.

With a line like that, she couldn't have resisted the temptation to lie in his arms even if she had wanted to. For these few hours, she could let go and pretend the world wasn't waiting for them, that there was no hurt in the past, and this pocket of time was theirs forever.

As she listened to his heartbeat and the steady rhythm of his breathing, she thought of love. It was a strange word, a beautiful word, but odd nonetheless. It was a single syllable, and a word that could be said in a simple breath. It could mean a thousand different things: an emphasis added flippantly to everything from pizza to lovers, or it could be a whispered promise of forever, or it could be shouted to the heavens as a way to say goodbye. To every person, every relationship, every moment, it meant something different.

Their love, that love of the past, was gone. They had carried its weight together for years. Sometimes it had been like a feather, while at others it had been like a bag of stones—one that threatened to drown them in the depths of life.

Once she had let it go, *that* love was gone, forever.

She liked to think they could find a new definition for the feelings that welled within her as he ran his fingers down the length of her arm, making goose bumps rise on her skin.

But she wasn't sure if she was ready, as love could also be defined as fear.

Chapter Twelve

He had made so many mistakes in his life, but none had been greater than watching Zoey leave him and doing nothing about it. They had both been hurting, and yet instead of moving closer to her, he had felt himself growing further away. At the time, he thought it would protect him, but he had also thought it would protect her. He had so much anger in those days.

That anger had quickly turned to rage and destruction— but the one thing he hadn't wanted to bring down and destroy was what they had built together.

Once he had heard a statistic that couples that experienced a stillbirth were twenty-two percent more likely than the average couple to break up.

They had never really talked about having children, but when he learned he was to be a father the world shifted beneath him. Colors were brighter. Food tasted better. It was easier to get through the day. His anxiety lessened. Everything, even down to the way he brushed his teeth, changed. With the knowledge that they were having a baby came the feeling that his life now truly held purpose. It was strange, but he found comfort in the idea that he had been put on this planet to do something more. He was a father.

During those few blissful months, nothing else mattered—only them, their love and the family they were going to build.

And just like that, when he saw the pale, lifeless face of his daughter, it was all stripped away.

Though years had passed, there was still an ache in his heart as he recalled all they had lost.

Though there was no going back in time and there was no fixing the hurt that still lay between them, as he touched her skin, he allowed himself to pretend the well of pain had finally run dry.

He kissed the top of her head and she sighed, the sound relaxed and pleased. She must have felt as safe as he did. They had found one another again.

She moved against him, lifting his hand to her lips and kissing his fingers. Her touch was so unexpectedly sensual that his body stirred to life. He ran his thumb over the soft pink curves of her lips and as he did, she smiled and looked up at him.

He knew that look. Oh, that saucy, sexy look. Any resistance his body had in awakening fell away.

He wanted her. And there was no doubt in his mind that she wanted him.

They could surrender to this moment and let it erase the last bits of their feelings from the past. But there would be no going back if they went down this wonderful, erotic path.

Zoey had always been an animal in bed. Hands down the best he'd ever had.

When she made love, her body was like rose petals opening and curling as they came into the rays of ecstasy.

In watching her body move, he had always been

forced to be mindful as he feared letting himself go and cutting short the beauty before him.

If he could spend a million lifetimes watching her atop of him, it would still not have been long enough.

There was nothing, and no one who could compare to her.

Part of what made her who she was were also a few broken pieces. Some of those pieces were from family, friends and former lovers, but too many of the cracks were put there by him. If he wanted a future with her, he needed to work to help her heal those parts or he would risk losing her again.

The thought of never having her in his arms had haunted him for too long as it was. He couldn't go back to living that way. If that meant not having sex with her, or limiting how far they went right now, it was a sacrifice he was willing to make.

He needed her. Forever.

And though they were close right now, one misstep, and Zoey would pull away. It was what she did. It had taken him so long to break down those walls the last time, and he had been foolish enough to allow them to be rebuilt in his absence.

He would need to be careful doing what he knew needed to be done. He didn't want her to feel rejected. That was the last thing that he could allow to happen. She could be so strong, so resilient, but if he chipped at her ego there was no question that she would resent him for it.

She moved her body up his, rubbing her hand over his pants in her ascent. "Did you ever think of me when we were apart?" she cooed.

"Every minute of every day."

She paused for a moment, reading his face like she wasn't sure whether or not she could believe him.

Didn't she know he wasn't like other dudes? He didn't need one-liners to get a woman in bed.

"Did you think of this?" she whispered, her breath brushing against his lips even more gently than his finger had brushed over hers.

She leaned in, and their lips met. Bursts of endorphins exploded in his brain, making him feel as though little fireworks were going off throughout his body. Though it felt amazing, he was certain that if he allowed them to continue, he would undoubtedly get burned.

But he couldn't pull away.

Not yet.

He reached up, spreading his fingers through her loose hair as he cupped her face in his hands.

She tasted of vodka, ginger, the past and a hint of the future. He had almost forgotten what it felt like to kiss her, the way she sucked in a breath and released it as a low, throaty moan as her body moved against him.

Climbing atop him, she straddled him and rocked her hips.

Damn.

He wanted to rip off her clothes and take her there. Forget the consequences. Just feel her. All of her.

She rolled again, and her breasts rubbed against his cheek as she moved.

He couldn't stop his tender, lusty hum as he buried his face in her cleavage. She smelled of sweet sweat and the fragrance he knew so well.

It was all too much. If he didn't turn away now, he would never be able to.

If he took the risk and made love to her, so many things could go wrong.

He kissed the supple skin of her left breast, then the right in greeting. It had been so long and after tonight, he might never have the chance to be this close to her heart again.

His lips grazed her cashmere skin as he pulled back and lowered his head against her chest.

He wanted it all. Everything they had to offer. And, in the stolen moment, he knew that was more than either of them could give.

"You are fantastic." He exhaled, trying to gain control over his body and his mind.

"I can't believe we are here again. I've missed you." She ran her fingers through his hair, gently tugging as she moved.

"I've missed you, too," he said, hoping she would not misread what he needed to say. "Every day I thought of you and our child."

She leaned back from him, like the word *child* was an electric shock to her system. That wasn't the reaction he had wanted, but he wasn't surprised. There would always be pain there no matter how much time went by.

But they needed to move forward. Even if it wasn't together, a pain like that must be confronted, dealt with and then not allowed to embitter. If allowed, pain like that could break a person. He knew all too well, as it had broken him.

He would never forget the promises that had grown in her belly, and the dreams of a future that never came, but he couldn't keep reliving their loss. That was no kind of life.

She said nothing as she looked at him. In a way, he

was glad she did not want to talk about the baby, especially now. And perhaps he had made a mistake in bringing it up, but it had fallen from his lips thanks to the purple haze created in his mind by her touch.

"I want you," he said, his hands drifting down until they rested on her fleshy hips. She was so close to perfect, that it pained him to see her looking at him like that, like she was just waiting for the next zap.

Which made what he had to say that much harder. The old adage of *damned if you do, damned if you don't* popped into his head.

"You know I want you," he said, moving beneath her so she could feel exactly what she did to him. "But I'm… I think if we do this, you'll come to resent me."

She opened her mouth as if to speak, but slowly closed it again. It was as if she wanted to argue with him, to tell him what he was saying wasn't true, but she must have realized he was right.

"We only just came back into each other's lives, and I don't know that either one of us is healed enough. I'm afraid if we do this, and you let me back in your life like this, I'm going to want to stay in it. And I can't lose you. I can't go through that kind of heartache ever again. You tore out my heart."

There was a slight sheen to her eyes, and she blinked back the start of her tears. "I get it, Eli. I wish none of that had ever happened," she whispered.

He wanted to tell her that she had done nothing wrong, that he could understand her reaction and why she had screamed out of his life. However, he didn't completely understand. And even if she tried to explain it to him, he wasn't sure that would ever make it okay.

But what he did understand was that there was no going back in time. There were no redos.

There was only forgiveness.

"Thank you. And I'm sorry for pulling away. I just didn't know how to deal with everything."

"I didn't, either." She moved off him, saving him the agony of having to tell her that he couldn't make love to her right now. "I often wonder if our jobs destroy a certain element of our soul that makes us capable of being vulnerable. You know?" She moved to the couch beside him and picked up her drink, taking a long sip like it was a salve for the wounds that rested within her.

He wasn't sure he agreed. He felt pretty damned vulnerable right now.

She set her glass down, ice clinking against the sides of the cup like a bell tolling to mark a funeral. Sadness welled within him. Though logically he had known the decision to pull away was right, it felt as though he was losing her again as he watched her stand up and walked back to her seat.

Her movements carried an air of finality—an air he had seen before.

HE TRIED TO catch some sleep on the rest of the flight, but what little he had gotten was spent restless with dreams of firefights and lost battles. Every time he looked over at Zoey, she was clicking away on her computer and carefully ignoring him.

The ground they had gained in their friendship seemed lost.

Maybe it was better this way. Some hurts were just too big, too defining, too much.

As the wheels of the jet touched down, she finally

looked up at him. Her eyes were bloodshot, and he would have assumed she had been crying if he hadn't known better—she had never been the kind to shed a tear, not when she could stuff away emotions and try to forget they were there.

"We will find him," Eli said, decidedly turning the conversation away from them and back to just her. She and her family needed the most help right now. The rest could wait.

"I hope so. I looked everywhere, but found nothing." There was a depth in her voice that made him unsure exactly what she meant.

He wanted to tell her that life had a way of working things out as they should be, but even he didn't believe that. Life was a constant kick in the butt.

"We'll keep looking. We won't stop looking until we find him, I promise."

She smiled as she stood up and motioned for him to take the lead. As they made their way out of the plane, the Spanish heat washed over them. The city smelled of dust, poverty and the forgotten sea.

The airport staff loaded their luggage into the waiting car as they got in. It didn't take long to get on the highway that led to Sitges and their waiting hotel.

As they drove, they passed by the wall of catacombs, the few occupants of the city who seemed interested in the ocean that washed against the city's stony cliffs. The graves were walled in glass and as they passed by, curiosity drove him to search for the skeletons of the long dead.

The city of the dead was macabre and strangely beautiful, a far cry from the American style of death and memorial in which loved ones were forgotten and tucked away at the edges of society. Here, they were given a view, a place in everyday life, and thought of even by those, like him, who bore no ancestry.

As they twisted through the tunnels carved into the mountainsides, he thought about his searching of the graves. Perhaps there was something really wrong with him in the fact that instead of focusing on what could be, he found himself searching for ashes and bone.

When they arrived at the small European-style hotel, they were ushered in by staff and called by name. Zoey made a point of grabbing her bag, as though she were afraid someone might steal it.

As they checked in and followed the bellhop toward their room, she leaned into him and whispered, "Do you think everybody in Spain knows we're here?"

He chuckled, but beneath his mirth was the realization she may have been right. People were watching them as they strode through the lobby. "There's plenty of tourists that come to this area. We're going to blend right in."

She glanced around as they made their way up the set of double-winding staircases. The place was quiet, the only sounds besides their footsteps and the slight humming coming from the bellhop was the chatter from a small bar offset from the lobby.

He had made sure to get two rooms that adjoined one another thanks to a small interior door. He would leave it up to her whether or not she left the door unlocked. Either way, he wasn't sure he minded—by giving her the decision, it kept his mind from running in circles.

He watched her enter her room. With a nod, she closed the door behind her.

He had been wrong in thinking they could take their

relationship to the next level in the future. Though the world would always keep moving forward, and they could function as a team, they had proven that two people could go through the motions of the present and stay firmly entrenched in the past.

Chapter Thirteen

Zoey couldn't believe she had let things get that far with Eli yesterday. As fun as it was to fantasize about being with him again, reality was another thing entirely. There was a chasm of wounds between them that ran too deep and too wide for them to ever cross.

It was never her intention to hurt him, rather just save herself. She had known that there would be collateral damage when she left, but she had thought he was so much stronger than the man who had kissed her last night.

She looked at the door that rested between the two hotel rooms. For a second, she thought about going over there and opening the door and letting him back into her life. But she wasn't sure she was ready. Instead, she scrolled through her phone and looked for more search results in hopes of finding Chad. Nothing. Always nothing.

A few times throughout the night, she had wondered if the video they had seen at the bank was even real. It was almost as if he were a ghost, slipping in and out of this world and teasing her with his presence.

She pulled a hair dye kit out of her bag and went to the bathroom. The pink had started to fade in her hair, and though she knew she could fit in with any color hair here in Spain, she decided on brown teak. The color was bland and indistinguishable from the masses. Hopefully, she could dress down enough to disappear. The last thing she needed was for them to be spotted before they could get in touch with Chad.

There was a knock on the front door as she let the color set.

She took one look at herself in the mirror. There was nothing sexier than a woman wearing a clear plastic shower cap and yesterday's makeup. Maybe this was what Eli needed to see in order to bring him back into the reality of who she really was.

But as she walked to the door, she hurriedly tried to wipe the mascara from under her eyes.

There was another knock at the door, more impatient this time.

"I'm coming." She opened the door, and standing there in the hallway was room service complete with silver platters of Spanish pastries and silver-domed plates on a fully loaded rolling trolley.

"I have the breakfast your friend ordered," the man pushing the trolley said as he struggled to look anywhere but at the mess on her head.

She stepped back and motioned for him to bring the trolley into the room. As the man walked by her, the scent of oatmeal, coffee, sausage, beans and eggs wafted toward her and made her mouth water. She reached into her wallet and grabbed some cash for the man as he made his way out.

Eli must have known she would forget to order breakfast for herself. As she closed the door, she caught another glimpse of herself in the mirror. Perhaps she was getting to see who Eli really was, as well.

Washing the dye from her hair and face, she wrapped a towel around her head. The dye had done its job, and she couldn't help but notice she looked like her mother.

She went to the door between their rooms and knocked gently. She wasn't going to eat his breakfast alone. Not when he had been so thoughtful. It didn't escape her attention that he may well have done it on purpose to force her hand and invite him to her room. Either way, whether it was selfless or selfish, she couldn't deny the fact that she was glad to have him with her. Though he had implied that there was no room for a relationship between them, perhaps they could go on to be friends when this was all through.

She smiled at the thought just as the door opened. Eli was dressed for the day in a linen shirt, perfectly suited for the heat, and a pair of khaki utility shorts. There was a slight bulge at his waist. He was strapped.

The realization that he was carrying a gun came as a comfort.

He looked her over, his gaze settling on the towel still wrapped around her head. "Are we going for a more devil-may-care look today? Do I need to go back and change my clothes?" he teased, jabbing a thumb in the direction of his room.

"Actually—" she walked over to her bag and grabbed the bulletproof shirt she had brought along just for him "—put this on." She tossed him the pale blue button-up.

He caught it midair. "Crap, was I supposed to bring you an outfit, too? Or is this a new uniform style for STEALTH?"

He slipped off his linen shirt, throwing it onto his

bed. She tried not to look at his faintly lined abs and thick-muscled arms before he pulled on the new shirt.

"Just consider yourself lucky," she said. "Now, shut up and get in here and eat breakfast."

He laughed as he stepped into her room and closed his door behind him. He walked over to the tray of food and started lifting off some of the domes and lids. There was a medley of foods from fruit and meats, to grains and cheeses. "I know you're normally just a coffee girl in the morning, but I wanted to make sure you ate well. I don't know when we'll get a chance to grab some lunch."

She stepped over to the trays and poured each of them a cup of coffee.

He grabbed a plate and started stacking food on it, and she followed suit. After the long flight and all the time changes, her body was begging for food.

As she lifted the last lid to peek inside, she dropped the silver dome with a clatter. Eli stopped. He picked up the lid exposing what lay underneath. Upon a plate, garnished with parsley and decorative orange slices, was the tip of a man's trigger finger. Next to it on the plate was a simple note that read Welcome to Spain.

"Son of a—" Zoey said under her breath.

Their arrival hadn't gone unnoticed. Someone was tracking them.

"I can't wait to see what they put in my eggs," Eli said, laughing as he set the lid on the cart next to the plate.

"Wow, so glad you haven't matured at all since the last time we were together," she said, but couldn't help the little giggle that escaped her. Truth be told, she had always loved the fact that he could take the darkest moments of their jobs and relieve the stress by making a joke of it. "Who do you think the finger belongs to?"

Eli shrugged. "I have no idea."

She took a picture and sent it to Mindy and Sabrina with a text asking them to pull anything they could from it. "You don't think it's Chad's, do you?"

His face pinched, making it clear he thought that it was her brother's.

No.

She forgot about the food as she threw on a pair of cutoff jeans and her Nirvana tank top. She slipped her phone into the back of her shorts pocket, covering it with her T-shirt. "Let's go."

He didn't argue, thankfully. They had no real starting point, no direction and no idea what the future would bring, but they couldn't sit in their hotel room and just fester. If she had to go house by house and knock on every door in the entire country of Spain to get Chad back and to ensure he was safe, she would do it.

As she moved to the door of her room, Eli stopped her. "There's still a towel on your head."

She huffed. Of course there was. She pulled it off and rubbed the last bit of wetness from her hair and threw the towel to the floor. Not bothering to look at herself in the mirror, she grabbed her bags and checked out of the hotel and headed out the door, Eli close on her heels.

Pulling up an encrypted map, she led the way toward the bank. The streets were narrow, just wide enough in most places to accommodate a single car or gaggle of tourists. She looked up at the historic buildings around her, hoping to see cameras installed sporadically, but she found none. No wonder she had a hard time finding images of Chad. Perhaps he was still here.

The bank was located near the main thoroughfare in the small town. From the street in front, she could see the Mediterranean. At the beach, children were laughing as they played and splashed in the water.

What it would have been like to have another life.

She walked to the front door of the bank, and tried to open the door, but it was locked. It wasn't until now that she realized how early it was. They wouldn't be open for another fifteen minutes.

Though it was stupid, she couldn't help feeling like she had failed. She always thought she was so smart, so strong, and yet here they stood in the middle of a foreign city with nothing but days-old information. She had to do better.

She hated to think of what Eli thought of her ineptitude. He had come all this way to help her, and there she was, unable to help herself.

It was a good thing she wasn't a crier.

"It's going to be okay," he said as he stepped close, running his fingers through her hair and taking a moment to fix what she assumed was her best attempt at a rat's nest.

Though she knew the sweet action was meant to soothe, she was so annoyed with herself that she stepped back and out of his touch. As she moved, she noticed the bulge under Eli's shirt and a thought crossed her mind.

"Are you all right?" Eli asked, seeming surprised by her edginess.

Opening up her phone. She looked up at him and smiled. "Yeah, I just had an idea." She clicked on the video of her brother and zoomed in on the woman in the background and skipped ahead to the moment the girl turned from the frame. At the woman's waist was a small bulge. As Zoey moved the video clip by clip, a small black handgun briefly came into view.

She zoomed down even further.

She knew that gun, or at least she was almost certain she did.

It looked like the ones used in the phony arms deals with the Gray Wolves. They had been promised as part of the shipments that they had used to lure the Gray Wolves into the trap they were planning before everything went haywire and Trish was killed.

Which meant…

She clapped her hand over her mouth with excitement as she hopped from one foot to the other. Though she probably looked like a madwoman dancing around in the city streets, she didn't care. Finally, they had a break.

She turned the phone for Eli to see and pointed at the gun. As she did, she glanced up and stopped as she realized that, just like with Chad, this bank was rolling footage. Thankfully, her phone's screen was turned away from the cameras. Her face on the other hand…

"We have to go." She nodded in the direction of the cameras and Eli's gaze instinctively moved toward them.

Without another word, they made their way from the bank, going in the opposite direction from which they came in the event anyone was watching. Not that it probably mattered—someone already knew they were there and was likely just waiting for the perfect moment to strike them down.

They made their way several blocks from the bank before slowing down. She kept checking over her shoulder, making sure they weren't being followed, but everyone around them seemed caught up in their own comings and goings and not focused on them.

The finger in the room was just a threat. If whoever had sent it had wanted her dead, she would've been dead by now. Obviously, they had access to her room, so it had to be some type of message.

"Now what were you going to tell me?" Eli asked.

"The gun in the video, it has a tracker in it. When we were doing the gun deal with the Gray Wolves, we had all the guns we were going to sell them implanted with GPS devices." Pulling out her phone, she clicked to the locator.

"How do you know it's one of your guns?" Eli asked.

"I don't for certain, but it's the best damn thing I can think of right now." Her stomach flopped like an undercooked pancake.

Going back to the enhanced video, she tried to read the serial number stamped into the barrel, but she could only pull the first four digits. Hopefully, it would be enough.

They walked around aimlessly as she tapped away on her phone, moving down the list of possible serial numbers of the guns they had planted with the trackers. After a few minutes, she came up with a list of twenty-five possible guns.

They stopped in front of the Iglesia de San Bartolome y Santa Tecla Catholic church, and with an acknowledging look, they ducked inside. In the church, they would be safe from prying eyes.

Their footsteps echoed on the stone floors, reverberating against the walls and echoing back at them thanks to the large domed ceiling and empty expanses. The cathedral was awe-inspiring with its breathtaking gold-inlaid ceiling, grand organ and pristine marble-white walls. It was different from the other churches she had seen in her years spent around Europe in its fine crafts-manship but simple design.

Genuflecting, they made their way to a pew in the back of the church and sat down. The pews creaked as they moved, making the room seem even emptier than it was.

"Take half the list, see if you can pinpoint the track-ers to anywhere within three hundred miles." She mir-rored her phone to his.

"What if we are just chasing our tails?" he asked.

She bit back the urge to be annoyed. "Do you have a better idea?"

He looked like she had struck him, and she instantly regretted saying anything. But seriously, why would he speak out? She was doing the best she could. And damn him if it wasn't good enough.

He tapped on his phone. "I'm going to send the pro-tective ops STEALTH team into our hotel. Maybe they can get the finger and see if they can pull some DNA or something. At least that way, we can know that it isn't Chad's."

That test would take weeks, they both knew it, but she appreciated his efforts. "Hopefully we have Chad back long before the results."

He nodded and the defeat in his eyes grew like a storm cloud just waiting to break loose. "Are you upset with me?" he asked.

She sighed as she put her phone down in her lap. She hadn't been after a fight, not in the slightest, but he seemed to be gearing himself up for one. Though she didn't have the wherewithal to deal with it, she had little choice. If they were going to continue working together, they were going to have to talk about the elephant in the room. "I'm not upset."

"Then what is going on with you? Did I do something wrong? If so, seriously, I apologize." He leaned closer to her and took her hand in his.

She wasn't sure what to do with it, but she liked the fact that in one moment he could be pulling the trigger and killing the enemy, and holding her hand as if it were a Fabergé egg in the next. He was the best of both worlds—lethal and protective.

It seemed impossible, but in the years that had passed, he had become even more like her dream man.

"You're good. I'm just…" *protecting my heart…terrified of falling in love…worried about my brother… scared of losing even more…* She could think of a hundred ways to end her sentence, but none of her many thoughts pressed past her lips. Being so open with him would not serve any purpose. "I'm just trying to focus on Chad." She squeezed his fingers, then let go of his hand.

No matter how great Eli was or how badly she wanted to live in the fuzzy, warm safe haven provided by his kiss, there wasn't room in her heart for anything right now—not with her brother and her family in mortal danger. For now, her only focus could be on survival.

Chapter Fourteen

Though he'd thought he had made the right choice by not having sex with her on the plane, now he wasn't so sure. She had taken it as a rejection, just as he had feared she would. There was no going back for another chance—especially sitting in the middle of the church. It had felt taboo even taking her hand in the sacred place.

He took one more look at her hand as he tapped on his phone, trying to find the location of the weapon the woman with Chad had been carrying.

He had been stupid for saying anything to Zoey about her idea. She was frazzled. He'd seen the desperation in her eyes the moment he opened the door between their rooms this morning and when they had found the finger... Well, that had definitely pushed her over the edge.

In all likelihood, and as much as he didn't want to admit it to Zoey, the finger belonged to Chad. Why else would anyone leave such a macabre threat for them to find?

The only time he'd ever seen anything like that, aside from mob movies, was when a member of his team had found a bloody foot stuffed in their duffel bag. Two weeks later the guy had been killed in action by a stray bullet. Everyone on his assigned team had their suspicions about why the bullet had found him, specifically that someone within their crew had a bone to pick. But he had always doubted the likelihood of something like that happening. His teams were always the best of the best—friendly fire wasn't in their vocabulary.

He moved to the tenth serial number on his list of guns. Tapping the number into the search, a green dot appeared on his map. There, in the center of Sitges, just blocks from where they sat, he had found a possible location. "Holy—" He stopped before the rest of the words fell from his mouth and landed like a thud in the center of the pew.

"Huh?" she asked, looking up from her screen.

"You were right," he whispered, glancing around and ensuring that they were still alone.

He could have sworn a light shone down as he said those words to the woman sitting next to him.

"Um, what? Do you want to repeat that?" she said, raising one eyebrow. "Did you just say I was *right*?"

"Live it up," he said, teasing back. "Look." He lifted his phone for her to see the little green speck on his screen.

She jumped to her feet. "I knew it!" A smile spread across her face and finally some of the darkness faded from her features. "He's here. I knew he was here."

Just because they were close to that dot didn't mean they were any closer to reaching finding Chad or finding him *alive*.

But Eli had already been wrong once. Hopefully he would be wrong again.

She took his phone out of his hand and, without missing a beat, flew through the doors of the church and out onto the street in the direction of the dot.

He followed along, watching her hair glistening in the morning sun. The new color was beautiful on her and, as she moved, the sunlight picked up bits of burgundy like her hair was imbued with rubies.

She was nearly running as she made her way around a corner and toward the apartment building in the distance where the dot was centered. The building had clean, clear lines and was painted a vibrant yellow with black art deco accents. At each arched window sat wrought-iron balconies. It was a place where only the well-heeled could afford to reside—a far cry from the derelict back alley room where he would have expected Chad to have been held hostage.

He touched Zoey's arm, stopping her midstride. "Wait."

"What? He's waiting," she said, nudging her chin in the direction of the building just half a block down the avenue.

"We can't just run in there half-cocked. Who knows what, or who, will be in there."

Her face fell. "Do you think we should call Trevor and Jarrod, let them know what we've found? See if they want to fly over?"

He shrugged. More wasn't necessarily better in this situation. "Let's just keep an eye on this place, see who's coming and going. I would hate it if we walked into a trap."

She chewed on her lip and nodded. Taking one last look at the building, she walked down an alley to their right, and out of view of whoever could have been inside the building in question.

"Lucky for us, I have friends in the NSA who understand our need to glean information from their drones on occasion... Without asking permission... Or actually telling them..." She tapped on the screen, pulling up what he was absolutely certain were illegal images from her near and dear "friends" within USCYBERCOM.

He chuckled. That was the Zoey he knew, doing anything she needed to do to take care of business. The Watch Dogs had an IT crew, a faceless man he had never met, and their intel collection was good, but it was nothing like Zoey on a mission.

Once again, he found himself missing his old role as Zoey's attaché.

For a moment, he considered what it would be like if they could go back in time and revisit the mistakes of his past. If they hadn't risked their friendship by moving things to the next level, they would probably still have been working in the same group, united against one enemy. She would know, without a doubt, that he was someone she could turn to and trust. Instead he'd let his body take the lead, and it had led them straight into disaster.

"Getting anything?" he asked.

Looking at her screen, he could just make out the area where they stood from the eye in the sky, he could see her new brown locks and what he feared was a possible future bald spot on the crown of his head. He was surprised everything was so immediate, so real-time. Out of curiosity, he raised his hand and instantly he watched himself doing it on her phone. If they had had this tech five years ago—heck, even two years ago—many of their failed missions surely would've turned out differently.

"Damn, I had no idea our government had come this far." He gave a little whistle.

She looked up from the screen and nodded. "Doesn't your new team have access to any kind of technology, Jiminy Cricket?"

She said *new team* like it was the name of his new girlfriend.

"Why, Ms. Zoey Martin, are you jealous?" he asked with a smirk.

"Why would I be jealous of some two-bit operation that can't even hack their way into the most basic of the government's databases?"

If she thought that the NSA's drone encryption keys were basic, he couldn't help but wonder what the more complicated ones were hiding.

He resisted the urge to ask if she could rewind it, fearing that he would sound like he was a thousand years old and from a different planet.

"Here we go," she said, moving closer to him so they could watch the screen side by side. "This was from early this morning."

She clicked Play. There was the normal movement of people up and down the street in front of the apartment building where the GPS device was located—nothing stood out. She skipped ahead two minutes. A woman wearing a light gray peacoat stepped out of the front doors of the building. The woman was alone. Even though she was wearing large welding mask–sized sunglasses, it was easy to recognize her as the woman from the bank's video.

The woman stopped and reached for something in her tiny purse and then started walking toward where he and Zoey now stood. He looked up from the phone, half expecting the woman in the coat to be standing directly in front of him. Instead, there was the buzz of car horns in the distance and the shuffle of feet on the cobblestone as people walked past.

The woman pranced like a well-trained and expensive dog.

"Do you see the handbag she's carrying?" Zoey asked, zooming in on the brown bag. It had a silver chain as the strap and it looked strange on the tiny briefcase-looking purse.

"What about it? I mean, besides being stupid-looking." He never understood what women saw in purses. As far as he was concerned, a purse was a purse was a purse. It was just a place to put their crap until they needed their crap. Really, a paper sack would do in a pinch.

"First, it isn't *stupid*-looking." She gave him a quick look up and down. "You are hardly one to judge, Mr. Cargo Shorts and a button-up."

"It's practical," he argued, but was stopped by the wave of her hand.

"More importantly," she continued, "the bag she is carrying is Jean Vitton. It's this year's Petite Malle mini bag."

"That doesn't change the fact that it looks like something from the bargain bin at the dollar store."

She huffed, clearly annoyed with his commentary on fashion. "Regardless of what you feel about this purse, it's amazing."

He cocked his head and gave her a disapproving look. "Really? You *like* the purse? It looks like a dude's shrunken briefcase. And I know for a fact that you are more comfortable carrying around a rucksack than you are an expensive purse."

"A rucksack is *practical*," she said, smirking as she threw his words back at him. "That being said, I am still a woman. While this one may not exactly be my style it doesn't change the fact that it is Vitton's most expensive purse this season and it isn't even available in stores yet."

"Oh, fancy."

"Actually, yeah, it is." She smiled like she knew something he didn't. "With a bag like that, we can probably figure out who she is. They only give those bags out to the rich and famous."

"Sounds like you just want to make a stop at Jean Vitton."

"So what if I do? But I think I can get what we need without going there." She pulled up a new window on her phone and set to work, starting at the Jean Vitton website. From there, she broke into their mainframe, hacking her way straight into the sales records.

It wasn't the first time she'd terrified him. With a tiny bit of information this woman could do almost anything—and put nearly any federal agent to shame. If anything, she'd gotten even better at her job since the last time he'd seen her. It had to be so hard doing what she did, constantly being on the forefront of technology, a world that changed nearly every second. He would happily remain a point man for as long as he still had a job.

"So according to their sales records, they've only sold five of these purses so far. They've given three away. And there is a wait list." She looked up. "I bet if I put my address in here, they would send us one for free." Her fingers trembled over the screen like she was seriously contemplating using her skill set to rig the system for herself. "The first person on the wait list is Gigi Hadid. Think about it, I can have the same purse as Gigi."

"I have no idea who that even is." He reached over and took the phone from her. "I still don't get it. I mean, how much is this purse worth anyways?"

"Twenty Gs." There was a breathless air to her words.

He handed the phone back to her like by simply touching the phone he was implicating himself in the theft of something so expensive. Now he *really* didn't get it. "You do know, for that kind of money you could get yourself a hell of a tactical setup."

She laughed. "I am more than a little aware of that." She gave him a look like he was the dumbest man on the planet.

"Oh, yeah. I bet you can get your tac gear on the cheap. But still, I would much rather have good gear than some stupid purse."

"Call it a stupid purse again and I am going to do the active-round testing of my next tactical line on you." There was fire in her eyes, but he knew she was teasing.

"Okay, so there's some things I don't understand. I'm sure I'll never get it." He put his hands up in surrender. "As for this fine specimen of fashion that is this purse, who are the five lucky souls chosen to possess such magnificence?"

She couldn't keep a straight face, no matter how badly she wanted to continue chastising him for his bad taste. "There are several socialites, one Hollywood star and one that interests me," she said.

"And that is?"

"According to this, there was one that was sold to a foreign buyer. Looks like it was picked up in Dubai."

"What was the name of the foreign buyer?" he asked.

"It was bought by a woman named Shaye Griest."

That name meant nothing to him. "Okay?" he said.

"You ever heard of Kristen Griest or Shaye Haver?"

He shook his head.

"Kristin and Shaye were the only women ever to graduate from the army ranger school. These are two badass women."

"I don't understand what two rangers have to do with one purse." He racked his brain in trying to put it together.

"When I was poking around about the Algerian prime minister and his family, I found that his oldest daughter used to be active on social media. She tweeted about Kristin and Shaye and what it means to her that these two women were able to develop their skills in such a prestigious and competitive location."

He still didn't get it, and apparently the look on his face must've said as much.

"That's the pseudonym for the prime minister's daughter, *dude*." She shook her head in exasperation.

"Oh," he grumbled, trying to cover his embarrassment. Hopefully she'd never realized how much better a catch she was than him. If she did, he would never have a chance in getting her back.

"Do you think that Chad is shacking up with the Algerian prime minister's daughter?" Eli asked.

"Or she kidnapped him." Zoey shrugged.

"Something about all of this isn't making sense. Why would the Algerian government put a hit out on Chad if he was with the Algerian prime minister's daughter? Wouldn't it put her in danger?"

Zoey nodded. "I know. I was thinking the same thing."

"Are you sure the woman carrying the bag is the PM's daughter?"

"So far, in every video I've seen of her, this girl has been very careful to cover her face—it's like she knows people will be using facial recognition to look for her," Zoey said. She started pulling up videos and images of the woman on her phone.

The woman had long dark, almost black hair in the most recent official government photos posted by the Algerians. However, the woman standing outside the building with the big sunglasses was unquestionably blonde. As he stared at the images in front of him, he could make out the same subtle curves of her jaw. And her nose was blunt and slightly upturned like a short ski jump. He couldn't say with one hundred percent certainty that the woman from the drone's image and the Algerian prime minister's daughter were the same woman, but he couldn't deny it, either. It was certainly within the realm of possibility.

"Did you see anything on the video about Chad?" he asked.

She gave a resigned sigh. "Not yet, but that doesn't mean he's not holed up in there."

There was the clatter of the metal gate being pushed up as the bistro behind them opened up for lunch. The woman who must've worked there gave them a smile and said something in Spanish to which Zoey replied.

They needed to get out of there, before they were

tracked down again. Zoey turned off her phone and stashed it in her pocket.

They couldn't go back to their hotel and they couldn't keep running. He wasn't sure what they should do next, but inaction was almost more dangerous than moving on their target. "Can you do facial recognition on the video from the drone for Chad?"

"Already done. Nothing came up, but he could have gone in the building during the night or when the drone wasn't posted at this location." There was a desperation to her voice.

Her unchecked emotions made Eli that much more on edge. It wasn't like Zoey to just say what she was feeling or even not bother to disguise it... She was hurting, which made pain rise within him. In a way, the situation reminded him of the last time they'd been together with their baby.

If he failed her, if Chad was hurt or killed, he would feel just as guilty as he had that day. Though he was certain he was doing the right thing, he hadn't taken all of the consequences into consideration. Here he was thinking about coming back to work with the Martins, but he was far more likely to find himself back on Zoey's persona non grata list than back in her life.

Maybe he would've been better off getting her flowers instead of chasing her halfway across the state in order to catch a glimpse of her. As he chuckled at the thought, he knew he was lying to himself. He would give up his last breath for her. No matter how this went down, there was no way he could stop loving her.

"What's the prime minister's daughter's real name?" he asked.

"Nihad Almaz," she said without a pause. "She is one

of three daughters and a son. The son is involved with the Algerian military, and there is talk that he will one day run the country in his father's footsteps."

"Is there any talk about how his daughters feel about that?" Eli took her hand and they started slowly walking around the city, keeping the apartment building in view.

"They haven't said anything publicly about the situation, but it looks as though they are going to act as ambassadors for the country until the time of their marriages."

"None of them are married?" Eli thought of Chad.

What if this wasn't a kidnapping, but rather an elopement? Though Zoey seemed to be convinced that this wasn't a romance. But if it *was*, it would explain why the prime minister would put out large sums of money for Chad's head.

But that didn't explain the severed finger that had been served to them this morning beside their toast and eggs. Or why the PM would put his own flesh and blood in the line of fire. That was, unless the man didn't care about his daughter's welfare. It wasn't unheard of for a father to disown a daughter, or son who moved against the family.

Chad had to know they were looking for him, and he wouldn't just run off with a woman and not give his family a heads-up. There were so many things that just weren't making sense.

Zoey gave him a look like she was trying to figure out what he was thinking, but he wasn't sure he wanted to give his theory any more air than necessary.

The last thing he wanted to do was give Zoey false hope when it came to finding her brother alive—

especially given the fact they hadn't found any trace of him in the last forty-eight hours.

Eli nodded. Yes, there was no way his stupid theory was right. And besides, Chad was far from being the romantic in the family. This wasn't a case of love making life go off the rails. Instead, the faceless enemy that was gnawing at their heels had to be something different, something not quite as dangerous as love but likely far more lethal.

Chapter Fifteen

She couldn't stand the inaction. As she stared down the alley in the direction of the apartment building, she had never felt more impotent. They had to act. Now. She didn't care about the danger it would put her in. She was willing and ready to kill any jackass who stood between her and her brother.

But she couldn't put Eli or her brother in danger by being impetuous. They had to be careful, to play this smart.

At the same time, she'd never been known for being overly cautious.

She gave Eli an impish grin as she thought about their next move. "Eli, what size dress do you wear?"

"What?" Eli asked looking at her like she'd lost her mind.

"I'm serious," she said as a wave of excitement pulsed through her. "Think about it—we allowed room service to come into our hotel room without question. We didn't even think about it, or at least I didn't. If you dressed like a cleaning woman, you could probably walk right in," she teased. "You might be our best chance to get in there."

"No." He shook his head.

Zoey laughed at his obvious discomfort. "You don't want to get in touch with your feminine side?" She feigned a look of disappointment. "I always like a man who has a certain gentleness."

"I always knew that," he teased. "Especially when we were elbow deep in the blood of our enemies in Tikrit."

"Absolutely," she said with a chuckle. "There's nothing more feminine than a little spatter on your cargo shorts… Well, that is, except for you dressing up like a cleaning lady. That would make me *hot*."

He snorted in derision. "I can get you hotter than that in plenty of other ways. I don't need to lace up a corset and wear stockings to make you want me."

She paused for a moment, not quite sure what to say. He didn't seem to notice. Instead, he continued, "But if dressing up like a woman is what I need to do to get back into your good graces, then I'll do it. Strap on the Betty Boop wig." His booming laugh bounced off the walls of the buildings surrounding them like a rubber ball until it rolled to a stop at her feet.

She wasn't laughing. Rather, she was thinking of what he had said. "You think you're not in my good graces?"

His face dropped, and the smile faded from his lips. He shoved his hand in his pocket, the simple motion reminding her of a man in the midst of interrogation. "Zoey, from the moment I came back and saw you in Billings, I wanted to be back in your life. Thought I made that obvious."

She hadn't questioned that. "I know, and I appreciate your help. I really do."

"So, you're not upset with me? You know, after what

happened on the plane?" He looked at her like he was just waiting for the whip to fall.

Maybe she had made a mistake in bringing this up. It would've been so much easier to just buy him a dress and let him traipse around the apartments like a cleaning woman—at least they would've been laughing. Instead, here they were once again dealing with the awkwardness that came with their relationship.

"I'm not upset with you. But I was embarrassed. I deserved being rejected by you after everything I put you through, but—"

"Stop right there." He moved closer to her. So close that she could smell the sweet scent of the nervous sweat on his skin. "What happened in the past between us—well, it can't be undone. But I would never hold a grudge against you for decisions you made back then. We were both hurting."

Pangs of love rippled through her chest, like his words were a pebble dropped into the smooth surface of a lake.

Dammit, why did he have to be so perfect? It was just too bad perfect wasn't what she wanted in her life. She needed a man who would make mistakes, just like her. It was too much pressure if he was perfect and she was always trying to be deserving of his love. She needed someone just as screwed up as her or a relationship would never work. They had been proof of that.

"Eli—"

Before she could say anything, he pressed her up against the building behind them and took her lips with his. It was so unexpected, so surprising, that she didn't know what to do. Part of her wanted to push him away, but at the same time she wanted the feeling of his lips pressed against hers and his tongue caressing the edges of her mouth like he was tasting her lips.

She closed her eyes, and let it be. Nothing else mattered.

That was, until he broke free of her kiss.

She grabbed his shirt and moved to draw him closer to her, but he stopped and looked over his shoulder. "Did you see her?" he whispered.

"See who?" she asked, momentarily forgetting everything that was happening in their lives.

"The woman from the video, Shaye." He nudged his chin in the direction of a small farmer's market that was set up to the left of where they stood.

There were at least a dozen vendors selling everything from plump, juicy-looking grapes to freshly roasted almonds. A woman passed by them, holding the hand of a young boy who was greedily stuffing bits of what must have been contraband chocolate into his mouth. He looked up at the woman, making sure she wasn't watching as he stuffed his pudgy fingers back into the pocket of his jacket and drew out another fistful of candy.

That woman could have been her...in a different life.

"There," Eli said, pulling her back. "She's at the far stand."

There, barely visible through the throngs of people who walked among the stalls was a tall woman with slender hands. She was pointing at something Zoey couldn't see. The woman was wearing face-shielding sunglasses and a checkered scarf over her hair, giving her an Audrey Hepburn–esque look.

The word *classy* came to mind. Followed on its heels was *kidnapper*, but it seemed like a word that would only be used when explaining what happened to a woman like her, not something the woman was capable of.

In a way, the woman reminded Zoey of herself, all the contrasting parts of her life. On one hand, she was capable of being so incredibly strong and resourceful, resilient in the face of extreme odds and hardship. And yet, when it came to her personal life, she was a bundle of nerves. Eli could almost bring her to her knees with the simple touch of his hand to her cheek.

Strong and sensitive…and completely unsure of herself when it came to pulling the trigger. Maybe she wasn't as much like the bureaucrat's daughter as she believed. The woman standing in front of her would probably kill in an instant.

"We have to get to that apartment," Zoey urged, spinning around on her heel and moving away from the woman.

Eli stopped her with a touch of his hand. "What if we took her?"

She stared at him, hardly able to believe his suggestion. "If we kidnap her, we are no better than them."

"It's not about who is better or who is worse. It's about keeping your brother safe. If we grab her, at least we can negotiate a trade. Right now, all we have is the vague hope of finding your brother in that building. But what if he isn't there? What if he's been moved?"

She wasn't a fan of his plan, but he made a good point. If they took her, at least they had access to whoever was holding her brother. "We don't even have a place to stay. If we grab her, what are we going to do with her?"

"Just because we had to check out of our hotel,

doesn't mean we don't have a place to stay. We can figure this out." He was already moving in the direction of the woman.

She let him walk ahead of her. He feigned interest in the stalls as he meandered toward the woman in his best attempt to not look suspicious.

As they drew nearer, Zoey stopped at the fruit stand and picked up an orange. She handed the vendor some change, but didn't take her eyes off their target. Eli glanced back at her, checking her position before he advanced.

Shaye turned toward them as she completed her purchase. She dropped a few Euros into her purse, the same purse from the video. This was definitely their target, but the woman seemed almost at ease flitting through the market stalls.

Shaye drifted to the next stall and smiled at the man standing behind his table of trinkets. She picked up a keyring and inspected it.

She acted nothing like a woman holding a man hostage.

There was something wrong. Something just didn't feel right.

Eli made his way to the woman, but instead of taking her by the arm and dragging her into an alley, he stopped beside her and picked up a hand fan.

From where she stood Zoey couldn't hear what Eli was saying, but as he spoke the woman smiled.

Zoey had never been an accomplice in a kidnapping before, but she wasn't sure that smiles and laughter were supposed to be part of it. An odd sensation of jealousy crept through her as she watched the woman lean toward Eli and touch him gently on the shoulder.

Zoey glanced around, searching the crowd for anyone that appeared to be standing guard for the woman, or anything that would help her make sense of why Eli was flirting rather than grabbing her and making off like a caveman.

He had to be seeing something different than she was, something that made him use this approach. Zoey wished she had been more adamant in her refusal of kidnapping the bureaucrat's daughter.

She dug her nails into the skin of the innocent orange. Sure, it hadn't done anything to her, but it was the nearest thing to a stress ball she had.

The skin popped under her nails as she pried it loose in one complete, long peel. Dumping the peel in a bin, she popped the first bite into her mouth. The tangy citrus flavor exploded in her mouth. It tasted of the sweet, warm sunshine and dark, languid earth.

There was a forbidden quality to the acidic nectar that dotted her lips, and as she licked the flavor away, it reminded her ever so slightly of Eli's kiss… A kiss she had momentarily claimed, but had no future hold on.

Besides, it didn't make sense to listen to the gnashing, teeth-baring lioness that roared with anger within her. There was no call to be jealous. Zoey had released her claim on him and with it she had also released the right to feel anything beyond civility toward the man.

He glanced in her general direction and the smile on his lips disappeared. A thin layer of sweat appeared on his forehead, but it couldn't have been from the fall heat.

Eli said something to the woman and, taking her hand, he escorted her toward a small café that sat at the corner of the intersection. He sat down with Shaye at a small metal bistro table and picked up the menu like they were on a midmorning date. Shaye took off her headscarf and flipped her hair back over her shoulder as she sat down with her back to Zoey.

Though they weren't close, Zoey could make out the ring of the woman's laugh as she crossed her ankles and leaned into Eli.

Enough was enough.

Unable to hold back the roaring lioness any longer, Zoey pushed her way through the crowd, garnering more than a few frowns and mumblings in Spanish from strangers, but she didn't care. Whatever he was doing, he was doing it wrong.

As she neared the table, he excused himself and headed her off, grabbing her by the arm and leading her inside the café and out of view of the woman.

"What are you doing?" he fumed, as he glanced over his shoulder in the direction of his waiting date.

"Seriously, what am *I* doing?" She glared at him.

He wrapped his hand around the back of his neck and he let go of her hand. "I couldn't just grab her off the street. How would that look—a woman kicking and screaming as I drag her away from the crowd? I don't know about you, but I don't want to end up in a Spanish prison. I don't have to kidnap a woman to keep her occupied."

"And just how do you plan to keep her occupied?" she spat. "You think she'll bring you to her apartment as her new lover?" She tried to not sound bitter, but she couldn't keep her feelings from flecking her words.

Eli reached down, took hold of her hand and gave it a light squeeze. "I don't want a *new* lover. All I want is you. You know that. Or at least you *should* know that. From the moment this all started, all I've wanted is you."

And with just a few words, she once again felt cut off at her knees.

She sucked in a long breath and followed it with an equally long exhale. "Then what are you thinking?" she asked, sidestepping around his declaration. Though it had been exactly what she had wanted him to say, she wasn't prepared to respond.

"I want you to go to this address." He slipped her a note with an address. "There you'll find a friend of mine. A guy from my Watch Dog team. He will go with you and together you can get into the apartment. I'll keep her busy."

"There is no goddamned way I'm letting you go off alone with this woman while you foist me off on some stranger." She wadded up the piece of paper and threw it on the ground.

If they were separated, there was no telling what would happen. For all they knew, the bureaucrat's daughter knew exactly who they were and Eli was walking straight into a trap.

"I'm staying right here," Zoey said. "That is, unless you are trying to get her to take you home."

His face reddened. "Actually, if you're so adamant that you won't go to the apartment without me, what better way could there be to get into her building to look around for Chad?"

Screw that. She hated the idea of them flirting their way toward the bedroom.

"Not gonna happen." She shook her head like she could shake away the image.

"You aren't jealous, are you?" he asked. "I told you how I feel about you."

She didn't want to be needy, or to make a scene, but she felt herself steadily approaching a precipice. If they were going to be a team, she was going to have to trust him. He had said he cared only for her, that he *wanted* her. It may not have been a proclamation of love and forever, but it was more than she had expected.

She bent down and picked up the address he had given her and stuffed it into her pocket. Though she had no intention of going to a stranger to get help, she would do what she had to do to ensure they all remained safe…or as safe as they could be.

"I'm not jealous," she said, feeling the weight of her lie as she forced herself to stand tall in front of him. "You go ahead, but instead of taking her back to her apartment, keep her here."

His eyebrow rose as he must have seen through her dishonesty. It wasn't pettiness, but the primal need to protect the thing she cared for most…even if that thing—rather, that *person*—was a full-grown man.

He nodded, but said nothing and instead stared at her like he was waiting for a "but." Instead, she said nothing. She would choose to trust that whatever happened in that café was for Chad's benefit.

"Do whatever you need to do to remain safe."

He opened his mouth to speak, but she stopped him with a slight shake of her head. They didn't need to talk about her unspoken meaning.

"Call my friend. His name is Frogger."

"I've got this." With that, she turned, walking out of the café and away from the faux date.

With every step it felt as if her heart were a piece of

putty being stretched and pulled into a long strand that connected them wherever they went. No matter what, no matter how thin the thread became, or how immense the distance, she would never let their bond be broken.

Chapter Sixteen

The last time he had seen Zoey look that torn was the moment she had told him she was pregnant. He could feel her confusion like it was a fog that had rolled in off the sea and settled over them. It had been stupid of him to befriend the prime minister's daughter, but it was the only thing he could think of in a pinch.

He wanted to run after Zoey, to make sure that she wasn't walking out of his life again, but he stopped himself. Desperate was never a good look on anyone. She had to know that he never wanted to do anything that would compromise their burgeoning friendship. If anything, he had been the one to lay himself out there and tell her that he wanted her, and she had said…nothing.

If anyone should have been walking off, hurt by the other, it was him. He was here for her. He was always there for her. He would give everything that he owned to be with her. And she was always breaking his heart.

All he wanted, and had ever wanted, was to be hers.

He rubbed his neck as he walked back toward Shaye. He wasn't sure how, but now he was even more at a loss than when he had chatted her up. At that moment, at least he had his best friend at his back. Now, he was alone. And he was the one who had sent Zoey away.

He was screwing it up all over again.

He sat down and forced his face to smile. "Sorry about that. I saw someone I knew from college."

"Oh, yeah," Shaye said, twisting her pearl earring. "Where did you go to school?"

"Notre Dame. In the States," he lied. He had never gone to college, not with a father like his; instead, he had been forced to go into the military or get a job.

How little he had known about the world then.

It was a stark contrast to his reality now. The only perspective that hadn't changed from his formative years was that the world was a deadly and evil place, and the scavengers were always waiting in the shadows to pick his bones clean.

"Eli?" Shaye asked, sounding as though she had asked him a question he had failed to hear.

"Sorry, what?" He forced himself to concentrate on the woman sitting across the table from him.

"Who's the woman?"

He could feel the blood rushing from his face. "Huh? What woman?" he said, trying to play dumb, but looking in the direction that Zoey had disappeared.

"You know, the woman you are thinking about?"

He sat dumbfounded, saying nothing as he stared at Shaye.

"It's okay." Her English was accented with the slightest trill, and the effect made her sound like something out of a fairy tale, nothing like the big bad wolf that they had made her out to be. "I know the look of love in a man's eyes. I have seen it many times in my life."

"It sounds like you've been incredibly lucky in love."

As she took a sip of her espresso, her hand shook, making a dribble twist down from the corner of her mouth. Her cup clanked against the plate as she put it back down and wiped the offending drop from her chin. "I suppose my success would depend on who you asked," she said daintily placing her linen napkin back in her lap.

"I must admit, when I first spotted you at the market, I thought you were incredibly beautiful and vaguely *familiar*."

She looked at him for a long moment like she was trying to decide whether or not he knew who she was. Like Icarus, he had flown too close.

"You belong on a runway rather than sitting here with me," he added, hoping he could keep her from shutting down on him before he got the information that he needed from her or worse, leaving and going back to the apartment and compromising Zoey's position.

He had to keep Shaye here as long as he could in order to keep the woman he loved safe. It felt strange being on a pseudo date with a bureaucrat's daughter, but thinking only about Zoey. Oh, the things he did for her.

"Actually, I'm here in Spain with a man." She picked at a piece of bread the waiter had left at the table, rolling the dough between her fingers until the bits became shaped like little grenades that she could use to destroy him.

If he had been on a real date with her and hadn't known the story behind her appearance in this marketplace, he would've been hurt that she was shooting him down.

"And who is the man?" Eli asked. "You love him?"

She tore off another piece of bread as she dropped the first doughy grenade on the table. She must have wanted to create a full arsenal.

"It doesn't matter who I love." The waiter strode over and placed a bowl of olives beside the bread.

They each gave him their order, for him paella and her a caprese salad. As the waiter strode from the table, Eli turned back to her. "If you're here with another man, why did you agree to have lunch with me?" he asked, hoping that the question would sound like a man who wanted to date her.

She looked torn, but he didn't know why. Perhaps it had something to do with Chad, and knowing that she was holding him hostage somewhere. The thought reminded Eli that regardless of how amiable the woman seemed, or how pretty her face, he was dealing with a potential killer. It was often the ones like her, women with an abundance of physical assets, who flew well above anyone's radar.

But he couldn't forget.

"I agreed to come along with you because you looked interesting." She moved slightly in her seat, turning her knees away from him as though she were closing a part of herself off.

He'd seen people use this subtle body language many times when he had been tasked with interrogating. It was the body's equivalent of saying there wasn't a chance in hell of his getting whatever information he wanted—the interrogation was over.

He had to get her to open up to him again.

"I looked interesting, huh?" He tried to give her his sexiest grin. "I'll take it."

She quirked an eyebrow. "Has anyone ever told you that you are not a humble man?"

"I hear there are worse things to be." He popped an

olive into his mouth and chomped on it like it was a grain of truth.

Shaye laughed. "I'm glad I'm not in danger of falling for your charms."

"If I were a lesser man, I would be deeply hurt. However, I believe I do love a woman. You are safe from whatever charms you think I have." Eli looked down at Shaye's hands, half expecting to see something that would give away all the evil things she had done. Instead, she had the long, manicured nails of a woman who wasn't accustomed to manual labor.

These were not the hands of a woman who had cut off Chad's finger. However, just because she hadn't wielded the knife, didn't mean she wasn't the one responsible for the amputation.

"What do you think of corporal punishment?" Once again, he could feel his wings starting to melt as he neared the sun.

"Well—" She sat in stunned silence for a moment. "It appears you are far more interesting than I had initially assumed. Now, I cannot help wondering if I should have stayed far away from you. I fear you are a dangerous man." She stood up, picking up her scarf from the table and swiftly wrapping it over her hair, like a symbolic white flag.

He fell back down to earth. He stood up and threw a bit of money on the table as he moved after her. "Stop, please," he called.

She didn't even look back at him as she strode away in the direction of the apartment. Eli wasn't sure if he should go after her and grab her, as in the initial plan, or if he should simply let her go. For all he knew, Zoey was in her apartment with Chad right now. If Shaye found her there, and if Chad wasn't already dead, she would likely kill them both.

The only thing Eli could do was what he had planned in the first place.

The prime minister's daughter was about a half block from him as he started to jog after her. As she approached the end of the street, he spotted Zoey as she came out and jabbed the woman with the tip of a pen.

Clever girl.

Though they had often talked about the best methods to drug an enemy, they had never used the old Russian Cold War trick in practice—until now.

He slowed to a walk as Shaye said something to Zoey, no doubt chastising her. Undoubtedly, no one on the street had noticed what Zoey had done, except him. Zoey looked back at him as the woman crossed the street ahead of them. They likely had only minutes before the prime minister's daughter would feel any ill effects from the drug. After that, they would have to swiftly remove her from prying eyes.

As he caught up to Zoey, he couldn't help but wonder why the bureaucrat's daughter in a foreign land had not only agreed to have lunch with him, but also been devoid of any security personnel. Either she was impetuous and stupid, or her father had wanted her to disappear. Was it possible that this young girl had a contract out on her head, as well?

One thing was certain, in coming to Spain and allowing them access, the woman had made a mistake—a mistake that was to their advantage.

Chapter Seventeen

Sometimes being bad felt so good. Zoey wrapped her arm under Shaye's as the prime minister's daughter began to list forward. "Come now, Shaye, I'll take you back to your apartment. I bet my brother's waiting."

The woman looked at her through cloudy eyes, like she was trying to make sense of the words that were coming out of Zoey's mouth. "What?" Shaye asked, her speech slurred.

Eli took the woman by the other arm, and as he grabbed her, it was as if she were suddenly weightless.

"You couldn't drug her a little bit closer to her apartment?" Eli asked, sending her an approving grin.

"Well, if your Prince Charming act had worked, I wouldn't have had to drug her at all. This is really on you." Zoey glanced down the street—they were only a few buildings from the apartments.

"Look in her purse," Eli said, motioning toward the expensive bag on her arm. "We are going to need her keys to get into the building."

Careful not to let the princess fall, she rifled around in her bag until she found a key ring, complete with a small mink fur ball.

She lifted the keys with a jingle for Eli to see. "We're in like Flynn."

He cringed. "You just jinxed us. Why did you just jinx us?"

She rolled her eyes, the gesture suddenly making her feel more like the girl at Victoria's Secret. "Don't be so superstitious."

They stopped in front of the apartment building where they had last traced the GPS device. She lifted the keys, hoping it would be easy to pick which one belonged in the lock, before anyone would suspect their being there. However, as she moved closer to the glass doors, there was no area for a key, rather there was only an electronic keypad.

Crap.

Maybe she really had jinxed them. What were they going to do now?

She turned to the nearly unconscious woman. "What's your access pin?"

Shaye mumbled and her chin dropped down to her chest.

"Can you do some super tech genius thing and get us in?" Eli asked, taking hold of Shaye so Zoey could work.

She was capable of doing many things when it came to tech and breaking into tech-based security systems, but she didn't have any of her supplies. "If I had a paperclip, a contact lens and a wad of chewing gum I might be able to do something."

Eli reached into his pocket and shuffled around. "I think I have a piece of gum in my pocket somewhere." He sounded excited, and it only made her feel bad.

"I was kidding, Eli." She gave him an apologetic

smile. "Knowing this lady, though, the number is probably something stupid. It's probably a number that's always right there in her life, like a birthday or—"

"How many people she's killed," Eli said, finishing her sentence.

"If that's the case, then I hope the number is zero." She gave him a warning look, but she could tell from the look on his face what he really meant was that they could be walking into a situation where she would find her brother deceased in the girl's apartment.

Zoey didn't need a reminder.

"Do you know anything about this building?" Eli asked. "Maybe if we can pull something about the owners…" He stopped talking, like he realized he was grasping at straws.

Think, Zoey, think.

She nibbled on her lip, wishing she had brought a larger kit with her, but she hadn't anticipated breaking and entering. "Seriously, though, if we had a rare earth magnet and a sock, we could break the keypad and get in." She could hear herself sounding more and more like Eli as the nervous excitement started to swell within her. She glanced at him, but he shrugged like he didn't even know what a rare earth magnet was. "If there's a hardware store around here…" She paused. "Actually, I think I saw one near the bank."

This was doable. They could get in. They would just have to be creative.

They couldn't leave Shaye here by herself, and there was no way they could drag her through town and to the hardware store in the state she was in. If they got an Uber or a taxi, they'd have to explain their drunk friend and she wasn't sure she wanted to do that, either.

Their best bet was for her to head to the hardware store to get what she needed. And Eli could wait for her to return; or, if they got lucky, for another person who lived in the building to show up and then they could copy their access code. But there was no telling when another person would come to the building, and time was slipping by.

"Dude," Eli said, moving to the door. "I have an idea. What was the amount of that wire transfer?"

"$500,226.23. Why?"

He pressed 2-2-6-2 into the keypad. The red light flashed. He huffed. Then pressed 2-6-2-3. The green light flashed and the door's lock clicked open.

With a beaming smile, he settled Shaye against him and opened the door. "After you, my lady."

"Nicely done, MacGyver." She giggled.

Making her way inside, she glanced around the lobby of the building, making sure there were no active cameras. Luckily, it appeared this building was managed by people who honored the privacy of their renters. The door clicked shut behind them and their footfalls echoed against the stone floors. Inside the lobby was a seating area set around a crackling fire. It was cool, making her wonder if it was nothing more than show.

She pressed the only button on the elevator bank, going up. "And what about what floor to find Chad on? Did he tell you that in his mysterious wire transfer numbers, as well?" She quirked her brow playfully, thankful that Eli had gotten them the break they so desperately needed.

He made a show of pressing the button for the second floor as they got into the elevator with the unconscious Shaye. He laughed as he turned to her. "I think that's it, but honestly I have no idea if that's the right floor or not."

"Here's hoping your good luck lasts," Zoey said, crossing her fingers. The doors to the elevator bank closed, and as they ascended, Zoey's nerves began to rise, as well. She couldn't stand the thought of what would happen if she got into that room and found herself in a situation like the one they had with Trish. If there was a firefight, Zoey wasn't sure she could pull the trigger.

If she couldn't, and if one of them or Chad was hurt or killed, she would be the one who would have to tell the rest of the family. She was already on thin ice with her brothers, who were dealing with Trish's death in their own stoic ways. In fact, Chad had seemed like the only one who had been doing relatively well—at least until Trevor and Jarrod had met their fiancées.

She glanced over at Eli. He was staring up at the number near the elevator doors as it dinged to the second floor. He lifted Shaye up into his arms as they got out of the elevator, like he was cradling a small child instead of a possible killer. They walked to the only door on the floor. There was another keypad. She gave Eli a weary look as she punched in the same code, hoping it would work as well as it had last time.

There was the click and slide as the door unlocked. She wasn't sure she had ever been more grateful. All they had to do now was grab Chad, deal with Shaye and get the hell out of there.

As she touched the doorknob, moving to open it, Eli cleared his throat. She looked at him and realized that he was silently chastising her. He motioned toward the gun he knew she carried in her purse. She cringed.

They couldn't walk in there unprepared and unarmed. He was right. There was no telling who, or what they would find, and the last thing she wanted was to walk into the middle of a trap. But the thought of getting close to someone, looking them in the eye and pulling the trigger, made her stomach churn. And that reaction made her a liability. And Eli had to have known it, too.

Zoey quietly drew the gun from her bag. She jacked the round in the chamber and drew her weapon, readying herself. Eli gave her a stiff nod. She opened the door only slightly, scanning the room for any visible threat before opening it wider so that Eli and Shaye could move through.

Inside, she could see a long hallway, and at the end of it was a set of double doors that led into what looked like a living room with books adorning the walls. There were several doors on each side of the hall that must have led to the rest of the enormous apartment. Though she didn't see anyone here, there may well have been an entire crew of people hiding throughout the complex. However, for now it appeared that they were alone.

The door was silent as she closed it behind them. Making their way deeper into the apartment, she heard the sound of a TV from inside one of the many rooms. Their footfalls sounded only slightly as they made their way down the marble hall. The apartment was sparsely decorated, as though Shaye had only just moved in or was almost done moving out. There was nothing on the walls, and there were boxes stacked here and there outside of the doors. The place must have been newly renovated as it still carried the smell of fresh paint and wood.

They crept down the hallway toward the sound of

the television. Maybe Shaye had left Chad in the care of a bodyguard and they had been keeping him entertained. The fact that there was a TV on had to be a good sign—at least there weren't the subtle sounds of someone being tortured or the rat-a-tat-tat of gunfire. Things could've been so much worse.

On the other hand, it was almost a little too quiet. If her brother was here, and still alive, he would be fighting or making a plan to escape.

Martins weren't quitters. They weren't the kind of family who let others tromp all over them. And they certainly weren't the kind of people to act as quiet hostages. Her stomach tied into knots and her heartbeat was so loud in her ears that it almost sounded as if someone were beating on the closed door to her right.

Chad was going to be okay. He had to be okay. And if he wasn't okay—she glanced over at their newest acquisition and stared at her closed eyes—Shaye was going to die.

She opened her mouth, considering calling out. But she stopped herself. If there were other people in this apartment, she couldn't alert them to her presence. For now, they had the element of surprise.

She concentrated on her breathing as her body tightened, readying itself for a fight. The gun in her hands trembled ever so slightly. She had spent many hours at the range firing her Glock, but she would never get over the nerves that came with facing an adversary. She should've been the one trudging Shaye around so Eli could take point.

She turned to him. His body brushed against her as he moved to her side. Shaye's cheek was pressed against Eli's chest, just where Zoey had curled against him on the plane. That familiar sensation of jealousy crept up on her. If she closed her eyes and thought back, she could still hear the beating of his heart and could feel the hard muscles of his core as she traced her fingers over his skin.

They should have slept together. If they had, and this went all kinds of haywire, at least she could have been with him one more time.

But she couldn't focus on him right now or the way she felt. She had to leave the past in the past and focus on the hunt for her brother and hope it wouldn't end in a bloodbath.

As for Shaye, Eli could keep carrying her. As much as Zoey hated the thought of killing someone, if she needed the impetus for pulling the trigger, all she had to do was take one look at the woman in Eli's arms—she had to protect those she cared for.

"It's going to be okay," Eli whispered, almost imperceptibly, as they neared the living room.

He stopped and gently set Shaye down on the floor, her head bowing to one side as she settled against the wainscoting. As Eli stood, he pulled his gun from his holster. He didn't jack a round in the chamber, which made her wonder if he had been walking around with a live round the entire time. He was always the tough one, but he was a stickler when it came to safety. If he was strapped and loaded, then he was definitely feeling more antsy than he had let on.

There was a dating game on the television. And as they pressed against the wall near the door, a woman was chatting in English, talking about how she hated men who wore their socks to bed. She giggled as she spoke, as if drunk on the audience's attention.

Zoey smirked. If that was all the woman had to worry about, she'd clearly never been four seconds from a likely gun battle. That woman needed some perspective in her life.

Eli placed his back against the wall and pivoted into the living room. He cleared the room, covering the left side of the room as she cleared the right. There was a couch at the center of the room, facing the television.

"Get down!" Eli called, aiming his gun at the couch.

The back of the couch flexed as a man sat up and looked over the top at them. "What in the hell?" he said with a faint Spanish accent.

"Get on the ground," Eli commanded, his tone deep and threatening.

The man dropped to the ground in front of the leather couch and put his hands on the back of his head.

She side-stepped around the couch, aiming at the man's back. He was wearing a gray T-shirt, sweatpants, and had on a black knit hat—even though it was warm in the house. There was a half-eaten bag of chips and a can of Coke on the table beside him.

"Who in the hell are you?" the guy asked, looking up from the ground. "I didn't do anything. How did you get in here?"

Zoey had been prepared for a variety of situations, but not barging in on an innocent man hanging out in his pajamas and watching TV. Had they just invaded a blameless guy's apartment? Was their assumption about Chad's location wrong? If it was, that meant they were back to square one.

"Where's Chad?" Eli asked, his voice the human equivalent of a German shepherd.

The guy looked up at them with a confused expression on his face. "Chad's back there." He nudged his chin in the direction from which they had come.

Feeling returned to Zoey's body as relief flooded through her. Chad was here. They had been right. She was going to save him. Everything was okay—or so she hoped.

"If you bastards hurt one freaking hair on his head…" Zoey started.

"You can take it up with him," the guy said, gesturing in the direction he had said her brother was being kept.

Was Chad even a hostage? The guy in his pajamas wasn't carrying a weapon. And if he was a bodyguard, he was doing a crappy job. And yet Chad had gone completely silent, which had to mean something was wrong. It was against every protocol in STEALTH to go missing and cut off all communication—silence always meant their operative was in trouble or dead.

As mad as she was at the thought of Chad being here on his own accord, she hoped that was the case, and Chad had just made a mistake in keeping quiet.

On the other hand, if that was what had happened, she was going to kill Chad herself. Really, it would be a justifiable homicide.

"Stay here with this guy. I'll go get Chad." Zoey started to move away. "Find out what this guy knows about Sleeping Beauty out there, and why she was packing one of our black market weapons."

Eli nodded, but she could tell from the pinched look on his face that he didn't like the idea.

"Don't worry, I'll be fine," she said, lifting her Glock a little higher so he knew she meant business. Though she had tried to comfort him, the look on his face remained. No matter what he thought, she was going to be okay. Even if she didn't pull the trigger, she could kick some ass.

Then again, perhaps he had seen her hands trembling when she had pulled her weapon on the attacker at the Widow Maker. He knew her demons just as well as she had once known his.

Before he could stop her, she made her way out into the hall. She stepped over Shaye's sprawled legs and around a stack of boxes.

Though she was almost certain they were nearly alone in the apartment with Chad, and her only concern was Sir Pajamas out in the living room, she was careful to be quiet as she crept to the next room. They should've cleared this whole place when they had come in, but just like the rest of this, nothing was going as planned. They were flying this operation by the seat of their pants.

She quietly clicked open the door on her right. Inside was a large chef's kitchen with stainless steel appliances and quartz countertops. Atop the stove was a single pot and spoon, and a stack of plates sat on the island. Aside from the meager assembly of dishes, the place was empty.

She stepped out and made her way to the next room, a deserted library. The empty bookshelves made the room feel gloomy. If she owned this place, they would have been filled to the brim.

Closing the door to the barren library, she wondered if Chad was even in the apartment. What if the guy had lied to get Eli alone so he could have a fighting chance instead of standing two against one? She glanced down toward the living room, but it was quiet. Hopefully Eli had everything under control.

At the end of the hall, she came to another door. She raised her gun, anticipating this room was empty like those before it. As she clicked open the door, she found herself in a man's bedroom. There was a pair of cowboy boots beside the bed and a ripped and bloodied flannel was thrown in a heap in the corner of the room. It looked like something Chad would wear.

As she stepped into the room to get a better look at the shirt, the door slipped shut behind her. As she turned, there was the sound of someone rushing toward her.

Pain erupted from her head as an object connected with the side of her face. The blow reverberated through her bones, making it sound like she had been hit by something metal. She turned slightly, but as she tried to catch sight of who or what had struck her, the world turned into a swirling mass of colors.

She tried to take control of herself and override the pain that threatened to overwhelm her. *Pain is just a signal from the body that there is something wrong*, she tried to tell herself. But the thought was as sluggish and weaving as the world around her.

Push past it. She told herself. *Focus.*

As she tried to center herself, another blow struck her from behind, making the same metallic, reverberating sound.

The swirling mass of white walls and gray bedding mixed with bright sunshine and dark shadows, becoming a vortex.

She didn't know how she found herself on the floor,

but she felt the cool tiles pressed against her throbbing cheek.

Blinking, the vortex of color turned into a black hole, sucking her into its gaping maw. No matter how hard she tried to focus on the floor, she felt herself slipping deeper and deeper into the abyss. She sucked in a breath, fearing that this was it. Death had found her.

Then there was nothing.

Chapter Eighteen

What was taking Zoey so long?

Eli pulled a set of zip ties from his pack and, pressing the man's hands and feet together, hog-tied him. "What's your name?" he asked.

The man said nothing.

"Don't make me have to repeat myself." Eli pulled the zip ties tight enough that they bit into the man's wrists to act as a warning.

"You are the one standing in my living room. Don't you think I should be asking the questions?" the man said, pulling against the restraints on his wrists in a feeble attempt to free himself.

"You know," Eli said, moving to the couch and sitting, "I have yet to find myself in your position—hog-tied and forced into submission—but I think if I were you, the last thing I would be doing is acting like a smartass."

"If I get my hands on you, you will get your chance to test your theory," the man said, rolling to his side to face him.

"I highly doubt that," Eli said, picking up the remote and changing the channel off the dating show. He flipped to the news.

The last thing he needed right now was to learn more about some woman's dating preferences when he had more than enough relationship drama of his own to worry about. He had never really understood the allure of watching dating shows—they seemed fake and manipulated. But when he and Zoey had been together, he had sat through more than his fair share of them in order to make her happy.

That sacrifice, in hindsight, seemed far more real than anything a television show could come up with. For him, love was the little things…not some grand gesture.

There was the cacophony of firearms as the reporter spoke of an ongoing conflict somewhere else on the globe. Eli found that the sound was far more appealing than listening to the news. The sounds of gunfire definitely made him feel less on edge.

The guy at his feet sighed, like being on the floor was merely an annoyance instead of the life-threatening proposition Eli had intended. "Can I get you something to drink? How about a Coke?" Eli said sarcastically, motioning to the can on the table.

His inflection must've been lost on the man.

"Actually, that sounds good." The man perked up.

"Yeah, right. You can want in one hand…" Eli snarled. "In case you forgot, I'm the one sitting here with the gun. Try giving me the information I need and maybe we can get out of here. Then you can go back to watching whatever that was."

The man prickled, but Eli could see that he was trying to remain calm, though he clearly wanted to come up off the floor and deck him. "What exactly are you here for?" the man asked.

Eli wasn't sure whether or not he should say anything

to the man about their true reason for being here. By now, he knew they were looking for Chad— they had said as much. But if the man didn't know about the contract out on Chad, Eli wasn't about to tell him about it.

"How did you get brought into all of this?" Eli asked. He was the one asking the questions.

The man shifted slightly on the floor, trying to find a comfortable position while they danced around one another. "I'm just here to do a job." The man paused. "You are Eli Wayne, right?"

Eli hated that the man knew who he was, and he had no idea who he was dealing with.

The man's beanie was coming off, revealing a head of red hair, the ruddy color bordering on strawberry blond. The dude looked nothing like he had any Spanish ancestry. It didn't mean he wasn't from Spain, but that and his slight Spanish accent made Eli wonder if he'd come from somewhere else—maybe even Algeria.

"I'm glad my reputation precedes me," Eli said, trying to sound far more confident than he was feeling.

He reminded himself that this man was his prisoner, not the other way around. The dude was trying to play head games with him. He couldn't allow himself to get sucked into his nonsense.

"With a reputation like yours, it's hard not to know about it," his hostage said.

"What the hell is that supposed to mean?"

So much for not pulled into his head games.

"That woman you came in with—I heard you got her pregnant…"

Eli's hands clenched and the remote in his hand cracked under the pressure. "Unless you don't want to make it out of here alive, I recommend you be *real* careful how you talk about her."

The man snorted with derision. "I heard about how she kicked you to the curb."

Who in the hell was this guy who seem to know so much about them?

Eli stood up and threw the remote on the couch. He couldn't sit here and let this man get under his skin. They needed to get Chad and get the hell out of here.

Glancing over at the man, making sure he wasn't going anywhere, Eli walked out into the hallway. Shaye was still passed out, her body tucked into the corner. They were going to need to do something about her if they stayed much longer. As he looked at her, she moved slightly as though she was starting to come around.

At the far end of the hall there was a door open, leading into a bedroom. The place was quiet and a wave of panic overtook him. Where was Zoey? She had said she was just going to get Chad. It'd been stupid of him to let her go by herself. He should've hog-tied that bastard sooner and come with her to find her brother. But as he chastised himself, he thought of the look Zoey had given him, that "I don't need a man to keep me safe" expression.

She was strong, but that didn't mean she didn't need help. He tried to respect her boundaries and her desires, but no matter what she thought, everyone needed help sometimes.

He passed two closed doors as he made his way down the hall. Entering the bedroom, nothing appeared out of place. Where had she gone? He was tempted to call for her, but he stopped himself.

He moved to step back out into the hall when there

was a creak in the floorboard behind him. He turned
as the bedroom's closet door swung open and a man
stepped out. Eli reached for his gun, but as he moved,
the man pointed a yellow Taser at his chest. Eli turned
to run, hoping that he could get outside of the shooting distance of the Taser before the man had a chance
to pull the trigger.

It was no use.

There was the pop of the gun, the spray of confetti,
and the sharp pinch of the barbs of the Taser as they
bore into the skin of his ass. It felt as if he had accidentally sat on a 110-volt line. Debilitating pain coursed
through him, dropping him to his knees.

Click. Click. Click. The electric current flowed
through him with each sound.

A strange cry that filled the air, an odd mix between
mewing and a screech, the noise like a hurt animal.

Click. Click. Click.

With the second round of clicks, Eli realized the
sound was actually coming from him.

As his crying stopped, he tried to rise to his knees
and get away, but found himself completely incapacitated. Then there was another round of that terrifying
noise.

He had forgotten how bad this hurt. He had gone
through a round of training in which they had been
forced to take a hit from a Taser, then receive a round
of OC spray—aka pepper spray—and then complete
an obstacle course. The OC spray was the worst. Once
this Taser was done pulsing, it would be over. The effects of OC spray could last for hours.

Click. Click. Click.

He could feel his heart fluttering as the electric current pulsed through every muscle in his body.

Five seconds. It would last only five seconds.

How long had he been on the ground? He prayed for this to be over. It felt like it had been going on for hours.

Had his attacker struck him with another set of barbs?

Maybe this was it. This would be how he went out. Attacked by a faceless enemy while trying to help the love of his life.

He collapsed as the pulse of electricity stopped coursing through his system.

He sucked in a breath, finally able to control his breathing again.

His body was exhausted, and as he lay there on the floor and tried to regain control of his faculties, half wondering if he'd peed himself, he noticed a set of feet across the floor. From where he lay, he could see only the soles and the sides of the brown leather shoes, but he recognized them as Zoey's.

Had she been shot with a Taser, too? Was she still alive?

He should have never let her go through the rest of the apartment alone. Why had he been so freaking stupid? Why didn't he listen to that little voice in his head that had told him she needed him? Why?

He choked on his breath, coughing and sputtering as his body flamed back to life. He had to get up. He had to get to her. Though he may have made a mistake, he had a chance now to make it right. To get her out of here. To keep her alive.

"Zoey," he called, his voice hoarse and raspy like he had taken the Taser barbs straight to the throat.

He moved to stand up, but as he struggled, there was the sound of footfalls from behind. Turning to look, he saw the quick brown flash of a man's boot as it connected with his head near the temple. There was the crunch of steel on bone and he bit his tongue, tasting the copper-rich stickiness as his body recoiled from the impact.

As bad as the Taser had been, he wished it had been the current that struck him rather than the kick. He collapsed, reality bleeding away.

Chapter Nineteen

They had walked straight into the snare. How had she not seen this coming? Getting in here had almost been too easy. She had been blinded by the hope of her brother leaving her secret messages and hints as to where to find him alive. But it could have been someone using him to get her to this point. Someone else must have known she would be searching for Chad and she would do anything to get to him.

Now, they were probably using her and Eli as bait. Hopefully they intended on keeping them alive. Bayural and his men were likely behind this. Just like them, he must've heard about the contract out on Chad's head. Using that knowledge, he must have set up this elaborate ruse, hoping it would flush them out of hiding.

At least she had told her brothers and their fiancées to stay away so the Gray Wolves wouldn't get the chance to kill them all in one fell swoop.

Zoey looked across the room at the bloodied and battered Eli. From where she lay on the floor, pretending to be passed out, she could make out the subtle rise and fall of Eli's chest. The man in the brown boots kicked him again. She wanted to jump up and pummel the man for hurting Eli, but knew it was no use. In the state that she was in, it would have been irrational to make a move.

Though she could kick some ass when necessary, with Eli out of the game she wouldn't stand a chance of making it out of here. Even if she did manage to somehow take down the man who had just taken both her and Eli out, there was no way she would leave Eli behind. For all she knew, their enemies could be hiding out in the apartment. The man turned on the heel of his boot, and as he moved Zoey shut her eyes.

Playing possum was her only defense. Even with that, the man may well choose to come over here and continue beating her. If he did, she would have to fight. She'd have to get up. She might even have to kill the man. Summoning what strength she had left, she vowed to do whatever she had to do to stay alive.

The man said something in Spanish she couldn't understand, but it sounded like expletives.

Good. At least he was as pissed off as she was. She would have hated it if taking them down had been easy on the man.

She wished she had put up more of a fight, but even now, as she forced her eyes to stay closed, there was a throbbing in her head. With each throb, a burst of light filled her darkened vision. *Boom. Boom. Boom.*

The sound reminded her of the clicks she had awoken to.

The sound of the Taser and Eli's cry was something she was never going to forget. Though without it, she wasn't sure whether or not she would have regained consciousness.

The man's footsteps moved toward the door and then it slammed shut. There was a click of a lock.

His footfalls cascaded down the hall as the man yelled something.

With the sounds of his voice growing more distant, Zoey was tempted to open her eyes and go check on Eli. Before she did, she held her breath and listened for anyone else in the room. She had only seen the one man who had taken her down—the bastard in the boots—but that didn't mean there wasn't someone else.

The only sound she heard was the slow, methodical breathing of Eli.

Thank all that was good he was alive.

She would have to try her damnedest to keep it that way.

Zoey peeked out from beneath her eyelashes. Eli wasn't moving, but there was a rigidity in his body that made her wonder if he was faking unconsciousness.

"Eli?" she whispered. "You okay?"

He didn't answer.

She must have seen something that wasn't truly there. She scooted her body across the floor and as she moved, the thundering in her head amplified. In all likelihood she had a concussion, but there was nothing she could do about it now. All she could focus on was the here and now, and getting them both to safety.

She leaned over Eli. He smelled of sweat and pain. Running her fingers through his hair, she tried to comfort him and draw him back to the present. "Eli, come back to me. Baby, I need you. Please," she cooed, but as she spoke, her voice cracked with emotion.

She swallowed back the feelings that betrayed her. She needed unwavering strength.

Eli's eyelids fluttered and a cute half grin peppered his face. "I need you, too."

She leaned in and kissed Eli's soft lips. As they fell into one another, a tear slipped down her cheek.

He was okay. They were together.

They could get out of this place alive.

She hoped.

Reaching up, Eli cupped her face and wiped away the tear on her cheek with his thumb. "You don't need to worry. I've got you, honey. I've always got you." He sat up and wrapped his arms around her.

In that moment, blanketed in his warm touch, she felt comfort. Their lives were in danger, and the world threatened to come crashing down on them, but she had fallen into the safety and security of the only man she had ever truly loved.

Though many things had turned her heart cold in the past, sitting here in his arms her heart was reawakened. They may never make it out of this room, but she finally truly had come back to her center—and to her home—in his arms.

If she lived or died, at least in this one moment she was nearly complete.

At the same time, though, there was no question of whether she loved him. She couldn't tell him—not now and probably not ever. To tell him how she felt was to put him in even further danger. If she opened herself up to him and then something happened to her, it would only hold him back. If he was the only one to make it out of this room alive, she wanted him to move into the future with an open heart…a heart that was free to find love and a life that brought him joy—even if that life wasn't with her.

She took a breath, absorbing everything she could about him, from the sound of his heart, to the heat of his touch, to the subtle scent of his cologne mixed with sweat. If this was the last time she found herself in his arms, she had to remember it all.

Dusk had started to settle on the world outside their barred window. Soon, night would be upon them and with that, a sense of foreboding.

Eli moved to stand, his feet unsteady beneath him. He extended his hand to help her to her feet. Taking his proffered hand, she stood. The throbbing in her head had subsided with each second she'd stayed in his arms.

"You check the window." He motioned toward it as he stepped toward the door.

He pressed his ear against the wood, listening for any sign that they were being monitored. Then, seeming confident that they were safe, he twisted the door handle. It made a *chunk* sound as if it were locked from the outside.

"Dammit," he said. The window provided no escape, either. In addition to being barred, it had been painted shut likely decades ago. Their assailants had chosen this room well.

"Did you see any sign of Chad when you looked around the apartment?" he asked.

"I saw a shirt with blood on it, but I couldn't tell if it was his." She walked over to the corner of the room to the flannel shirt. Pinching its sleeve in a place that wasn't stained with blood, she lifted it. It was an extra-large. She wasn't sure, but she could have sworn Chad wore a medium. Even if that were true, it didn't stop her from thinking the worst.

"Do you think this was what he was wearing when they cut off his finger?" Her voice sounded tinny and foreign, like it was coming from someone else. She dropped the shirt.

Eli shrugged. "We don't know anything for sure yet. Don't worry. I'm sure he's fine."

He was lying, but she appreciated that he was making an attempt to lessen her panic.

Eli patted his pockets until he found his phone.

It was ridiculous, but for a moment she hoped he was calling someone to help. But who was there to call? They were here in Spain alone, and their closest ally was her family in Sweden. It would take them at least half a day to get to them. By then, she and Eli were likely to be killed.

Besides, the last people they could call was her family. If the Turkish terrorist group was behind their abduction, then they couldn't risk getting all of her family together in one place. Actually, it didn't even matter who had set them up to walk into this trap. They couldn't allow her family to follow suit.

She remembered Eli's team member—the one he'd asked her to find before coming here.

"Are you going to call Watch Dog?" she asked, pulling her own phone from her pocket.

At some point the screen had been cracked, most likely when she had fallen to the floor or perhaps when the man had kicked her while she had been down.

"Yeah, Frogger is nearby." Eli tapped on the screen. "He can put together a team and extricate us before morning, I'm sure."

Though she was relieved that they had an exit strategy, she wasn't sure how it would look that another team was going to bring them to safety. If it got out that Watch Dogs had saved her, a member of STEALTH, her family's company would lose their hard-nosed edge in the contractor market.

But what did it really matter, as long as they made it out alive?

Ego didn't have a place when it came to life and death.

Watch Dog could have this victory. She would even send them a gift basket. Maybe something from their new line of tactical wear.

She chuckled at the thought.

Eli glanced over at her and furrowed his brow. "What's so funny?"

Checking her smile, she stopped, but not before glancing at his blue button-up. "Nothing. I must be tired."

She turned back to her phone and texted Jarrod an encrypted message.

Eli and I have a situation here in Spain. Going to call in Watch Dog. You all need to stay away. We will get out of this. But in case we don't, give my little Anya and the rest of the family hugs for me. Love you all.

After she hit Send, she turned off her phone, hoping to save the battery and, admittedly, she wasn't sure she wanted to see her brother's response. No doubt he would flip out.

Hopefully everything would turn out all right and soon they would all be back home at the ranch, out of danger and celebrating the holidays.

She closed her eyes and thought of it now. In her fantasy Christmas, Eli was sitting next to her opening presents as they drank eggnog and laughed about all the trouble they had found this year. They would talk about Trish and how, when she was young, she had loved *Teenage Mutant Ninja Turtles*. Michelangelo had always been her favorite.

And this was the first year they were going to get the chance to spend Christmas with Anya. Though she had only just recently entered their lives, she had changed everything. That girl was incredible. She had an extra chromosome, which made her extra in every way— and none more than her ability to bring joy to the family. She was the light in everyone's eyes. One minute around Anya and it was easy to forget your troubles and just enjoy the moment. She was the linchpin that kept every one of them grounded and centered. She needed them just as much as they needed her.

The thought of everyone made Zoey ache with longing.

She and Eli should have never come here. They should have just waited until they had found more evidence about Chad's location. They should have played it smart. But no, she had been in such a damned rush to get to him that she had brushed their rules and protocols to the side.

Now it was not only going to cost her, but it was going to cost Eli everything, as well.

There was the sound of men talking from outside the door, and she and Eli stopped moving. They both slipped their phones away.

Her heart skipped a beat with the turn of the doorknob.

"We need to kill them."

"No," the second man said, his voice thick with an

accent that she couldn't place. "We need them at least until Chad arrives. Then you can kill them for all I care."

She felt the blood rush from her face and she sank down onto the edge of the bed that sat at the center of the room.

"As long as Chad *thinks* they are here, we're covered," the second man continued. "If we keep them alive, they are nothing more than a liability."

"I said no," the first man growled. "If we kill them and Chad somehow finds out, we will be back to having nothing. We need them as leverage. That's an order."

Were these men military? They had to have some sort of hierarchy. Maybe they were operatives just like them.

She choked on the urge to cry. It was nothing more than frustration, she reminded herself. That was all. She just had to keep from losing her cool and everything would be okay.

The second man let loose a string of expletives at the man's refusal. Yeah, maybe they weren't military after all, but it didn't eliminate the likelihood that they were contractors. Which meant they were looking to score the bounty on Chad's head.

"Just leave them for tonight. Tomorrow, if we haven't heard back from him, we will kill them," the first man said.

She could almost hear her clock ticking down to zero hour.

As their footfalls moved away from the door, she looked around the room for anything that could help them get out of there. The window bars refused to budge and there were no grates or openings in the floor or ceiling large enough for them to slip through. All they had were their cell phones and their wits.

"Tell your guy we're going to need him here sooner rather than later," she said, turning back to Eli, who was currently staring at his phone.

"Already done." Eli sighed. "But he's not at the address I gave you. He's traveling—and still a ways out. Until then, he told us to stay put."

She laughed at the idea that they had any other option.

Her headache worsened and she lay down on the bed, pulling up the down comforter around her tired body.

Eli dropped the phone onto the floor beside the bed and moved in next to her. "I'm sorry I got us in this mess," he said.

"What?" she said, sitting up slightly so she could look him in the eye. "You aren't the one who went all gung ho into this. If I would've stopped to think for more than three seconds, and not let my emotions get away from me, we wouldn't be here. This is all my fault. Not yours."

"Yours weren't the only choices made. We did this together. This isn't just on you."

It was strange, but she felt a bit stripped of her strength by him taking some of the blame. She wasn't sure that she liked the sensation. She deserved to feel responsible for all the bad things that were coming their way after all she had put Eli through.

He motioned for her to fold into his arms. "You don't get to carry the burden of guilt all by yourself, my love," he added.

She laid her head against him, finding comfort in

the melodic rise and fall of his chest. *My love*, he had said. Was that his hint that he was falling for her again?

She ran her fingers over the buttons of his shirt and made small swirls on the fabric. This, being with him in bed, was something she had missed after they had gone their separate ways. Was she ready to open her heart up and let this happen—if they got out of here alive?

He kissed the top of her head and drew in a long breath. "You know I love you, don't you?" he whispered into her hair.

Her entire body tightened. It wasn't that she didn't want to hear those words, it was just that they came as a surprise. Sure, there were feelings between them, but love? Maybe he meant the kind of *comfortable* love that came with time and two people who became accustomed to one another.

Just because he said he loved her, it didn't mean his feelings were a *romantic* love, the kind for which people sacrificed and gave everything they had for the other: sleep, money, time, opinions and even habits…

He was certainly sacrificing everything he had for her right now.

She wanted to tell him that she loved him, too. But she had to stick to her guns. She couldn't get them out of their predicament, so the best thing she could do to protect him was to keep the truth away from him. At least until they were on the outside. But that didn't mean she couldn't take this chance to show him how she felt.

This was their night…their one last chance together. For all she knew, it could be their final goodbye. And if all they had were these few, precious hours, she was going to make the most of it.

She gazed up at him and gave him the look that had

always been her cue to make love. In their past life, she had given him this look what must've been thousands of times, but none of them felt as important as this moment. This last moment.

She regretted all the mistakes she had made when it came to him. "Eli, I'm so sorry. I'm sorry I left you back then." The lump formed in her throat and she tried to swallow it back, but it refused to budge. "I never wanted to break your heart. But after we lost the baby... it changed me."

He tightened under her, but said nothing.

"Every time I closed my eyes, all I saw were the swirls of her dark brown hair—your hair. And her big green eyes—she had your eyes. And that sweet little pointed nose—she had my nose." She swallowed back the lump in her throat. "I never knew I could know such love and such heartache all at the same time."

"She was beautiful, just like her mommy." Eli ran his fingers through her hair, comforting her. "When she died, so did a piece of me... And then when you split, the rest of me withered away."

"I'm so sorry." Her voice was raspy with unshed tears. "I felt like I wasn't myself anymore. I was just a shell. But I feared that if I stayed, I would be constantly reminded of the future we could have had, just by looking in your eyes—her eyes."

He nodded, but was silent for a long moment. "You weren't the only one hurting, Zoey."

"I know." She wished she could go back in time and correct her wrongs. "And I also know that no amount of apologizing will ever be enough." She put her hand over his heart. "I was so myopic. All I could do was concentrate on my own pain and agony. I just shut down."

"Do you know that when you disappeared, I didn't stop looking for you until I knew where you had gone and that you were safe?"

She hadn't thought of the days after she had left him and run to a cabin in the Rockies in a long time. She had holed up for nearly six months. She'd only let Trish know where she was, so they wouldn't come looking for her.

Once in a while, her sister would bring her food and check on her to make sure she was still alive; but beyond that Zoey had seen no one. Even with Trish, she had barely spoken a word, but her sister hadn't forced her to make conversation. Instead, Trish had just talked to her about what the family was working on, and assignments that they had taken.

The only thing Zoey had been capable of doing was continuing her drone strikes and IT work—which she did with manic diligence.

"Did Trish tell you where I was?" she asked.

Eli gave her a guilty look. "She knew how concerned I was about your safety." He drew in a long breath.

"Just so you know, if I could go back in time and make things right, I would. I would never run away from you like that again... No matter how badly our hearts get broken by the world." She moved atop him, straddling her legs around him.

He slipped her fingers between his and raised her hands so she was kneeling over him. He reached up and kissed her lips. In his kiss was a deep sadness and an equally deep well of desire.

"Make me a promise..." he said, his breath caressing her lips. "And we can start over, no guilt."

"What?" she asked, her voice as smooth and supplicating as his touch.

"Promise me that if we make it out of here alive, we can quit screwing around."

She smiled as she kissed his lips. "And what is that supposed to mean?"

"Let's get married."

She stopped moving and stared into his emerald eyes. He was being serious. A gust of joy breezed throughout her body. She wanted to say yes, a thousand times yes, but she stopped herself from getting too excited.

Though she feared her own demise, and what it would do if she told Eli the truth, he was going to hurt either way. He *loved* her. He wanted to *marry* her.

If she agreed, they could revel in the joy that came with promises of forever—at least for one night.

"Yes, Eli." As she answered, she realized she had never told him that she loved him, but he didn't seem to care. It was almost as if she didn't have to put words to her feelings as he already knew how she felt.

He took hold of her and pulled her down hard, his lips crushing against hers in his excitement.

Whether she ever had the chance to tell him or not, she loved this man. She would love him until the end of time and then probably even long after. He was hers and she was his, and she never wanted it any other way.

He pushed up her shirt and lifted it over her head, exposing her naked breasts. He cupped them in his hands as he sat up and moved to take her nipple in his mouth. She savored the feel of his mouth on her and how he tenderly thrilled his tongue against her sensitive nub.

She bit back a moan.

They would have to be quiet. Silent even, in their

lovemaking. Their silence, mixed with the threat of danger, swirled together into a heady elixir of desire.

She hurried, taking off his pants and his shirt; stripping him of all of his underclothes in her rush to feel him.

This was it, their last moments together. This was the only future they were promised.

She kissed him, trailing her mouth down his chest until she found him. He tilted his head back into the pillow and she could hear his breath quicken as she swirled her mouth around him.

"Zoey," he said as she tasted him. "I want you. I've wanted you every moment…of every day…" His voice was faint, slipping into the euphoria.

She would be lying if she tried to tell him that it had been any different for her.

He was her everything, just as he always had been.

His body grew harder and impossibly harder as she played.

"Come here," he said, calling her to move atop him. "I need to feel you. I've missed you for so long."

She moved over him, slipping him into her gently as she rocked her hips back and forth. Their movement was easy and unrushed, as if they were both savoring the limited time they had together, and every thrust, every circle and nudge of her hips was a day they had been apart.

Their lips met as he sat up and pulled her into his lap, their knees pointing toward the ceiling. As he drove deeper and deeper into her, she thought of how much time she had missed by making one stupid decision and running away.

At least for this one day, this one moment, they could have the past that she had so foolishly stripped away.

Her breathing quickened, and she tried to force her body to listen to her mind. She wanted this moment to last—she couldn't let herself go. Not yet. But he felt so good. Being in his arms. Feeling him inside of her.

She buried her face into his neck in order to try and quiet her throaty moan as her body released, giving in to the ecstasy of being with him.

As she collected herself, she started to move again. This time, just for him.

Tonight, they would have everything the other offered—love above all.

Chapter Twenty

The next morning, before dawn, the door to their bed-room flew open. Zoey pulled herself out of Eli's arms, afraid that if their enemies saw them together they would know the most effective way to hurt her. Pajama dude was still wearing the beanie from the night before, but instead of looking bored and confused by their presence, now he looked pissed off.

"Get in there," he ordered, shoving Shaye into the room with them.

She turned back as soon as he threw her inside. "No. These people will kill me. You can't put me in here with them," she pleaded to the man as he slammed the door shut.

There was the click of the lock. Shaye screamed after the man. "Come back! No! This is absolutely unaccept-able. Just wait until my father hears about what you have done." She stopped for a moment as she stared at the door. "You will be dead before nightfall!"

Ever so slowly, she turned around to face them, a look of disgust and anger burned across her beauti-ful face.

"What in the hell are you doing in here?" Zoey asked, staring daggers at her.

She was definitely the kind of woman that Chad would go for. She was curvy and there was a dimple in her chin. Her long blond hair was free and falling in loose waves over her shoulders. Zoey hadn't noticed before, but the woman had eyes the color of blue glacial ice. As angry as she was, Zoey was surprised that the heat of her stare didn't cause the icy color to melt and become the hot orange hue of flames. Fire and ice… Chad's MO when it came to the women he had dated in the past.

Zoey wanted to get up and shake her to get the answers they so desperately needed, but at the same time she wasn't sure approaching the Algerian snow beast was the best option. She looked as though she was ready to scratch their eyes out.

The woman must have been put in here to act as a spy. This was her apartment and they were her men—weren't they?

As Zoey sat up, she straightened out her shirt. Luckily, both she and Eli had slipped back into their clothes after they had made love. She drew in a long breath as her thoughts drifted back to last night.

She loved the fact that his scent still perfumed her skin.

It was just a pity that she had to spend the afterglow with the woman who had been enemy number one for the last week.

"If you lay one finger on me, you will be added to *his* list," Shaye said, indicating the closed door and the men outside.

"We have no intention of doing anything of the sort," Eli said.

Zoey wanted to tell him to speak for himself—she

was more than willing to take this woman down if it led to Chad.

"Is that right?" Shaye spat, pulling her hair back like she wanted to put it up, but stopped as she must have realized it was a nervous tic that made her look weaker. "Is that why you drugged me and forced me to come back here?"

Forced her? "Isn't this your apartment?" Zoey asked. Eli set his hand on her thigh, a subtle reminder that they had to be careful about what they did and didn't say.

She needed no reminding.

"It's my friend's apartment, but I had no intention of coming back after—" She went silent.

"After what?" Eli asked, his voice taking on a soft, caring tone that Zoey couldn't have conjured even for all the wealth in the world.

Shaye walked across the room and stared out the window, suddenly acting like she couldn't hear them.

"Is my brother Chad still alive?"

"He's your *brother*?" Shaye asked, turning with a start. "Odd."

Her surprise made Zoey wonder if her and Chad's relationship wasn't what she had assumed. If Chad was dating this woman, he wouldn't hesitate to tell her about his siblings—though none of them were normally particularly forthcoming about the family business.

"Yes. Now, is he alive?" she asked, trying hard not to grit her teeth.

"As far as I know. Why wouldn't he be?" Some of the anger seemed to drift out of Shaye's features. "What in the hell is going on?"

"We wanted to ask you the same thing," Eli said.

The woman sat down on the window's ledge, giving

one more forlorn glance at the bars before looking back at them. "I don't know who you really are, or how you found me, but even if you hadn't drugged me, I wouldn't have anything to say to you."

Zoey moved to stand up, but Eli shook his head almost imperceptibly. Instead, he rose to his feet. He must have known she was close to losing her cool.

"Look," Eli said, meandering over toward her like she was a stray cat who might run away if he moved too quickly. "We didn't want to drug you. All we wanted to do was—"

"Pick me up," she said, staring at him.

"No, I just wanted to get to the bottom of a few things. And to find Chad. We know he was here...with you. We saw you together." Eli stopped about halfway to her and crossed his arms over his chest.

Her eyebrows rose and she mumbled something unintelligible under her breath. "Your brother was fine when I left him yesterday. He was supposed to meet me at the Maricel Museum, but he never showed up."

"A museum?" Zoey asked before thinking. "He wasn't your hostage?"

"What?" Shaye scoffed. "No. Of course not. Why would you think I... Wait. Is that what all your nonsense was about? You thought I'd *kidnapped* Chad so you kidnapped me?" She gave a disbelieving shake of her head. "Americans."

Ignoring her disdain, Zoey tried to collect her thoughts. "If you didn't kidnap him and take him hostage, then what were you doing with my brother?"

"He was working for me," she said, but there was a bit of color in her cheeks.

"Doing what?" Eli asked, moving to the wall on the other side of the window from Shaye.

Shaye tapped her perfectly manicured nails against the windowsill. "Is she the woman you were thinking about when we were at the café?" She motioned toward Zoey.

Eli smiled and gave a nod. "Yes. That obvious, huh?"

The remaining anger disappeared from Shaye's face. "Even if I hadn't seen you sitting in bed with one another." Shaye blushed ever so slightly. "How long have you been together?"

Eli shifted his weight. "On and off for a few years now."

Zoey just wished she knew if it was going to be on or off when they walked out of this room—or rather, *if* they walked out of this room. In the light of day his marriage proposal last night seemed absurd. Had he really been serious?

"You said you were here with a man. Were you talking about a boyfriend or Chad?" Eli asked.

Shaye sighed. "I don't have a boyfriend. At least, not anymore."

"Did you hire Chad to kill him?" Zoey asked. It sounded odd when it escaped her lips, but what else would the woman have hired him for?

Shaye laughed. "No. Hardly. But my ex is the reason we had to leave Algeria."

The sounds of men yelling came from outside the bedroom, and they all went deathly silent. There was a tirade of obscenities coming from the other room, but she couldn't quite make out what they were fighting about. It likely had something to do with how to handle their hostages.

"Is that why your father put out a contract on Chad's head?" Zoey asked in a whisper, hoping to get as much information from the woman before the door opened and shots were fired. "Because he was involved with your ex?"

Shaye shook her head. "My father had my ex murdered about six months ago when he learned that we were thinking about getting engaged. I can't prove it, but my father hated him."

"What's your ex's name?" Zoey asked, pulling out her phone and turning it on.

"Raj Assaf. He was a fisherman's son, and my father thought he wasn't good enough for me. I didn't care what he thought. I used to think I had the right to love who I wanted. My father taught me otherwise." Shaye cupped her hands over her face as if by covering her mouth she could make the words she had just said disappear.

Zoey went to work researching the man's name. In a matter of moments, she had pulled up the contract released for the man's death. Again, it carried the mark of the black star. And though she couldn't find out the source of the contract, the language was similar to her brother's hit.

Shaye was telling the truth, and likely right about her father.

"How did Chad get dragged into all of this? What did you hire him for?" Zoey asked, dropping her phone into her lap.

"He was friends with Raj. When I told him about what had happened, he said he would be happy to kill my father to avenge his death." She looked down at her hands. "He and Raj had talked just a day before he was killed. I think your brother felt guilty about not knowing about the hit and not being able to save him."

"So, basically, you hired Chad to kill your father?" Eli asked.

"No," she said, shaking her head. "After Raj's death, my father found a man he thought was a better match and he and the man's parents arranged for us to wed. I met him. We went to coffee. While we were there, he was texting other women. When I asked him about it, he told me that he never intended on a "true" marriage. For him, when we wed, it would be nothing more than a business arrangement. My father had even agreed to give him a job in his counsel for my dowry."

Zoey hadn't seen anything online about the arranged marriage. Just that she and her sisters were single.

"I don't want my father to die," Shaye continued. "He's old-fashioned and a bit chauvinistic, but I don't want him dead. I just want him to see that I'm my own woman. That I should be trusted to make my own decisions, and can't be treated as chattel. So, I hired Chad to kill Sami, the man I was supposed to marry."

The men outside stopped yelling and there was the sound of furniture being moved about in another room.

"Why didn't you just tell your father or Sami that you didn't want to get married? Jumping to murder seems a bit drastic," Zoey said, slipping her feet out of bed and putting on her shoes.

"I tried. Neither would hear of it. I turned to Sami's mother and father but even they dismissed my wishes— they told me marriage has never been anything other than a business transaction. For me to think otherwise was foolish." Shaye's voice was strong but laced with pain.

Zoey could understand the extreme measures. If

she had ever found herself in that situation, she would have made the same choice. She couldn't even stomach the thought of what the future would bring for a woman placed in such a situation. What of love? Freedom? Choices? And what about having children with a man who treated her as nothing more than a way to get ahead?

The thought revolted her.

"Did Chad get it done?" Zoey asked, half wondering if she needed to assign the hit to someone else on her team.

She shook her head. "He tried, but Sami caught wind of my plan. My father was furious."

"And that was why he put the hit out on Chad," Eli said, finishing her thought.

Shaye stared at him. "So, he did it, then? My father ordered him killed? He had threatened, but…"

Zoey nodded.

"I'm so sorry." Shaye put her head in her hands. "I should never have brought Chad into this. He is just someone I knew I could trust. That I liked. Someone who knew Raj and wanted revenge as badly as I did."

Zoey knew all about feeling inadequate. It was the one thing she was good at.

"Chad knows the risks he faces anytime he takes a job," Zoey said, trying to comfort her. "The only mistake he made was not letting his family in on his plans."

"He mentioned that he was taking the job on the down low. I think he didn't want anyone telling him it was a bad idea. Something about keeping a low profile, but he didn't elaborate."

Chad had been right. She would have never signed

off on this. Not with everything going on with the Gray Wolves.

On the other hand, she, too, had gone against her better judgment when she went to the trade show. Maybe they had all gotten a little bit too comfortable with being in danger.

The yelling started again outside the room. This time she could make out something about Chad. She listened harder, but had a hard time understanding the broken Spanish jargon the men were using.

Zoey ran her fingers through her hair, trying to pull the rat's nests out. It was far easier to untangle a days' worth of unbrushed hair than it was to untangle her brother's affairs. As she worked her fingers through her hair, she glanced over at Eli. He looked nothing like the wreck she was sure she was.

"What about these guys?" Eli asked. "Are they part of your father's crew?"

She shook her head. "My father made it clear that I'm not welcome back until I'm ready to marry Sami. If I don't return, I will be stripped of everything."

"So, you are going to go back?" Zoey asked pensively.

"Absolutely not. I have everything I need to survive. I don't need my father's wealth or his taking control of my life."

"Then were these men sent here to bring you back against your will?"

"My father wouldn't allow this." She lifted up the sleeve of her shirt, exposing a large ripening bruise. "He would never agree with them treating me like this."

Apparently, a contractor being physically aggressive

to his daughter was too much for the prime minister to accept, but purchasing a groom who didn't care about his daughter was just fine.

Zoey shook her head in disbelief. "So your father didn't put out the contract on Chad?"

Shaye shrugged. "He may have, but if so, his plans have gone off the rails. These people, whoever are holding us, they will be made to pay for raising a hand against me."

Zoey phone pinged from her lap.

There was a flurry of texts from her family as her phone picked up its messages after restarting. The first she read were from Jarrod, time-stamped throughout the night.

How are you doing?

Are you okay? Text me.

We are catching a flight to get to you now.

Calling in reinforcements.

Chad still MIA. We will find him.

Get out of there.

Text us.

We're worried.

The texts from her brother went on and on, and were followed by many just like it from Trevor. At the bottom of the list of people texting her, she found Mindy's notes. Most mirrored her brother's sentiments, but the last stood out. It read:

Severed fingerprint scanned and matched to CIA database. Belongs to one Demetri Johnson. Know him?

She had no idea who that was and as she pulled up records on the man, no one with that name looked or sounded familiar.

"My family is freaking out. I think they're on their way here." Zoey looked up at Eli. "Have you gotten an update from your people at Watch Dogs? They coming soon?"

Eli glanced down at his phone and tapped a few buttons. "Radio silence. So far as I know, my buddy should have been here by now."

"Okay." As Zoey spoke, she wondered why his team was running late in extricating them. STEALTH worked nothing like that. If they made a plan for extraction, they had it planned to the second a door opened. "It sounds like my brothers are looking into Chad's disappearance. Do you have any idea where he would have gone, Shaye?"

She shook her head. "He's always been really good about being on time and being where he says he is going to be. All I can think is that these guys must've also gotten him."

"No," Eli said. "They're looking for him, too. That's the only reason we're still alive. They're using us as bait to entice Chad back here."

Who in the hell were these guys who were keeping them prisoner?

"Have you ever heard of Demetri Johnson?" Zoey asked them.

Eli blanched. "Why? What happened to him? Is he okay?"

He sounded worried, which concerned her. She didn't want to be the one to tell him what her brother's fiancée had told her.

"He is the owner of the finger we found in a hotel room," she said.

"You found a *finger*?" Shaye asked.

"Yes," Eli said. "And hopefully the man it belongs to is still alive. As it is, I think we have bigger problems than we anticipated."

"Why? Who is he?" Zoey asked.

Eli looked at her, and the expression on his face made her blood run cold. "Demetri is my friend. His call sign is Frogger. I've been talking to him ever since Billings. He was the man from Watch Dogs who I have been working with. If he's been brought into this, it could only mean one thing… My bosses have been spying on us, and they used him to send me a message. They know I've gone rogue." He paused. "I fear my involvement in this situation has been compromised and I have brought hell to our doorstep."

Chapter Twenty-One

Frogger had to be dead. And what was worse, their employer was likely behind it. He had been warned, and so had Frogger, that they were never to move against Watch Dogs. He had been crazy to think they wouldn't act against him for going rogue when it came to Chad's contract. They must've been following him every step of the way.

He was the reason they were stuck in this apartment. He was the reason they were likely going to die. And it was all because he had gotten involved in Zoey's life.

And he had to tell Zoey the truth. She was going to hate him. As it was, up until last night, she had been on the fence about ever getting close to him again. Finally, they had a breakthrough, and now here they were... going back to square one.

Crap.

"I'm so sorry, Zoey. I had no idea this was going to happen. I thought my new bosses were more like you guys. I thought that they had honor. Turns out, they're all about the money." He moved over to her and sat down beside her on the bed. Lacing his fingers through hers, he gave them a light squeeze as he stared down at the space where their skin touched.

He would hate himself forever if this was the last time he got to touch her.

Zoey sat in silence for a long moment. Shaye squirmed as she gazed out the window.

Finally, Zoey cleared her throat. "Eli, this was never going to be a mission that was cut-and-dried. You and I both know sometimes things don't go as we plan. Everything we've ever done together we've done to the best of our abilities. Well, except, *you know*... If I had done things differently during the pregnancy and then just dealt with things when it all went wrong, maybe life would've been different."

The last thing he wanted was for her to feel guilty or bad for what had happened. It hadn't been her fault. Their baby girl had just not been meant to grow up in their lives. If anything, she had been sent to become their guardian angel. And as much as he had always thought of her loss as a curse, looking at it from this perspective, maybe she had really been the greatest gift they had ever been given.

Life always had a way of self-correcting. Nothing could take away the pain and loss they had gone through, but time had proven they were better as a team.

Eli jumped up from the bed as footfalls, like that of someone running, came from outside the bedroom door. He stood with his back against the wall beside the door, grabbing the only thing that was close to him—a small bedside table.

The door flew open, smashing against the wall. There was a barrel of a gun, pointing directly at Zoey. Before he could even think, Eli swung the table. It hit with a crack and smattering of splintered wood as it connected with the beanie man's face.

He dropped to the ground with a yelp of pain. Blood poured from a gash near his eye. Though the table was in pieces, Eli swung again, hitting the man in the back of the head over and over until all Eli was holding were two broken legs and the beanie the man had been wearing was coated with blood.

Zoey ran over and picked up the man's gun. With a click, she checked to make sure it was loaded. "Let's go," she said, motioning for Shaye to follow them.

Eli took the lead and they rushed down the hall. A second man, tall and muscular, stepped out of the living room. He looked frazzled, like he was running from something and had no idea he was about to come upon them.

As he spotted Eli, he drew his weapon. But before Eli could react, a shot rippled through the air.

It whizzed toward him, striking him at full force in the chest. He looked down where the bullet had hit him. Blood seeped through the blue fabric, and he struggled to breathe, but the bullet hadn't penetrated through the shirt.

"Dang. That's going to leave a mark," he said, wheezing.

There was the boom of another shot. Eli looked up just in time to see the man who had shot him crumple to his knees. He looked surprised as his body thumped forward, his face hitting the floor.

In all the years Eli and Zoey had been together, he had never seen her pull the trigger. As he looked over at her, she stood calm, still aiming the gun at the fallen man.

She had just killed a guy, at close range, for him. If that wasn't love, he didn't know what was.

He gently pulled the gun from her hands, and she didn't fight it. "Thank you, Zoey. I've got it from here."

From the voices they had heard, there had to be at least one more man in the apartment. They had to kill him.

He quietly cleared the rooms they passed before getting to the man Zoey had shot. Blood had started to pool around his head.

He was surprised the third man hadn't come to check things out after the sound of the gunshots. If Eli had been leading this team of operatives, he would've been on that.

Something was up. This was out of character and training.

Maybe the third man had bugged out. Nothing would surprise him now that he knew the true nature of his employer—or rather, *former* employer.

He stepped over the dead man and into the living room. The television was off and it was eerily quiet in the room.

There was a man was sitting in a chair in the corner. Saliva was dripping down from his mouth and there was a long, oozing laceration around his throat indicative of strangulation. His face was a bit swollen and languid, but Eli recognized him.

Frogger.

He looked away from his friend's body.

His going rogue had cost Frogger his life.

Fury raced through him. His former bosses would pay. One way or another, he would never let them get away with coming after them.

"Brother," Eli said, his voice barely above a whisper as he genuflected out of respect for his fallen comrade.

"Brother? Is this what you Watch Dogs do to your

brothers?" Stepping out of the shadows behind Frogger was Chad. "I hate to imagine what you've done to my sister."

Of course, he would think he was still working for Watch Dogs, and therefore an enemy. Eli dropped his gun and put his hands up. "No, man. I would never hurt Zoey. I love her."

As Zoey stepped into the room, Chad spotted her. "Zoey? I'm so glad you're okay," Chad sighed with relief. "You are okay, aren't you?" He nudged his chin in Eli's direction like a protective father.

"I'm fine," Zoey said, looking over at Eli. "In fact, if we get out of here alive, *we* will be even more than fine."

Eli couldn't control the wide grin that took over his face. Was that her way of saying she still wanted to marry him? Damn, he hoped so. He wanted to spend every minute of every single day with her…the woman who had saved his life.

Eli gave him a nod. "It's okay, Chad. We were here to rescue you."

Chad chuckled as he stepped around the dead man and stripped off his leather gloves. "And yet, here I am saving you."

"This fight isn't over yet," Eli said, picking up his gun.

"The place should be clear." Chad walked over and took the gun from him. "I was hoping this would prove useful in case of emergencies." He pointed to a small indentation in the gun's handle.

"Is that our gun? The one with the GPS?" Zoey asked, reaching for it. Chad gave it back to her.

"It was how I tracked the crew after me. I left it be-

hind when Shaye and I bugged out. I knew that they had
our location and I was hoping to use it to find whoever
was tracking me."

"So, you knew that there was money on your head?"
Eli asked.

Chad nodded. "Yeah, sucks to know I'm worth a hell
of a lot more dead than I am alive. I was half tempted to
stage my own death and cash in on the bounty."

Zoey smirked as she glanced in Eli's direction, then
to Chad. "Why don't you? We could give the money to
Shaye. It seems only right, and it would be kinda perfect if her father *paid* for his sins."

"Actually, that was what the wire transfer was for.
I knew you'd be okay with me helping out my friend's
family. Raj's parents lost everything, their business,
their son and any chance they had of survival, all thanks
to the prime minister." Chad sighed. "I will pay the
company back. It was just the only place I knew I could
pull a large sum of coded money and also let you know
that I was alive."

Zoey nodded. "Don't worry about the company's
money. Right now, I think we have a death to stage.
That is, if you're in."

"I'm in. Raj's family and Shaye…they are going to
need help getting on their feet," Chad said, walking over
and taking Shaye's hand. "What do you say? Want to
make your father give something back for all that he's
taken from you?"

Shaye's eyes welled up with tears. "I… You guys…
You be careful when dealing with my father."

"We will be. And you will get what you deserve for
everything your father has put you through." Chad put
his arm over her shoulder and hugged her tight to him.

"One thing about us Martins, we believe in picking the right side—the side of justice—especially when that involves taking out the bastards who wish to hurt the people we love."

Chapter Twenty-Two

It didn't take a hell of a lot of work to get a little DNA evidence and "prove" that Chad had been taken out by a contract killer.

The money was in their bank account the very next day when they arrived back at the Widow Maker Ranch. Hopefully their home would be safe now that the hit had been closed on Chad's head, but they were hardly out of the woods. If Zoey had done everything right, Bayural was probably looking for them somewhere in the middle of Norway right now and anyone who had been tracking Chad was off the scent.

Only time would tell.

She sat back on the velvet sofa and looked over the top of her computer at Eli. He was staring at her, making her wonder if it was the feel of his gaze that had made her look up in the first place.

"You gonna stare at me all day?" she asked with a smile.

"If I get my way, I sure as hell will," he said. "What are you doing?"

"Making sure that everything is clear. Just made it look like Shaye was taking a flight out of Sitges headed to Paris. She is going to send her father a letter ceding from the family." She made a long face. "It's going to be harder for her than she anticipates, I think. She's gone through a lot."

"I know. But she is a strong woman, kind of like you." Eli stood up and walked over. She gently pushed her computer closed and moved it off her lap. Then he extended his hand. "Will you do me the honor?"

She slipped her hand into his and he helped her to her feet. "Where are we going? Am I going to need to grab my jacket?"

He laughed, giving her a soft smile. "That's not what I meant."

She stopped. He wasn't going to do what she thought he was going to do, was he? Her entire body clenched with anticipation.

He dropped to one knee. Reaching into his pocket, he pulled out a red velvet box. "I had this made especially for you a long time ago. I've kept it with me ever since. Just like you, it's one of a kind."

He opened up the ring box. Inside was a simple platinum band with a sapphire set into its center.

He must have been carrying it for her for some time. The thought melted her. Even when she was adrift, he had loved her. And she had loved him.

"Will you marry me?"

"I love you, Eli. I love you so much. I'll love you until I take my last breath."

"Is that a yes?" he asked, looking up at her.

"A deal is a deal," she said, giving him a playful smile. "We got out of there alive. I mean…thanks to me, but…yes, I will marry you."

As he moved to stand up, she stopped him and put her hand over her mouth. "Wait."

"What, honey?" he asked, taking her hands from her face and holding them. "What's wrong?"

"What about trying again…you know…for a family?" She wasn't sure what she wanted him to say. And she wasn't sure she was ready to go down that road once again.

He stood up and wrapped his arms around her. "For now, all I want is for you to be my forever. I am yours and you are mine," he whispered into her hair. "If someday it happens, then yes…and if we choose not to, then no. But no matter what life brings, I just want us to face it together."

Together. There was no sweeter word. Or perhaps there was one—*forever.*

* * * * *

COLTON FAMILY BODYGUARD

JENNIFER MOREY

For my family, for always supporting me and
the time I spend writing.

Chapter One

Why did every woman he met and thought might be the one always announce at the worst possible time that she wanted babies? Callum Colton walked along a street at the edge of Mustang Valley, Arizona, on a sunny, early spring day. He had just left his now ex-girlfriend, Cindy, in tears because he'd had to tell her he was never going to have any children. He'd explained that to her at the beginning but she must have thought she could change his mind. He'd had to remind her he meant what he'd said. In truth, he felt so rotten, ending the relationship like that. She'd told him she understood and held no animosity toward him, but she was obviously very hurt.

Callum stepped into Executive Protection Services, LLC still lamenting what had happened. What else could he have done? He would have hurt his ex-girlfriend more had he continued on with her. When Cindy sat him down for The Serious Talk, she'd told him she wanted children and she wanted them with him. She loved him, and her biological clock ticked on and she felt she had to move now. That convinced him they weren't right for each other. She had hoped he felt the same as her and that he would give her children. She hadn't anticipated how unbending he was on the matter. And the truth was that he did not love her. They would have ended their relationship eventually, since she wanted a family. Why drag it out? He never had serious relationships with women he dated. How had she gotten the impression he would with her? He had told her as much. He almost shuddered as the door closed behind him and he walked through the entry with its vacant reception desk toward an office in the back.

He had enough going on without having to now feel guilty for hurting Cindy. He was still reeling from the news that his half brother, Ace, had been switched at birth and wasn't really his biological sibling. Not by blood. Who would do such a thing and why? The why of it really twisted his mind. Charles, the owner, chief executive officer, president and whatever other titles a guy like him liked to have, looked up from behind his metal-and-glass desk. The lack of clutter and nearly bare walls pretty much described him. Focused. Nothing personal. Good business head. That's why Callum had agreed to work for him. Callum had no liking for paperwork. Charles did.

"It's about time you got here." Charles stood and moved around his desk.

"I had to take care of something." Cindy's tear-damp cheeks flashed through his mind. Chaos had reigned recently in his life, ever since an email had made the rounds of his family's company, Colton Oil, saying that his oldest brother, Ace, was not a biological Colton. Since then, his father, Payne, had been shot—and now the cops even suspected Ace.

Charles stopped before him and cocked his head. "Well, that sounds like you. When you need to take care of something, nothing keeps you from doing it—not even your boss."

"I broke up with my girlfriend," Callum said.

"Another one? The hot blonde? What's wrong with you?"

Callum put his hands up. "She wanted kids."

Charles's brow creased a little. "What is it with you and kids? They're harmless and adorable. Who wouldn't want them?"

"Not me."

"Why not? They can be challenging sometimes but the rewards far outweigh that."

Charles had two young kids. He had a wife and a nice house. A real family man. "Why did you call me here?" Callum asked in irritation.

After considering him awhile, Charles said, "You never talk about anything, do you realize that?"

Callum angled his head in silent warning.

"Keeping things bottled up is unhealthy. I worry about you."

Callum said nothing and continued to look at him.

"Why do you think I called you here?" Charles asked.

Callum had a pretty good idea why. And he also thought this was going to be a waste of time. "I got the job done and the client is alive." He'd done a job as a bodyguard for an executive who had a stalker.

"I'm not telling you to change your ways." Charles scoffed. "I couldn't anyway. But for the welfare of this company, I am telling you to be more careful. I almost couldn't convince the police you didn't break the law."

The stalker had gotten too close to his delicate female client and Callum had given him a clear...message. Someone must have called 911 because the police had arrived after Callum and his client left.

"You were lucky the stalker was wanted for sexual assault on another woman. If they hadn't been able to arrest him, they probably wouldn't have let you go with just a warning," his boss said.

Callum walked over to the window and passively watched cars go by and a man walking his dog on the sidewalk.

"Seriously, Callum, you can't make up your own rules as you go."

Why was Charles rambling on so long about that? Hopefully Callum had knocked some sense into him. Charles was just uncomfortable about employing a man who wasn't afraid to cross boundaries.

"I'll be careful, Charles," Callum said.

"Why does that sound so half-baked?"

Callum glanced back with a rueful grin. "Because it is. Stop worrying so much. You're not the one who would have been arrested, and protecting our clients won't damage our reputation. If anything, it will get us more business."

"You can't protect anyone if you're in jail."

Turning back to the window, Callum said, "I didn't cross the line. We advertise elite services, don't we?" The view distracted him a moment. Charles had rented an office in an attractive one-story mall with a restaurant and a gas station beside the parking lot. The back of the building faced a quiet, tree-lined road. Across the street an upscale subdivision sprawled.

"Okay, but just don't get caught."

"I knew that stalker was wanted for assault. I found out two days ago."

"You still could have been arrested, Callum. Even criminals have rights."

"I'll keep that in mind." Or not. Callum's first priority was protecting his clients. He had a strong conviction about that. Victims didn't deserve to be forced into being victims. The menace that threatened them was a cancer that had to be carved out and stopped. That's what had led him to a career as a bodyguard, and back home to support his family in a time of crisis.

"It turns out that's not the only reason I asked you to stop by. I've got another case for you. Ever hear of the country singer Blake Reynolds?"

"No." Callum liked country but didn't pay attention to the artists' names.

Outside, a black Mercedes SUV—one of the more economical versions—pulled to a stop on the side of the street. Callum caught sight of a woman with long dark hair in the driver's seat. She had a fantastic profile. At the same time, a car stopped on the side of the street about two houses down.

Callum listened to Charles explain the new case while he turned back to the woman, who climbed out of the SUV and opened the back door. She worked to free a little girl from a car seat. Normally this was when he would have turned away from the sight of a mother and her child, but something about the woman made him keep watching—and stop listening to Charles. Maybe it was that tight body in those dressy black pants, or the curve of that slender waist, or the way her those perfectly shaped breasts strained against the white blouse.

She lifted the girl from the seat and lowered her to the ground. Holding a stuffed Cookie Monster in one arm, the child looked up at her mother and said something, to which the woman shook her head. The little girl didn't appear to like the answer, an adorable pout forming beneath scrunching eyebrows, and she hugged the stuffed toy against the white top of a cute flaring black skirt. He felt an automatic pang at the adorable mother-daughter duo.

The mother went to the back of the Mercedes and lifted the hatch. Callum got a really nice view of her frame as she leaned in and retrieved two recyclable grocery bags. Setting those on the pavement, she reached in again and handed a plastic container to the little girl, who still frowned and continued to argue with her mother.

The beautiful woman crouched before her, her facial features striking him to the core. She spoke to the girl, whose frown finally smoothed.

Standing, the woman closed the hatch and lifted the bags, talking with the young girl. The child walked with short, clumsy steps beside her mother up the driveway to the front door of a house. When they disappeared inside, Callum realized how immersed he'd become in watching the woman and child. His stomach fell.

Then he looked down the street and saw the car that had pulled over was still there, with someone sitting in the driver's seat. A man. He appeared to be watching the woman's house, though he was too far away to get a good look inside. Out of habit, Callum checked the license plate but it was too far away to make out.

Charles appeared beside him, looking from the house across the street to him. "Have you heard a single word I've said?"

"Sorry, no." Callum turned away from the window.

"The singer had a girlfriend who's gone off the deep end. He's afraid she'll go after him."

"Another one of those cases?" Only this time it would be a man he protected.

"They were together for six months and she started to get too clingy, so he ended it. He said he noticed other things, too, like catching her in lies. She told her friends they were getting married. She also told him she was pregnant but she wasn't. He made her do a test and it was negative. When he asked why she lied, she said she was afraid she was going to lose him."

"Does he have any kids?" Callum asked.

"No. You've made it perfectly clear you don't want those kinds of cases—which you still haven't told me why." Charles looked out the window again. "I meant what I said about keeping things bottled up, Callum."

"When do I go?" He didn't like talking about why he never took mother-child cases. Charles tried to get him to every once in a while and Callum believed that Charles was concerned about him. He had become a good friend, aside from being Callum's boss.

"He's local. That's how he heard of you."

"Me?"

"Yeah. He asked for you by name. You'll be working with his usual security team."

"He doesn't think his own team will be enough?" What kind of woman had this new client broken up with?

Charles walked back to his desk and picked up a folder. "I printed these out for you. I also emailed them. You'll understand more after you read it. He's out of the country right now, but asked if you could stay at his place next month."

Callum took the file. "Thanks." Charles knew he liked studying cases on paper more than on a screen. Some things were still better offline, like holding a book instead of a tablet.

"Any news on your father?" Charles asked.

"He's still in a coma. I'm heading over to the hospital after I go see my brother." Payne Colton had been shot after receiving a bizarre email containing the shocking news about Ace. He didn't say which brother he was going to see, since Ace was still a suspect in Payne's shooting. When Callum and his twin sister—current Colton Oil CEO Marlowe—had visited Mustang Valley General Hospital last month, they were told that a fire broke out the morning of Ace's birth and destroyed all records.

With one more look out the window that told him the car and the man were still there, Callum bade Charles farewell and left the building. But he couldn't stop thinking about that parent and child. He couldn't explain why he needed to make sure she was all right. A sixth sense told him something was off about the stranger in the car. Even though he had sworn off guarding families, he couldn't ignore this. He'd make sure the woman and her daughter were okay and then he'd be on his way.

HAZEL HART TOOK her now-cheerful daughter's hand and walked with her toward the SUV. Earlier Evie had fussed about being told she could not go for ice cream today. Hazel's schedule was far too busy. But Evie liked passing out cookies to Hazel's clients. Hazel had told her five-year-old she could sample one with them. That had taken care of the ice cream tantrum.

Hazel glanced around. The street was quiet. This area of town didn't get much traffic. On the edge of Mustang Valley, there was a lot of new development and not much commercial business. The back of the strip mall across the street hid most of the activity there, though landscaping along the sidewalk made it more palatable for residents. The client she'd just left enjoyed the convenience of Hazel's home deliveries, especially since she had been taken ill with breast cancer. The woman was going to be all right, but had hired Hazel to provide her meals while she recovered. The woman had family but they all lived out of state and she didn't like the food her neighbors prepared.

Hazel had left her job at an upscale restaurant several months ago to go off on her own as a personal chef. She preferred the independence and not having to work under someone else's thumb. Plus, she could always be with Evie, which was her most favorite thing in the world.

Reaching the SUV, Hazel unlocked it and had her hand on the back seat door handle when Evie said, "Mommy, what is that man doing?"

Hazel looked in the direction Evie pointed and saw a man in a blue sedan, wearing sunglasses and a baseball cap.

"Why did he hit that man over the head with a rock and put him in the car?"

Hazel turned sharply to Evie. "What?" She looked around and didn't see anything.

Evie pointed. "That man put another man in the trunk, Mommy."

Hazel felt a wave of apprehension sweep through her as she stared at the sedan. If the driver had struck a man unconscious and put him into the trunk, he could not have any good intentions. He started pulling out into the street way too quickly for Hazel's comfort.

Hazel memorized the license plate as the man began driving along the street, right toward them.

Reaching for Evie's hand, she went to pull her daughter onto the sidewalk. Evie dropped her Cookie Monster and bent to pick it up. Horror flared up in Hazel. She glanced up and saw the car was almost on them! They'd be run over!

"Evie—" Just then someone swooped Evie up and grabbed Hazel's hand, yanking her backward.

The stranger in the sedan continued to race for them. Hazel screamed, as did Evie, as a man hauled them behind her Mercedes and up onto the sidewalk. The other car whizzed past, taking out her Mercedes' driver-side mirror.

"Are you all right?"

Hazel pulled her hand from the man's, heart flying and struggling to catch her breath. A car had just tried to mow them down! The sound of the Mercedes mirror being torn off kept echoing in her mind.

She reached for a crying Evie. The heroic man handed her daughter over and Hazel held her tightly. "It's okay, baby. We're all right." She looked at the man as she answered his question.

Hazel checked up the street and saw no sign of the driver. Then she turned back to her hero. "Thank you."

He took out his phone and called 911.

Her adrenaline began to abate as Evie's crying softened. Smoothing the few tendrils of brunette hair that had fallen free from the two ponytails sticking out from the sides of Evie's head, she wiped her daughter's cheeks.

Looking over the child's shoulder, she saw the man as more than her rescuer. His reddish-blond hair was slightly wavy and he had strong facial features. He wore dark slacks with black leather loafers that had thick soles, and between the lapels of his black jacket she could see he had on a white shirt with the first two buttons undone. He finished telling the operator where they were and disconnected. Towering above her, he was probably six-three and had an athletic build.

"I'm Callum Colton," the handsome man said.

"Hazel Hart, and this is Evie, short for Evelyn."

Evie turned her head, still pouting, and looked at Callum.

"Hi, Evie. Are you okay?" Callum asked.

Evie nodded.

"That's an awfully cute stuffed monster you have there," he said.

"Her name is Cookie," Evie said, brightening.

He chuckled and glanced at Hazel, who became transfixed by his smile. "That's appropriate."

Well, whether he was a kid person or not, his tactics worked. Ever since Ed ran out on her after hearing she was pregnant, Hazel always wondered whether or not a man who caught her eyes liked children.

"I think Evie saw something," Hazel said. "She said a man hit another one over the head with a rock and put him into the trunk."

The faint sound of sirens joined the gentle hum of distant town movements. Hazel put Evie down and held her hand, needing to have contact with her. Having nearly been run down by a car had rattled them both. To think Evie could have been hurt, or worse...

"Did you see him, too?" Callum asked.

She shook her head. "He was in the car already when I saw him. I didn't get a good look at him. I did get the plate number, though."

"That's great." Then he asked Evie, "Can you describe the man?"

The little girl nodded. "Mm-hmm. He looked really mad."

"Mad?" Hazel asked, prompting her to elaborate.

Evie crowded her tiny eyebrows over eyes that were greener than her mother's. "Yeah." Evie nodded. "He looked like the man at the mall, Mommy."

Hazel met her daughter's round, innocent eyes, heart melting as usual at Evie's adorableness and also searching for the memory. Then she recalled a homeless man they had encountered at the edge of the parking lot. He had been dressed in heavy clothing and had a beard, a dark beard.

"Was the man you saw as hairy as the man in the parking lot earlier?" Hazel asked.

"No, he was not skinny. And no hair on his face."

The homeless man had been slim and had a beard. "The man she saw was average in height and weight," Hazel said.

The sirens were now a blaring howl and seconds later, fire trucks, police cars and ambulances converged upon them.

"I hope this doesn't take long." Hazel had to prepare meals for tomorrow's deliveries.

"You witnessed a crime," Callum said. "The man

got away. What if he comes after you again? We need to catch this guy."

Hazel hadn't considered that. Police approached and, filled with intensifying apprehension, she had to turn away from Callum's unmistakable concern. Her meals could wait. She could get up early tomorrow and prepare them.

A woman in a tan blazer approached, her strides graceful, auburn hair flowing.

"Kerry," Callum greeted her. "Good to see you again."

"Callum, what are you doing here?" Kerry's blue eyes were direct and exuded confidence.

"My office is across the street. I saw a man in a car and thought it was suspicious."

He had? Hazel looked across the street at the one-story strip mall. One of the spaces must be where Callum worked.

"This is Hazel and Evie Hart," Callum said. "This is Detective Kerry Wilder. She's also my brother Rafe's fiancée."

Hazel shook the pretty woman's hand.

"Evie here saw the man when he got out of the car," Callum said.

"You did?" Kerry asked in a lighthearted tone, crouching before the girl. "What did you see?"

Evie huddled closer to Hazel's leg, bringing Cookie up to her face. She got bashful sometimes.

"She saw the driver of the car hit another man on the head and put him in the trunk," Hazel answered for her daughter.

Kerry straightened and began writing on a small notepad.

The detective with Kerry went to take photos of Hazel's broken mirror while Hazel described the man who had almost run them down. Then she gave the detective his plate number.

"All right. We're going to talk to neighbors and tenants of the commercial building to see if there are any other witnesses," Kerry said. "Why don't you stop by the station later so we can have a sketch artist draw the man you saw?"

Hazel nodded.

"Callum, you should come, too. You can probably help with the description."

Callum nodded once.

Detective Wilder put away her notepad. "Meanwhile, we'll have officers on the lookout for this car."

And whatever he had done with the man in his trunk. Hazel warded off a shiver. If he could hurt someone like that, what would he do to Evie?

"You should be careful until we locate him. Are you or your husband armed?"

"I'm not married," Hazel said, then saw Callum glance at her at that revelation.

"Maybe you should stay somewhere else," Kerry said. Then to Callum, "I don't think they should be alone tonight."

Callum looked a little startled by the suggestion, or that Kerry had directed the declaration at him, as though he should be the one to take care of them for the night.

"Do you have any family you can stay with?" Kerry asked Hazel.

They were all far away except her brother, but he was a two hour drive from here. She shook her head.

"Friends?"

All out of state. She didn't know anyone well enough here to impose on them like that. Again, she shook her head. "All my close friends are in Colorado and I haven't had time to make any here." She looked down at Evie, who consumed every spare moment she wasn't working.

"That man could have gotten your plate number the same as you got his. He might have a way to find out where you live," the detective said. "Maybe I'm being overly paranoid, but I'd rather you be safe."

That certainly unsettled her.

Detective Wilder smiled. "I'll let you be on your way. Think about staying somewhere other than your house tonight after we finish up with the sketch, okay? Maybe get a room at the Dales Inn."

"Okay."

"What about letting Evie go to the station with Kerry for her safety? In the meantime, I'll take you home to pack bags for both of you," Callum said.

Oh. Hazel hated being separated from Evie under such dire circumstances, but her daughter seemed entranced by Kerry's shiny badge and getting her own detective shield sticker.

Hazel hesitated. "Detective Wilder is the one with the gun…"

Kerry chimed in, "Maybe Callum can help out. He's an ex-Navy SEAL turned professional bodyguard."

Evie looked at Callum. "Are you going to catch the bad man?"

Callum didn't respond, just stared at Evie as though flustered. What about her question had caused such a reaction? He seemed to be frozen.

"What if he comes after us, like you said?" Evie asked.

"I shouldn't have said that in front of you," Callum said.

"Honey, Callum isn't a policeman. He is a bodyguard," Hazel said.

"What's a bodyguard?" Evie asked.

"Someone who protects people from bad men," Callum said.

Evie smiled big and again Hazel noticed a change in Callum, the way his body stiffened. "Then you can protect me and my mommy."

He smiled down at her. "I'll try."

Evie glanced down at her toy. "It's okay, Cookie," she said. "You're all right now. Just remember, it's wrong to hit and push. You should always be nice to other people."

Hazel reached over and put her hand on Evie's. "Now you're going to the station and I will go home and pack clothing for us."

"Okay, Mommy."

It was getting late, past six in the evening. "All right," Hazel said. "Let's go."

Detective Wilder joined her partner and Evie as they walked up the street.

"Let's go to your place," Callum suggested.

The abruptness stopped Hazel short. This man was a complete stranger.

"I'd like to talk a little more," he said. "And Kerry has a point. I'm worried that man will come after you. You got his plate number. He probably got yours. He could find you."

Why was he so concerned about her? He didn't even

know her. "I'm a newbie with all this. What kinds of people do you usually work with?"

"My next client is Blake Reynolds."

"The country singer? Really? You must be some bodyguard. Are all your clients celebrities?"

"Oh, all right. Let's go."

The police were still working the neighborhood but the emergency vehicles had left a while ago. Callum drove Hazel in silence to her apartment, located above a bakery. Callum had arranged for someone to take her car in for repairs. She had left a key under the mat. She might drive a Mercedes but it was the lower end model and she had saved for a long time for a decent down payment. The money she made was just enough for her and Evie to get by. So far, being a personal chef didn't earn her huge income. Her business showed signs of picking up but she wasn't quite there yet.

When they arrived at her apartment, Callum passed the front and turned to go around to the back.

The first floor of the older building was a charming little bakery with a neon Open/Closed sign on the door, four old-fashioned, small round tables in the dining area and two booths against the window. The main feature was the display case…and, of course, the kitchen. The owner of Jasmine's Bakery let her cook her biggest batches there for a modest fee.

After Callum parked, Hazel walked from the rear parking space up the iron stairs. Unlocking her apartment door, she flipped on a light and entered, Callum behind her. "It isn't much. Just two bedrooms and not very big." She didn't know why she felt the need to explain that.

Callum didn't say anything as he stepped inside, looking around.

"When my ex, Ed, walked, I started saving for a house, but I also want money tucked away for Evie's college education."

Hazel found herself looking at him, his rugged, stubbly jaw, his thick, reddish-blond hair. Her gaze moved to his bright blue eyes…and stayed. He had been watching her study his face and now his eyes flared with something more than friendliness. A spark of heat flashed inside her.

How could just a look do that to her? Did he feel it too? Granted, he was hot, but she had seen other attractive men, and none of them had caused this reaction.

"So, you're an ex-Navy SEAL and now you're a bodyguard," Hazel said by way of breaking the awkward moment. "If you're going to protect me and my daughter, I should know more than that about you."

"I'm surprised that's all you know about me," he said. "I am, after all, a Colton."

The name did sound familiar but not familiar enough. "I may have heard the name before. I haven't lived here my whole life."

"Given the news lately, you probably have. Payne Colton is my father."

Hazel searched her memory but still nothing stuck. "I'm sorry. I don't watch the news. I try to keep it away from Evie. I don't think it's healthy for a five-year-old to hear about murders and lying politicians. And besides that, I have a very busy schedule. We do watch a lot of family movies and listen to country, though." She smiled. "You might have to introduce us to Blake Reynolds."

He chuckled. "I can't believe it."

What couldn't he believe? That she didn't watch the news or that she didn't know him by name? She couldn't detect conceit. He wasn't bragging about being a Colton, just surprised she hadn't heard of them.

"My father is chairman of the board of Colton Oil and owns Rattlesnake Ridge Ranch just outside of town. But we do all work hard for our money," he said.

Then it dawned on her. She had heard of a man who had been shot and was now in a coma, a prominent local rancher and businessman gunned down for no apparent reason. She hadn't paid any further attention to the story. Until now.

"Oh, I'm so sorry," she finally said. Callum came from lots of money, then. Hazel felt herself stiffen and erect a barrier. She was from a very humble background and her last encounter with a rich guy hadn't turned out so great.

"Don't be."

"I grew up in a small Colorado mountain town where everyone knew everyone and there were no conveniences, no big-box stores, no chain restaurants or movie theaters. We lived outside of town on several acres in a small colonial. I spent my childhood reading or watching satellite television and going to community events with my older brother and our parents."

"Sounds charming."

His handsome grin disarmed her a moment. She should go pack but she didn't feel she knew enough about him to stay with him yet. And if her daughter was going to be near him for the unforeseeable future...

"In some ways. But growing up that way made me a little naive. I met Evie's father, Ed, when I went to college and moved to Arizona with him. When I got pregnant, he left."

"How does that make you naive?"

Edgar Lovett had lied to her about almost everything about himself. The only thing he hadn't lied about was his college degree. "I should have known he wasn't reliable. I had never met anyone so experienced at duping people. He wasn't at all what he pretended to be. He told me he came from an average family and that his parents were dead."

He also told her that he had never been married before. "I didn't find out until after he left that he was the son of a wealthy Arizona senator and his parents were very much alive. He also was married before we met in college. He divorced his secret wife before I met him and we moved to Arizona."

Hazel didn't know why he had lied. She could only guess he had done so because he was afraid she was using him for his money. The last she had heard, he was living in Florida off his trust fund. Hazel had tried to get child support but he always evaded the attempts. Eventually she gave up and chalked him up as a deadbeat dad, albeit a wealthy one. She didn't have to be told he had abandoned her and Evie because he was incapable of accepting any real responsibility. She wanted to thank him for leaving instead of putting her through a life of struggle with a man like him. She also held a lot of animosity toward him, a man who could have easily afforded to help her out but had not. What kind of person did that? And how had she never seen that about him?

"You weren't naive," Callum said. "I bet he liked you, maybe even loved you, but he must have known you had higher expectations than he could deliver on when it comes to making a family. He misled you because he was probably tired of being identified as a senator's son."

Of course, she thought the same, except her expectations were pretty simple. She didn't require anyone rich or anyone with specific personality traits. She only wanted someone decent. She had told Ed she wanted a good and honest man like her father had been, like so many other men she had grown up around.

"Why bother lying, though, about who he was and about his ex-wife?" Hazel still wanted to know, to this day. "He must have known the truth would come out eventually." Hazel would have left him after learning about his deception.

"You're a beautiful woman, Hazel. Any man would be a fool not to want you."

Ed had lied in order to have her, even if for just a little while. He had never talked about marriage with her, a fact she'd only thought of after he was gone. Then she realized what Callum had just said. Did *he* want her?

"What about you?" she asked, flirting back.

"I've never been married," he said, "and I'm not lying about that." He grinned.

She laughed lightly and briefly, believing him. It was easy to talk with him. Feeling much more comfortable with him, she stopped herself from enjoying this too much. Hadn't she just finished telling him about the biggest mistake she ever made with a man? She would never regret Evie, obviously, but Evie's father was nothing to brag about. She'd rather not wind up having to say the same thing about

Callum—or any man. And despite knowing she was biased, she didn't trust anyone wealthy.

"You better get packing," Callum said.

Yes. They'd better pack—rather than play on their attraction to one other.

Chapter Two

Callum leaned against the door frame of Evie's bedroom, watching Hazel pack a bag. She glanced up and saw him.

"Bored?" Her eyes glowed a green hint of her name. Long and dark, finger-tempting wavy hair fell over slender shoulders and framed a remarkably pretty face. Tendrils of that silky splendor curled around melon-shaped breasts. He felt his defenses rise. She had a *daughter*. A really cute one.

"No." He would just rather stare at her. This sudden chemistry threw him off balance.

With a soft smile, she resumed packing.

In just the brief time he had been around Evie—rescuing her, watching her fascination with Kerry and then her bravery in going with the detective—the child had already touched his heart. Now he knew more than ever why he tried so hard to avoid protecting kids. The mothers were another issue completely.

Evie had punched her way through his usual, iron-walled barrier. She was about the same age his daughter would have been, had she and her mother survived. Callum shook off the thoughts. He was better shutting that off, contrary to what Charles said. Despite his cardinal rule never to protect mothers with kids, to leave that up to other bodyguards who didn't share a history similar to his, he could not leave them at the mercy of a man who knew Evie had witnessed him dump a body in a trunk. Now here he was, in Hazel and Evie's apartment, about to take them to the Dales Inn and live with them for however long it took to catch the bad guy.

HAZEL FINISHED PACKING for Evie and went into her bedroom to do the same for herself. Callum followed, she wasn't sure whether out of boredom or because he just enjoyed watching her. The way he did made her acutely aware of him as a man.

"I bet my room is much smaller than the one you sleep in," she said, still self-conscious of his wealth and her bad experience with a man with money.

Callum eyed her peculiarly. "It's a nice apartment. And even though I'm a Colton, I don't dwell on the wealth of my family."

She believed that, but he also must have a sizable bank account, maybe a trust fund or something like that. Just like Ed. That put a sour taste in her mouth.

Taking the bags to the dining area next to the back entry, she saw Callum go to the mantel above the gas fireplace. She had an electronic photo album there. He gestured with his hand to it.

"These are great."

There were lots of pictures of Evie doing all things Evie. Evie with a toothy smile and mouth smeared with ice cream. Evie holding a bunny rabbit. Evie riding a pony with Hazel. Evie and a friend dressed identically and striking a pose. Hazel and Evie cheek to cheek in a selfie. And so many more. Vacations Hazel had saved for, trips to Disney World and Yellowstone. Them at community events.

As he watched the pictures change, his expression changed. What about these photos put such a look of sadness on his face? She wanted to ask but didn't.

"She's the best thing that ever happened to me," she said instead. "Ed taking off the way he did doesn't even matter anymore. I mean, it did when I was pregnant. What kind of man can abandon their unborn baby?"

Callum didn't say anything, just continued to look at the pictures.

"As soon as Evie was born, everything changed. I didn't care about Ed anymore. She became my world. And she's such a good kid. Even when she was a baby. She didn't cry much, only when she needed something. She slept all night and still does. She rarely has tantrums and when she does, they're over pretty quickly. I'm a lucky mom."

Callum turned to look at her, some of the sadness leaving his eyes. "She's an adorable girl."

"Do you want kids some day?"

"I travel a lot. Usually I'm out of the country on assignments."

He must be some bodyguard. "Do you protect a lot of affluent people?"

"Yes, and high targets for kidnapping in countries where that sort of thing happens."

Dignitaries, politicians and executives for big companies, she supposed.

"I'm only here now to be near my father."

His father had been shot. That must be so difficult, not knowing whether his dad would wake up or not. Callum must be close to his father if he'd changed his work schedule to be by the man's side. She wondered if he regretted helping her, since she obviously was taking time away from his hospital visits.

"If you need to be with him…"

"I'll visit him. I don't have to be with him all the time. I do still have to work, after all. Just not out of state."

Hazel smiled because this was the chattiest he had been since they met.

"You must be close to him," Hazel said, thinking she had made an accurate observation.

"Actually, I'm not," he said, and regret seemed to come over him.

With him out of the country so much, Hazel could see why, but what about when he had been younger? "Was it always that way?"

"Yes. When I was a kid he was always working, and I had my own ideas about what I wanted to do with my life. I knew early on that I never would be an executive like he was." He paused. "Is."

She felt terrible. "If not for me, you would be with him right now."

"No. I was going to visit my brother, but I saw you and…"

And what? He saw her when? Before she had gone into her client's house? And then he had seen that car. She'd changed his plans for the day.

"Which brother?"

"Ace." He shook his head and scratched his forehead in angst. "He's a suspect in my father's shooting. We were never close, either, like with Dad. He followed my dad into the oil business. But I feel for him, you know? He just found out he's not a Colton by blood and there's this clause in the Colton Oil bylaws that says the CEO must be a Colton by blood, and then Dad got shot and everybody thinks he did it—geez, why am I telling you all of this?" He walked toward the back door and the luggage.

Hazel caught up to him and put her hand on his forearm, stopping him from bending to pick up one of the bags. "Hey, it's okay. I like hearing this."

"You like hearing about all my family drama?"

That's all he worried about? She breathed a laugh. "Every family has drama. Why is your brother a suspect?"

"My father had to fire him because of the bylaws. He did it in front of the board, and Ace didn't react well. He threatened my dad."

"How did he threaten him?" With a gun? Had he said he'd better watch his back or something? Ruin his reputation?

"Ace told Dad he would regret it and stormed out of the room."

"That doesn't mean he shot him."

"I know. I don't think he did, but he shouldn't have threatened him like that, and in front of the board."

Hazel could see he was genuinely concerned for his half brother, despite his claim of not being close to Ace. Just because he had spent a lot of time overseas didn't necessarily mean a family bond didn't exist. Hazel wondered if they were closer than he thought.

"You're easy to talk to," he said after a while, his smile rueful. Did he not open up to anyone? Why had he done so with her?

"Evie doesn't think so."

He chuckled a little. "I saw her arguing with you

when you first got to your client's house. I think she does listen to you."

"Like I said, she's a good kid."

"She must have a good mother."

Hazel fell into his eyes, the warm regard there, the attraction. She felt it, too, these underlying sparks that had grown since the moment she saw him.

Once again stopping the sparks, Hazel asked, "So, tell me about this family of yours. You seemed to know that detective, Kerry."

"I come from a large blended family. My father married three times. I have a half sister and two half brothers—including Ace—from the first marriage. He had none with the second, and my mother had me and my twin sister, Marlowe, plus our brother, Asher. Rafe is my younger adopted brother. He's engaged to Kerry. That's how I know her."

"Ah. She's part of the family now. She's very pretty," Hazel said.

"And smart. And tenacious. She's a rookie but Rafe swears she's as good as a seasoned detective."

"I did get that impression of her, well, short of knowing her, that is. She just had a way about her."

"If anybody can find the man who almost ran you down, she can."

Hazel fell silent, not liking the thought of that. A man capable of hurting or killing another human—especially a child—was a dangerous one, for sure.

"You're a twin?" Hazel asked. "What is that like?"

"We're more like a regular brother and sister, but closer. We were close growing up and still are."

"Are you similar?"

He chuckled at that. "Not at all. Her hair is blonder

than mine and she has brown eyes. She's now the CEO of Colton Oil, an executive type. Workaholic." Callum was definitely not an executive type. He was driven in different ways. "But she's pregnant and engaged now, so that will probably change. She's still going to keep her job but she's starting a day-care program."

Hazel seemed to ponder that awhile, as though doubtful that a woman like that could change.

"I technically have one less sibling now—even though I still consider Ace my half brother. Ace's switch has caused a bit of chaos in the family," he said.

She breathed a tiny laugh at his sarcastic tone. "It sounds dramatic. Who switched him and why?"

"We don't know yet."

"That must be hard for him to face," Hazel said.

He fell silent and Hazel sensed he had given out enough family information for now. Then he just nodded and said, "Yes, it is."

"What made you decide to leave the navy and become a bodyguard?" Hazel asked to change the subject.

"I was getting too old to be a SEAL."

At his short, simplistic reply, she wondered if he didn't want to discuss this. He seemed reluctant to talk about anything personal.

"How old is too old?" she asked anyway.

"I'm thirty-two. Right now, I'm not taking out-of-state assignments, so I can be close to my dad."

"I'm twenty-five," she said. "Have you been married or in any serious relationships?"

She had confessed her failed serious relationship, so that justified her asking the question. "No to marriage. Yes to a relationship, but it didn't work out."

"What happened?"

"It didn't work out," he repeated, turning his head and not looking at her anymore.

She watched the tension on his face for a few seconds, then said, "Sorry. I didn't mean to pry."

"We should get going to the police station. Why don't we go get her and head to the hotel?" Callum said.

She wanted to get to Evie as soon as possible—and slow down whatever was happening between her and Callum.

Waiting for Hazel to finish getting ready to leave, Callum struggled with what her questions had brought to the surface. Shortly after he had left the SEAL team, he had lost Annabel. He never talked about her and their unborn baby. After she died, he had told everyone they'd broken up. He couldn't bear to face the truth and he didn't like people asking him about her. No one had enquired about her in a long time, which probably explained the heavy emotion he felt right now.

When Hazel joined him at the back door, Callum left the apartment, carrying two of her bags with one hand, leaving the other free. He searched the parking area behind the bakery and at first everything seemed quiet. But then he saw someone sitting in a car parked at the end of one of the rows. It was different than the one that had nearly mowed down Evie and Hazel; this one was white with tinted windows. He couldn't see the person inside, but the shape had the form of a man.

Alarmed that someone might try to harm Hazel again, he said, "Go back inside, Hazel."

"What?" Her eyes searched his face beneath lowered eyebrows.

"I need to check out that car over there. Go back

inside." He had to keep her safe and she'd be safest in there for now.

Hazel looked out into the parking lot. "Oh, no."

"It might not be anything. Just let me check it out," he said as reassuringly as he could. He didn't mean to frighten her.

She turned and went back inside. He saw her go to the window next to the door and watch.

Callum stepped down the stairs, leaving the bags on the landing by the door. He walked to his truck and started it, then drove closer to the building. There, he waited a few moments. The driver of the other car pulled out of the parking space and drove down the alley toward the street.

Getting out of the truck, Callum went to help Hazel as she came out of the apartment and locked the door. He searched the parking lot and alley, keeping his body between the direction the car had gone and Hazel. He picked up the two bags and followed her down. At the passenger door, he opened that and waited for her to get in, continuing to watch for the mysterious car.

Putting the bags in the back seat, he got behind the wheel and started driving.

At the street he pulled out into traffic, glancing frequently into the rearview mirror. As he suspected, the stranger had waited for them.

Hazel twisted to look behind them. "Is that car following us?"

"Yes."

"Is it the same man?"

"I don't know." Callum turned a corner to see if the stranger would follow.

He did.

Callum turned another corner and the stranger turned, too. He was two vehicles behind them. Callum couldn't see the man clearly.

He decided to drive to the police station. Who in their right mind would try anything in front of a police station? Someone out of their mind...?

Hoping to get a better look at the man, Callum slowed down.

"What are you doing?" Hazel asked in a scared tone.

"I want to see if we can identify him." He watched in the rearview mirror as the vehicle behind him got into the right lane and passed them. The second car moved over next. The white sedan slowed with Callum, maintaining distance. Whoever was driving wouldn't risk being seen up close.

Not wanting to incite the man into drawing a gun or doing anything else that might endanger Hazel, Callum sped up and drove the rest of the way to the station. As they made the turn into the parking lot, the other car drove by. Callum stopped his truck and looked out his window. He saw a man who probably was about six feet tall. He had a hoodie and wore sunglasses—at night—and looked right at him, lights from the dash meagerly reflecting on him.

Callum waited until the white car disappeared from view, having memorized the plate number.

He parked. "Wait for me. Don't get out."

Hazel stayed in the truck and Callum opened the door for her, looking for the white car. Then he put his arm around her and walked with her to the front entrance. Inside, he turned to the glass doors and watched for a few minutes. The car didn't reappear.

He heard Hazel ask for Detective Wilder and turned

from the door. A short while later Kerry appeared from a hallway.

"Evie is looking at mugshots," Kerry said. "I thought you both should have a look as well. Right this way." She waved her hand in encouragement.

Callum followed Hazel and Kerry down a hall to an office where Evie was perched on a desk chair that all but swallowed her. Seeing her mother, she hopped down and ran over on her little legs.

"Mommy!"

Hazel picked her up for a hug. "Hi, sweetie. Did you have fun?"

"Yes. The artist is really good. He said he likes his job." Her innocent eyes were wide with excitement.

"Oh, really?"

"And I looked at pictures of bad people."

The kid would probably go down hard when Hazel put her to bed. Who needed sugar when you had such an active imagination? Evie definitely needed a lot of stimulation mentally. She would probably do great in school. He often wondered what his daughter would have been like. Who would she have been? What would her personality have been like? His personality or her mother's?

Callum went over to Kerry and told her about the white car, glad for the distraction. She went to the computer where Evie had been "working" and must have navigated somewhere that would tell her about the car.

"Reported stolen this afternoon," she said.

Damn. The stranger was being very careful. Callum didn't like how he had followed them. He had found where Hazel lived. What if he found them at the inn? He felt enormous pressure to keep Hazel and Evie safe, more so than his usual clients. This seemed more personal.

Before that thought could cause him some heartburn, he went with Hazel to the computer, where Kerry brought up the mugshots. They spent about an hour going through those, but none of them looked familiar. They also couldn't say with any certainty that any of those who had the same type of build might be a potential suspect. Evie's assessment was their best shot at this point.

He'd been so consumed with protecting Hazel and Evie that he hadn't asked Kerry about the progress of the investigation into his father's shooting.

"Hey, have you gotten any further on finding Nan Gelman?" Nan was a nurse who'd been working on the maternity ward at Mustang Valley General Hospital the day Ace had been born—and swapped with another baby. Though the hospital's records had burned, the Coltons were trying to track down Nan to find out what had happened that day.

Kerry made a disgruntled sound. "No. I found a Gelman living in Mountain Valley, but they aren't related to Nan. No one in that family worked at the hospital."

Maybe he'd see what he could dig up. "I might be able to help. My company has resources that you may not have access to."

She brightened. "That would be great."

"Detective Wilder?" Callum looked up and saw an officer in the doorway. "We have a body. It might be related to the near hit and run."

Kerry indicated for Callum and Hazel to follow.

Hazel looked at Callum. "Evie should probably have

a tour of the station or something." She should not hear about a dead body.

An officer approached at Kerry's gesture and Evie happily went off to resume her fun-filled day at the police station.

Callum and Hazel went into a conference room, where other detectives had gathered.

"Kerry's here now," the chief of police, Al Barco, said. Fifty-two, mostly bald and with a slight paunch, he had calm, kind green eyes, despite his commanding nature.

And a man started talking through the speakerphone on the long table. "Hi, Kerry. It's Dane Howman."

"Hey, Howman. What have you got for me?"

"A hiker found a body on the banks of a river a few miles from where Evie saw him put in the trunk. Preliminary forensics suggests the cause of death was blunt force trauma to the head. He had a wallet and an ID. It's Nate Blurge."

"I know that guy," one of the other officers in the room said. "He's a wild twenty-six-year-old, been arrested three times for drunk and disorderly conduct. Practically lives at Joe's Bar and always gets into fights."

"Could one of the people he crossed have killed him?" Hazel asked.

"That's a possibility," Kerry said. "It's where we'll start in the investigation."

Hazel looked over at Callum and he could feel her worry. How long would the investigation take? How long would she have to be on high alert?

"I'll find the killer as fast as I can so you and Evie can have your lives back," Kerry said.

Hazel answered with a slight smile that was more of a silent thank-you than anything else. The reassurance didn't alleviate the fear, and Callum's determination to protect them with all the skill he'd gained over the years redoubled.

REJOINING EVIE, HAZEL flashed back to Callum's reaction when she had asked him about his past relationships. Clearly something bad. It bothered her that he had trouble talking about something personal like that and also made her doubly curious.

Again, both she and Callum added what little information they could to the description of the killer. Right now her daughter was transfixed by Kerry's badge.

"I've booked out one of the two-bedroom suites at the Dales Inn," Callum said.

Hazel looked at him, startled. "You mean…you and me and…" In one suite? "I can't afford that."

"I can. Don't worry."

She kind of did worry, but she decided not to argue. Keeping Evie safe was most important to her. He put his hand over his chest. "I'm a bodyguard. Consider this a professional courtesy. No charge." Now he opened his arms in offering, and oh, what an offering.

She stared at him for long seconds. "Oh, I don't—"

Hazel felt some trepidation at staying with a man she had only just met. Nearly being killed had frightened her but this was all happening so fast. Her routine had been disrupted.

"Actually," Detective Wilder said, removing her badge and handing it to Evie, who took it and felt the top, "Until we find Blurge's killer, I think you should stay at the Dales Inn with Callum."

More than one night? "I don't—"

"I've already offered my services as a bodyguard," Callum cut in again.

Hazel hesitated.

"You're in good hands, Hazel. He is one of the best bodyguards in the country. His company is known for that. They have a solid reputation. You can trust him."

That made her feel marginally better, but it seemed excessive. And with a stranger.

Bodyguard.

She supposed if she thought of him that way...

"You would be my bodyguard?" she asked him.

"Yours and Evie's."

Hazel glanced at Kerry, still uncertain but wavering. "He isn't a policeman." Callum might be six-three and solid muscle, but cops carried guns.

"He's licensed to carry a firearm." Kerry looked at Callum, who moved his jacket aside to reveal the gun in a hip holster.

When Hazel said nothing, just looked over at Evie, Kerry added, "There isn't an officer in this department who wouldn't vouch for him. He does work for a top personal protection agency. Really, I can't say enough good about him."

Hazel put her hand to her forehead. "This is so sudden." She lowered her hand and looked at Evie. The sketch artist handed her a detective shield sticker, which put a big smile on her face. She peeled the back off the sticker and stuck it to the left side of her chest.

"Hey, Detective Evie." Hazel went to her and crouched where she sat at Kerry's desk. Evie beamed, no doubt imagining she was a detective and would go to work just now. "We're going to stay at a hotel tonight. It'll be a vacation."

Evie nodded, looking at Kerry, who had put her badge back on, clearly distracted.

Chapter Three

Having confirmation that the man Evie saw being dumped into a car trunk was dead unsettled Hazel much more than she'd anticipated. Evie had seen the man knocked over the head with a rock. They didn't know if that had killed him. Sure, she had contemplated the possibility, even the likelihood, but having it become fact put them up against a killer. *A killer!*

Callum held the station door for her and Evie, whom she held since her eyes were drooping with the late hour. She saw him scan their surroundings. He put his hand on her back protectively and then his head stopped moving. She followed his gaze and saw a white car drive past the station again and then turn the corner. Apparently the vehicle had been circling the block while they were inside.

"Go and get Kerry," Callum said. "Hurry."

Hazel turned and walked quickly back to the door. When inside, she saw Callum had drawn his gun and was watching the street.

"Is something wrong?"

Hazel heard Detective Wilder and faced her. "The white car that followed us here is still out there. He's going around the block." Just then Hazel spotted the car in front of the station on the street, driving slowly. Callum took cover behind his truck.

Kerry hollered for two other officers and ran out the front door.

"Mommy?" Evie said sleepily.

"It's okay, honey. Go back to sleep." Hazel hoped it would be all right.

Evie rested her head on Hazel's shoulder and closed her eyes. Hazel didn't have time to savor the sight.

Callum opened the station door as Hazel saw Kerry racing away in her car, two other officers following.

"Let's get you out of here," Callum said. "Kerry's on his tail."

She carried Evie out the door.

Callum stayed close to her side with his pistol. At his truck, he opened the back door and guarded them while Hazel put Evie in the car seat he had thoughtfully put in there. Then he opened the passenger door and guarded Hazel again while she got in. Going around to the other side, he got behind the wheel and drove quickly out of the parking lot.

A few minutes later they arrived at the Dales Inn. Hazel knew it was upscale but she had never been this close before. Its grandeur towered before her, the double wooden doors with oval windows welcoming guests to promised luxury. A parking valet gave Callum a ticket.

"Welcome, Mr. Colton," the valet said and then nodded to Hazel. "Ma'am."

"Callum Colton?" a bellboy asked.

"Yes," Callum answered.

"I'll take care of your bags."

"Thank you."

All Hazel had to do was carry a sleeping Evie inside.

The richness of majestic white columns and dark polished stone floors beneath a high, ornately trimmed ceiling engulfed her. Numbly she walked to the reception desk with Callum.

"We're checking in to a two-bedroom suite, please."

Hazel thought about protesting again, but her anxiety over the driver of the white car stopped her. That and Detective Wilder's unwavering praise of Callum's good character.

He took the room keys, then guided Hazel with his hand on her lower back, something that was becoming a habit for him. Strangely, Hazel didn't mind. She wasn't accustomed to a man doting on her the way Callum did. She had always taken care of herself. He might be doing all of that as her bodyguard, but she still liked it. She felt pampered.

They rode the elevator to the top floor with the bellboy and their luggage. Her luggage. Hazel looked at the cart the bellboy had gotten and saw two additional bags. She looked up at Callum in question, Evie's warm breaths touching her neck.

"I arranged for my things to be brought here."

Who had he called? And when? He must have done so while he waited for her to pack. No doubt his family had all kinds of people who did such things for them. Hazel had a funny feeling about that. Ed had hidden his wealth from her, so he had never taken her to places like this, but his lies had hurt. She wouldn't fall so easily for anyone again. Not that she was falling for Callum. He was extremely handsome, that's all. What woman could be immune to that? It was like staring at a beautiful painting, unable to look away until she'd had her fill of the pleasure.

In the posh hallway, Callum stopped at a room door and unlocked it. Then he held the door for Hazel and the bellboy.

"Go ahead and put my bags in the room with one king," Callum said to the bellboy.

"Yes, sir." The bellboy walked down the hall and Hazel followed.

Going into the other bedroom, Hazel drew the covers back on the far queen bed and gently laid Evie on the sheets. She touched her daughter's sleeping face as the bellboy brought in her bags.

"Thanks," she said.

"You're welcome. Enjoy your stay at the Dales Inn." The young man left and Hazel shut the door before undressing Evie.

It was a bit of a challenge to get her daughter into pj's but she finally succeeded without waking her. The poor kid was exhausted.

Hazel unpacked both of their bags, hanging some clothes and putting some in drawers. She put Evie's toys on one of the chairs in front of the draperies and then spread Evie's favorite soft blanket over her. Leaning down, she kissed her daughter's forehead.

Going out to the main room, she saw Callum on his phone, standing between a four-seater dining table and a sectional that faced a gas fireplace with a TV over it. He talked to someone as he faced the corner windows, Mustang Valley town lights sparkling outside.

There were some things on the table, a computer and other equipment. As she neared, she saw three GPS tracking devices, several USB drives. Some devices looked high tech, others had tiny screens, and she saw bulletproof vests, one small enough to fit Evie. Now she knew why he had two bags.

"All right. Keep me informed," he said and then disconnected.

Hazel went to the four bar stools at a marble-topped kitchen island with a sink in the middle. Three pretty orange-gold pendants hung from the ceiling. A four-burner gas stove with a microwave above was on the other side, and there were cabinets on both sides. It even had a pantry.

She put her hands on the back of one of the chairs. "This is very nice. I'm more of a two-or three-star hotel kind of girl." Not a fiver.

He chuckled. "We need the space and you need a kitchen. Think of it as a home away from home."

Hazel had told him she was a chef on the way to the Dales Inn but not much else. Leaving the chair, she went around the island and began going through the cabinets. The kitchen was fully stocked with all the equipment she would need. "The only things missing are food and spices."

"Make a list and I'll have that delivered in the morning."

With the snap of a finger he'd do that? "Then I'll pay you."

"No, you won't. I want you to relax and have as much semblance of your normal routine as possible. Don't worry about anything other than doing your job and taking care of Evie. I'll do the rest."

Finished checking out the kitchen, seeing it had pretty much everything, she walked to the impressive windows. Mustang Valley looked bigger than she had always thought of it from here.

"Why are you doing this?" she asked.

She heard him walk up behind her and stop beside her. "I was there when the man tried to run you over."

He had already indicated as much, but she wanted to know why he was here with her. Why had he offered his services, free of charge?

"Why this?" She turned as she swept her arm out into the room, facing him. "Why is it so important for you to help us?"

She met his incredibly blue eyes while he considered his reply.

"I don't know," he finally said. "When I first saw you, I had no intention of going out to meet you, but then I saw that car with the driver and instincts kicked in. This is what I do, Hazel."

That sounded truthful enough. Why, then, did she have this feeling that it was more personal than that?

"Kerry called. She lost the white car," Callum said, pulling her thoughts elsewhere. "She said the driver must know the town well. Otherwise he might not have gotten away as easily as he did."

Hazel bit her lower lip in consternation. The killer had gotten away. Where was he now? Lurking outside? Did he already know they were here? Picturing Evie's sweet sleeping face, she released her lip with a long sigh. If the killer knew the town well, he'd know the Dales Inn was the only hotel in Mustang Valley.

Feeling as though someone could see them through the windows, she went to stand by the dining table.

Callum went to the other side. "I sleep light, so don't worry. And if you have any lingering doubt as to why I'm doing this, now you shouldn't. I couldn't leave a dog in danger like this."

She believed that his work was second nature to him, but she still thought there was more to him than that, more that drew him to her and Evie, maybe even something he hadn't acknowledged himself. Yet.

Looking down at all the items on the table, she pointed to the vests. "I take it we're going to be wearing those?"

"Whenever we leave the inn. They're knife-and bulletproof and made with poly-cotton netting that breathes to keep you cool or warm, depending on the weather. You can wear them underneath your clothes. They're comfortable."

Very high tech. And she would feel so much better knowing Evie would be protected as best as she could.

"What will you do with the USB drives?" she asked.

"Some are listening devices, others are cameras. One is for deleted file recovery." He gestured to the USB devices. "We'll put a GPS in your car, purse and Evie's backpack. They all have extended battery life."

Hazel couldn't bear to think she or Evie might be abducted, but Callum would know where they were if it happened. He wasn't taking any chances. She couldn't imagine they would need to recover any deleted files in order to find the killer. Maybe that was another precautionary measure Callum had taken.

"I've got some night vision goggles and extra guns and ammo in the bag. I'll keep those in a safe place."

Out of Evie's curious hands. That was comforting. Hazel met his eyes, thinking she could never get tired of doing so. She could stare at them for an hour and float on a cloud of infatuation. How many other handsome men had she seen and not had such a strong reaction? She had been quite attracted to Ed, but she had

never felt this way with him. Callum might be rug-
gedly gorgeous but Hazel didn't think he'd be a good
match for her.

What made a good match? She did not know him at
all, at least, not very well. He physically attracted her.
What would she do with that? What if she had no control over what was between them?

WHY ARE YOU *doing this?*

Why is it so important for you to help us?

Those two questions that Hazel had asked kept re-
peating in his mind and he couldn't shut off the voice.
He was tired of hearing it. Mostly he was tired of wondering why and feeling somewhere deep inside that he
already knew the answers.

He opened the drawer of the built-in desk next to
the kitchen, looking for a notepad and pen. Hazel had
gone to sit on the sectional. It was getting late but she
needed to give him a list of kitchen necessaries so he
could have everything she needed by morning.

He had been truthful when he had told her instinct
had taken over. Instinct had made him walk across the
street to check on the mysterious car. He hadn't really
thought much beyond that, but now here he was, guarding a woman and her child.

Finding a notepad and pen, he brought it to Hazel and
sat beside her. "Here you go. Make your list."

She tapped the pen lightly against her lower lip
awhile before finally beginning to write down ingredients.

Callum studied her profile, sloping nose and full lips.
Long lashes low over hazel-green eyes. He let his gaze
travel lower, noticing a button on her white blouse had

come loose and exposed more of her cleavage. She was a stunning woman.

He turned his attention to her growing list.

"Do you have regulars?"

"Yes. I'm a personal chef," she answered without pausing in her writing.

Leaning over he started reading the list. "Are the ingredients all meat and potatoes?"

Smiling she slid a glance toward him. "No. Some are chicken and mashed potatoes."

He chuckled. "I could do that job."

"I also have clients who want things like shrimp and scallop scampi. Roasted chicken au jus. Seafood-stuffed salmon. Steak. Lobster. Vegetable dishes. Fruit."

He would like to try a few of her concoctions. But since he barely knew her, he didn't mention it.

"What made you decide to become a chef?" he asked.

She smiled softly. "My mother cooked all the time. I grew up with delicious smells wafting from the kitchen."

"You never told me about your family. You know all about mine and I know nothing about yours." That wasn't fair. He felt safe asking her, not too personal.

"Not much to tell," she said. "My parents are both from Pagosa Springs, Colorado. They knew each other in high school but didn't get together until after college. My brother is a cop and lives in Phoenix with his wife's family."

"I'm sure there is more to tell than that."

She smiled in that soft way again. "Are you looking for drama?"

"You did say every family has it." He was starting to love this banter.

She laughed once. "Um…let's see…well, there was the time when my brother skipped school to smoke pot with his friends. My parents flipped. They were afraid he would drop out of school or be kicked out and his whole future would be in ruins. But it turned out he just went through a phase. He rebelled for a year and then got his grades back up and went on to college."

To become a cop. Her family drama paled in comparison to his. "What about you? Did you ever rebel?"

"No. I was never good at math or the sciences, but I managed a B average. Art was my forte. I oil painted, drew in lead and colored pencils. My paintings were often displayed in the school hall outside the art room. My parents worried I'd never make a comfortable income. They sat me down for a talk my senior year and said, 'Hey, look, you might not be able to support yourself.' Their way of saying they were convinced I'd be the clichéd starving artist." She laughed. "I suppose I am still, in some ways."

He liked that she smiled and laughed so much. He smiled and laughed, too, at least he thought he did.

"You were an artist and became a chef," he said. "How did you go from one to the other?"

That made her think a moment, tipping her head up a bit, eyes lifting in search of an answer. He could see the flecks of green glowing.

"I think the talk with my parents influenced me," she said. "I went to college for interior design, but one of my optional classes was culinary. That's what changed everything. I loved the art of making plates look like colorful, abstract paintings. And then I fell in love with flavors and aromas. I dropped out of college after the first semester and went to culinary school."

She must have a knack for it, since she was so young and already striving for success. "You're self-employed. That's quite an accomplishment."

"I only recently went out on my own. I did my externship at Flemming's, a renowned restaurant here in Arizona."

"I've heard of it. Where did you go to school that got you that kind of externship?" he asked.

"The Culinary Institute of America."

He whistled. How had she been able to afford that? He didn't know the exact tuition but did know it was among the best culinary arts schools in the country, if not the world.

"My parents saved for my college education. They gave me almost half and I took out student loans for the rest. That and the externship got me my first job at a place called Carolyn's Kitchen. It was an upscale, home-style restaurant. I helped them spiff up their menu and some of the meals I created gave me the idea to go out on my own. Jasmine, the owner of the bakery, lets me cook in her kitchen when I have a big order or several all at once. I cook after the bakery closes at two."

She didn't appear to make a ton of money, living in the small apartment, but she had to be getting along just fine, making a decent income to support herself and Evie. Callum admired that. He admired ambition in anyone. Working hard was rewarding. It didn't matter if the hard work made a person wealthy. If Callum hadn't been born a Colton, he wouldn't be wealthy. He made a good income, more than an average bodyguard, but nothing approaching what his father made.

"What's your favorite food?" Hazel asked, handing him the notepad.

Taking it, his fingers brushed hers. She gave him the pen as their eyes met.

"Seafood. Clams. Scallops. That scallop recipe sounded really good."

"Clams. I could make you an outstanding clam dinner. We'd have to make something else for Evie. She doesn't like seafood."

"Does any kid?"

She took the pen and paper back and jotted down some more ingredients. Then she handed the list back to him. He put it on the coffee table.

"What are you going to make me?"

"Linguine with white clam sauce."

"Mmm." He couldn't wait for that. Spending time with her in the kitchen, too. Doing anything with her. He liked being with her. "How much time do you need to cook tomorrow?"

"Five or six hours."

Taking out his phone, he took a picture of the list then texted it to one of his agency's best personal staff and asked to have everything by nine in the morning. Patsy Cornwall responded a few seconds later. She was a night owl. Callum could always depend on her.

"Just like that, we'll get all the ingredients?" Hazel sounded amazed.

"Just like that. Patsy is paid very well for her services."

"Is she some kind of concierge?"

"She's a personal assistant. She works from home and runs errands for us when we need it. We all keep her pretty busy."

"Nice. Lucky me." Hazel gave him the pleasure of

one of her soft smiles and the color of her eyes spell-bound him.

She moved her head a fraction closer, as though she couldn't help it, stopping short and looking into his eyes.

Callum lifted his hand and placed his palm against her cheek, then, nearly involuntarily, pressed his mouth to hers. She immediately responded, her warm lips melding with his and sparking much more carnal urges. The intensity of sensations just a kiss caused in him made him withdraw.

She opened her eyes and he found himself trans-fixed again. He had only known her for about ten hours. With all that had happened, he felt he had known her a lot longer.

"I should get some sleep. Tomorrow is going to be a busy day," she said.

"Right. Yes." He stood with her, seeing her smooth her hair and press her lips together as though she could still feel him kissing her.

He walked behind her toward their bedrooms, she veering to the right and he to the left. When she reached her door, she slowed and looked at him. A moment of electrified attraction passed between them before she disappeared from view.

Callum entered his room and closed the door. While he undressed and got into bed, he imagined what it might be like to be naked with Hazel. On his back, he folded his arm under his head and stared at the dark ceiling, the passionate urges subsiding as the reality of starting something romantic with her set in. Hazel, single mother of Evie, an adorable little girl who re-minded him of what his own daughter might have been.

Daughter. He had never formed that word since his

girlfriend died. And now an intense sense of dread came over him. Dread and a horrible, defenseless feeling that swirled in his stomach.

Okay. He had gotten himself into this mess. He would treat it like any other job. Watch out for Hazel and Evie. Get them through what they had witnessed. Catch the bad guy. Move on to the next client. No more kissing Hazel.

Chapter Four

When Hazel woke, she didn't immediately know where she was. She had been so exhausted, she'd slept deeply. Now, pushing the covers off, she sat up to be surrounded by the luxury of the Dales Inn room. With white, brown and splashes of color in paintings, the room was immaculate and quiet. She stood and saw Evie had already gotten up.

Checking the time, she saw it was almost eight. Going to the door, she cracked it open and heard Evie chattering happily away. Assured her daughter was fine, Hazel hopped in the shower. Remembering kissing Callum, she tipped her face up into the spray, feeling him all over again. She'd had trouble falling asleep last night because of that. She couldn't even blame him, though, since she was the one who had leaned in. She had been so entranced by him, by his eyes and every feature of his face. The sound of his voice and the things they had talked about, the connection between them.

She dressed in gray slacks and a black blouse and left the room, hearing voices.

"I love strawberries."

"I can seen that you do," Callum said.

"I *looove* strawberries," Evie repeated.

Evie sat at the dining room table with a huge plate of strawberry crepes in front of her. The dish dwarfed her head and upper torso, just her shoulders cleared the height of the tabletop.

"What are you doing to my daughter?"

Callum looked up from the table, where he arranged two breakfast plates that still had silver covers on them.

He chuckled. "She said she was starving. I hope this is okay with you. I sort of winged it by ordering room service." He pointed to the plate at Evie's right. "That's yours. I'm glad I didn't have to wake you before it got cold."

"More than fine. I'm starving, too." She sat next to Evie and lifted the cover.

"It's a Santa Fe skillet," Callum said. "Wheat toast and fruit for sides. Evie picked it out for you. She said you liked food like that. There was a picture on the room service menu."

She did like food like this. Evie knew she loved green chilies.

He poured her a cup of steaming coffee. "Cream or sugar?"

"Yes, please, just creamer."

He handed her two small containers of creamer and she went about adding both to her coffee as Callum sat across from her and removed the silver cover from his plate. He had gotten a ham and cheese omelet with rye toast.

"Do you eat out a lot?" she asked.

With a bite of food, he nodded. Then after swallowing, added, "Bachelor."

She and Evie rarely ate out, but why would they, when Hazel cooked for a living?

"Evie told me the last man you were with was a… what did you call it?" He turned to Evie.

"A nerd." Evie giggled before shoveling another bite of crepe into her mouth.

"Evie was worried you were falling for him," Callum said.

Hazel saw his questioning look. She had dated James for a few weeks. She didn't like talking about him.

"Well, Evie, you're awfully chatty this morning," she said.

Evie giggled. "Cal-em is funny."

"Why is he funny?"

"I don't know. He's funny. He's not a nerd."

Gaze running over his shoulders and chest, Hazel had to agree. When she met his eyes, the same tingles of sexual awareness assaulted her, just as they had last night.

"Who is this nerd? He must have been important to you if you let him spend time with Evie."

"He didn't think Mommy was smart. He called her stupid once."

Callum's lower jaw dropped. "What?"

"She told him to leave. Except she used a bad word."

Hazel remembered the sting of James's condescension all too well. Just when she had begun to trust him, he'd turned on her. He had made her feel the same awful sense of betrayal that Ed had.

"He had a PhD in economics," she said. "Apparently he was very proud of that."

"Why did he call you stupid?" Callum asked, sounding incredulous.

"We were talking about retirement. I didn't have anything put away at the time. My sole focus was Evie, taking care of her, saving for her college, making sure she has medical insurance and good clothes and shoes and healthy food. It escalated to an argument and he called me stupid. He said I didn't know arithmetic or anything about science and all I did know was how to cook."

As she talked Callum's brows gradually rose with each insult. "The man is clearly mad. And completely blinded by his own self-interests."

She wasn't sure she could have said that better.

"Just because you're more inclined to the arts doesn't make you stupid," Callum said. "A person doesn't have to be a genius in math or any of the hard sciences to be intelligent." He shook his head. "I can't believe anyone would say that to another person."

"I thought he was a decent man, just like Ed." She glanced at Evie. The little girl didn't yet understand what had happened between her mother and father, but some day Hazel would have to have that talk with her. She wouldn't disparage Ed's character, just state the facts. What she dreaded most was that Evie would feel her father never loved her, even though he hadn't. He didn't. He didn't care about Evie. He didn't even know her name. Maybe she could tell Evie someday that her father never knew her, but that if he ever did, or took the time to, then he would love her.

When Hazel turned back to Callum, she saw he had caught her meaning. She was no good at assessing men, at predicting their characters. She had always been trusting, had had no reason not to be, having been surrounded by good people, raised in a stable family.

"I've always thought relationships were based on trial and error," he finally said. "Sometimes the trials go well but you learn the person isn't right for you and you respectfully part ways. Sometimes the trials go badly and end up a mistake. But eventually, with a little luck, you find a person who works."

Works? He sounded as though he believed what he said, or had at one point. "What kind of trials have you had?"

"Ones where I learned something, and some that were a mistake."

"What did you learn?" She'd start with the easier question to answer.

His shrewd mind must be at work. He eyed her with subtle suspicion mixed with intrigue, perhaps, and then his head cocked ever so slightly.

"Too personal?" she asked, half teasing.

A one-sided grin was his initial response, then he said, "I learned that some women are more interested in their own gain, and others aren't certain enough about what kind of man they're searching for or don't care as long as he is kind and capable of providing. I've learned those kinds of women aren't for me."

Oh, my. This man knew what he wanted. He sounded so candid. She didn't doubt he had learned what he claimed, but what about the mistakes? Maybe there had been only one.

"What about your mistakes?" she dared to ask.

Going still, he just looked at her.

A knock on the door interrupted. Callum went to the door and in came carts of groceries and supplies.

"Whoa!" Evie exclaimed, holding a sticky fork and sporting a strawberry-stained mouth. She put her utensil down, prongs up, on the table, watching the assistant roll bags of food into the suite.

"I'll help put all of this away," Patsy said. A woman

of average height with wavy brown hair and blue eyes, she had an energy about her that radiated efficiency.

Evie got off the chair. "Are we going to cook, Mommy?"

"*I'm* going to cook. You're going to go take a bath." She stood. "Come on. I'll get you started."

Hazel saw the assistant begin to put groceries away and Callum lending a hand. The refrigerator would be bursting by the time they finished.

In their en suite, Hazel started the bath and then went to Evie's stash of toys and found her floating Barbie boat and doll. Returning to the bathroom, she discovered Evie had removed her clothes and stepped into the filling tub.

Seeing Hazel had her favorite toys, she smiled and reached up for them. "Yes."

Hazel laughed with the affection that filled her. She handed her daughter the toys and Evie went instantly into playtime mode. Leaving the door open so she could hear her if anything happened, Hazel left the room and saw that Patsy had gone and Callum was removing cooking pans from a box. Patsy must have brought them, since the inn only had a minimal collection.

"You're going to help?" Hazel asked, going to the sink to wash her hands.

"I wouldn't want to ruin anything. I'll keep you company. I have nothing else to do until I make all your deliveries."

"I make the deliveries. It's good PR."

"No, I'll make them. You stay here, where you and Evie will be safe."

She had spoken without thinking, distracted with getting ready to cook for a few hours.

"I'll tell your customers Evie is sick and you sent me instead," he said. "I'll be charming. You won't lose any business."

Was he a good liar? She wished she could be there to hear him so she could make that assessment. Then again, she was never any good at detecting falsehoods.

While Callum made a call to Kerry to ask her to post an officer outside the inn while he made deliveries, Hazel decided to start with the pork chops. Brining them first, she felt Callum observing her work. While the chops soaked for thirty minutes, she moved on to the chicken and broccoli. Turning on the oven, she put the meat in a bowl, seasoned it and drizzled the cutlets with olive oil. All the while she contemplated picking up her conversation with Callum. She was beyond curious over what mistakes he had made. She knew there was one, probably a big one that he had trouble talking about.

She placed the broccoli on one baking pan and the chicken on another, then put both into the oven. Next, she began preparing spaghetti sauce, cooking the meat first.

"Mommy," Evie called from the room. She must be finished with her bath.

"I'll watch the meat." Callum took her place at the stove.

Hazel hurried to the room and helped Evie dry off, giving her hair a rub with the towel. "Get dressed, honey."

Evie went to the drawers where Hazel had placed her clothes and began digging through them. She'd make a mess and take forever to find something she liked. For the last year Evie had insisted on dressing herself. Usually she didn't match very well, but she always looked cute.

Back in the kitchen, Hazel took over at the stove, Callum moving aside. He leaned his hip on the counter and again Hazel became aware of his more than casual observation of her. She resumed preparing the meals.

A while later, Evie emerged from the room, half skipping her way toward them, her hair an utter mess. In the kitchen, she stopped next to Hazel.

"Mommy." She lifted the brush.

Callum stepped around Hazel and took the brush. "I'll do it. Your mother is working."

Picking her up, Callum took her to the other side of the kitchen island and sat her on a tall stool. Hazel had a great view of her as he began to brush her long hair. Evie brushed her Barbie doll's hair at the same time.

"How long are you going to be with my mommy?" Evie asked Callum.

"I don't know, Evie. It depends on how long it takes to catch that bad man," he said, struggling with a tangle.

His big body and manly hands running the brush through a five-year-old's hair touched Hazel for some reason.

"Are you and Mommy going to be friends after?"

Callum's hand paused in brushing her hair. "Do you want me to be?"

Evie shrugged. "Are you working for her?"

"Yes, I am."

"But you're her friend, too."

It was Hazel's turn to pause in her task. Why had her daughter asked such a question?

"We just met yesterday, but yes, she is a friend." Callum looked at Hazel with a grin, clearly enjoying this conversation. He began brushing again.

"Mommy needs more boy friends." She tipped her head up. "I don't have a daddy."

"You do have a daddy, Evie, he just isn't here," Hazel said. Why was her daughter bringing this up now? She wasn't prepared to have this talk so soon.

"Where is he?" Evie resumed brushing her doll's hair.

"He...wasn't interested in being with me."

"Does he know about me?"

"Yes, but he has never met you." Hazel glanced at Callum, who looked back at her somberly.

Evie lowered the doll and looked at Hazel. "Why not?"

"He left me, Evie. It had nothing to do with you."

"But...doesn't he want to meet me?"

"You're awfully inquisitive for a young girl," Hazel said.

"Some people aren't prepared to raise kids," Callum said. "Sometimes they aren't ready until much later in life. He doesn't know you, but if he did, he would see what a special girl you are."

Hazel's heart burst with appreciation and awe that, without prompting, Callum had told Evie something similar to what she had thought she would say.

"Do you have a daddy?"

"I do. We aren't very close, though."

That had surprised Hazel when he'd told her before. He seemed so concerned over his father. If they weren't close, why weren't they? Evie had looked up at him with his answer and Hazel could see a connection forming.

Did Evie relate her lack of a relationship with her father to his?

"Do you have any kids?" Evie asked, a fountain of questions.

Callum finished brushing her hair and put down the brush. "No."

"Are you going to?"

Hazel watched him tense up. She wondered—if it had been anyone other than a child asking, would he have retorted something to stop this grilling? She also began to worry about Evie's unabashed curiosity about Callum. She seemed to have taken a liking to him rather quickly, which might not be a good thing.

"Evie, that's enough. We barely know Callum. It isn't polite to ask so many personal questions," Hazel said, sure that Evie's Curious George mode was too much for Callum.

Evie's lower lip puffed out a little in a pout, but then she brightened quickly enough. "Can I go watch cartoons?"

"Sure," Hazel said.

Callum helped her get the television on and tuned to the right channel and then returned to the kitchen island. Hazel had put the chicken into the oven and gone to work on the chops, getting a pan ready to sear them.

She busied herself in the kitchen for the next few hours. Callum had gone into the living room to watch television with Evie. The two were getting chummy in there. Callum had found a good family movie that adults could enjoy.

Hazel began putting food into microwavable containers and then into the refrigerator. Her customers could freeze what they wouldn't use in the next day or two. Instant, delicious meals for busy workers or the elderly.

"Will you write down the addresses?" Callum asked. "The officer is outside. I checked."

While that was reassuring, he couldn't keep her penned up in here until the killer was caught. She had a life to live. But dragging Evie around with them wasn't a wise idea, either. Damn that stranger. He was taking her freedom from her. She needed her freedom, but she was no fighter like Callum. Better that he did what he could. He was right. She and Evie were safer here.

"You're doing an awful lot to keep us safe," she said.

Callum stepped closer to her. He put his fingers beneath her chin. Heat coursed through her as she tried to figure out why he had touched her this way.

"It's more than wanting you safe, Hazel. I have a personal reason for doing so. You see, I normally don't take the cases involving women and children. Protecting them. It just so happens that I fell into protecting you and Evie and now I cannot turn my back. I have to see this through."

He seemed to be trying to make her understand why it was so important to him that she stay here in their suite. She still didn't get it. He had to see this through…but why *him*? Why didn't he take cases involving women and children? Why make such a pledge?

"I can't explain it right now. All I ask is you trust me," he said.

After a moment of stunned perplexity, she nodded. She wouldn't press him now, but the need to know would gnaw at her until he told her everything. If he ever did…

MYSTIFIED OVER HOW close he had come to telling Hazel his darkest secret, Callum began loading the containers of food into his truck. What really got him was that he had felt as though he *could* tell her. And that maybe a huge burden might be lifted if he did. Maybe Charles was right. Maybe keeping all of that bottled up was doing more harm than good.

Memories of when he had first met Annabel flooded him. He had been at a home improvement store looking at wood-saw blades to remodel his bathrooms. Annabel had been looking at the drills. He'd found that interesting. It wasn't every day a guy saw a woman buying tools, unless it was for her man. Callum hadn't seen a ring, so he had gone over to her.

"Are you a carpenter?" he had asked.

Her head had come up and she looked at him for endless seconds. She had long dark hair and dark eyes. Very beautiful.

"No." She had held up a drill in her hand. "Replacing old doors in my house."

"You don't hire out for that?"

"Why? Because I'm a woman?"

From that moment on, he had fallen hard for her. They talked for hours. They spent quiet times together, just comfortable in each other's company. Callum had thought they had the makings of something special, but he hadn't had time to really get to know her. They had only begun to explore. They hadn't been together long before—

He could not let his mind dwell any more on that. A deep sorrow penetrated his usual wall of carefully crafted indifference. He finished putting the food in the truck and closed the door.

As he walked to the rear of the truck on the way to the other side, he spotted a black SUV. That in and of itself didn't alert him, but the man sitting in the driver's seat did. The guy was just sitting in a vehicle.

The passenger window rolled down and he barely noticed the muzzle of a gun before diving for cover. He just made it around the side of his truck before bullets hit the bumper and rear tailgate.

He drew his own weapon and inched up enough to see the shooter. He took aim and fired before ducking as more bullets hit his truck. Hearing the SUV's engine rev and tires squeal, Callum tried again to shoot the driver. He had to take cover again as the SUV raced by and bullets pummeled the truck.

When the volley subsided, Callum got into the truck from the passenger side and crawled behind the wheel, fleetingly seeing a couple crouching at the entrance of the inn, one of them with a cellphone to his ear. Starting the truck, he peeled out of the parking space and chased after the SUV. He veered in and out of traffic, seeing the vehicle several car lengths ahead.

The shooter turned a corner. Callum was slowed by traffic and when he made the turn, he didn't see the SUV. He searched side streets as he weaved, earning honks from a few drivers. Looking left, he spotted the SUV and nearly sideswiped an oncoming car as he swerved into the turn. He gave the truck full gas, no cars in his way, and careened into another turn. The SUV had vanished again, but Callum saw an alley. Swerving into the turn, he gained on the SUV. The shooter flung out into traffic on a busier street. Other traffic veered out of the way as the driver maneuvered around them, Callum not far behind.

There was no plate on the SUV.

The shooter craned back to fire his weapon again and bullets struck Callum's windshield. He crouched low and stuck his pistol out his window, firing back. The shooter drove erratically and made a sharp right turn, causing a delivery truck to brake hard and swerve.

With the delivery truck in his way Callum had to stop and then drive around. People scattered on the sidewalk. The SUV had distance on him again. The shooter turned a corner about a block and a half ahead.

But when Callum reached the street, he didn't see the SUV. He searched until he reached another road. He checked both ways, but the SUV was nowhere in sight. Making a guess, he drove left. A few minutes later it became apparent he would not find the shooter.

His cell rang. Seeing it was Hazel, he answered.

"Are you all right?" she asked. "There are a bunch of police out front and someone said there was a shooting."

"I'm okay. Stay in the room. The shooter came after me. I tried to chase him but he got away."

She was silent for a while. "I'll stay in the room. Be careful."

"I'll be back soon." He liked the concern for his welfare in her voice but not her worry. He thought about rushing back to Hazel, but she was safe in the inn, which had solid security. There were security cameras everywhere and a security team. That was probably why the shooter had waited outside. He knew if he tried to go inside and kill anyone, he'd be captured on video. Besides, the police were there now.

He called Kerry.

She answered on the second ring.

"The killer tried to shoot me just now," Callum said.

"I heard."

He explained what had happened and that he didn't get a plate number this time.

"Well, we can pretty much assume he's stealing vehicles to avoid identification," she said.

"He's getting bold. He waited for us outside the inn. How did he know we were there? How did he find out so fast?"

"Mustang Valley isn't very big. Dales Inn is the only hotel in town. I'm sure he deduced you and Hazel would go there if you weren't at her place."

"What about the ranch?"

"I'm sure he checked there, too."

Callum ran his fingers through his hair as he drove to the address of the first delivery.

"I'll put out a BOLO on the SUV and check for any reported stolen vehicles," Kerry said. "Be careful."

Nobody had to tell him that. Ending the call, he gathered the bag with all the containers for Emily Watson, one of Hazel's elderly clients. With glasses on a chain, her silver hair in stiff curls and a face covered in peach fuzz, Emily smiled her welcome in a floral house dress. Callum was immediately charmed.

She glanced down at the bag he held. "Where is Hazel?"

"She's not feeling well so I'm making her deliveries for her. My name is Callum."

"Come in, come in." Emma stepped aside and checked him out. "My, my, aren't you a handsome fellow."

Callum entered the older Victorian, dark wood floors creaking, letting her comment go.

Emily shut the door and led him into the kitchen. "Go

ahead and put them in the freezer. That's what Hazel always does. I still have one of her delicious meals in the refrigerator and with it just being me, that lasts a few days. My Irwin passed a few years ago and the kids don't come around as often as I'd like."

She must be lonely and starved for adult conversation. Callum opened the freezer drawer and began rearranging the contents to make room for a week's worth of meals.

"Irwin was an engineer and retired a vice president of his department," Emma said. "He was a good provider. What is it that you do, Mr...?"

"Colton. I'm a personal protection officer." That always sounded more palatable than *bodyguard*.

"Oh, you're a security guard?" Emily asked, going to a glass-faced cabinet. "Would you like something to drink?"

She didn't recognize his last name. Maybe it was her age. "No, thank you. No, I'm not a security guard."

Emma filled a glass with tap water. "Hazel never told me about you. She and I have such lovely talks when she's here."

Callum imagined Emily talked anyone's ear off when they visited. Plumbers. Electricians. Maybe the mail carrier. And her kids when they came over.

"She is such a dear," Emily said. "I know she doesn't have to stay when she delivers my meals, but she does. She genuinely cares about me. She's become a friend of mine even if she doesn't consider me one of hers."

"I'm sure she does."

"She's a very good chef." Emily patted her tummy, which wasn't protruding much at all. "She felt so bad for leaving that job of hers, but she belongs on her own."

"She felt bad?" Hazel hadn't mentioned that.

"Oh, yes. Hazel is such a conscientious person. She wouldn't hurt a flea. She worried about the owner of that restaurant…what was it called? Carolyn's Kitchen. She and Carolyn were good friends. Carolyn didn't want her to leave but Hazel followed her heart, and good thing she did. She's going to be very successful someday. You wait and see."

"She already seems to be."

"It's nice to see that she's finally found a husband and father for Evie. I'm going to have to ask her why she didn't tell me."

Husband and father? Callum stood, finished putting the containers into the freezer, feeling a lump form in his throat. He swallowed.

Emily smiled fondly at him, making him more uncomfortable. "I always knew it would only be a matter of time. Hazel is so pretty and nice. And her daughter is sweet as can be. But I'm sure you already know that."

"Hazel and I aren't married," he said.

Emily waved her hand in dismissal. "You don't have to get married to be a family these days. Look at Kurt Russell and Goldie Hawn. They're a model of how healthy families survive without being taken down by old traditions."

Her refreshing outlook did little to calm his inner turmoil. Being a part of Hazel's family would bring heavy responsibility. Callum would go crazy worrying for their well-being. His line of work brought plenty of danger. The people he protected clients against might go after his family to get to him.

Emily stepped closer and gave his forearm a few pats. "If you aren't romantic with her yet, you will be.

I'm good at reading people and you seem like a decent man. Unlike Evie's father. Hazel says she won't go for the gorgeous and rich types ever again." She observed him critically. "You're gorgeous, but I bet you aren't rich. Bodyguards don't make that much, do they?"

What did she mean by that? Hazel had told her she would never be with anyone wealthy?

"I don't make millions protecting my clients, but I make more than average," he said, not going into any details of the company that employed him—or the fact that he was a Colton. This woman was already making him talk too much.

"I better get back to Hazel and Evie." He began to back off.

"Yes, I'm sure they are anxiously waiting your return. It was very nice to meet you, Mr. Colton." Emily's face sobered as though something dawned on her. "Colton. You're Payne Colton's son?"

"I am." Maybe she wouldn't be so quick to pair him with Hazel now.

"I heard about the shooting. Who would do such a thing? And how is he doing? Is he going to survive?"

"We don't know yet." Reminded of his father, he planned to go see him in the morning.

Emily's mouth pursed as though mulling over something troubling. "What I said before about Hazel not seeing anyone rich... I didn't mean..."

Callum held his hand up. "Don't worry about it. Hazel and I aren't together that way."

"Are you working for her? She hired you? Is she in danger?"

"Evie witnessed a crime. I'm staying with her until the suspect is captured."

Emily put her hand over her mouth with a sharp inhale. Lowering her hand, she asked, "Is she all right?"

"Yes."

"Because you're watching over her." Emily smiled. "You might come from wealth but you're not the same ilk as Edgar. I can tell."

Right. Because she was good at reading people. Maybe that was true. When a person lived as long as Emily had, they grew wise. She had no magical insight. And Callum would not give credence to anything she had shared with him today. Even if he secretly wanted to.

EVIE WOULDN'T EAT her vegetables. Hazel had neared her limit of tolerance just when Callum reentered the suite. She quelled the surge of gladness seeing him made her feel. Evie, on the other hand, did nothing to hide hers. She jumped off the chair and ran to him with a squeal and a loud "Cal-em!"

He bent as she crashed into him, tiny arms going around his torso, reaching his sides and no farther. Callum lifted her and carried her to the table.

"Mommy and I made cookies today. Chocolate."

"Chocolate chip," Hazel corrected.

"And we watched *Frozen*."

"For the thirtieth time," Hazel quipped.

"Hectic day?" Callum asked her.

Seeing his teasing grin, she said, "Evie wanted to go for ice cream. I've been arguing with her all afternoon. Now she won't eat her vegetables."

Callum put Evie down. "Why don't you go do as your mother says? You don't want to grow up short and puny, do you?"

Hazel had to hide a laugh.

"What's puny?" Evie asked.

"Littler than everyone else your age. Go on."

"Will you read to me first?"

Hazel rolled her eyes behind her daughter's back. What a manipulator. But even at her worst, Evie was the most precious thing ever.

"After you do as your mother says and finish your dinner."

With a pout and much slower steps back to the table, Evie climbed up onto the chair and picked up her fork. As she began eating, Hazel opened her mouth in awe and looked at Callum.

"The man with the magical touch," she said, and then regretted letting that slip. It sounded so sexual.

His eyes heated as he appeared to register the same meaning.

"How did it go today?" Hazel asked, going into the kitchen to resume preparing dinner for herself and Callum.

"Good. Emily Watson is quite the character." He followed her, inspecting what she was doing.

She was making linguine and clams. After that exchange she hoped he didn't guess that she had chosen this recipe because he had said it sounded good.

With everything out and ready to go, she started the gas stove burner and cooked the garlic.

"Is that going to be what I think it's going to be?" he asked, standing close behind her and to her left, looking over her shoulder.

She turned her head, her face inches from his. He smelled like outside and subtle cologne.

"Yes." Her voice sounded sultry to her own ears.

His eyes shifted to hers, then lowered to look at her mouth.

"Are you making that for me?"

"We all have to eat," she said.

He grinned, as if to tell her he knew better.

When the garlic cloves browned, she removed them and dumped them in the sink. They had served their purpose. In their place went three and a half dozen clams, some wine and water. She covered the pan and soon the suite began to smell like the beginnings of a delicious seafood plate.

"Can I help?" he asked.

"Sure. I need a big pan of boiling water."

While he did that, she saw the clams had opened and removed them to cool. She reduced the remaining liquid in the pan, feeling Callum watch her.

"The clams need to be removed from their shells," she said, uncomfortable with the manly way he regarded her, eyes warmer than enjoying the preparation of a good meal would cause. "But leave a few of them in their shells for garnish."

"Roger that." He began removing the clams and she salted the boiling water and added linguine.

"Now what?" he asked.

She put butter into the sauté pan, poured in the clams and added seasoning. Once the ingredients began to boil, she reduced the heat and waited until the pasta was al dente. She strained the pasta and combined it with the sauce. After cooking that awhile, she turned off the heat and tossed in grated Parmigiano-Reggiano.

"Voilà," she said.

He reached past her and picked up a clam.

Hazel swatted his hand. "Contamination."

"I used to do that growing up. Drove the cooks mad."

"It drives me mad. You should have sat through the food safety class I had in college." Spooning the pasta onto two plates, she put the clams in shells on each and then sprinkled a little more Parmigiano-Reggiano on top. She handed Callum a plate and took hers to the table.

Evie had finished her dinner and immersed herself in a coloring book. Hazel and Callum ate in silence for a time.

"This is fantastic," Callum said. "Whoever marries you will have a tough time keeping the pounds off."

Whoever? A quick flash of his being that person made her pause in taking her next bite. Cooking for him would be fun. Among other things…like sex.

"It promotes exercise," she said.

"Is that how you stay in shape?"

"Mommy takes me on bike rides," Evie said as she colored. "We go camping, too."

"Horseback riding," Hazel said. "I used to hike when I lived in Colorado." Having a child disrupted a routine.

"You like sports?" Callum asked.

"Not softball or football or things like that. Just hiking, biking."

"I want a horse," Evie said with a glance at Callum. "Mommy says I'm not old enough."

"You probably aren't. You could get hurt pretty bad if you fall off."

"I still want a horse."

Hazel had adored horses when she was a kid, too. What wasn't to love? They were beautiful animals. She had gotten Evie some books on horses, along with some model horses that she played with often.

"Well, when you're old enough to take care of it yourself, then we'll talk," Hazel said.

Evie looked at her mother and saw she meant it and didn't argue. She went back to drawing.

"Why didn't you go back to Colorado after you had Evie?" Callum asked Hazel.

She wondered over the suddenness of his question. He must have been thinking about it before Evie had joined the conversation. Was he trying to learn more about her? Was he interested?

"I like it here. I like the community and the climate. It's warmer and drier here. We go back to Pagosa Springs to see my parents, usually on the holidays."

"Don't you want to be closer to your family?" he asked. "Especially with Evie?"

He had hit on one of the things that had kept her away. "Actually, I love my parents but they can be intrusive. My mother would be at my house daily or demand I come see her. She already does that now. She complains she doesn't see us enough. It's like she has a hard time letting us go as kids. We're adults now, with our own lives and aspirations. I wish she'd treat us that way."

"Have you told her that?"

"Yes. She just says she loves me and wants to see me as much as possible. It's better that I'm in Arizona and she's in Colorado, at least for now. I might want to change that as Evie gets older. We'll see. What about you? What kind of relationship do you have with your family?"

"You said you would read to me," Evie interrupted.

"Go get your jammies on," Hazel said.

"Aww," Evie complained, but she went to do as told.

"I'm not very close to them, except Marlowe. I never talked much with my parents. I don't know if that's because my father was so busy working at Colton Oil. I would like to change that, though. Ever since my dad was shot, I've thought about that. I want to be closer to him and the rest of my family."

Hazel thought that was quite sentimental of him. She liked that.

Just then Evie bounded into the room in her pj's.

"Are you ready now?" Callum stood and went to the sofa. Evie grabbed a book from the coffee table and sat right next to him.

Evie's easy acceptance of Callum troubled Hazel. What if she got too attached and then the time to part ways came? Regardless, seeing her daughter bonding with a father figure warmed her and made her yearn to give her that all the time.

She watched as Evie tipped her head to the side to see the pages better and listened to Callum's deep voice reading the children's book. She could feel his affection, hear it in his animated tone. She cleaned the kitchen with a soft smile, not wanting to fall for Callum but afraid she would if he continued to befriend Evie.

Thirty minutes later, Evie's head rested on his shoulder, her eyes closed. Callum put the book on the sofa beside him and carefully lifted the child, cradling her and standing. He looked to Hazel, who led the way to their room. She pulled back the covers and Callum laid her down. Hazel tucked her in.

Then she joined Callum at the foot of the bed. He wore an awed look, no sign of his usual tensing. Evie was working her magic on him. Hazel wasn't sure if just any child could have done that for him. She hoped he would someday get over whatever had happened to make him decide not to protect women and children.

"She's something," Callum said.

"Yes. Of course, she is to me. I'm her mother."

"She seems smart for five. Her understanding of words is really good. Advanced."

His fondness sank into her as she sensed his genuine reaction. He sounded like a proud father. Hazel had noticed Evie was a quick learner, too.

They stood there awhile, until Hazel's awareness of him changed. His feelings for Evie melted her, lowered her guard. An intimate connection grew out of their mutual appreciation of her daughter. Her insides reacted, sparked, and instinct nearly made her move closer. But with him she needed to be careful. She would not make the same mistake she had made with Ed.

She couldn't look away. He lifted his hand and curled it behind her neck. Unprepared for this, she let him lean in and kiss her. His mouth pressed firmly to hers as inexplicable chemistry took over. She put her body against his as she slid her hands up his chest. With that encouragement, he turned the kiss into a flaming ball of passion, pressing harder as they added tongues to the erotic play.

Hazel could barely catch her breath as he devoured her. Callum had his hands on her back, holding her against him. He all but danced her around and guided her through the doorway, into the hallway—and away from Evie—until she came against the wall. Hazel had enough presence of mind to be thankful for that.

Now his hands were free to caress her elsewhere, and he wasted no time running them over her breasts. She had a crazy thought that making a baby with him would be wild and wonderful. He unbuttoned her blouse. Exposing her bra, he touched her again.

He worked the front clasp and once he had her bared, he stopped kissing her and lowered his head to her left nipple. Next, he lifted her off the floor to bring her more to his level, planting his mouth on her right nipple. Hazel wrapped her legs around him and gripped his head, urging him to her mouth. She wasn't ready to stop kissing him.

Callum pressed his lips to hers and she fell into a whirlwind of torrid desire. She fumbled with his shirt, needing more than anything to have her hands on his chest—a chest she had only been able to look at up until now. Slipping her hands under the material, using the wall for support, she had to draw away to catch her breath.

As she reveled in the hard panel of muscle under smooth skin, Callum kissed her neck and jaw before taking her mouth again.

"Mommy?"

Jarred from this uncontrollable state of sexual frenzy, Hazel jerked her hands from underneath Callum's shirt as he abruptly stepped away and her feet lowered to the floor. He stared at her, visibly stunned but his gaze still lustful.

Appalled by her behavior—just outside the room where Evie slept—Hazel put her clothes back together and rushed into the room, trying to calm her racing heart and breath.

"Yes, honey?"

Evie blinked up at her sleepily, thankfully oblivious to what had occurred in the hall. "Will you turn off the light?"

Seeing the lamp between the two queen beds was on, she bent and turned it off. Then she went to Evie and kissed her forehead. "Go back to sleep, sweetie."

But Evie had already done so, slumbering peacefully. Hazel pulled the blankets up over her tiny shoulders and then returned to the hall, where Callum still stood. He looked much more composed now. In fact, he looked downright aloof.

"Everything okay?" he asked.

"Yes. She just wanted the light off." She studied him carefully. His eyes were a mask now, almost cold they were so remote. He had withdrawn. Granted, that hot encounter had shaken her to her core as well, but he seemed to have withdrawn much more than was warranted. Didn't he marvel over how spectacular it had felt? She did. And she felt slighted that he might reduce it to something meaningless.

"Look... I'm sorry about..." Callum began.

He couldn't even put what happened into words. Maybe he refused to, because doing so would add meaning to it.

"Good night, Callum." Miffed, she went into her room and shut the door, wishing she could slam it. But she didn't want to wake up Evie.

She jerked herself into her pajamas, muttering, "Imbecile," before getting into bed. She turned on the television. It would be a long time before she settled down enough to sleep.

Emily must have given him an earful about her and Evie, in particular about how Ed had run off after discovering Hazel was pregnant. Emily herself had a blended family, having remarried after divorcing her first husband, whom she had met when she was a teenager. No one should ever marry at such a young age. People, at least in Hazel's opinion, needed time to grow before they made such a huge commitment. Spending your entire life with someone was kind of an important decision. Emily strongly opposed a too-impulsive marriage, saying it was just a legality, when love was the thing that kept couples together, not a piece of paper and a few laws.

Whatever Emily had planted in his head, it had made him think. It had brought him closer to Evie, a child and Hazel's daughter, two things he had for some reason sworn off.

Trying to get distracted by the nature program she had turned to a low volume on television, Hazel failed miserably. Her spirits sank when she considered how she'd celebrated the fantastic feeling of kissing Callum, while he apparently shunned such an emotion. The cops had better find that shooter soon. Hazel needed to get away from a man like Callum Colton. She'd be better off with someone more in her league.

Chapter Five

The next afternoon, Callum arranged for a car rental and went to visit a comatose Payne at the hospital. He brought with him Hazel and Evie, who skipped beside Hazel on their way toward the entrance. Callum had noticed a distinct change in Hazel this morning. He wondered if he had mistaken the way she'd said good night and shut the door before he could even respond. Was she upset that he had kissed her? He'd rather have this resolved before going in to see his father. Some of his family would be there and he didn't need to have to explain Hazel's mood.

He stopped her on the cement in front of the doors. "Is something wrong?"

Evie's head tipped up and she looked at him.

"No," Hazel said.

"Last night…"

Evie turned to her mother.

"Don't worry about it. We'll wait for Kerry to find and catch the shooter and then we can both get back to our lives."

Callum met Evie's eyes as she glanced back at him and then she asked her mother, "Mommy, are you mad?"

"Not now, Evie."

Callum could see Hazel was quite upset, her keen gaze firing arrows at him. "I didn't mean to hurt you. It just—"

"Do we have to talk about this now?" Hazel interrupted.

It might not be appropriate to talk in front of Evie, but he doubted she'd really understand and he wasn't going to say anything grossly offensive. "I'm sorry, that's all."

"Yes, I could tell you were."

She thought he was sorry for kissing her? But was he? "Sorry" wasn't the right word. *Concerned* would be a better choice but he couldn't tell her that.

"Don't worry," she repeated, sounding more sincere now. "Whatever you're going through, I get it. I don't need to get involved with another rich guy, so let's just make the best of this situation, okay?"

"Who is Rich?" Evie asked.

Callum almost smiled. Evie thought Rich was a man.

"You're judging me because my family has money?"

"*You* have money. I don't mean to judge. I don't know you well enough. All I can do right now is go on what I do know."

"My *parents* are rich."

"They don't share any of it with you?" Hazel asked, more of a challenge.

He didn't like what she was implying. "We all have trust funds, but—"

"Well, there you go." Hazel resumed walking toward the door, Evie in tow.

Evie looked back at him and then up at her mother. In the elevator, she asked, "Why are you mad, Mommy?"

"I'm not mad."

Callum watched her as he stood beside her, clearly disagreeing.

Hazel felt a little contrite over her reaction. She couldn't blame him for not feeling what she'd felt in that kiss. Some men treated women poorly, without empathy, and others didn't intend to cause harm. Callum hadn't meant to snub her, humiliate her or make her feel rejected. Even though, absurdly, she had experienced all of those emotions. Or maybe she was just mad for putting herself into a situation that resembled that with Ed far too much.

Callum entered the hospital room first. Hazel was struck by the extent of the medical equipment and the tubes coming from Payne Colton. She had never been this close to someone in such critical condition. She had seen a coma patient on television, of course, but the real thing came with a considerably larger impact.

There were three others in the room, two men and a woman.

"Mommy?" Evie said in a quiet tone, tugging on her sleeve.

"Yes, Evie?" Hazel noticed that everyone except Payne had turned toward Evie, who was oblivious to the attention she'd gained.

"I like Cal-em," Evie said.

"I know you do." Hazel saw a good-looking, dirty-blond-haired man on the other side of Payne's hospital bed smile slightly.

"Don't be mad at him," Evie said, eyebrows arched upward in earnest appeal.

The striking woman with light blond hair looked very businesslike and snickered a bit, while the man next to her in a suit smiled.

"I'm not mad at him," Hazel said, glancing at Callum, whose eyes held a teasingly smug glint.

Evie's expression said she didn't understand. "You were mad."

"Evie, not now," Hazel said sternly.

Evie went into one of her lower-lipped pouts.

"Is my brother stirring up trouble?" the woman asked Evie.

"No," Evie retorted, eliciting a round of laughter.

"How did you manage to make such a fine friend, Callum?" the woman asked.

"Hazel, this is my twin sister, Marlowe," Callum said. "That's her fiancé, Bowie."

"Hello, very nice to meet you. Callum told me about you," Hazel said to Marlowe. She liked that Callum had such a high regard for his twin.

"And this gentleman over here is Rafe," Callum said, "my younger brother. He's also Detective Wilder's fiancé."

The adopted brother. Hazel recalled Callum telling her that. Not only were the Coltons wealthy, they were all so good-looking! Hotness filled the room. And even though Bowie wasn't a Colton, he was also quite a treat for the eyes.

"I'm going to go get a soda," Bowie said. "Does anyone else want anything?"

"Juice," Evie said.

"A punch or mixed berry is fine," Hazel said.

Everyone else declined and Bowie started for the door. "One juice coming right up," he said.

"How is he today?" Callum gestured toward Payne.

"The same," Rafe said.

They all fell into somber silence.

"What do the police think happened?" Hazel asked.

"He received an email saying Ace was switched at birth and isn't a Colton by blood," Marlowe said. "Naturally, Ace wasn't happy to hear about that."

"The police think Ace tried to kill Payne?" Hazel asked.

"He's the only one who appears to have a motive," Callum said. "But I don't think he did it."

"I don't, either," Rafe said.

"He's our brother," Marlowe said. "Of course he didn't try to kill Dad."

"He said he was home the night of the shooting," Callum said. "There's no video surveillance supporting that."

"Isn't Kerry looking for someone shorter?" Callum said.

"Yes," Marlowe answered.

Callum moved closer to Payne. Hazel watched him take hold of his hand.

"I wish you'd wake up, Dad," he said. "You could tell us yourself who shot you."

Could the shooting have something to do with Ace being switched at birth? Maybe the culprit didn't want to be discovered. Then why send an email making that announcement? Unless the one who had actually swapped the babies wasn't the one who sent the email.

"Do you know who sent the email?" she asked.

"No. I have someone from IT at Colton Oil looking into that," Marlowe said.

"Hey, Callum, how long are you going to be in town?" Rafe asked.

"Indefinitely. I have a new job starting at the end of the month but it is local. I'm free until then."

Marlowe turned her gaze to Hazel, appearing to grow more curious. "When did you two meet? Callum never tells me when he has a new girlfriend."

Why did Callum's twin think Hazel and Callum were together like that?

"Kerry is investigating a murder that Hazel's daughter witnessed," Rafe said. "Callum is protecting them."

"Oh." Marlowe looked from Hazel to her twin. "And you already made her mad?"

"Marlowe…" Callum protested.

"Sorry, brother. I'm not buying it. You look at her like she's more than a client," Marlowe said.

Hazel turned to Callum. He looked at her in a particular way? She hadn't noticed. But then, she hadn't glanced at him much since they entered the hospital room. Every time she did she felt an unwelcome spark, which only brought her back to his regrets over kissing her. She could not afford to want something he would never give.

LATER THAT DAY, Callum couldn't stop thinking about what Marlowe had said—that he had looked at Hazel in such a way that gave Marlowe the impression they were an item. He hadn't been aware that he had done that. If he had no control over the way he regarded Hazel, wasn't aware of how she affected him, how could he control how he felt about this relationship? Was he calling it a relationship? A zap of alarm pricked him as he realized they were starting to have one. How could he call it anything else? They had kissed. They had almost had sex. They'd have a casual relationship, then.

He walked with her into the inn. They'd go back to their suite and be alone again, except for Evie.

Halfway through the lobby, Hazel stopped, Evie by her side.

"Carolyn?" Hazel asked.

Callum followed her gaze to a woman standing by a cart full of food chafing dishes. A blonde with a bob in a smart black skirt suit with a white top, she seemed surprised to see Hazel.

He stopped next to Hazel as she leaned in for a hug. Obviously the two knew each other, and judging by the catering supplies, they shared food as an interest. Had Hazel worked with this woman in the past?

"What are you doing here?" Carolyn asked, moving back from the hug, smiling as her eyes roamed over Hazel's face.

"I'm staying here."

"We're being protected," Evie said in her cute voice.

Carolyn crouched down to the girl's level. "Well, hello, Evie. You've grown since the last time I saw you."

"I'm five."

Carolyn laughed a little and stood, sending Hazel a questioning look. "Why are you being protected?" She glanced at Callum.

"It's a long story," Hazel said.

"I saw a man get hit in the head with a rock and he died," Evie said.

Carolyn looked down at her. "Oh, my." Then she returned her attention to Hazel. "Are you all right?"

"Cal-em is protecting us," Evie said.

"That's enough, Evie."

Hazel must say that a lot to her daughter. The more time he spent with them, the more he learned of their close connection. He had always thought a mother and a daughter must have a special bond. Then his Annabel had died and he'd avoided anything mother-daughter altogether.

"What happened?" Carolyn asked.

Who was this woman and how did Hazel know her? He waited for Hazel to give a quick summary of why they had ended up here and then she finally turned to him.

"Callum is a bodyguard."

"Oh." Carolyn sounded impressed. "A bodyguard, huh? You must be special now."

"Not really." Hazel smiled humbly.

"Yes, she is," Evie said, hanging onto Hazel's arm.

"Callum Colton." He held out his hand to the woman. "And you are…?"

Carolyn's mouth dropped open. "Colton? As in Colton Oil?"

He had grown accustomed to people recognizing him by his surname. They were sort of like celebrities in town; some regarded them in awe and some in loathing, depending on which Colton's path they had crossed. "Payne Colton is my father."

"Oh, yes. I'm so sorry. I heard about your father. My deepest condolences."

What had she heard? "He isn't dead yet."

"But in a coma, right? That's terrible." Carolyn looked from him to Hazel. "How did you manage to meet up with a Colton bodyguard?"

"Completely by accident," Hazel said. "He was across the street when the man was struck and came to help us."

"Aren't you the lucky one?" Carolyn smiled.

"How long have you and Hazel known each other?" Callum asked.

Hazel put her hand to her forehead. "I'm sorry. How rude of me. Callum, this is Carolyn Johnson. She owns Carolyn's Kitchen. I told you about working for her."

"Yes, I remember. Very nice to meet you."

After a moment where she seemed miffed that her friend hadn't mentioned her, Carolyn looked at Hazel. "She was one of the best chefs I've ever had."

Callum thought she sounded wry, even cynical, and wondered why.

"Thank you, Carolyn. You always treated me so well. Restaurants can be so stressful, but you were always calm and courteous."

Hazel didn't seem to notice her friend's tone. Pleasing customers with food did seem demanding, as did the work hours. Service jobs were unfortunately thankless, most of the time. A shame, given how enjoyable going out for dinner or whatnot was.

"We have to keep customers coming back." Carolyn sounded faintly derisive.

Hazel looked at the cart behind her. "You're making a catering delivery? You normally have others do that."

"Yes, normally."

Hazel hesitated, finally registering Carolyn's sarcasm. "How are you doing? H-how's the restaurant?"

"Oh, I had to close it."

That came as a total shock to Hazel, Callum saw by her rounded eyes and dropped jaw. "No. What happened? You were doing so well."

"Yes. After you left, I couldn't find another chef as good as you. And me?" She lifted her eyes and glanced at Callum ruefully. "I am not a cook. I'm a businesswoman. This lady, however..." She gestured toward Hazel. "She is *amazing*."

She sounded different now, not so brash. Did she mean the compliment?

"Carolyn. I'm so sorry. I had no idea. You should have called me." Hazel seemed genuinely remorseful, as though she felt responsible for the closure.

"You made your decision and you gave me more than enough notice." Carolyn shrugged. "The luck of the draw, I guess. The chefs I hired after you left couldn't prepare the meals the way you did. Customers slowly stopped coming. And then I had a bad review and it was all over. I got out before it ruined me completely. Now I work for a catering company." She gestured back at the cart. "A tough transition, going from entrepreneur to servant."

Callum was good at reading people and he could tell her transition had been especially difficult. Carolyn made a good show of being a good sport but the loss had to be painful. Who wouldn't feel that way after accomplishing so much, just to lose it? He felt bad for her. He couldn't imagine how Hazel felt.

"Is there anything I can do to help?" Hazel asked.

"No. Don't worry about me. It's been really great to see you again. How is your food delivery service going?"

Hazel paused before saying, "It's going all right. I wouldn't say I'm a raging success. I'm staying afloat."

Carolyn smiled. "I'm sure it's just a matter of time before you are a raging success, artist that you are. I know firsthand how your cooking can make a big impact on revenue."

"Oh, my gosh, Carolyn. I never intended to cause you to lose business. I set everything up so the recipes would be easy to follow. You shouldn't have suffered at all."

Carolyn shrugged again. "You made quite an impression for me, you know."

Hazel seemed confused. "No, I didn't know that."

"I don't see how. Patrons asked to thank you personally all the time. They complimented your cooking to me more times than you know. I didn't tell you at the time, but I was very worried about how things would go after you left. I respected your decision, though, and didn't want to influence you. You were my friend more than you were my chef."

"Oh." Hazel leaned in and hugged Carolyn again. "I wish you would have told me. I could have worked part-time for you or something. Anything to help you not lose your restaurant. I know how much it meant to you."

Moving back, Hazel looked at Carolyn with heartfelt sympathy and regret.

Carolyn met the emotion with stiffening aloofness. She didn't like pity, that much Callum could see. Neither did he.

"Really, Hazel. I'm a grown woman. I can take care of myself. I'll do the servant thing for a while and then start up a new venture. You know me. I'm no quitter."

Callum believed that. He didn't really know the other woman but she had an indomitable energy about her. No wonder she and Hazel were such good friends. While Hazel wasn't aggressive, she had tenacity and ambition as well as talent.

"No, you are not. And you are a smart business-woman. You belong in your own element."

"Ms. Johnson?" a voice interrupted.

Callum saw a hotel worker approach Carolyn.

"We're ready for you," the hotel worker said.

Carolyn turned to Hazel. "Have to go now. So nice running into you."

"You, too." Hazel touched her arm before Carolyn pushed the cart, following the hotel worker, probably to a conference room.

It took Hazel a few long seconds to start walking toward the elevator with Callum. She apparently had fallen into melancholic thought.

"Why do people always think it's their fault when decisions they make result in others having a run of bad luck?" he asked.

That pulled her out of her reverie. "W-what?"

"You aren't responsible for other people's misfortunes."

They stepped into the elevator, Evie holding Hazel's hand, head tipped back as usual. Her curiosity made her listen intently to everything said by the adults around her.

"I created the recipes," Hazel said.

"Which should have helped her."

"It did, but you heard her. The chefs she hired after me couldn't replicate them."

He took a moment to marvel that she didn't see what he did. "You're an artist first, Hazel."

She blinked a few times as though startled by what he brought to light.

"Your passion went into every one of those recipes, those meals you oversaw in the kitchen," he said.

"But…they had the recipes and I wrote detailed instructions."

"*But* they didn't have the heart. Only you had that. You made Carolyn's Kitchen."

"No. Carolyn made Carolyn's Kitchen," Hazel argued. "She was an aggressive businesswoman. Driven. Smart. She hired me to help her make her dream a reality. She was a good person."

"Then she should have gone to culinary school if she wanted to run a restaurant," he said.

Hazel rubbed her forehead with two fingers.

The elevator doors opened and Evie tugged Hazel toward the exit. Callum wanted to say more, do more about this discussion. But he walked to their suite, mindful of the energetic Evie, and let them inside.

Evie bounded toward the television and Hazel set her up with an animated show. Then Hazel walked into the kitchen—and took out a pizza from the freezer. No gourmet meal for tonight.

Glad Evie's overactive mind had something to keep her occupied, Callum joined Hazel behind the island, where Hazel had picked up a pen and hovered the point over a notepad.

He wasn't fooled. She used idle tasks to help ease her tormented thoughts.

Putting his hands on her upper arms, he asked, "Did you leave on bad terms?"

She shook her head. "I gave her a lot of notice."

"Then why are you beating yourself up over this?"

She put down the pen and ran her hand over the top of her hair. Facing the living room where Evie watched television, she stilled. Callum didn't think she registered Evie's presence all that much, so absorbed did she appear to be in her separation with Carolyn.

Finally, she turned to him. "I left for selfish reasons. I had Evie and…"

"You had to look out for your own."

"Yes, but Carolyn would have never betrayed me."

Callum moved to stand near her, gripping her shoulders and making her face him. "It's okay to want to forge your own way in life. You don't have to work hard to make others succeed. I think, deep down, you knew you had greater potential than what you got working for your friend."

Hazel's captivating, green-gold eyes met his soulfully, and she added a slow and telling shake of her head. He had nailed what she felt.

"Am I right?" he asked to make her confront it.

With teary eyes she nodded.

He drew her into an embrace. "You followed your heart, Hazel. No one can condemn you for that, least of all me. I did the same."

His father hadn't been happy with his decision not to join the Colton Oil team. Neither had his mother. "I know what it's like to want something others don't understand or expect from you."

"I just hate to see good people fail," Hazel said.

"I bet she'll have a comeback. Maybe she won't open another restaurant but she'll find success somewhere."

At last the first glimmer of a smile emerged on her pretty face. She had her hair back today, exposing her expressive eyes, prominent cheekbones and full lips he longed to kiss right then.

"That's better. A woman like you should never be sad," he said.

Her smile expanded. "Why me?"

Why indeed? He had to think a minute as to why he'd even said such a thing. Although he inwardly cringed with the truth, he said, "You're beautiful inside and out."

"Wow, the last man who said something that nice to me probably lied."

He was glad she made light of such a serious compliment. "Ed?"

"Yes. He said sweet nothings to me a lot. He had me really believing I was special."

Wait a second. Was she making light or did she think Callum had just said something nice and was being insincere about it?

"Surely you've had others. I can't be the only one who complimented you over the last five-plus years."

"No." She shook her head and moved into the kitchen. "No one."

He followed her, leaning against the island counter as she began to prepare dinner. "No one?" There had to have been *someone*.

"No one serious," she said.

But she had dated. "How many have you dated?"

She made a funny face. "You make it sound like I slept with all of them."

"Unintended. How many guys have you been out with?" He discovered he really wanted to know.

"Not many. Three. No, four. Two were one date and the other relationships lasted a few weeks."

He reflected on his own experiences. Annabel had died almost five years ago. He and Hazel had been single and getting past old hurts for the same length of time. Maybe for too long. Hazel had a better excuse than he did. She had Evie to keep her busy, and it would be a lot harder for her to find a man suitable to take over a father role.

Father role.

"What about you?"

Hazel's question spared him from painful memories. He had already faced more of those than he could deal with.

"Girlfriends?" Had she capitalized on the direction of their conversation?

"How many have you *had* since your last serious relationship?" She grinned before opening the oven to check on the pizza.

Wily woman. Lucky for her, this was something he could talk about.

"Not many. Seven."

She planted her hands on the counter beside him. "Seven?"

That was a lot to her? "Yes. Minimal dates."

She mouthed *minimal dates* and scrunched up her brow in question. "You cannot tell me that some of those women didn't mean something more than a date."

As she chopped lettuce for what he presumed would be a healthy salad to go with their not-so-healthy pizza, he realized she had concluded he had had not more than a casual fling in the past five years. How could she? She knew nothing about him, really.

"What happened to you?"

Her earnest question put him at odds with how to respond. "Nothing."

She chopped a carrot, the knife hitting the cutting board hard. "Did any of them matter?"

"They all mattered."

She continued chopping and, without looking at him, said, "No. Really matter."

He had to be honest. "They all mattered, Hazel. They just deserved better than what I could give."

"How many were you serious with?"

Why did she ask? Why was that important to her? Was she trying to find out what she was up against?

"Five or six. Some lasted a few months, others a week or two. One pretty recent." When it got too serious, then he walked.

She stopped chopping the poor carrot, her head bowing slightly and her shoulders slumping equally indiscriminately. Still keeping the knife on the cutting board, flush with a carrot, she turned her head to see him. "What happened, Callum?"

He silently cursed. No one had ever pushed him like this. He glanced over at Evie, who was still engrossed in her movie and not paying them any attention.

He had never told anyone about Annabel. Few knew she had been his girlfriend. Back then, he had been mainly in Texas, but he worked a lot. He had drifted away from his family, only seeing them on Christmas and Thanksgiving. He had brought Annabel to both holidays that last year. When asked later if he was still seeing her, he had only said no. Now he was about to tell Hazel. Why her?

He met her eyes and could feel his soul pouring out through his. She blinked solemnly, putting down the knife and facing him. She put her hand on his cheek. "It's okay. You don't have to tell me."

The selflessness of her saying that tore through all of his resistance. She meant it. She respected his sensitivities. The connection between them strengthened, his to her, anyway. She was someone he could trust. Maybe it was timing more than anything else. Maybe, finally, he was ready to put in words what he had so far kept to himself.

"She died nearly five years ago." Saying that felt like

a regurgitation, it came up from inside him like sour milk. He felt sick. He put both hands on the kitchen island counter and lowered his head. "I've never told anyone this."

Hazel's hand touched his back, high and on the left. She caressed him in comfort. She didn't press him, just waited. He could go on or he could stop right there. She wouldn't force anything out of him.

"She was pregnant." Callum choked back a powerful wave of anguish.

"Oh," she breathed in heartfelt empathy. Not pity, no sympathy, just a profound understanding. She was a mother. She must know how terrible it would be to lose her child.

"We knew it was going to be a girl," he said, barely getting the words out before his anguish became too unbearable.

Unable to continue, he pushed off the counter and walked toward his room.

Chapter Six

Hazel ordered room service the next morning. She had picked at her dinner the night before while Evie devoured hers. Callum had not come out of his room the rest of the night. Hazel had lost her appetite after hearing his gut-wrenching confession. She could not imagine the awfulness of losing a person you loved and a child all in one fell swoop. She had to assume he had really cared for the woman. Such crushing emotion would not have overcome him had he not.

She prepared Evie's breakfast of cereal and fruit. Evie had complained about the fruit but Hazel said that after junking it up last night, she had to eat healthy today.

Hazel sat down at the dining table and began eating with her daughter. Looking at Evie's innocent face as she scooped milky bites into her mouth, Hazel thought again about how difficult it must be for Callum to be around them. She had thought about that a lot since the previous night. She also had so many questions she would never be able to ask, would not ask. How had the woman died? How long were they together? Were they engaged? Did he love her as much as he appeared to? Now she understood why he usually refused to take cases involving families.

He had broken down just voicing that she had died and their unborn baby girl along with her. Callum was not a weak man mentally. He was tough, fearless. Look at his profession. He was a bodyguard, one of the best in the world. But talking about the woman from his past had brought him to his knees.

And then there were the other thoughts she had. The selfish ones, like, what did his loss mean for her, Hazel? She could no longer deny she had begun to have feelings for him. What would it do to her if he decided to turn away? He had already withdrawn and it had been nearly five years since the tragedy. *Five years.* Something terrible must have happened. Something sudden. A car accident? No one ever got over losing love—or a child.

"Mommy?"

Grateful to be pulled out of her never-ending contemplations, she looked at Evie.

"You're not eating."

Hazel hadn't touched her cereal. She still wasn't hungry. "I know."

"How come?" Evie swung her legs under the chair and table.

"I have a lot on my mind."

"Cal-em?"

"Finish eating, Evie." Dang if her daughter wasn't a perceptive little thing.

"Were you mad at him again?"

"No."

"Good, because I want him to be my daddy."

Where had that come from? Daddy?

"He's not your daddy, Evie."

"But I want him to be. I want a daddy. Everybody else has one. Why can't I?"

"Someday you might." Hazel couldn't predict when and she wouldn't rush into anything. The man she married would have to prove himself a good person and role model for Evie.

Callum could be.

Hearing Callum enter the room, Hazel hoped Evie would stop asking all her questions and expressing that she wanted a father.

"Good morning," Hazel said.

Callum was all cleaned up and ready for the day in jeans and a long-sleeved white button-up. Sexy as hell. He didn't seem reluctant to see her after what he'd told her. He seemed back to his normal self—and guarded again.

"Good morning." He picked up the box of cereal Hazel had left out and poured some into a bowl she had also had ready for him. Then he sat across from Evie, who sent him a big smile.

"Somebody got plenty of sleep last night," he said to her, smiling back.

Evie giggled as she chewed a mouthful of cereal.

Callum reached over and put his hand over Hazel's, catching her by surprise. She met his sobering eyes.

"I'm sorry for leaving you the way I did last night," he said. "I've never told anyone about Annabel."

Hazel sensed she had a chance to ask questions. She'd be careful not to push him. "Not even your family?"

He shook his head. "They knew I was seeing her, but they don't know she died."

Her heart went out to him. He had suffered for so long in silence. "Callum, why?"

Pulling his hand away, he looked down at the bowl of cereal. "I...couldn't."

Until now, with her. He had told her.

"Were you engaged?" Hazel asked.

"Not yet. I was going to propose the next weekend."

Seeing him drift off into that dark place, Hazel refrained from asking how the woman and the baby had died. This time she put her hand on his. "Thank you for telling me, Callum. I know how difficult that was for you." He looked at her, the darkness fading. "I want you to know if you ever need someone to just listen, I can be that person for you."

He took her hand in his. "I know you can, but I'm not sure I'll ever be able to talk about her again."

After long seconds of staring into his candid eyes, Hazel nodded. "Okay."

"Are you going to be my daddy?" Evie blurted out.

"Evie," Hazel admonished. "That is rude." Clearly she hadn't understood anything Hazel and Callum had just said. Adult talk.

Callum chuckled. "What makes you ask that, Evie?" Callum asked.

"You keep touching my mommy."

"Your mother is a very good friend of mine."

"I would like you to be my daddy," Evie said.

"Evie, that is enough."

Callum chuckled again and Hazel realized he had done so because she repeated "that's enough" to Evie a lot. She smiled at him and then Evie.

The suite phone rang and Hazel went to answer it.

"Ms. Hart?"

"Yes?"

"We have a package that was delivered by courier for you at the front desk."

That was odd. She hadn't forwarded her mail, but was having it held at the post office. She'd pick it up there on occasion.

"All right. Could you have someone bring it up?" She hung up and faced Callum, who looked at her in question.

"There's a package for me at the front desk."

He immediately looked concerned.

Moments later a hotel worker knocked on the door. Callum answered, taking a cardboard overnight delivery envelope.

Well, it couldn't be a bomb. It was too thin, and looked like it contained a letter.

He inspected it and then ripped open the top, taking out a typed letter. After he read it, he handed it to her.

In capital letters it said:

I WOULDN'T GET TOO COMFORTABLE IF I WERE YOU. JUST BECAUSE YOU'RE WITH A COLTON NOW DOESN'T MEAN YOU'RE INVULNERABLE.

She looked up at him. "The shooter knows we're here." This was a small town and the Dales Inn the only hotel, but being stalked like this scared her.

Nowhere she and Evie went would be safe. The shooter would find them. Hazel looked at her daughter, who had moved into the living room and was watching a cartoon. If anything happened to her...

Hazel recalled how devastated Callum had looked

when he told her his baby girl had died with her mother. Hazel wouldn't survive losing Evie.

He took out his phone. "Hello, Kerry. Someone sent Hazel a threatening letter." When he disconnected he said to Hazel, "She's on her way."

Hazel looked at her daughter again, imagining the shooter hitting her over the head with a rock or shooting her little body. She dropped the letter and put her hand to her mouth.

Callum came to her and pulled her into his arms. "I won't let anything happen to her."

"We can't stay in this inn forever."

"You won't have to. Kerry will find him."

"In the meantime, what if he gets to us? He seemed certain."

He rubbed her back. "I won't let him hurt you. He'll have to get past me to get to you and I won't let that happen."

She believed him, but even with his expertise, he couldn't be one hundred percent sure. She leaned back and met his eyes. Pressed this close to him, with his arms still around her, and especially with their deepened connection, her sexual reaction to him was stronger than ever before. His eyes grew darker with passion. He had to feel the same.

If Evie hadn't been in the room, she would have kissed him. Last night and this morning, Hazel had been tempted to take a chance on him. She had never met a man since Ed who made her feel they could have something lasting.

Easing away, she took a seat at the kitchen island. Callum bent to pick up the letter and placed it on the counter. They waited a few minutes and Kerry called

Callum to say she was on her way up. Moments later, he let her into the room.

"Hey, Evie. I've got something for you." Evie turned from the television as Kerry went to her and handed her a MVPD baseball hat.

Evie inspected it and then put it on her head with a giant smile.

"What do you say, Evie?" Hazel said.

"Thank you!"

Kerry straightened and walked over to the island, where Callum handed her the letter.

She read it and frowned.

Callum gave her the envelope, handling it lightly to preserve fingerprints—if there were any.

"I'll run some forensics on this but my guess is whoever typed this was careful not to leave any traces," Kerry said. "I will check security and can track down where the envelope was mailed from and maybe find out something that way. It might take me some time, though."

"Whatever you can do," Callum said.

THE NEXT FEW days were anticlimactic in that no one sent any more threats and they saw no suspicious characters in the few people who visited their suite. Callum decided it was time for a surprise to break up the monotony—and provide some relief from the constant awareness of Hazel and how much he would like to stop fighting to keep things professional.

A sudden knock on the door signaled the arrival of the surprise.

Hazel looked up from her work in the kitchen, preparing another week's worth of food deliveries while wearing a sexy blue flowing sundress and no shoes. He loved a barefoot chef. He held back a smile as he went to the door to let Patsy Cornwall inside. The assistant led a hotel bellboy into the suite. The bellboy pushed a cart that held a big box and some bags of other items.

"Something for a young girl," he said.

As soon as Evie spotted the packages, she squealed and charged to the entry. The box contained a finished dollhouse mansion. The bags contained everything to furnish it.

He put the box in the living room and let Evie go through all the accessories.

"You didn't."

Glancing up, he saw Hazel had left the kitchen to get a closer look. "I did."

"Callum, this is too much."

"No, it's not. We're cooped up in here. We'll all get a kick out of this." The dollhouse had turrets, curving staircases going up three levels and two porches. The miniature house had incredible detail, from the exterior Victorian trim to interior wallpaper and paint. Evie was going to have a blast.

Callum sent Hazel a mischievous glance.

She looked at her daughter, who was ecstatic over the plethora of doll items.

"You're going to spoil her."

He wanted to spoil her. After seeing her play with her Barbie and how her imagination soon soared, he knew he had to get her one. He had asked Patsy to get every piece of furniture she could find and to include the little things, like dishes. Patsy had it overnighted from a store willing to work with them in a hurry. He had requested it a few days ago. She might break a few things at her age but she'd have this for years, maybe even into adulthood.

It took him a while to set up the dollhouse. Evie had all the accessories scattered on the floor behind the house, which she'd already begun to fill with furniture.

This is what it would have been like with his daughter, had she lived. Callum pushed those thoughts away and went around to the back of the house to help Evie arrange the rooms.

She let him take over and began dressing two Barbie dolls.

"This is Angie," Evie said, showing him the doll dressed in a sparkly dress.

"She's pretty, like you."

Evie beamed up at him before going back to her dolls. He finished arranging furniture and got out of her way.

She instantly dove into playtime, speaking in a low voice, pretending the dolls were talking about going to their new house.

He left her to it and went to the kitchen, where Hazel was cleaning up after a day of cooking. "What's for dinner?"

"Spaghetti."

"Nothing too fancy. Too bad." He dipped his finger into the sauce for a taste.

She swatted the top of his hand. "Raised the way you must have been, you didn't spend much time in a kitchen."

They'd had servants to do the cooking and serving. "Your cooking is irresistible." He could get accustomed to this, a delicious meal every day...and a beautiful woman by his side.

That thought came unbidden. She *was* a beautiful woman, no denying that. And he could get accustomed to a delicious meal every day. What troubled him was much more than how those two things appealed to him. The idea of living with them made him feel good. Too good.

"Why don't you set the table?" Hazel asked.

Callum did so, enjoying the sense of being part of a family unit. Hazel put food on the table and had to force Evie away from the dollhouse. They all sat together, something he hadn't often done with his family growing up. The Coltons had formal gatherings and sat together on holidays. He and his siblings had tremendous respect and love for one another, but Callum had drifted apart from them after Annabel passed. Since he'd been back in town, he had grown closer to Marlowe and Bowie. And he couldn't imagine Ace could ever have shot their father…

He ate dinner without talking, because he feared he could not survive the cost to his heart. Despite all his efforts to steer clear of women with children, he was falling headfirst into a powerfully moving relationship with Hazel and Evie. Where had all his resolve gone?

HAZEL TUCKED EVIE in to the sound of Callum cleaning the kitchen. She hadn't missed his joy in seeing Evie's excitement over receiving the extravagant gift. Sharing dinner tonight had been especially poignant. He genuinely adored Evie. He looked at her as though they had been a family for years. When he let his guard down— unaware or not—he was a phenomenal man. Evie could look up to someone like him.

That terrified Hazel.

She had to know more about him before they sank into a lovestruck quicksand.

"I'd like a glass of wine before we turn in," she said. "You?"

A few seconds passed before he said a tentative, "Sure."

After she had two glasses on the counter, she took out a chardonnay from the cooler and found an opener. Manly hands took over from behind her. Putting her hands on the counter, she watched him open the bottle, feeling his arms on each side of her.

After he uncaged her with one arm, she rolled to lean on her lower back against the counter.

He handed her a glass.

Taking it, she said, "Princesses all over the world must have cast a spell on you."

"I've protected many princesses."

His deep, chocolaty voice and intimate tone riveted her. "You have? Like who?"

"They were from Morocco, Spain, Japan and Sweden. Most of them are repeat clients and usually need me when they travel."

Which must be often. He lived such a glamorous life. He came from a wealthy and prominent family and he protected affluent people. But then, he must be used to that way of life.

He was so different from the kind of man she had envisioned for herself after Ed ran off. She couldn't forget the promise she had made. Up until Ed, she had left her fate to chance, believing that everything happened for a reason and that the right man would come along naturally. Well, Ed had come along naturally, all right, but he'd turned out to be all wrong. Nothing should be left to chance. Maybe some things happened for a reason, but finding a good man was not one of them.

After sipping some wine, she asked, "What made you decide to become a bodyguard?"

He took a moment before he answered. "I was on a mission in Ukraine and noticed two men waiting outside of an apartment building. A young woman came out and they abducted her. I followed them. Watched them force her out of the vehicle and into a house. They had her blindfolded and tied."

Hazel listened with increasing horror.

"I went to the door and knocked. One of them answered and I gave him a throat strike." He gestured with his hand, putting his fingers to her throat. "I heard the girl screaming down the hall and the other man yelling for her to shut up. I heard him hit her and tell her he'd kill her if she didn't be quiet. By then I was at the doorway. He had already torn her shirt and was trying to remove her jeans. He saw me and stopped and asked who the hell I was. I told him I would be the last person he'd ever see alive if he didn't get off the girl." He stopped as though back in the scene.

"What happened?" she asked.

"He got off her and lunged for his gun. I threw it out of reach and gave him a good beating. Just before I knocked him unconscious, I told him if he ever hurt another woman again I'd come back and finish him off." He drank some wine.

"Then what?"

"I called the police and told them what happened. The two were arrested and sent to prison."

"What happened with the girl?" Had she been the woman he had lost?

He shrugged. "She thanked me and I never saw her again. That was my last mission before my service ended and I left the navy."

Callum had done a very heroic thing and that woman had to have been so grateful. If that had happened to Hazel, she would have wanted to find the man who saved her from rape and possibly murder, to thank him when she wasn't traumatized.

Looking at him and his handsome face and messy hair and into his blue eyes, she fell for him even more. Although she tried to ward the feeling off, the warmth mushroomed and gave her a tickle in her stomach.

"When I returned to the States, I didn't know what I wanted to do with the rest of my life. All I knew was I didn't want to work at a corporation, especially Colton Oil."

Hazel hadn't expected him to continue talking, but welcomed it.

"Being a SEAL taught me how to fight and use guns and do both really well. That was my skill set. I ran into an old friend who told me about Executive Protection and put me in touch with the CEO."

"And the rest, as they say, is history," she said, admiring his tall, muscular frame and his SEAL background that he put to good use. She sipped wine and put down her glass on the kitchen counter.

"A little more history than I like," he said.

Could it be he'd talk about the woman he had lost?

"I almost stopped working for Executive Protection a year after I joined."

"Because of her?" she asked quietly.

He nodded, the mood turning darker. Putting his

glass beside hers, he walked into the living room and stopped before the windows.

Hazel followed, standing beside him and resting her hand on his forearm, urging him to face her.

He did.

"Tell me, Callum." It would help him if he talked about it. And since she was losing her fight not to fall madly in love with him, her best interest was to help him help himself.

"I was protecting a witness in the trial of a drug dealer who murdered someone," he said. "I did my job and saw that the witness made it to court, testified and sent the dealer to prison." He stopped.

Hazel could see he had come to the most difficult part. She stepped closer and put her hands on his impressive chest, encouraging him without words. The painful storm in his eyes eased a little.

"No one knew he wasn't just any dealer. He was high level and dangerous, with ties to one of Mexico's most notorious cartels. Living in the shadows of the underworld. I was seeing Annabel during the trial. She lived in the city where we met. The dealer must have found out. She was run off the road and killed."

Hazel felt his pain, shared it and wished she could take it away.

"I protected the witness but I couldn't protect Annabel or our unborn child," he said, grinding out the words with deep and barely leashed anger.

"Listen to me, Callum." Hazel had to reach him now. He was vulnerable. "You didn't know he would send someone to kill her. It is not your fault."

"The person who ran her off the road was never found. I tried, but…"

Hazel touched both sides of his face. "You didn't kill her. The drug dealer did."

"He did it to get even with me. To make me pay."

"It is not your fault." She stopped him from turning away. "I know people say that too much, but it's true, Callum. An evil man killed her, not you."

"I vowed to never protect women and children after that."

Hazel slid her hands to his shoulders. "But you protected princesses."

"That was different."

"How?" She watched him ponder that. Princesses were women. Some of them had to have kids.

"I don't know. They didn't make me think about Annabel."

She had a question she dreaded to ask because she was pretty sure she'd hate the answer. "Do I make you think about Annabel?"

"You make me have to try very hard *not* to. You and Evie both."

Well, that was better than an all-out yes. "You need to confront your grief, Callum. Have you talked with Annabel's family?"

"Not since the funeral."

"Maybe you should. It might give you closure."

"They blame me."

"That's what they said? Are you sure they really blame you? Any parent would be distraught over losing their child. Have they tried to contact you?"

"They invited me to a gathering they planned on the one-year anniversary of her death, but I didn't go. Even if I'd wanted to, I was out of the country. I didn't get the invitation until after the memorial."

"Do they know about the baby?" she asked.

"Yes. Annabel told them."

"And no one in your family knew you went to her funeral?"

He shook his head. "At the time all I thought about was getting away."

He had submerged himself in work, traveling all over the world, never taking a break to be with family or friends. What a lonely existence. And the burden he had carried with him must have been suffocating at times. Hazel couldn't believe he hadn't told anyone about the baby. Well, maybe she could. He hadn't been able to talk about them.

Until now. With her.

Hazel became aware of his hands on her hips. At some point during their exchange he'd placed them there. Her body pressed against his. Her gaze melded with his, seeing into him without barriers. He'd opened himself to her and their connection blossomed.

"Why me?" she asked, her voice low with rising desire.

"I wish I knew." He lowered his head and kissed her. His lips touched hers, featherlight, brushing over them and then taking her mouth for an intimate mating.

After he had poured out his heart to her, Hazel felt secure in giving herself to him. Everything.

Chapter Seven

Hazel looked up at Callum when he broke from another impassioned kiss. His eyes burned with lust, fueled by the significance of what he had confided, as though freed. She reveled in the deep meaning in his next kiss, and was glad she had put Evie to bed. She had the night with Callum. With his arms around her back, she looped hers over his shoulders.

He lifted her and she wrapped her legs around him as he carried her to his room, kissing all the way to the bed.

Hazel had to fight for a few seconds of clarity before this continued.

"Callum, I'm not on the Pill."

He rose above her, looking intently into her eyes. She didn't want him to stop but they had to behave like adults.

"I don't have anything, either. I have something at home but I didn't bring it."

Neither one of them had thought they'd end up in the same bed, especially this soon. She did some quick calculations.

"I just had my period. We should be safe."

She spent a long moment wavering between temptation and logic. He had to be thinking the same thing. What if she got pregnant? How would she feel about that? Was this worth the risk?

Her heart charged forward with an affirmative while her brain cautioned to slow this down. Lying here like this, with him hovering over her and her hands on his hard chest and the vision of his face, so manly and full of desire, temptation hummed into a roar. She could feel his member against her. Kissing had made her hot; this wasn't lessening the effect.

"Are you sure?"

He wasn't asking if she was sure about the timing. He asked if she was sure if she wanted to take this risk.

"Are you?"

He lowered his mouth to hers for a soft kiss. "I asked you first."

"I'm sure." Especially now that he had resumed kissing her.

"Me, too." He kissed her harder, lowering his body onto hers and sending lightning bolts of sensation through her.

She sank her fingers into his thick hair and moaned. In response to that sound, he moved against her, teasing, hinting at what would come.

Sliding her hands down to his T-shirt, she lifted the hem. He moved back and removed the shirt the rest of the way, sending it sailing to the floor while his eyes devoured the sight of her. The blue sundress dipped modestly low in the front, but there was enough cleavage to show off.

He lifted the dress up and she sat up as he pulled it over her head and dropped it on top of his shirt. His eyes took their fill of her naked breasts before he came down and sampled one in his mouth, flicking the nipple while his hand ran over the other breast.

Eager to see him, she tugged at his jeans' button. He withdrew and helped her, having to get up to take them off. Convenient that they were both already barefoot. She kicked off her underwear and waited for him to climb back on top of her. She was traditional that way. She loved the feel of a man's weight on her before he entered. While that was her favorite position, it most certainly wasn't the only one she enjoyed.

Callum crawled over her and slowly lowered his body onto hers. A delicious shiver coursed through her. He kissed her softly for endless moments before kneeing her legs apart. She was ready to give herself to him, more ready than she had been for any man in a long time.

He guided himself to her and slowly pushed into her, filling her deliciously. The initial friction against her sensitive spot drove her to near orgasm.

"Wait. Wait," she rasped.

He stilled above her, his breathing faster and his eyes ablaze.

Hazel dug her head into the pillow against unbearable pleasure. She didn't want her first orgasm to end so quickly. But he turned her on so incredibly much!

Callum groaned. "I can barely hold still when you look so sexy and beautiful." He withdrew and thrust into her and then repeated the action over and over, moving her body on the bed and sending tingles of ecstasy radiating from her abdomen all the way out to her limbs.

She bit back a cry as she came on an explosion of

orgasmic fireworks. He groaned again and slowed as he experienced his own release.

Then he put his head beside hers, each of them catching their breath.

"That was incredible," he said next to her ear.

"Like the Kentucky Derby, except the most exciting two minutes in sex."

He chuckled, then rolled off her to prop his head on his hand. "Are you usually this responsive?"

"No. Ed had to work at it for at least fifteen." Suddenly disturbed by that revelation, Hazel averted her eyes from Callum. What was different about Callum?

After a moment, she turned her head and saw his thoughts had taken a sober turn as well. Not wanting this moment or the beauty of what had just transpired to fade yet, she rolled onto her side with her back to him.

"We can at least spoon for a while, can't we?" she asked.

After a few brief seconds, he moved closer and said above her ear, "Yes."

The feel of him against her calmed her and enveloped her in warmth. When his hand caressed her arm and he planted a soft kiss on her cheek, she knew he had fallen under the same spell, the spell that had landed them in bed together. Tomorrow would bring whatever it brought.

CALLUM ORDERED ROOM service the next morning. Hazel had gotten up after him and gone into her room before Evie woke. Now Evie was busy with her dollhouse and Hazel was finishing getting ready. He'd heard her shower turn off a few minutes ago.

When he had first awakened to Hazel's sleeping face

on the same pillow as his, he had been overcome with affection and arousal. Her ankle was over his calf. Her plump breasts were molded into tempting mounds above the sheet and blanket. He could start every morning like that.

And that was precisely the thought that had sent him careening back to reality. Annabel's face rushed forth. He didn't feel guilty or that he had betrayed her. It had been too long since she had died. It was more of a threatening feeling. He was in danger of welcoming a woman and her five-year-old girl into his life. He had failed at protecting the last mother and daughter he had been involved with. Did he want to take that risk? No. At least not now. He didn't know if he'd ever be ready for that.

Hazel's responsiveness to him had only increased his pleasure and, if he were brutally honest, the bond he felt with her. It was too overwhelming. Too potent.

He had told her what he had told *no one*, not a living soul other than Annabel's family. He recalled the day of her funeral, when her father had asked why no one from his family had attended. He had said they couldn't make it. Annabel's father had looked at him strangely. He didn't know it at the time, but all Callum had wanted was to leave and be as far away from any reminders of Annabel as he could.

Annabel's murder had occurred in another city, not Mustang Valley. Another police force and even the feds had investigated but with no real zest. It had been assumed her killer had fled to Mexico. It hadn't made big news. No one in his family or circle of friends had heard about it, by some miracle. He had needed to be left alone.

No one would have understood. No one who hadn't gone through what he had would be able to understand. The terribleness of her murder. The helplessness of not being able to find her killer. The knowledge that her murder and the killing of their unborn child would never be solved.

There wasn't a day that passed when he didn't think about that. Who was her killer and where was he today? Did anyone know what he had done and could it lead police to him? Was there a way to extradite him to the States if he was abroad?

Maybe that was what he needed. Annabel's cold case solved. Maybe then he could move on. Maybe then he wouldn't think about what was taken from him so violently whenever he spent time around women with children. Pregnant women got to him the most. He had missed out on that.

One could argue he could find another woman and start a family, but for him it wasn't that simple. Not only had Annabel and their unborn baby been taken from him, so had all of the first-time experiences and the happiness. The wonder of the creation of life, the stages of pregnancy, the anticipation of the birth. Looking up names. Imagining being a family—a *close* family.

Everything good about being with a woman who was pregnant with his child had been destroyed. All that came to his mind now in connection with pregnant women was Annabel's lifeless and abused form on the coroner's table, the baby bump still there, but full of death now.

He had put up with enough when it came to family, so why did he have to go through that? His was not an idyllic family. His former stepmother, Selina, loved drama and enjoyed driving wedges between his siblings. Callum never understood why his father allowed her to keep her job at Colton Oil. Everyone thought she must have something on Payne. She also kept jovially reminding everyone of the Colton Oil bylaws that said the CEO had to be a Colton by blood. With the discovery that Ace was switched at birth, that presented a significant problem. Her heartless pokes reminded Callum of his estrangement from his father and how terrible it would be if Payne never woke up from his coma.

He snapped back to the present and poured Evie some cereal. "Evie, come get breakfast."

Saying that made him feel like a father figure. Taking care of Evie came so naturally. How had that happened? Would he ever be the same after this?

Just then Hazel appeared in jeans that hugged her slender hips and a silky white top. She eyed him peculiarly and he knew she wondered why he'd gotten out of bed before she woke. Was she gauging him? Maybe she hoped he was an early riser. More likely she thought he had run away.

He put the room service on the table. "Coffee?"

"Sure."

He felt her continue to evaluate him as he finished getting their breakfast spread out on the table.

"I'd like to talk with Kerry about what we can do to help with the investigation." He watched her ascertain why he was so anxious to help. Or maybe she wondered why he'd so abruptly made that announcement. He needed something to do and he needed to get away from her as fast as possible.

"Okay," she said slowly. She sat and sipped the coffee he'd poured.

He sat across from her. Evie bounded to the table and took her seat, oblivious to the tension between her mother and Callum. She scooped up her cereal and looked toward the television.

"What did you have in mind on the investigation?" Hazel asked.

"Nate Blurge was the murder victim Evie saw being kidnapped. Maybe we can find out more about him."

She nodded a couple of times. "Okay."

"Did you know him or of him at all?"

"No. I never went to bars like Joe's."

Of course, she wouldn't. Not only did she have a young child, she wasn't the kind of woman who would frequent places like that. Maybe he had asked just for something to say that wasn't related to last night.

"You were up early," Hazel said.

"Yeah. I couldn't go back to sleep."

"Something troubling you?" She took another sip, doing a poor job of appearing nonchalant.

"No." He ate his breakfast, hoping she'd just let it drop.

Turned out, she did, but she was way too quiet as they left the inn to go to the police station.

Outside, he gave the valet his ticket.

Evie clung to Hazel, trying to swing off her mother's arm.

His rental arrived and he opened the back door for Hazel to get Evie in her car seat. Then he opened the front passenger side and went around to get behind the wheel. She was still quiet as they headed out, but only for five minutes.

"Did you love her?" Hazel asked.

He had often thought of that. He hadn't known Annabel long before she had become pregnant, but as time passed and the birth of their child drew nearer, he'd thought he could love her. They never had the passion he and Hazel shared last night. That confused him.

"I have to believe I did, yes."

"Do you still?"

That stopped him for a few seconds. He hadn't really contemplated that since she died. Now as he reflected on it, he realized he did not.

"No," he finally said.

"Then...why?"

She was reading too much into him getting up before her. He got it that she was suspicious, but why grill him like this?

"I just woke up before you, Hazel. Did you want me to wake you?"

She didn't answer right away and he let her take her time in contemplating what he'd said.

"I wouldn't have been with you had I thought you'd turn me away the next day," she said at last.

Where had that notion come from? "I didn't turn you away." Was she the cuddling type? He used to be.

Evie's father must have really done a number on her. Was Callum another mistake to her?

"You seem different this morning," she said.

"I don't mean to be." He wished she wouldn't push the issue.

"Are you okay with us?"

He glanced in the rearview mirror and saw Evie fast asleep in her car seat. No wonder Hazel was talking so freely. Now he had to answer, and he hesitated because he had to be honest.

"I take it by your silence that you aren't. I'm sorry

for making such a big issue about it, but I need to be sure about how to handle this going forward."

He heard sincerity in her voice. She didn't like asking all these questions. She just felt she had to. "Everything is going so fast between us. I haven't had time to process it. Have you?"

She breathed a laugh of relief. "No. We can slow it down. Is that what you want? I have Evie to think about. She's already so fond of you. I worry about her when it comes time to part ways—if that happens."

"I don't ever want to hurt Evie, so I'll do whatever you think is best when it comes to her."

"What about me? Will you do what you think is best when it comes to me?" She said it lightly, but he sensed she actually needed to know.

"It isn't my intention to hurt you. I'm trying to be honest with you."

"I appreciate that, but I'm a little disappointed in myself for not thinking this through better. We rushed into this and now I wish I hadn't."

They had rushed into sleeping together. Could they have done anything to prevent their attraction? He couldn't blame her for being regretful or concerned. They barely knew each other. About the only things they did know were a little background information and that they had a hot physical chemistry that was apparently uncontrollable.

"I don't regret last night at all," he said. "In fact, that's what has me in such a conundrum today. I have never had such an amazing time, except maybe my first time."

She averted her head, propping her elbow on the door

frame and curling her fingers against her chin. "That has me in a conundrum, too."

Her quiet, soft tone revealed her vulnerability. He reached over and covered her hand with his. "We'll cool this off for a while. Get to know each other more."

She looked at him as though having serious doubts as to whether either one of them could cool this off.

Suddenly, the glass of Callum's window shattered as a bullet flew past him and went through the passenger window. An instant later, he realized someone had shot at them, narrowly missing him and Hazel. "Get down!" he shouted, looking in the back at Evie, who had slouched enough in her sleep to be below the door frame but now began to wake.

As he took out his pistol, his heart pounded as he urgently searched for the shooter. An SUV had fallen back in the other lane but sped up as Callum had done the moment the bullet had penetrated.

He weaved in and out of traffic, putting more distance between them and the shooter.

"Call 911," Callum said to Hazel, who had already taken out her phone.

He slowed enough to make the next turn, trying not to frighten Evie more than she already was. She had begun to cry. Cars ahead blocked his way. This wasn't a movie—he couldn't drive up onto the sidewalk.

Hazel finished talking to the dispatcher.

The gunman began to gain on them. Callum's fear that Evie would be harmed intensified.

"Callum." Hazel sounded terrified. "Evie."

"I know."

He tried to veer out into the oncoming traffic to get around a car. He had to steer back into the lane. The car passed and Callum would have tried again but the gunman was beside them in a big black SUV. The shooter aimed. Callum pressed on the brakes. The other man did too and then rammed into them.

"Evie, stay down!" Hazel hollered, dropping the phone.

"Mommy?"

"Just stay down."

Callum didn't want to shoot unless he had to, not with a child in the truck. The traffic began to clear. He drove into the oncoming lane and gunned the truck, passing two cars before getting back over as another vehicle approached, horn honking. With some clear road, Callum raced toward the police station, unable to believe they were being chased again, that he had allowed it to happen.

If he hadn't been distracted by Hazel and their night together, he could have stayed focused and prevented this—at the very least putting Evie in less danger.

He made the last turn to reach the station. In the rearview mirror he saw the SUV pass without turning. The gunman knew they were headed for the police. He also must know the police would come after him if he tried to wait for them again.

"He's gone," Callum said.

Hazel breathed heavily and put her head back.

He drove into the police station parking lot and parked.

Hazel jumped out and hastily removed Evie from the car seat. When she had her daughter in her arms she asked, "Are you all right?"

"I'm fine, Mommy. Did we almost have an accident?"

"Yes, sweetie. Mommy just had a big scare."

Callum put his hand on her back as she scanned the area. "Let's get inside."

They walked inside. Kerry would be expecting them. Callum had phoned ahead. A few minutes later, she appeared, sporting her badge on her belt.

"How are you doing?" Kerry asked.

"We were chased again and shot at," Hazel said, putting Evie down.

"Where is he? I'll get some cars out there."

"It's too late. He didn't follow us all the way to the station," Callum said.

"I'll have them be on the lookout for the vehicle."

Hazel gave her the plate number, surprising Callum with her stealthy observation and thinking. She went on to describe the SUV, including the damage to the passenger side when the shooter had rammed into them.

"What brought you here today? Not drawing the shooter out and trying to run you down?"

"We'd like to help with the investigation. Speed it up if we can."

Kerry looked from Hazel to Callum and then Evie. "We've questioned some of the workers at Joe's Bar. Nothing very concrete has come up. We did learn that Nate Blurge's wife works there and he had a reputation for flirting with a lot of women, many of them the waitresses there. Apparently he made a lot of husbands angry. If the killer was one of them, he might show up. If you could watch the place, see if you can find out anything about who might want him dead. If you help out with that, I can pay more attention to his family."

Callum nodded. "We can do that, but not with Evie."

Hazel shook her head. "No, not with Evie."

"Is there anywhere you can take her?" Callum asked. "Didn't you say you had a brother who was a cop in Phoenix?"

"I did. His wife is a cop, too."

"That sounds about as perfect as it gets," Kerry said. "I agree. Evie is in too much danger if you keep her here. Every time you leave the inn you're at risk. Whoever is after you is watching that place very close."

"I hate the idea of parting company with my daughter but I can't argue she's in danger. She'd be safe with my brother and his wife."

Callum liked that idea. Not only would it keep him from bonding even more with the girl, he wouldn't have to worry about protecting her *and* her mother.

"Why don't you go back to the inn?" Kerry said. "I can have an officer escort you."

"That won't be necessary," Callum said.

"Are you sure? It's too dangerous for you to come and go from the inn and I'm concerned next time you won't get away without being harmed."

Or killed. Although she didn't say so, Callum knew she worried they could very well be murdered.

"I'm sure." He would not let his guard down again.

"We need to come up with a way to get you out of the inn and Evie somewhere safe." She tapped her lower lip with her forefinger and then lowered her hand. "How about if I have someone drop off some disguises so you can get Evie out safely? Then I can arrange for undercover officers to watch you and make sure you get on your way."

Callum grinned. "I like that idea. In fact, I know the perfect disguises." He leaned close to Kerry's ear and told her in a low voice what to get for them.

Kerry smiled and glanced at Hazel.

"What are you up to?" Hazel asked Callum.

"You'll see." Then to Kerry, he said, "Just ask Patsy to pick them up. She'll have fun with that."

He gave Kerry Patsy's contact information, looking forward to the trip to Hazel's brother. All that time they would spend together as a family… And then he would be alone with Hazel after they dropped Evie off. That came with so many conflicting emotions. Leaving Evie would be sad, but being alone with Hazel gave him all kinds of unwelcome thoughts…and welcome ones, too.

Chapter Eight

Later the next morning, Hazel couldn't believe what she had allowed Callum to talk her into wearing. She looked at herself in the mirror. The studded leather sleeveless top zipped up to just above her breasts and the low-hipped leather pants hugged her shape. The jewel encrusted shoes with four-inch heels would bring her much closer to Callum's height. A blond wig completed the ensemble.

Beside her Evie giggled. She had a wig, too, also blond, and wore an adorable biker girl T-shirt with leather pants—not skintight like her mother's. Patsy had also gotten her a fun metal rivet and leather wrap bracelet and a pair of black boots.

Evie posed in front of the bathroom mirror, only her head above the sink counter.

Hazel chuckled. "Come on, Evie."

They left the bathroom. Callum waited for them in the kitchen, leaning against the island counter, holding his phone. His eyes lifted as they approached, frozen in that pose as his gaze roamed down Hazel and then back up.

"I'm a biker girl!" Evie jumped and stopped in front of him.

"You sure are. Looking good, too."

"Hopefully you haven't ruined her future," Hazel said with humor, enjoying this and feeling like they were a family getting ready to go on an outing. She wouldn't even analyze that right now.

She did have a moment where she had to stare at him, though. Dark blue jeans that cupped his crotch and a leather jacket over a gray T-shirt that had a black print on the front. He also had on glasses to ramp him up from lowly biker to biker with money. She liked his wig, black with a tasteful ponytail.

"Are we ready?" he asked.

"Yeah!" Evie called out cheerily.

"Let me check outside first. I have my rental car waiting in front of the inn," he said.

He had prepared well for this. And even though her disguise was a bit sexy, all of them were convincing. They looked completely different than they had this morning.

IN THE LOBBY, Hazel took Evie's hand, and Callum noticed a man walking with another woman staring at her.

She looked away, stopping before following Callum through the doors. He covertly checked the front of the inn and beyond and then turned, still holding the door open, not saying he'd spotted a dark SUV across the street. The driver turned their way, stared a few seconds then turned away. A man and a woman with a child wasn't unusual. They might stand out as a biker family but they looked nothing like they usually did. Callum was pleased the man apparently hadn't caught on to their disguises.

Hazel stepped outside with Evie. The car was right

in front of them, a valet having already opened the back door.

Ushering Evie into the seat, Callum let Hazel bend to buckle her in. She looked through the opposite window at an SUV. The driver still wasn't even paying attention to them. Callum saw he wore a cap and sunglasses, so recognizing him was still impossible. Callum thought it might be the same man who'd come after them before.

He saw another man ogling her as she got in the front passenger seat. Callum got behind the wheel, looking over at the SUV. The driver glanced their way but didn't seem to have any peculiar reaction.

"This costume is attracting too much attention," she said.

"Good, nobody is going to guess it's you."

"Evie might have made that SUV driver suspicious," she said.

"Evie won't be with us after today."

As they moved out of the inn's parking area, Callum glanced once more at the SUV. The driver paid them no attention as they passed. Evie would be safe. Callum leaned back, savoring the victory. He didn't understand why or how, but Hazel and Evie were so important to him. His job of protecting them was so important to him. He looked over at Hazel, gorgeous and content in their successful getaway. He'd seen her satisfied in another way, too, and struggled to ward off the temptation to see that again.

"Hazel?"

Hazel's brother was a couple of inches over six feet and built like a linebacker. Off duty, he sported jeans and a Kansas City Chiefs T-shirt. Callum could see the resemblance to Hazel in his thick dark hair and hazel-green eyes.

"Is that you?" her brother asked.

Hazel smiled big. She had called ahead to make sure Owen could take in Evie but she must look so different than her usual self right now. "Yes."

"And Evie?"

Evie giggled. "Yes."

"What's with the look?" Her brother opened the door wider to let them in.

"I'll explain." Hazel entered the house.

After a two hour drive they'd arrived in this neat and tidy suburb of modern homes, some stucco, some more traditional, all with big front windows. Hazel's brother's house was two stories with a covered porch and a three-car garage.

The grayish-brown wooden floor of the foyer opened to a formal living room, with the kitchen and dining areas to the left. Stairs led up to the second level beyond the dining room.

"Callum, this is Owen and Jessica, my brother and his wife." Hazel introduced them.

Callum shook Owen's hand as his wife walked up beside him, a stunning woman with long dark hair and brown eyes. They made a handsome couple.

"Hi," Jessica said with a wide, toothy smile.

"Hey there, Evie." Owen crouched to Evie's level, who clung to her mother's leg in a sudden show of shyness.

"You remember your uncle, Evie," Hazel said. "Say hello."

"Hi," Evie said quietly.

Hazel laughed, her affection and adoration coming out in the sound.

Callum hadn't thought Evie had a shy bone in her body but meeting new people apparently made her withdraw. She'd done the same to him when they had first met. Kids.

"You've grown since I last saw you," Owen said.

A beagle came trotting up with a wagging tail.

"Do you remember Olive?" Jessica asked.

"Yes." Evie crept out from behind Hazel's leg and knelt down before the beagle.

Eager for attention, the dog jumped up on her, paws on her legs. Evie giggled and collapsed onto her rear. When she crawled on hands and knees into the living room, Callum knew she'd be preoccupied for a while.

"We were surprised you were coming up today," Owen said. "Such spontaneity isn't like you. We were glad we're both off duty today. Is everything all right?"

"There's a good reason for us showing up on such short notice, and looking like this," Hazel said. "Evie saw a man get hit on the head with a rock and his body was found."

Jessica inhaled sharply. "Oh, no. She saw that?" She glanced back at Evie as though wondering if she was okay.

"Evie seems fine," Hazel said. "She seems unaffected."

"She's probably too young to fully understand what happened," Callum said. "The problem is the police haven't caught the killer yet, and he knows where we're staying."

"He's tried more than once to get us."

Owen kept an unreadable but somber face but Jessica's jaw fell.

"Evie?" Jessica asked, incredulous.

Hazel nodded. "That's why we're here." She looked at her brother. "I need a huge favor."

"You want us to watch Evie? You don't even have to ask," he said. "Of course we'll do it."

"And she'll be safe," Jessica said. "We're both armed and have licenses to carry."

"She'll be guarded at all times," Owen said.

Callum saw Hazel's shoulders slump in relief. "I can't thank you enough," she said. "You don't know how much it means to me to know she'll be with two cops. I won't have to worry about her the way I have been."

"Of course," Owen said. "We'll love having her." He glanced over at Evie and Olive, who were rolling around the living room in play. "And so will Olive, it would seem."

Hazel laughed and Callum smiled a little at the cute sight of Evie and the dog.

"Do the police have any solid leads?" Jessica asked.

"We're looking into the murder victim right now. Hopefully that will point us to a suspect," Callum said.

"Where are you staying?" Owen asked. "Is there security?"

"Callum is a bodyguard." She explained how they met and how Callum had saved her and Evie. "He's kindly agreed to protect me until the killer is caught."

"Bodyguard, huh?" Owen said, checking Callum out. "Do you work for a security service?"

"I work for Executive Protection Services. It's an international personal protection agency."

Owen's brow lifted and he seemed impressed. "Sounds flashy."

"He's protected princesses," Hazel said. "Not your everyday bodyguard."

The way she looked at him snared his attention. He doubted she meant to reveal her admiration so guilelessly.

"So it would seem," Owen said.

"We were just about to have lunch," Jessica said. "Are you hungry?"

Callum wasn't but Hazel glanced at Evie and said, "Evie hasn't eaten yet."

"I hope chili cheese dogs are okay." Jessica led the way into the open, bright kitchen.

"*Yaaay*, hot dogs!" Evie bounded into the kitchen and took a seat at the table, Olive right by her side, sitting on the floor beside the chair.

Jessica prepared some paper plates, serving Evie first and then the men at the kitchen island.

Hazel sat at the table with Jessica.

Callum wasn't very hungry so he knifed off one bite and set down his utensils.

"So, a bodyguard, huh?" Owen asked, picking at his food.

"Yes."

"What's your story? How'd you get into that profession?"

"I was a Navy SEAL before that and the opportunity presented itself when I left."

"SEAL. Not many can make it through that training," Jessica said, sounding impressed.

"No." No point in denying it. SEAL training was beyond extreme.

"What made you decide to be a SEAL?" This question came from Hazel.

He hadn't thought about that in a really long time. Growing up he hadn't always aspired to be a SEAL. "I was an aggressive kid. Always getting into fights.

Staying out late and getting in trouble. I was never arrested, just kind of...wild. My last year in high school I wondered what I wanted to do with my life. Not follow my father. A friend of mine suggested the military. He had a good point. If I continued on my path of aggression, maybe I would have ended up in jail. When I was a kid, I would play with toy soldiers. The army didn't appeal to me but the navy did. The SEALs always fascinated me. The challenge of becoming one satisfied my headstrong nature. So I tried out and made the team."

"You were wild?" Hazel asked. "You're so level-headed now. So calm."

"I thank the discipline of training for that. It changed my life." The years he had been active had been enough. When he left, he was ready for something different. Being a SEAL had served its purpose. He had learned how to channel his aggression, put it to good use. Being a bodyguard continued to do that for him. He felt fortunate to have found his true calling in life. Not many people did. He would have been a lost soul if he had chosen to work an office job.

"You said you were staying somewhere together?" Owen asked.

"At the Dales Inn," Hazel said.

"You're staying with my sister?" Owen asked Callum.

"For her protection. And Evie's, up until now."

Owen glanced from him to Hazel and back again. "Are you sure there isn't another reason?"

Was he being a protective older brother?

"Owen," Hazel said in a cautionary tone.

"Are you seeing him?"

"What difference does that make?" she asked.

"So you are?" Owen looked at Callum.

"No. We aren't *seeing* each other. He's helping me, that's all." But Hazel averted her head, a dead giveaway that she wasn't being completely truthful.

"Hazel has been through a lot," Owen said to Callum. "Did she tell you about Ed?"

"She did."

"So you understand she needs a man she can depend on."

"Owen, stop." Jessica laughed a little. "He's always been protective of Hazel. Don't mind him. I'm sure you're a decent guy and wouldn't hurt her."

"I wasn't there for her when Ed left her. That won't happen again." Owen said the last directly to Hazel.

"Everything is all right, Owen," Hazel said. "I'm not doing anything I don't want and I won't do anything that will hurt me or Evie." She turned to Callum. "Especially Evie."

Callum put his hands up. "I am a decent guy and I would never harm Hazel or Evie." He looked at Hazel. "Not intentionally."

He couldn't promise she wouldn't end up with hurt feelings after this was over. He couldn't predict the future, much less their chemistry. That had a mind of its own.

"All I ask is you don't tell anyone Evie is staying here."

"We would never put her in that kind of danger," Owen said, Jessica shaking her head in full agreement.

They finished eating and now it was time to go. Callum saw how difficult this was going to be for Hazel. She watched Evie play with Olive with somber eyes.

"She'll be fine," Jessica said. "We have toys for my

nieces and nephews, my siblings' kids, so she'll have plenty to do."

Hazel sent her a grateful but bittersweet smile. "I've never been away from her like this before."

Jessica put her hand on Hazel's shoulder. "You'll see her again before you know it."

Hazel nodded, wiping her eye even though no tears had fallen. She did look a little misty, though. She went to Evie and crouched.

"Hey, Evie. Mommy's going to go now. I'll be back to get you as soon as I can, okay?"

"Okay." Evie stood and turned to hug her mother, not seeming at all afraid to stay with her aunt and uncle— and their cute beagle.

Hazel kissed her head. "You be good for Aunt Jessica and Uncle Owen, okay?"

"Okay." Evie plopped back down by Olive, whose tail wagged and head moved forward for a quick lick on Evie's face.

Evie giggled and petted the dog.

Hazel stood and walked to the entry where Callum waited. She glanced back once more before saying goodbye to her brother and Jessica.

Just then, Evie bounded over, throwing her arms around one of Callum's legs. "Bye, Cal-em."

Callum knelt before her and she hugged him around his neck. "Bye, Evie. We'll see you soon."

"'Kay." With that, she ran back to the dog.

"How long did you say you two have been living together?" Owen asked incredulously.

"Not long. A week or so," Hazel said.

"You must be good with kids," Jessica said.

"Maybe so. Evie is a good girl," Callum said, seeing Hazel wasn't amused. She was probably concerned over how Evie would react if he left them.

Callum couldn't do anything about how much Evie liked him. He could be careful with her, though—and Hazel.

They left the house.

Outside, Hazel rubbed under her nose as though the sting of tears threatened her composure. "Is she even going to miss me?"

Callum chuckled. "She'll have a lot of new things to keep her preoccupied. But yes, she'll miss you and she'll be so excited to see you again."

Hazel smiled slightly. "And you, it would seem."

"I'll be mindful of that, Hazel."

"She's already so attached to you."

"She likes me. I haven't been around her long enough to make that big of an impact. It will be the same as saying goodbye to a friend at school."

"It *will*?"

He hadn't meant to sound as though he had already decided to part ways with her when this was over.

"If this doesn't end up turning into something more," he said.

She glanced at him with appreciation for the clarification. As they reached the car, Callum wondered why he had reassured her. The prospect of their becoming a real couple—maybe even a family—gave him a sick feeling. He would never forget the way he had felt when Annabel died, along with their unborn baby. His soul had been ripped from him. He hadn't been able to function. He had wondered if he would ever make it through.

No more talk about the future for him and Hazel. He'd make sure she was safe and then that would be that.

SINCE THEY WERE already dressed in disguise, Callum suggested they start staking out Joe's Bar. Nate Blurge was known to have spent a lot of time there, as Kerry had said. Someone had to know something that might lead to a break in the case. Hazel stepped into the dimly lit bar with Callum. Right away her first impression was that the lights were low to conceal the disrepair. A melting pot of people half-filled the place with its dirty, worn floor, and scratched and chipped tables and chairs. The ceiling had water stains and dirt caked the twenty-plus year old trim.

"Have a seat anywhere," the bartender called out.

No Wait to Be Seated sign here.

Two young couples laughed at a table. Solitary patrons at the bar watched the television that hung above shelves of liquor or stared at their drinks. A group of scary-looking biker men loitered around a pool table. The tallest one zeroed in on Hazel, making no effort to hide his ogling.

Callum chose a table in the middle of the bar. Hazel sat adjacent to him. Moments later a scantily clad waitress approached with a name tag that said Shelly. Callum ordered a beer and Hazel ordered a chardonnay.

"Hey, isn't this the place where that man who was murdered hung out?" Callum asked.

Hazel was amazed at how quickly he went to work.

"Nate?" the waitress replied. "Yeah. He was here most nights. Been kind of peaceful without him."

"Oh, really? Why is that?" Callum asked.

"He liked to flirt with all of us girls. Nate wasn't the handsomest man you ever saw. Shame he was killed and all, but I didn't know him very well. I'll be back with your drinks." She left for the bar.

Hazel watched her get their drinks from the bartender and walk back over to them.

"Did Nate sleep with any of the waitresses?" Callum asked.

Shelly slowed as she placed the glass of wine in front of Hazel. "Why do you want to know?"

Callum shrugged dismissively. "Maybe that has something to do with why he was murdered."

"Police already came in asking questions." She set a bottle of beer in front of Callum.

"Did they talk to anyone who had relations with him?"

"Don't know for sure. He bragged to me once that he had a thing going with Candace."

"Candace?"

"Yeah. She works two jobs. Has a day job in town."

"Is she here now?" Hazel asked.

"She only works weekends here," Shelly said.

"Did he engage with anyone else?" Callum asked.

"I didn't keep track of his love interests. He mostly annoyed me and the other girls."

Kerry hadn't mentioned anyone named Candace. Could it be they had stumbled upon something?

The waitress left to visit other tables.

Hazel looked around the bar, at the bikers who gave her an uneasy feeling, at the cheerful pair of couples and the line of solitary men at the bar. She was about to turn back to Callum when she noticed one of the men at the bar was staring at the waitress who had just served them.

The waitress turned from a table and the man quickly averted his head. As she passed behind him, he looked at her again and watched as she retrieved more drinks from the bartender and then walked to the table of couples.

"What is it?" Callum glanced behind him and saw the man. He followed his gaze and also where Hazel looked.

"That man," she said. "He's watching that waitress."

The waitress returned to the bar, going behind it. She smiled at the man who had been staring at her and they began to converse.

"They seem to know each other," Callum said.

The man at the bar reached over and touched the woman's hand and she smiled differently now, much more warmly. Then she glanced at the bartender as though making sure she hadn't been seen. The man seemed to respect that and pretended to pay attention to his bottle of beer.

"The ghost of Nate Blurge?" Hazel said.

Callum chuckled. "Yes. He might be flirting vicariously through that guy." If the woman Blurge had flirted with was the killer's wife, maybe that was why Nate was murdered. And maybe the new man who flirted with her would draw the killer out.

"I have to go to the bathroom." She stood and made her way to the back corner, having to pass the group of bikers on the way.

She ignored the tall biker, aware that he followed her movement. She finished her business in the bathroom, washed her hands and left.

As she walked past the pool table, the tall biker stepped in her path. She stopped.

He wore a sleazy grin, or at least that's how she interpreted it.

"Hey, how about a game of pool? You can invite

your friend over." He gestured toward Callum. "Is he your boyfriend?"

She contemplated lying. "No."

"Oh." His gaze roamed down her body and back up again. "What's your name, pretty lady?"

"Excuse me." She moved to go around him but he blocked her way.

"If not tonight, then maybe another night?" He gestured toward Callum again. "Maybe when he isn't around?"

"No, thanks."

"At least tell me your name. Can I have your number? I think we should get to know each other."

"Look, I'm not interested." Hazel stepped aside.

The tall biker took hold of her arm and she got a whiff of his breath. He had been drinking for some time.

"Let go of my arm." She jerked her arm and he held firm.

"Tell me your name."

Just then Callum's hand flattened on the man's chest. "What do you think you're doing?"

"Hey." The tall biker stumbled back with Callum's shove. "I was just talking to the lady. She said you and her weren't a couple."

"She also told you she wasn't interested. Is there a problem?"

The tall biker shook his head, feigning nonchalance and acting as though he wasn't afraid. "No problem."

"It looked like you weren't letting the lady pass."

"I would have let her pass. What business is it of yours anyway?" The man stepped forward, as though trying to intimidate Callum.

Callum stood at least an inch or two taller than the

biker. "She's with me. And even if she wasn't, I can tell when a woman doesn't want to talk to a man and she doesn't want anything to do with you."

"You don't know that. And you don't own her."

"Come on, Callum." Hazel put her hand on his forearm. "Let's go."

"You gonna hide behind a woman now?" The tall biker stepped even closer. "You should have stayed out of this. If you hadn't shown up, I'd have her number by now."

"She wouldn't have given you her number."

"Well aren't you a cocky bastard. Maybe somebody needs to put you in your place."

"Maybe you should quit drinking and go home. I don't want any trouble. I was a Navy SEAL, so you should think twice about starting something with me."

Callum didn't brag. He sounded calm and as though he had given the man a courteous warning.

But the tall biker smirked and glanced back at his cohorts. "Did you hear that? This jerk is a SEAL. He thinks he's better than all of us."

"I'll warn you once more. You don't want to start anything with me."

Hazel backed up a little. This could get ugly. She had no doubt whatsoever that Callum could take on all of the bikers. Maybe if they were sober the other men would have had a chance, but all of them looked inebriated.

Two of the bikers stepped forward, one holding a pool cue.

"You don't look like you ride. You're too pretty," the tall biker said. "What makes you think you can come in here and get between me and a lady?"

"She doesn't want to talk to you," Callum said.

"I'm getting tired of you saying that." The tall biker took a swing, which Callum easily avoided. He ducked another attempt and then delivered a hard uppercut to the jaw.

The tall biker stumbled backward and the one with a pool cue tried to jab Callum.

Callum blocked that and outmaneuvered him for control of the stick. He swung the cue, knocked the third man on the head and then kicked the taller one, sending him flying back onto the pool table.

This was turning into a real bar fight. And Callum could really move. She almost wasn't afraid, she was so in awe of him.

Hazel backed up some more when the biker who had come after Callum with the cue charged. Using the stick, Callum blocked his punching fists and twisted to high-kick his face. When he landed he used the cue to poke the second man and then tossed it aside to hit the taller biker twice. His opponent fell down.

The other two backed off. Hazel noticed everyone in the bar had stopped to watch, even the bartender. Fighting must be the norm here, because no one interfered.

Callum waited for the taller man to decide what to do. He stared at Callum as he got to his feet, wiping blood off his lip.

"Come on, man. Let's play pool," said a biker who hadn't joined the fight.

The taller biker looked from Hazel to Callum and then finally swatted the air with his hand. "She ain't worth it." With that he faced his friends.

Callum turned and found Hazel, putting his hand on her lower back.

She walked with him toward the exit, Callum tossing money on their table on the way out.

"That was quite a spectacle back there," she said when they were outside.

"They were drunk."

"Clearly. You could have seriously hurt them."

"Yes. I'm glad he chose not to engage anymore."

"Did you learn all those moves in the navy?"

"I refined them in the navy. I got into bar fights a lot when I was young."

"Right. Wild." She smiled and laughed a little, trying not to be so turned on by him.

Nobody had ever fought for her, least of all at a bar. She had not been the type of girl who hung out at such establishments, especially like this one. She had always been more of a wine bar kind of woman. Lunches with her girlfriends. Dates to nice restaurants.

Walking beside Callum, covertly taking in his long strides and his big shoulders, slightly swaying, she had never felt safer.

He caught her looking at him. "What?"

She shook her head, fumbling with brief self-consciousness. "Chivalry isn't dead."

"You liked it that I got into a fight back there?" He grinned teasingly. "I wasn't playing around."

"Oh, I know you weren't." She eyed him again, unable to stop her admiration.

At the car, he stopped her before she opened the door. "Maybe I should get into fights more often."

She tipped her head up, falling into this flirtation far too easily.

"And you in this outfit doesn't help matters." He

touched beneath her chin. "I've been dying to do this all day."

He kissed her, soft and slow. Then the flames took over and he deepened the caress. He didn't touch his tongue to hers, just gave her a long and reverent kiss.

She was beginning to think avoiding another tumble in bed would be impossible. And as for avoiding falling for Callum? That was becoming even more impossible by the moment.

Chapter Nine

Back at the Dales Inn, Callum saw that same SUV out front with someone inside. Funny, now that he had a closer look, this man didn't appear as large as the one who had shot at them. He must have been mistaken about the suggestion that this was their shooter.

"We should be fine. Just don't look at him." If it was a man. Callum wondered if it could be a female.

Up in the suite, he called Kerry, who told him she was on her way to check on them.

"Is there anyone else you can think of who has a grudge against you?" he asked Hazel.

Her head popped up from the tablet she had been playing around with. "What?"

He went over and sat beside her. "It just occurred to me that the person who's been sitting out in front of this inn might be a woman."

Her brow scrunched in confusion. "But the person who almost ran me and Evie over was a man. I know it."

"I know that, too."

"Well…what are you suggesting?"

"Maybe nothing. I'm more thinking out loud." He ran his fingers through his hair. "I just have this feeling that there is someone else seeking you out. The person who sits outside the inn doesn't shoot at us."

"We were in disguise."

Yes, but every time? What if Callum hadn't noticed the driver of the SUV before today?

"Can you think of anyone who might have a reason to be angry with you?" he asked.

She frowned in confusion. "Callum, I don't understand why you're asking me that. You think there is someone else—besides the kidnapper Evie witnessed—who is after me?"

"Yes, and no. Like I said, I'm thinking out loud, making sure I cover every angle."

After a moment she slowly shook her head. "No."

She seemed hesitant.

"What about your ex-boss? Carolyn Johnson?" The woman had lost everything after Hazel left her restaurant. People murdered for different reasons and revenge was one of them. Not that he could say for certain that Carolyn would try to kill Hazel. Maybe she stewed over her losses and blamed Hazel, but hadn't gone over the edge yet.

"Carolyn wouldn't do that," Hazel finally said. "She isn't that kind of person."

"People respond differently to life situations. What did that restaurant mean to her?"

When Hazel looked away, Callum already had his answer. The restaurant had meant everything to Carolyn.

"That's why I felt so terrible," Hazel said.

And Carolyn had seemed gracious and forgiving. Even accepting, maybe overly so. "Let's talk to her again. Maybe keep an eye on her."

"You mean…do surveillance on her?"

"Yes."

After a while she shook her head. "I don't know. I can't believe she'd do something like that."

"Let's hope not. Let's hope Carolyn is not somehow associated with the killer."

"What if whoever you saw out there wasn't Carolyn and was just waiting for someone else?"

That was possible, but Callum wouldn't take any chances.

"I need to be sure, okay?" He met her eyes in a silent plea to heed him.

She blinked in concession. "Okay." Then she gave him a faint smile that told him she appreciated his careful concern.

He heard his phone go off, indicating he had received a text message. It was from Kerry. She was five minutes out from the inn and she asked him to meet her in the parking lot.

After they each changed into normal clothes, he went back into the main room. "You wait here," he said to Hazel. "There's another officer outside on guard. I'm going to go down and meet Kerry."

"All right." Hazel sounded distracted, possibly weighed down by thoughts of Carolyn retaliating.

Assured that Hazel would stay put and she'd be safe in the suite, Callum rode the elevator down and went outside.

He spotted Kerry getting out of her vehicle. He also searched for the mysterious SUV and didn't find it. The driver must have given up and gone for the day.

He looked around for any other signs of danger. A man wheeled his luggage toward the inn entrance and a car left the parking lot. Movement drew his attention to a tree off to the side of the front doors, where a man smoked a cigarette and looked back at him. He was about the same build as the man he had seen who'd shoved a body into his trunk. It was hard to say, though, because this man stood and the other had been in the car. Could they be the same man?

"Do you see that?" Kerry asked.

"Sure do." He looked like a stalker. A few months ago, a creep had stalked Marlowe until he'd been caught.

"Let's go see if he'll talk to us."

Callum started for the man with her by his side. The man continued to smoke and watch them.

Kerry took out her badge and showed it to him. "Detective Kerry Wilder. Are you staying here?"

The man glanced at Callum and back at her, blowing smoke out and then dropping his cigarette onto the ground.

"No. I'm waiting for someone."

"What's your name?"

"Joseph Smith."

"Do you have any ID?" Callum asked.

The man removed his wallet and showed them his driver's license. It said Joseph Smith but any person, even a man who stole cars and committed murder, could come up with a fake one.

"Who are you waiting for?" Kerry asked.

"No one who's staying here. We just agreed to meet in this parking lot because it's halfway between where we live."

"What is the person's name who you're meeting?" Callum asked.

"You a cop like her?" Joseph asked.

"No. There's been suspicious characters loitering around this inn."

Joseph didn't respond right away but then he said, "Her name is Eleanor and I'd rather not tell you her last name. She's married. I don't want to get her in trouble."

Callum halfway believed this guy. Just when he was about to interrogate him some more, a gunshot rang out and a bullet splintered the bark of the tree.

"Holy...!" Joseph dove for the ground as Kerry and Callum drew their weapons and took cover, she behind the tree trunk and he behind another nearby.

He searched the parking lot and saw no moving vehicles or anyone inside a vehicle. Most notably, there was no sign of the SUV.

He spotted something in the trees surrounding the inn. "Over there!" He pointed.

Kerry nodded and yelled, "You stay here!" then sprinted for the trees.

Callum followed. He couldn't in good conscience allow her to track down a killer on her own. But she was the detective.

The shooter had a good head start, but he ducked behind a tree trunk and poked his head out to shoot at them. He missed Kerry by inches.

Callum fired back, forcing the man to retreat. He got a good enough look at him to know this person was bigger than the one in the SUV. Whoever this person was, he was very desperate to silence anyone who could track him down.

He and Kerry emerged from the trees where they had taken cover and ran to two others closer to their target.

The shooter fled. Callum didn't have a good shot, but

Kerry did. She fired and must have gotten the man's leg because he stumbled and then limped away.

Callum lost sight of him in the trees, but they soon reached a clearing and the highway. An older model Camaro was parked at the side of the road and the shooter got inside. By the time Callum and Kerry broke free of the trees, he had the car racing away. Kerry took aim and fired twice, breaking the back window but missing the driver.

She stood on the side of the highway staring after the vanishing car, putting her gun away.

Callum did the same.

"He's a slippery one, isn't he?" she said.

"Why did he shoot at us?" Callum asked.

"He was trying to shoot you," Kerry said.

He had shot at Kerry, too. Had he gone insane?

The detective called in the incident, which would bring in other officers. "I've got something else to discuss with you. Why don't you come up so Hazel can listen in?"

"All right. Is there more going on between you two than a mad shooter?"

He walked with her up through the trees—all part of the landscaping of the inn's grounds. "Unfortunately, yes." He was more convinced of that than ever.

HAZEL HEARD THE door open and looked up from the book she had been reading. She had to keep her mind off Evie. Kerry followed Callum into the suite.

Hazel stood from the sofa as they approached. "Did you find out who was out there?"

"That SUV was gone but someone started firing at us," Callum said.

"We were questioning a man who was standing outside the inn looking suspicious when we were shot at," Kerry added.

Hazel looked from her to Callum, confused as to who could have shot at them. "Was it the person in the SUV?" Maybe they had parked somewhere else.

Callum shook his head. "No. I'm sure of it. The gunman was bigger than the person in the SUV. I'm sure they're two different people."

"The person in the SUV is watching you?" Kerry asked. "Is it the stolen one from before?"

"No, this one was a charcoal gray and that other one was black. I didn't get a plate number, but I don't think that person is the same as the shooter. It's just suspicious. The gray SUV was parked out there a long time."

Kerry nodded. "Well, let me know if something changes or you see it parked out there again. And try to get a plate number. If it's someone different than our shooter, then maybe they won't be as careful." She glanced at Hazel. "Like, if it's someone you know." Looking back at Callum, she said, "I'll keep an undercover cop outside. I would suggest going somewhere else to stay, but given how brazen the shooter is, he will most likely come back. We could catch him if you keep drawing him here."

Callum told Kerry about Carolyn.

"Then your suspicion is definitely warranted. She may seem rational to your face but you never know what she's thinking or doing when no one is around."

Hazel didn't like imagining Carolyn capable of stalking her or something more, but she would keep an open mind.

"I should get going," Kerry said. "It's a really busy

day." She stopped at the door. "Hey, did you have any luck tracking down Nan Gelman?"

Judging by Callum's frown, he hadn't done anything yet and felt bad. "I'm sorry, with everything going on…"

"It would be great if you could do that."

"I'll see what I can come up with in the next few days for you about Nan."

"Thank you," Kerry said. With that, Kerry left.

Alone with Callum, Hazel began to get uncomfortable, as she usually did, because she had such a hard time controlling her attraction to him. He was just so nice to look at. She even loved the sound of his manly voice. And she couldn't forget the frequent reminders of how good they were together in bed.

"I've got to cook some meals. Can you start looking for this Nan person?"

"I need access to some systems through work. I can call Charles and get something going."

Hazel went into the kitchen to start cooking, ever aware of Callum as he made a call to Charles, who must have been his boss. She listened to him make a request for remote access and Hazel gleaned from the call that Charles would have what he needed delivered later that day. Just like that, he'd be connected.

Callum sat on the sofa and saw her book. Picking that up, he read the title, then the back cover. "You like thrillers?"

"I like any action-packed murder mystery." She watched a lot of the murder case shows on television.

"I like those, too."

She sneaked a look at him. Pretty soon they'd be watching television together like a couple who'd been together for years. It already felt like she knew him that well.

He put the book down and flipped channels, stopping on a local one showing a reddish-blond-haired woman with blue eyes talking on a news program. She stood in front of the Colton Oil offices, so Hazel assumed she was a member of the family. She was quite attractive and looked to be in her late forties. The banner beneath her image read Selina Barnes Colton, VP and Public Relations Director of Colton Oil.

"Ace Colton is innocent until proven guilty," she said to a group of reporters.

"Have you seen or spoken to him since he's become a suspect?" a reporter asked.

"No, I have not, and I am sure he will be exonerated very soon." She flashed a megawatt smile for the cameras.

Hazel got the impression that she liked attention. She did not sound very sincere. One look at Callum and she knew he had similar sentiments about the woman.

She gave a wave to the reporters and walked like a movie star to her Mercedes—a much, much, much more expensive one than Hazel drove. Hazel experienced a few seconds of envy but she knew she would never be happy with that kind of lifestyle. Just looking at the woman gave her more than enough information. That woman thrived on attention and material things, expensive things, unattainable things for most people. Hazel thrived on her daughter and the everyday routine. She paid no heed to what strangers observed in her. They either accepted her or they did not. No bother to her.

Caring about all that would take too much energy.

Energy better spent on what truly mattered. Evie. And real life. Real relationships.

Meeting genuine people was rare. Something to be cherished. Dear friends didn't come along at will.

Neither did meeting Mr. Right...

She saw Callum's expression had grown stormier.

Hazel finished with her recipe and put the freezable casserole into the oven. Cooking always lulled her into a state of artistic creation. She believed that the activity warded off stress and prolonged life because of that.

As she finished putting the food she had prepared into containers, she noticed Callum half-heartedly watching the newscast.

She put the Tupperware containers into the freezer, barely fitting them, and decided to delay cleaning the kitchen.

Going to where he sat, she plopped down beside him. "Everything okay?"

She saw his tension release. He leaned back and sighed. "Selina is kind of a loose cannon, in my opinion."

"Who is she to you?"

He let out another stress relieving breath. "Sorry. Selina Barnes Colton. She's vice president and director of public relations at Colton Oil. Also, my father's second ex-wife."

The way he said that piqued Hazel's curiosity. "Not well liked among the family?"

He grunted and looked at her. "No. My mother hates her. None of my brothers and sisters care for her much, either. We always were suspicious of her hold over him, why he keeps her on at Colton Oil."

Hazel saw him drift off into reflection. "She seems very good at her job. She put on a good show on that news segment. She might come across as lofty but I bet people buy into her game."

His demeanor smoothed some more and he looked at her again, this time much more warmly. "Yes, that is exactly how I would describe her. And I do think she is good at her job, but I also think she has something on my father and that is why he had to keep her on as an employee. She creates a lot of friction there—or so I'm told."

"But she's good at her job," Hazel summarized for him.

"She is good at her job."

"And you and your brothers and sisters are stuck with her."

"We are stuck with her." He met her eyes with warm regard.

As their uncontrollable chemistry heated up, he stretched his arm out behind her.

After a few simmering, electrically charged moments had passed, he said, "Selina hasn't let it leak to the press that Ace was ousted from the board."

Hazel didn't understand the significance of that. "Why wouldn't you want anyone to know?" Anyone paying attention to Payne's shooting in the news would know Ace was a suspect.

"The company bylaws say only a Colton by blood can be CEO."

That certainly held significance, but she thought of something else that might hold even more. "He wasn't ousted because he is a suspect in your father's shooting. He was ousted because he isn't a Colton by blood?"

Callum turned his head, his eyes going all shrewd

and sexy. "No one knows Ace was let go because of the bylaws. She's trying to protect the company."

"That's a good thing, right?"

"Yes. It would seem so. Although I don't trust Selina. I never have."

"What if she's the one who sent that email?" Maybe she had learned Ace wasn't a Colton by blood. But then why shoot Payne?

Hazel didn't think Ace had a strong enough motive to shoot Payne. All his father had done was remove him as CEO. Having thought about it that way, though, Hazel changed her mind. Maybe Ace did have motive. In the throes of bitter emotions of loss and betrayal, he could have snapped.

"What kind of relationship did Ace have with Payne?" she asked.

"Not bad. Dad can be tough and isn't one you'd want to cross, but Ace was his son in every way. Ace *is* his son."

His cell chimed, indicating a text message had arrived. He read it and then got up to go to his laptop on the table. His boss must have come through with a way to track down the woman named Nan.

She followed, sitting beside him, seeing him navigate from his email to a browser. "What are you doing?"

"I couldn't find her in a regular search. She doesn't work as a nurse anymore, from what I can tell. Charles found a good way to search the web."

"What is that? A search engine?"

"No, it's not a search engine like what you're accustomed to using. It's more like a repository of archived data. It accesses content that search sites can't or that have removed the information because it is old. Hundreds of times more in volume."

That sounded intriguing.

"How can it do that?"

"They're databases, not websites. It's content that is invisible to normal search engines."

She watched as he typed in Nan's name, which produced a daunting amount of results. Callum didn't seem bothered. He worked intently.

In just a few minutes he brought up a file that looked like a photo of announcements. He scrolled to a twenty-year-old wedding announcement for Nancy and Herman Hersh. In the text, Nancy's maiden name was listed: Gelman.

"You found her!" Hazel exclaimed, amazed and impressed.

"Maybe." He went back to searching. "Nancy Gelman might not be our Nan Gelman."

The Dark Web had brought forth information on a Nancy Gelman. Callum needed to find a link to Nan the nurse.

After a few more minutes he found the obituary of Samuel Gelman that listed the surviving family, with Nancy Hersh as one of them. He did additional searches and found that Nancy Hersh was the same person as Nan Gelman, a nurse who'd worked in the maternity ward at Mustang Valley General Hospital.

"She lives three towns over, in Mountain Valley," Callum said. "She's not related to the Gelmans from forty years ago that Kerry found in the census, though."

"We should tell Kerry."

While Callum called the detective, she called to check on Evie. She missed her daughter so terribly.

"Kerry is unavailable." He looked at Hazel after he hung up and she could see him contemplating going to see Nan himself. What could it hurt? They would help the investigation if they did and also save time.

"Let's go," Hazel said.

NANCY HERSH LIVED in a neighborhood one would expect of an average, everyday working family. Neat and tidy, green grass and no rundown vehicles or junk lying around. Callum walked with Hazel up to the door and rang the bell.

No one answered, so he rang the bell again.

Still, no answer. No one was home. After 6 p.m., it was late enough in the day that someone should be there after work.

"You looking for Nancy and Herman?" a woman called from the house next door.

Callum looked there and walked with Hazel into the woman's front yard. In jeans and an Arizona Cardinals T-shirt, the neighbor was in her forties with dark hair and rectangular glasses. He'd take advantage of her willingness to talk.

"Yes."

"They went to Europe. Just left yesterday. Won't be home for ten more days. Asked me to keep an eye on the place." She eyed them suspiciously. "Who are you?"

"They don't know us. We were hoping to ask Nancy a few questions," Callum said.

"About what?"

Was the woman being nosy or did she plan on reporting back to Nancy when she returned? Callum wasn't sure how much to reveal at this point. If Nancy had switched babies all those years ago when she worked at the hospital, had she suddenly vanished out of fear of prosecution—if she *was* the one who switched the babies? And why would anyone do that in the first place?

"We're reporters doing a story on the history of Mustang Valley General Hospital," Hazel said.

Callum inwardly cheered at her cleverness. "There was a fire there and we heard that Nancy was working around that time."

The woman's mouth spread into a smile. "Reporters, huh?"

She seemed happy that her friend and neighbor would get a little notoriety for a story about a historic hospital.

"We're freelancers, but yes, the article would appear in the paper," Hazel said.

And again, Callum was captivated by her ingenuity. He had a sudden urge to do something romantic with her tonight. Maybe dinner in a dimly lit restaurant followed by a quiet night at the inn.

"We'll come back when she's home."

"I can tell her you stopped by," the woman said as they headed back for the car. "What're your names?"

Callum waved farewell and didn't answer, hoping the woman wouldn't grow suspicious again.

"Why don't we grab dinner while we're here?" he asked when they were in the car. "I know a great place." He knew they hadn't been followed, so he felt safe in spending a little quality time with Hazel. He wouldn't think about what that meant for the near future, how it might bring him closer to her.

"All right." She smiled over at him, the whole beautiful presentation sending sparks shooting through his chest.

HAZEL WAS STILL floating on air after dinner. They had talked about opinions on politics and religion. They shared a lot of the same views.

At the hotel, she walked with him toward the entrance and saw a toddler with her mother. Wearing a cute pink dress with white tights, the girl laughed up at her mother, who crouched before her in the stroller.

Hazel could see and feel the love. Reminded of Evie at that age and younger, a pang hit her. A glance at Callum told her he had fallen into regret, likely thinking of Annabel.

"Evie was so adorable at that age," she said. "I wish I could have recorded the first time she said 'Mommy.' We were at the grocery store and she stared at my face like she always did. I have never seen a kid study faces the way she did. All of the sudden, when I was picking out some apples, I heard, 'Mommy.'" She smiled and a gush of love suffused her.

Callum chuckled. "I wish I could have been there. I can imagine it, though."

"All those moments happen when you least expect them. Except when she learned to walk. I taught her and she picked up on it pretty quickly, taking those first stumbling steps." Now she chuckled.

Callum opened the door for her and they entered the hotel. It was late, so they'd booked a room at this place rather than drive back late at night. The place was a nice one but not a five star like the Dales Inn.

She saw him reflecting again, his lightness gone.

"Are you thinking about Annabel?" she asked.

He turned to her as they headed for the bar. "About what I missed out on."

"You could always have another family, with someone else." With her...

They checked in and then walked to the elevators.

She stepped inside and faced him. He stood before her, still somber over what she had said earlier. She wondered if he was pondering having a baby with her.

"The more time I spend with you and Evie, the more that seems like a possibility," he said.

"The more you feel you can?" she asked.

After a few seconds, he nodded. "Yes."

She met his heated gaze and stepped toward him. Deliberately avoiding thinking about what would happen when the case was solved, she put her hands on his face and kissed him.

She didn't mean for it to turn into a firestorm, but the instant their lips touched, passion flared and they kissed fervently. That made her glad she had gone on the Pill.

The elevator doors opened and that broke them apart.

Hazel saw an elderly couple waiting on the floor outside. They looked shocked.

Callum took Hazel's hand and led her down the hall to their door.

As he swiped the keycard to their room, she moved in front of him, not able to wait. She put her hands on his face again and kissed him. His hands flattened on her lower back and he pulled her against him.

Pushing the door open, he walked forward and she backward into the room, bumping into the door as it swung closed.

Hazel began to unbutton his blue shirt, spreading the material aside to put her hands on his bare chest. He pulled up her blouse and she moved back to lift her arms. He tossed that to the floor and removed his shirt. Then he unclasped her bra and she sent that to the floor as well.

Callum cupped her breasts. "I will never get tired of looking at these."

She liked the sound of that. *Never.* That implied a future.

He returned to kissing her, caressing her nipples as he did.

She ran her hands over his muscular chest and abdomen, then around to his back and up to his shoulders.

Callum lifted her and stepped to the bed, letting her down. He unbuttoned her jeans and she pushed them off her legs, along with her underwear, while he got out of his.

Both of them naked, he crawled on top of her. She wrapped her arms around him as he resumed kissing her.

Hazel lost herself in the feel of her hands on his skin, roaming down his back to his rear. Ending the kiss, he just looked down at her. The wonder of all this entranced her, too.

At last he kissed her again, and she opened her legs as he sought to enter her. For long, slow moments they moved together. Each gentle penetration stirred her senses higher and higher, until they both climaxed at the same time.

Afterward, he pulled her beside him and held her, kissing her forehead.

"What the hell is happening with us?" he asked softly. Although he swore, he sounded bewildered.

"I don't know."

She didn't admit aloud that this could be the makings of true love, and she sensed him doing the same.

Chapter Ten

Callum stepped into the lobby of the Dales Inn, holding Hazel's hand. He had taken it after they left the car, ignoring the realization that the action had been automatic, driven by his affection for her and the passionate night they had shared. He also didn't want to hurt her by abruptly letting go.

The reception desk was busy. It was close to checkout time, and people rolled luggage toward the exit and away from the reception desk. People's voices mixed with a ringing telephone. A lone man walked toward the exit with no luggage. Something about him looked familiar. He had on sunglasses and a Stetson. Wrangler jeans and cowboy boots completed the cowboy ensemble.

The man looked at Callum and both of their steps slowed.

Callum knew this man. He approached and when he saw his jawline and nose in more detail he recognized Ace.

"Ace?" Callum checked out his brother. Ace would normally be seen in very expensive suits. About the only thing cowboy about him normally was his slightly unruly light brown hair.

"Yes. Callum." He leaned in for a quick manly hug. "Good to see you. I didn't know you had a new girlfriend." Ace looked at Hazel.

"This is Hazel Hart," Callum said.

She smiled and shook his hand. "Hello."

"From what I can see, Callum is the lucky one."

"Thanks for the compliment," Hazel said.

And Callum had to agree. He was the lucky one. Or not, if things fell apart.

"What are you doing here?" Callum asked.

Ace sighed his frustration. "I can't believe this is happening to me. I didn't shoot Dad."

Although Callum didn't believe his brother would kill anyone, he often wondered if it was possible Ace had fallen into a rage and acted impulsively. A lot of murderers went to prison that way. They seemed like normal, everyday, rational people but something happened to make them lose control momentarily and in seconds the deed was done. They killed and instantly wished they could undo the act.

"Dad had a long list of enemies," Callum said. "I wouldn't even know where to start to look for suspects." That's why he was a bodyguard and not a detective.

"I can't risk coming out of hiding. There is too much publicity." Ace glanced around as he must do all the time. "I'm going out of my room to get food. Other than that, I stay hidden. I'm a little worried you recognized me."

"I'm family. Anyone who doesn't know you well wouldn't."

"There are rumors all over Rattlesnake Ridge Ranch and my condo, so I'm staying at the Dales Inn until all the nonsense dies down. I'm half tempted to leave town, even though the cops told me not to. I cannot be arrested."

"You should be fine if you lay low," Callum said.

Ace didn't look convinced. "I miss it," Ace said. "Running Colton Oil. It's in my blood." He stopped as though catching himself. "Even if Colton blood isn't running through me, I am a Colton."

Having been raised by Coltons and then entering into the world of Colton Oil, Ace's entire life revolved around the family name. Callum felt for him, that he faced losing so much.

"No argument from me," Callum said. "You're my brother no matter what." Even if his instinct said Ace didn't shoot Payne and he ended up being wrong, Ace would always be his brother.

"I appreciate the support, brother." Then he glanced at Hazel. "What are you doing here?"

"Someone is after Hazel. She and her daughter witnessed a murder." He went through a brief explanation, Ace listening.

"You're working," Ace said when he finished.

"In a way, yes."

"I saw you holding hands," Ace said. "So, it must be more than work."

"In a way," Hazel said, mimicking Callum's response.

Ace laughed, low and brief. "Love at first sight?"

Callum didn't have a comeback for that. Hazel must not have, either, because she also had nothing to say.

"It's about time you had a long-term relationship," Ace said. "It's been, what, almost five years now since Annabel?"

Callum nodded.

"I always wondered about that. She must have done a number on you. Weren't you the one who broke up with her?"

"It was mutual."

Callum half saw Hazel glance sharply at him. He shouldn't lie to his brother. Or his family. Not anymore.

"Actually, I lied about that, Ace."

Ace's expression sobered. "Why?"

"We didn't break up. She died in a car accident. I was protecting a witness testifying in the trial of someone who worked for a drug cartel. They found out I was dating Annabel and had her killed to intimidate me. Annabel was also pregnant."

Ace gaped at Callum in stunned silence.

"I'm sorry. I...couldn't talk about her." He looked at Hazel. "Not until I met Hazel."

Her eyes turned soft with deep gratitude and respect. He felt himself falling in love with her.

"Wow, Cal. I had no idea. You should have told someone."

He nodded. "Probably. But I just couldn't. It devastated me." Hell, it had changed him. He was not the same man as he was before that. He was a lot more cautious now. And better at his job. The one good thing that had come out of the experience.

"He blamed himself for her death," Hazel said to Ace. "She was murdered after the trial, when Callum was no longer watching over her."

"Then clearly it was not your fault."

"I should have checked out the suspect more. I should have known what kind of monster he worked for."

"You can't blame yourself for that. You aren't a cop. You're a bodyguard, and a damn good one." Ace did another check of the lobby and his eyes stopped short toward the entrance.

"Sorry to cut this short," Ace said. "I have to go now."

Callum followed his eyes and saw two police officers enter the lobby.

"You go back up to your suite. We'll bring food to you." Callum nudged his brother with a hand on his shoulder. "Hazel is a personal chef."

"I miss good food. The food here is good, but I mean my favorite restaurants."

Callum chuckled and gave his brother a pat on the back, letting him walk to the elevators. He wouldn't risk anyone exposing Ace.

"I HOPE I didn't sign you up for more work than you can handle," Callum said as they entered the suite.

Hazel walked in ahead of him, feeling him check out her butt. "It's a slow week. I have some pork chops to make today and that's pretty much it. I'd like some more to do."

"I'll pay you, of course. Can you come up with a week's menu?"

"What kind of food does Ace like?" she asked, turning in the living room to face him.

She saw him take in her face and chest. "He isn't picky. Seafood pasta, burgers, Mexican. Anything but Indian food."

"Easy enough. I'll write up a menu. I know a good weeklong plan."

Hazel used the same meals for certain types of people. In minutes she had a list and handed it to him.

"You're going to increase my revenue this month,"

she said. "There are perks to this relationship." She winked at him, making him want to take her into his arms and show her the other perks.

Hazel made a quick call to Evie, which she did each day. She went into the kitchen, hearing him phone Patsy. Once again she marveled over how quickly he could make things happen. He had people at his service with just a call. Money gave him that. As he talked to Patsy she admired his profile, from his sloping nose to his moving lips, and on down to his strong shoulders and chest, flat stomach…nice ass…and long, manly legs. He'd called Patsy for her. She had almost refused to let him pay her but she needed the money. And she also felt pampered and liked that.

Reminded of Ed, she cut short her too-trusting reaction. *Treat it like a business deal.* He wasn't asking her to prepare meals for his brother because he wanted her sexually. He'd asked for her business.

She started to prepare a pork chops recipe. Chops never turned out well if all you did was cook them in the oven. In culinary school she'd learned that the secret was to brine the pork first. Hazel had already done so and now got a pan out to sear the meat.

As she began to do that, Callum joined her in the kitchen. She retrieved the chops from the refrigerator, where they had been soaking in water and salt for three hours. Removing them from the solution, she placed them on a paper towel, flipping them to dry the other side.

Next, she brushed them with olive oil and then sprinkled them with garlic.

Callum joined in with the onion salt and she said, "Good," when he'd done enough on each chop.

She followed up with pepper, glancing up at him. His playful eyes caught hers. He enjoyed being close to her. The seasoning was just an excuse.

"If I stick with you I could learn how to cook," he said.

If he stuck with her? As in being girlfriend-boyfriend? She decided not to rein in her temptation to play along. This was too fun.

"I hope you're a fast learner, then." She let him interpret that any way he chose. She meant she hoped he'd learn to forgive himself for the deaths of his girlfriend and child and open himself up to new love. And quickly. Before Nate Blurge's murderer was caught.

"I fear you're the kind of woman who could make me one," he said.

He had interpreted what she had said exactly as she meant it. Tickled on the inside, she seared one side of the chops and then the other, feeling as hot as the pan right now.

After placing the chops on a pan, Callum put it into the oven. Then he straightened and faced her, the movement bringing him right before her.

She put her hands up against his chest, a reflexive reaction.

He didn't step away and she found herself melting into his eyes. The seconds ticked on but she was only aware of him and the heat rising.

"What's next?" he murmured.

"I…" Dazed by the fire coursing through her, she at first thought he referred to their close proximity.

"With the pork chops," he said.

"Oh." She breathed a laugh. "Three minutes on each side and then they're done. Then I need to make the vegetable. I already have the potatoes and gravy in the freezer."

Their room phone rang.

Hazel went to answer it. "Hello?"

"Hello," a man's voice said. "This is the front desk. We have a delivery here for Ms. Hart."

"Oh. A delivery?" She glanced at Callum, whose lighthearted expression turned to concern.

"Yes, ma'am."

"Okay. I'll be right down." She hung up and turned the stove off before going for the door. "There's something at the front desk for me."

Callum headed for the door ahead of her. "I'll go with you."

They took the elevator down.

In the lobby she walked with him to the front desk, where she already saw a vase full of flowers and a box of what had to be chocolates next to it.

"I take it you didn't send me those," she said, needing to keep the moment light.

"No, but maybe I should."

At the desk, she told the clerk her name. He slid the vase and box toward her.

Callum took the box and opened it. Inside were what appeared to be ordinary chocolates. She removed the card from the flowers.

Reading aloud, she said, "Thank you for preparing me all the wonderful meals. It's signed Abigail." She looked up at Callum. "That's my client who lives in the house where that man almost ran me and Evie over."

He took the box of chocolates. "We have to tell Kerry."

"Kerry...why?" Did he think Abigail sending these

was significant? That had been her first thought, as well, but would the killer be this subtle? He had already tried to run her down and shoot her. He must know Evie wasn't with her now. If the chocolates were poisoned, he would only take out Hazel, not the star witness.

"It may be nothing but we have to be sure. If they turn out to be all right, I'll replace the box of chocolates."

She glanced at the flowers. Was there a way to poison those?

"I think we'd all be dropping dead already if those were casting off any toxins," Callum said, having read her thoughts.

"Abigail is a new client. If these are from her, it's good to know I won't be losing her."

"This doesn't seem like the killer's MO," Callum said. "It's more like what an ex-boss would do for revenge."

"Carolyn?" She still could not imagine her capable of murder. Why would she try to kill Hazel for leaving the restaurant? Even if she blamed her for her ruin, would she really resort to murder?

A few days later, Kerry called with the results of toxicological testing done on the chocolates and they came back negative. She'd also confirmed that Abigail sent them.

Callum asked Patsy to bring a replacement box to the front desk of the inn without Hazel knowing and was waiting for her call.

Hazel stood behind the kitchen counter, where she had worked for hours on a new order. The flowers, now in a vase, were still fresh on the dining table.

"Callum?" Hazel asked.

Judging by her tone he sensed a serious question was on the way.

"Yes?"

"Can I ask you something about Annabel?"

Yup, here they went. Mentally preparing himself, he said, "Yes."

She set down the knife she'd been using in the kitchen. "Do you still keep in touch with any of the friends you had together?"

What made her ask that? "We didn't really have any friends in common, only mine and hers."

"Why haven't you spoken with her parents in all these years?"

"They don't want to hear from me."

"You indicated that before, but I have my doubts. If anything, they'd be more upset that you didn't keep in touch. You were the last person to be close to her. You were going to have a baby together. Don't you think they'd like to talk to you? You could tell them things about her in the days before she died. Was she happy? Maybe some special moment you two had. They probably needed that and you abandoned them."

"I didn't abandon them. I got their daughter killed. Seeing me would only remind them of that."

"Now, see, there's where I think you're wrong. You said they invited you to the one-year memorial and you didn't go."

"I couldn't go."

"Right. You were out of the country, but you could have called and told them that."

He looked over at her, unable to refute her point.

"Okay then, I couldn't have gone even if I was available."

"Now *that* I believe," she said. "You've been running all this time. You buried her and your emotions. You didn't even tell your own family about her death."

"I *couldn't*." Didn't she get it?

"But I bet you can now," she said quietly, gently.

It had been long enough now that he should be able to face Annabel's family. And funny how the thought of that wasn't as painful as it had been in the months after Annabel's death. He felt more open to the idea.

"It would help you move on, Callum," Hazel said. "And now that I have a vested interest in you, I encourage you to reach out to them."

She had a vested interest in him? He grinned over her choice in words.

"And I'm hoping you feel the same about me and will work on getting over Annabel's death."

She hoped he had a vested interest in her. Did he? He enjoyed her company. He felt an intense attraction to her. But he still couldn't think about any kind of long-term future with her.

His cell chimed and he was relieved for the interruption. He read a text from Patsy. The returned chocolates were downstairs.

"There's something for you at the desk again," he said to her.

"Again?"

"Maybe it's another admirer. Come on. Let's run down there."

She rinsed her hands and dried them and then adjusted one of the burners to low. Then she rode the elevator with him. In the lobby they were headed for the desk when he spotted a woman who looked vaguely familiar. She wore a baseball cap and sunglasses, but her hair was a blond bob. Carolyn. She wasn't dressed as smartly as when he'd first seen her. She wore jeans and a T-shirt today. Was she trying to disguise her appearance?

She turned her head and saw them. Callum pretended not to notice her and went to the desk with Hazel. The clerk gave her the new box of chocolates.

"Those are from me," Callum said. His voice sounded lower than normal and he had to attribute that to liking giving her something romantic.

Her mouth parted in surprise and she took them. "I didn't think you'd actually do this. Thank you."

He'd have to get her flowers, too, when the others wilted.

Carrying the box, she opened it a crack to retrieve one, popping it into her mouth as she walked away from the counter.

Callum looked toward Carolyn. She watched them. Was she trying to monitor their movements? If so, she was doing a terrible job. He looked through the front windows to the parking area and saw a dark SUV.

Taking Hazel's hand, he steered her toward Carolyn. Might as well confront her. Maybe it would dissuade her from any future attempts to do whatever she might intend against Hazel.

"That's Carolyn over there," he said to Hazel.

She searched the room until her gaze came back to the woman in the cap. "She never dresses like that."

"I didn't think so."

Carolyn stood as they approached, awkwardly removing her sunglasses as though feeling caught. "Well, fancy meeting you here again."

"Carolyn," Hazel said. "Why are you here?"

"I'm waiting to meet the manager about an upcoming catering event."

"Who are you catering for?" Callum asked.

"It's a local business," she said, sounding blasé. "An all-day meeting."

He doubted she had to meet in person to discuss what needed to be done in preparation for a business meeting.

"Why are you still here?" Carolyn asked. "Is that man not captured yet?"

"No, unfortunately."

"Where is Evie?" Carolyn asked. "I never see you without her."

With Hazel's hesitation, Callum knew she was thinking twice about telling her former boss. "She's somewhere safe."

Carolyn eyed her peculiarly, as though not missing that Hazel had chosen not to tell her. "This whole thing must be so disruptive to your business. Without a kitchen to handle all that cooking."

"Oh, no. It hasn't slowed me down at all," Hazel said. "Our suite has a full kitchen and Callum has lined me up with new customers."

Callum wondered if she was aware of how unabashedly excited and happy she sounded to be so busy.

"He has, has he?" Carolyn looked over at him and then back at her.

"I'm supplying one of his brothers with food this week and that has already led to other customers."

Ace had recommended a few to Callum, who had

made some calls. Hazel's business was thriving and would continue to do so.

"You always did seem charmed," Carolyn said with a hint of resentment. "Some people are just born with luck, aren't they? A great start to a new business and a handsome man to boot. Cute little girl. How do you do it? Is there a method?"

"I..." Hazel seemed perplexed. "I guess I just follow my heart."

"That's what I did and look where it got me."

Hazel studied her for several seconds. "Carolyn, you aren't angry with me for leaving your restaurant, are you?"

Carolyn waved her hand through the air. "Of course not. I understand people have their own lives to live."

Her answer fell flat because she seemed to be overdoing her sugary tone.

"Yes, but my leaving put you in a difficult position. I wish you would have told me."

"You were busy doing your thing. People do that. They move on without a second thought to those around them. I'm sure you did what was best for you and your daughter."

"Carolyn. Maybe we should talk. You're angry with me."

Carolyn shook her head. "No. I just understand people."

"People in the restaurant industry can be brutal. Not just cantankerous customers, either," Hazel said. "Executive management and coworkers. It's a highly stressful environment for a career. That was one of the reasons I left it. I'm not in a restaurant environment anymore. Maybe you should consider doing something similar."

Carolyn scoffed. "You told me that was one of your reasons. You had a daughter to look after and wanted to be with her more. But that kind of choice won't work for me. I'm not a chef."

Did Carolyn now feel trapped in an unsatisfying career? She must prefer being the boss. Short of owning a restaurant, she'd still have to report to someone. Nobody liked that but most of them had no choice. Callum was lucky to have a boss who let him do his job and didn't inflict any ego-driven power trips on him.

"The manager must be running late," Callum said.

Carolyn turned to him and he saw that she recognized he didn't believe her.

"I'm early."

"I mean it, Carolyn," Hazel said. "We should talk."

Callum would not allow that unless he was right next to her. Second nature in his line of work was not trusting anyone, especially when there appeared to be a good reason not to. Why would Hazel suggest such a thing? Why did she want to talk to her? He got it that she had empathy for the woman, but maybe she was trying a little bit too hard.

"We have talked. I don't think there's anything left to say."

But maybe there was something to *do*. And what would that be? What would Carolyn do in retaliation for Hazel causing the demise of her business?

Chapter Eleven

Hazel went with Callum to check on his father. There was still no change in his condition. Callum wanted to sit in the room awhile. Hazel sat on the couch, her bodyguard in a chair beside the bed, just watching his father's still and pale face. Machines hummed around him and lines hung from Payne's body.

Hazel could see Callum genuinely needed another chance to be close to Payne Colton. His tense mouth and eyes said that his thoughts ventured beyond worry.

"Who besides Ace do police think may have shot him?" she asked.

He looked at her, coming out of his deep thoughts. "They considered many, most in the family. They even considered Marlowe, since she is now CEO."

Hazel wondered if all of this was related to Ace being switched at birth. "It seems like too much of a coincidence that he was shot so soon after that email was sent about Ace not being a Colton by blood."

He nodded. "Yeah, I thought about that myself. We're all trying to figure out who switched him—and if that same person sent that email via the Dark Web. Marlowe and I tried to find hospital records, but a hospital administrator told us there was a fire on Christmas morning, the morning Ace was born. All the records were destroyed. We thought it too much of a coincidence that the fire broke out then."

"The person who did the switch must have set it," she said.

"Yes. It would seem that way. What we all can't understand is, why anyone would switch a healthy baby with one who wasn't?"

"The real Colton baby wasn't healthy?"

"No. He wasn't doing well. That's why Ace was called a Christmas miracle, because none of his symptoms were present the next day."

Further proof—if the DNA wasn't enough—that Ace had been switched. Someone really unbalanced must have done it. Hazel could see no other motive for Ace to shoot Payne than anger over being cast out of Colton Oil. Whoever had shot Payne had to have another reason—one related to the baby switching. Maybe she was wrong, she was no detective, but the motive had to be more complicated than that.

"Is there any evidence supporting Ace's innocence?" she asked. All the times she'd encountered him, he had not struck her as a violent man. She had a good barometer when it came to judging people. In the last two weeks they'd stopped by his room four times. Ace had never been anything but kind and gracious when she and Callum had delivered food.

"Not really," he said. "There's video footage showing a person who's around five-nine wearing a ski mask and black clothes near the crime scene. If it's a man he's not very big. Ace also doesn't own a gun. If anything, the evidence points toward him. It might not be Ace in the video but Ace had the resources and the motive to hire someone to shoot Payne. There's no video showing him coming home the night of the shooting but there is video showing other Coltons arriving home at the mansion."

"So, there was nothing wrong with the surveillance equipment." If Ace claimed to be home, which he must be doing, then the video evidence contradicted that. "And then there's the threat that the board all witnessed."

"Yes, the threat. And a cleaning woman named Joanne Bates, who found Payne's body, heard someone say *mom* just before he was shot." He looked back at his father, clearly frustrated that his brother had to be in such a perilous situation.

Hazel stood and went to him, putting her hand on his shoulder. He looked up and put his right hand over hers. Warm tingles spread through her as their gazes met and locked. She could feel him returning what she felt. With just a touch and the invisible energy linking them in a look, she fell into the magic of their chemistry.

If Evie had been there, she'd have acted as a buffer. Without her, there was none. Hazel might as well be floating through rapids toward a waterfall ahead. As soon as she reached the edge, there'd be no turning back.

CALLUM SPENT THE next two days thinking about what he and Hazel had discussed about going to talk with Annabel's parents. Avoiding them had been a burden in and of itself. Not telling anyone about Annabel's death had, too. He had to agree it was long past due that he go and see them.

He had just finished making a delivery for Hazel.

Driving in the car gave him more time to solidify his decision. He had also had time to make a few calls.

Entering the suite, he found Hazel relaxing on the sofa with her feet up. Something smelled really good.

"What's for dinner?"

"Truffled bay scallops with celery purée, buttery potatoes and snap peas."

"You're going to make me fat." He went to her, bent and planted a kiss on her mouth. It was something he had never done before—come home and kiss her, first thing. She looked up at him with startled but heated eyes.

"I made arrangements to fly to San Francisco to go see Annabel's parents. I decided not to tell them I'm coming."

After surprise turned to a warm glow of appreciation, she reached up and touched his cheek. "That's good, Callum."

"You're coming with me." He wouldn't let her out of his sight. "We'll be safer if we aren't here anyway."

"How long will we be there?"

"I got open tickets so we can come back when we need to. In case they aren't home when we go there."

"You want me to be with you? I don't think—"

"Yes. I want you there. You're the one who helped me get to this point. I want you with me."

She tipped her head back, seeking his mouth. Still bent over, he obliged and kissed her. He kept his mouth pressed to hers, feeling her breath and the sparks that always started with just this.

Reluctantly lifting his head, he looked into her sultry eyes. "Keep that up and you're going to rope this cowboy in."

She smiled. "You're not a cowboy."

He chuckled. "I can be for you." Seeing her smile slowly fade, he knew some sobering thought had caused it, something about the two of them. He walked around the sofa and sat beside her. "What's the long look for?"

She sighed and snuggled closer to him. He put his arm around her, feeling this was so right.

"I can see a weight has been lifted off you," she said.

It has. "I do feel that way. It feels good."

"I love this," she said. "You and me relating like we're a couple, like this could last."

He hadn't thought much about the future. He had only acted on how good it felt to look forward to resolving something he hadn't thought bothered him as much as it had.

"Well, what if things don't go the way you expect in San Francisco? What happens after this euphoria fades and you begin to think about how serious you and I are becoming?"

"Are we becoming serious?" He wasn't so sure. They had great sex. How could they know that would translate into compatibility in every other way? How did anyone know that without spending months, or even years, together?

She moved back from him. "Do you have any feelings for me?"

He knew he was falling for her and thought she was extremely beautiful. More. There was something about her that was different from any other woman. "I enjoy being with you." And he truly meant that. He loved spending time with her and Evie. "We seem to be hitting it off really well. You make me feel good and I hope I make you feel the same. So, yeah, I'd say I have feelings for you."

He didn't want to ask if she had feelings for him. He didn't want to know right now. What if something happened to her or Evie? He cringed with even the suggestion. He could not go through that again. Not ever. And given her situation, she was in a lot of danger. Something could easily happen to her.

Best to keep his distance—at least for a little while longer.

AFTER THEY LANDED in San Francisco, Hazel drove with Callum to their hotel. They checked in and then Callum drove their rental to Annabel's parents' house. She was probably as nervous as he was, but for a different reason. He was about to face the biggest demon from his past and she would find out if there was any hope for them as a couple.

On the way, she called Evie. Her brother answered.

"Hey, it's me," she said.

"Hazel. How are you?" Owen asked. "Is everything okay? I was about to call you to check."

"We're doing fine. We are going out of town for a little bit, hopefully to find information. How's Evie?"

"She's good. Keeping busy."

"Is that Mommy?" Hazel heard her daughter almost screech in excitement. She missed her so much.

"She's about to grab the phone from me." Owen chuckled as Hazel listened to him hand the phone to Evie.

"Mommy?"

"Yes. Hi, honey, how are you?" Being without her

had been a lot harder than she thought. Not having that bundle of energy around all the time created a big hole.

"I miss you. When are you coming to get me?"

"I can't yet, but I hope to real soon. Are you having fun?" She would try to steer her daughter away from talk of when she could go get her and bring her home.

"Yes. We went on a picnic and the movies. I got to see Tinkerbell."

"Oh yeah?" Adoration and love filled her to overflowing. And gratitude for her brother keeping Evie entertained.

"Yeah. And they took me to work. I got to ride in a police car."

"Wow. That's exciting." Owen wouldn't have taken her on any emergency calls. He must have just given her a ride.

"Mommy?"

"Yes, sweetie?"

"I want to be a police girl when I grow up."

Evie had been getting a lot of exposure to policewomen, first Kerry and now Jessica. "That's a good profession. You'd make a fine one. And you're already getting experience." Hazel believed that children could not get enough encouragement. It allowed them to focus more on the positive than the negative, what they could do as opposed to what they couldn't.

"I like Jessica. She bosses all the boys around."

Hazel laughed and saw Callum pull to the side of the street. They had arrived at Mark and Loretta's home.

"She's a good role model for you then. I've got to go, Evie. You be good for me."

"Okay, Mommy."

Hazel would never get tired of her kiddie voice, high and sweet. She'd miss that when Evie grew up. "I love you."

"Love you, too."

Hazel didn't hear any disconnect and in the next couple of seconds her brother came back on. "Hey," he said.

"She sounds really good."

"Yeah. She's a good kid. You're doing an amazing job with her."

"Give her a kiss and a hug for me."

"Will do. Are the police any closer to catching that shooter?"

"No. We're trying to track down information on the victim and hoping that will lead to something. All we know so far is he liked to flirt and he went to a bar a lot. The sooner we find out more, the better." She wanted Evie back by her side.

"Well, don't worry about Evie. She's warm, safe and dry here."

Warm, safe and dry. "I like that. Thanks, Owen."

"Take care."

She ended the call and looked over at Callum, who must have been watching her and listening the whole time. He had a soft expression, his eyes full of admiration or maybe envy. For a man who shied away from mothers and children, he sure seemed to yearn for exactly that type of family life.

"You ready?" she asked.

"Yes." He got out of the car and so did she.

They walked to the house, a three-thousand or so square foot two-story home. A rock water fountain bubbled beside the front door. Callum rang the bell. After a few moments a lanky man with a headful of gray hair appeared. He looked from Hazel to Callum and froze. He was surprised to see him.

"Hello, Mr. Rubio."

"Why are you here?" Mark asked.

"I'd like to talk if you're okay with that."

Mark Rubio stared at him awhile.

"This is Hazel Hart," Callum said without any further explanation as to why she was there with him.

"Who's here, Mark?" a woman called from inside.

A remarkably youthful woman appeared, blue eyes widening and then going rather chilly as she stopped beside her husband.

"Well, you're here, so you may as well come in." Mark moved aside.

"Thank you." Callum stepped in, putting his hand on Hazel's lower back.

She wasn't sure if the contact gave him reassurance or if it was an automatic gesture. Either way, she felt the touch all the way to her toes.

The house was clutter-free and painted in shades of gray and earthy tones with white trim. Mark led them into a formal living room toward the front of the house. Hazel got the distinct impression that was no mistake, as though Annabel's father did not want to welcome them into their home.

Mark and Loretta stood on the opposite side of the entry, facing Callum and Hazel.

"First, I want to apologize for not coming to see you sooner," Callum said. "When you sent that invitation to the year memorial of her death, I should have at least called you."

"You vanish from our lives as though Annabel didn't matter one bit and you expect us to believe you? You discarded her like trash. Were you glad she was gone? That's how it seemed to us."

Callum shook his head emphatically. "I never meant to make you think that. I just… I just couldn't…"

Mark's brow creased in confusion. "You had nothing to do with her murder."

"I should have protected her. I could have."

"How?" Mark asked.

Callum pinched the bridge of his nose and then let his hand drop. "I should have known she would still be in danger after I finished protecting that witness."

"You did your job."

"You should have been with us during that time," Loretta said. "You abandoned us. You were all we had left of her."

"I'm sorry." Callum breathed out. "I'm here now. I'm here the soonest I could be, largely thanks to this woman here." He put his arm around Hazel. "She helped me see what I had been doing, which was burying extreme pain."

"What do you think we were going through?" Loretta asked. "We lost our daughter and our grandchild. When you vanished we lost a son-in-law."

Callum hadn't married Annabel, but they must have thought of him as part of the family.

"He didn't tell anyone in his family Annabel died," Hazel said.

"No one?" Loretta asked, incredulous.

"I couldn't."

Loretta stepped forward then. "Oh, you poor man." She touched his face. "You should have come to see us. You could have talked to us about it. We needed that with you."

"I know that now. I'm sorry."

"This doesn't make things all right with us," Mark said. "You caused our grief to be worse by not being with us."

Hazel thought that was a little over-the-top. Mark must not be a very forgiving man, but his wife was.

"I know it's taken me too long to come and see you. If there's anything you want to talk about, I'm here now."

Loretta stepped back. "There is something I have wondered all this time." She folded her arms. "Annabel told us about the baby the day after she found out, the day after you both found out. But I didn't get to talk to her much before she died. She came to see me once and we talked about how good things were going between you two. She didn't know at that time whether you were having a boy or a girl, but I know she had an ultrasound scheduled."

Hazel wished she could give the three some privacy. She felt this was a very personal moment.

"She was at twenty weeks," Callum said. "There was no sign of a penis and the doctor said we were having a girl."

Loretta covered her mouth with her hand as a sob wrenched her.

Hazel lowered her gaze, feeling she intruded too much.

"She was thrilled," Callum said. "So was I."

Hazel looked at him and became captivated by the light in his eyes, the slight curve of his lips the memory brought. That had been a magical moment for him. Hazel remembered when that day had come for her. *Magical* didn't come close to describing what seeing the miracle of life could do to a person.

As she realized the depth of his emotional injury, the weight of the risk to her heart settled in. His journey to healing wasn't over. And she had been instrumental in guiding him onto this path. She might be the rebound woman.

The image of Evie's gap-toothed smile pierced her. Her innocent eyes. Her tiny, soft-skinned fingers. The way she sometimes skipped instead of walking. When she talked to bumblebees and ladybugs. Not spiders. Although she did respect the aphid eaters... She didn't want to involve her child in a tenuous relationship with a hopeful father figure who had so much weight to bear. But the more time she spent with Callum, the more she felt like it was out of her control.

Chapter Twelve

Callum knew Hazel had suffered at least some tension during that visit.

He might be a brawny workingman, but he did have a sensitive side. He was grateful for her support despite how she must have felt like an intruder. And hearing about his and Annabel's special moment could not have been easy.

She had been quiet all the way to the hotel near the airport and now surfed channels on the television. Their flight back to Arizona was in the morning. Callum couldn't explain his need to make it up to her, to tell her that Annabel's memory didn't loom large as much as it used to. A voice said Hazel mattered more but that scared him, so he didn't give it any credence.

Going to the suite phone, he called room service and ordered champagne with strawberries and requested a delayed dinner of steak and crab. When he hung up and turned to Hazel, he saw her looking at him peculiarly.

"I figured we could use a nice dinner tonight," he said.

Her eyes narrowed.

"Okay, I figure I owe you at least that, if not more, for what you did for me today."

"Me? I didn't do anything."

"You were there for me." He walked over to where she sat on the sofa and took a seat right next to her. Taking the remote, he searched for a classical music station and found one playing a piano dominant tune.

After a few minutes, she said, "I know what you meant about seeing the sex of the baby for the first time."

"Were you alone when you saw it?" he asked.

"Yes. My family was in Colorado. But I sent them copies of the sonogram."

"That kind of thing bonds the parents together," he said.

"So I gathered." She inched away from him on the sofa. "You and Annabel had a special thing going."

He had brought up the bonding on purpose. He intended to lead into what he really needed to say.

"We did bond over the baby, but that didn't change the way either one of us felt about each other. I told you I would like to believe I loved her, but after all this time and much reflection, I know I didn't love her as much as I could love a woman." He wouldn't say how he knew that. He knew because he could love Hazel ten times more. "I loved her enough to marry her and have a family, but at some point, it would have become clear that she wasn't the one for me, and I would always have wondered who the right woman would have been."

"Would you have stayed in the marriage?"

"With children involved? Yes. Annabel was a good person. Honest, full of integrity. There would have been no good reason to leave her."

"Other than not being happy," Hazel said.

"I would have been happy enough with her. It's not

like she made me miserable, nor do I think she ever would have." There were different degrees of happiness. People could find great joy even if they married someone they weren't madly in love with. As long as there was loyal companionship and friendship, marriage could work.

"I would have had plenty of good reasons to leave Ed, had he stayed and married me," Hazel said. "I'm not even sure I would have agreed to marry him."

Room service knocked and Callum let them in. The champagne was in an ice bucket and the strawberries in a bowl. The room service attendant put the tray on the coffee table. Callum tipped him and he left.

Going back to Hazel, he sat beside her. Leaning forward, he removed the bottle of champagne and easily and gently popped the cork, which didn't go flying. Setting that aside, he poured Hazel, then himself, some. Handing her a glass, he clinked his to hers.

"Here's to you being the amazing woman you are."

She smiled softly. "Thank you."

As she sipped, her golden-green eyes looked up at him suggestively, heatedly. When she lowered her glass, she said, "If you aren't careful, you might end up liking me too much to leave me when this is all over."

He'd rather not go there yet. "Maybe. I prefer to take it one day at a time."

"Me as well." She took a strawberry from the bowl and put it to his mouth.

He ate it and then took one for her, feeding her a strawberry.

"Mmm, there is something about strawberries and champagne," she said.

"It's the pairing of the sweetness in both." He sipped some champagne.

"What were you like before Annabel?" Hazel asked.

He wasn't sure what she wanted to know. "With women? The same."

"No, did you date a lot? My guess is you had girls crawling all over you in high school. After that you must have dated a lot."

He hadn't thought of that since Annabel was killed. He had been very different. "I did date a lot."

"Were you popular in high school?"

"I was a quarterback. I wouldn't say I was the most popular. I didn't get into school politics. That crowd seemed more popular."

She breathed a laugh, clearly disagreeing.

"What about you?" he asked.

"I was popular. I was a cheerleader and I dated the quarterback. He and I were king and queen at our senior prom."

"Do they still do that in school? Kings and queens." He grunted in humor. "Seems like another lifetime ago." He set aside his glass.

"Yes, and I'm only twenty-five."

More memories from that time came to him. He hadn't been popular with the good kids. He had run with a more rugged crowd.

"Back then I had more of a reputation as a bad boy," he said.

She nodded thoughtfully. "I can see that." She put her glass on the side table.

This conversation was far more interesting than sharing champagne and strawberries. "I started rebelling against my dad my sophomore year. That's when he began *prepping* me for joining the Colton Oil executives." He had not been executive material. Even as a kid he had always sought danger. Climbing trees. Riding motorcycles and mountain bikes. Rock climbing. Skiing. Anything exciting.

"I got into a lot of fights. Some of the other kids tried teasing me about being a Colton, a spoiled rich kid. Those kids usually got nosebleeds after I punched them. I almost was expelled. I think only my father's connections prevented that. He grounded me and tried reasoning with me, but I never listened. He never laid a hand on me but I bet he wanted to more than once."

"A bad boy. All because your dad wanted you to join Colton Oil?"

"Not just that. I aspired to a different existence. Something more earthy and adventurous."

"Hence the military and then personal protection." *Earthy and adventurous.*

He had never conveyed his life journey to anyone in that way. He left his thoughts to look at her, this magnificent woman. "I loved the navy, but not the discipline. Being a bodyguard suits me perfectly."

Hazel sat back and sipped her champagne, crossing one slender leg over the other. In admittedly selfish pleasure, he covertly took in the shape of her knee and the lines of her fit thighs and the side view of the curves of her butt.

"Mr. Callum Colton," she said, turning her head with just the right angle to give her eyes a sultry slant. "You are one sexy, successful man."

Her relaxed pose and flirtatious words and tone threw him. "And…you are…" What could he say? She had already trumped him. *She* was one sexy, successful woman. Taking a chance, he moved in, touching her cheek and kissing her.

He would have encouraged her for more but she drew back, almost flinching.

Opening his eyes, he searched hers.

After several seconds, she asked, "Would you ever be able to try having a family again?"

Her catching, whispered question speared him.

This conflict would not go away. She had been abandoned, pregnant with Evie, and he had lost the mother of his unborn child, and with her a baby girl he would never know.

He and Hazel had issues that meant they might never be able to work together to form a healthy, new relationship. Everything felt so good with her. Everything felt right and safe. But was it?

Callum could never go through what he'd gone through with Annabel ever again. He had to be honest here. People died. Hazel could die. Something could happen to both her and Evie. What if they had a child of their own? Something could happen to that child.

He imagined living with Hazel and Evie, having a blended family and living an everyday life together. Spending time in the evenings with them. Doing schoolwork. Going to bed every night with Hazel. He would fall in love with that life. He could already feel it to his core. And then, after growing more attached than he had ever been to Annabel, what if something tragic happened? Nothing and no one could predict life or what awaited everyone as time marched on.

"I don't know if I'm ready for that." Would he ever be?

His spirit plummeted as he saw Hazel's reaction. Her

face hardened to disappointed stone and she lowered her eyes in sadness before getting up from the sofa.

"Good night," she said.

The urge to go after her nearly brought him to his feet. That urge, foreign in its powerful, primal need. *Go after her. Take her.* Never let her out of his bed. Ever.

But therein lay the problem.

He'd only just begun to confront the tragedy of his past. If not for Hazel, he would not have gone to see Annabel's parents. He had blocked all emotion where his ex-girlfriend was concerned. Nearly five years later he still wasn't over his loss. It was unfair to lead Hazel on, to let her believe he was ready for a future with her and Evie.

Evie.

Oh.

He could not, he *would* not, hurt that wonderful child—or her amazing mother.

HAZEL HADN'T LIKED Callum's answer yesterday, but there was little she could do about it. There was even less she could do about how she was beginning to feel about him. Conversation had been limited on the way back from San Francisco. Now they were back at the inn and Patsy arrived with another food delivery. With the help of two hotel staff members, the goods were unloaded on the kitchen island counter.

"Thank you, Patsy. You sure are indispensable for Executive Protection…and now me." She smiled.

Patsy gave a quick, "No problem," and turned to leave.

Odd, the woman seemed to be behaving differently

than usual. She seemed awkward, as though something troubled her.

"Is everything all right, Patsy?"

"Yes, fine." She offered a half-hearted smile and left.

Hazel watched her go behind the hotel staffers and then turned to Callum, who sat at the dining room table in front of his laptop, digging up what he could on Nan, all the places she had lived, places she had worked, people she knew from her Facebook page and other social media sites.

"Patsy seems out of sorts today," she said.

He looked up. "How so?"

"I don't know. Does she have a happy home life?"

"As far as I know. She always seems happy to me."

"Hmm." She began putting food away, starting with the produce and perishables like milk. Next came the canned goods and other pantry items.

Lifting the jar of olive oil, her fingers came in contact with something grainy. Inspecting the jar, she saw traces of a white substance, a powdery film. And then she saw what appeared to be a fingerprint on the glass. Holding the jar closer to her eyes, she spotted undissolved white particles inside, floating in the olive oil. Twisting the cap, she found the seal had already been broken.

"Callum?"

He looked up again and then stood to come to her.

"This doesn't look good," she said.

He took the jar and placed it on the counter, then bent to examine it. "It looks like it might be poisonous."

Patsy's edgy demeanor came back to her. No. One of Callum's agency's assistants?

"You said Patsy was acting strange?" Callum asked.

"Yes."

"Someone could have paid her to try and poison us."

"Not me, my clients," she said. "I would have used this oil for recipes to be delivered."

His mouth flattened in consternation. "That doesn't sound like something the killer would do. He'd want *you* dead. You and Evie. Evie isn't here and he can't find her. While he must be getting impatient, I doubt he'd go after your clients."

Well, Hazel could think of only one other person who had a motive to see Hazel's clients die. Carolyn.

THE NEXT DAY Kerry reported the jar of olive oil had been tested. The liquid had been poisoned. Kerry also let them know she'd picked up Patsy and now had her in custody. Callum took Hazel to the police station. She entered the observation room with Callum and watched Kerry interrogate the nervous woman.

"This will go much easier for you if you cooperate," Kerry said. "Now, I'll ask you again. Why did you put poison in the olive oil that was delivered to Callum Colton and Hazel Hart's room at the Dales Inn?"

"I didn't put poison in it," Patsy said, wringing her hands.

"Then you must know who did, because you were the one who purchased the oil and helped deliver it."

"I don't."

Kerry sighed. "I know you do. I have enough to arrest you right now. We have a fingerprint on the jar. My guess is, it's yours. Do you really want to take that chance?"

"It's not mine," Patsy said. "I just made the delivery."

"How can you be so sure?"

Patsy continued to wring her hands and now added chewing her lower lip to her edgy movements.

"Whose fingerprint could it be?"

"If I tell you, are you going to arrest me?"

"I can't guarantee anything, but maybe I can ask our DA, Karly Fitzpatrick, to see if we can work out a deal with you. We might be able to get you probation instead of prison time, especially since this is your first offense."

Chewing on her lip, Patsy flattened her hands on the table as she mulled over her options and the consequences of whatever decision she made.

"All right. It was Carolyn Johnson. She said she saw me make other deliveries to Hazel and offered to pay me to deliver the olive oil. She didn't say she was going to poison it, but I'd suspected she did something to it. I didn't think she'd actually try and murder anyone."

Hazel glanced at Callum. Surely Patsy would have known Carolyn had intended something terrible.

"How did she come in contact with you?"

"She saw me going in and out of the inn and approached me one day. She asked if I was close to Hazel and I said I didn't know her, I was an assistant, who brought them things they needed. She then asked if I could use a little extra cash to deliver something to her."

"How much did she pay you?" Kerry asked.

"Five hundred."

"Why did you do it?"

"I needed money. The agency doesn't pay me very much. They could afford to pay me more but they don't. I'm behind on my bills."

"I can't believe that," Callum said. "We pay all our

employees top wages. What did you expect? Personal assistants don't make what executive bodyguards do."

"Desperate people do desperate things." Hazel was still reeling over her ex-boss trying to kill her clients. She must have intended for her to be accused of the murders. Revenge for causing her restaurant to fail? Since Carolyn had failed, Hazel should fail and her clients die?

"Is Kerry going to arrest Carolyn?" Hazel asked.

"If she can find her, I'm sure she will."

"You okay?" Callum held the station door for her as they walked to the rental.

She nodded. "Just shocked and disappointed."

She did seem pretty upset. Someone she had respected and might have even considered a friend or mentor had betrayed her in the worst possible way.

Today, they weren't in disguise, so extra precautions were in order. The emergency had prevented them from taking those precautions. He took care in looking around for potential threats.

No parked vehicles with anyone sitting inside.

No strangers walking dogs or sitting on benches—there were no benches.

Walkers didn't look their way. Drivers didn't either.

He escorted Hazel to the passenger side and then stepped up behind the wheel. He drove back toward the Dales Inn and thought again—as he had often since they talked—about whether or not he was ready for a serious relationship and even a family. With Hazel he would have one ready-made.

The more he considered that, the more the idea appealed to him, but he could not get past the fear of losing them in some horrible way. If he steered clear of ever having a family outside the one he already belonged to, he would spare himself nearly insurmountable anguish.

Just before they reached the inn, Callum saw a black SUV parked on a side road. The driver was bigger than the person in the gray SUV had been. This was not Carolyn. This was Nate's killer. He had waited there for them, most likely having seen them leave the inn and wisely not followed them as he had before.

Callum sped up, but the killer shot out one of Callum's tires. As he lost control of his vehicle, the right front tire caught on a pothole in the road. Callum could not correct the truck's path and they careened head-on into a tree. Momentarily dazed from the force of the airbag, he shoved the now deflating bag out of the way and saw Hazel doing the same.

"Are you all right?" He searched around for the killer and found him aiming a gun at him through the driver's side window.

He made a roll-the-window-down gesture.

Callum obliged.

"Where is the kid?" the man asked. He wore sunglasses and a beanie hat over longish brown hair. Around six feet tall and of average build, he had the appearance of a regular guy. No tattoos that Callum could see. Clean-shaven. Just as Evie had described to the sketch artist.

"I won't ask you again," the killer said. "Where is the kid?"

Callum had his hand on the door handle. He lifted his other, palm facing the man, more to distract him. "Just calm down."

At the same time that he opened the car door as fast

and hard as he could, he karate chopped the man's wrist, knocking his aim off.

The gun fired into the air as the man fell backward.

Callum propelled himself out of the car as the other man rose to his feet. Swinging his foot, Callum kicked the gun from the man's grip, sending it flying into the road. He began to draw his pistol but the other man produced a second gun he had tucked into his boot. Callum ducked behind the open car door in time before bullets struck the side.

Callum fired back when he could, seeing the killer limping from the wound Kerry had inflicted toward the SUV. He shot and missed.

The killer raced off in his SUV, another failed attempt to shoot them.

Looking into the truck, he saw Hazel crouched low, eyes big and dark and round with fear.

"He asked where Evie was," she said.

Neither of them had to ask why. The killer wanted both Hazel and Evie dead. The little girl would be a witness to testify in a trial, if it ever came to that. A familiar wave of dread washed through him. What would become of Hazel and Evie?

Chapter Thirteen

A few days later, Callum thought that Nancy Hersh should be back from her trip to Europe with her husband by now. Callum had told Hazel it would be good for them to be out of Mustang Valley. He was anxious to work more on finding out who shot his father and hopefully proving Ace didn't.

Once again, they stood at Nan's front door and this time she answered. Round faced with short hair dyed blond, she wore visible hearing aids.

"Nancy Hersh?" he asked.

"Yes?" She looked from him to Hazel and back to him. Then she snapped, "I have a No Soliciting sign on my door."

"We're not selling anything. We're trying to track down someone whose last known whereabouts was at Mustang Valley General Hospital forty years ago."

"My gosh, that's a long time ago."

"Did you go by the name Nan Gelman back then?"

He must want to be sure she was the maternity nurse who worked at the hospital the day of Ace's birth.

"Yes. Nan was a stupid nickname. I don't go by that anymore. People call me by my given name, Nancy.

I haven't been Gelman in a very long time. Divorced twice before I met my now-husband."

"So you did work at the hospital?" Hazel asked.

"Yes. I did. I worked on the maternity ward."

"Did you work Christmas Day forty years ago?"

Nancy rolled her eyes irritably. "Yes. In fact, that day forty years ago sticks out like a sore thumb." She told them the year. "For one, a fire broke out that morning and destroyed the nursery records and nurses' station. Also, my rotten supervisor wouldn't give me the day off. I had to work Christmas Eve night and Christmas Day morning. I couldn't stand working for her. She had all the holidays off. Talk about narcissistic. I wanted to give her an award for loving herself more than anyone else I've ever known. She's the reason I left."

Her life had gotten better, at least financially, if she'd just gone on a long European vacation. Hazel wouldn't judge, but many people she had come into contact with who had gotten divorced more than one time had personal issues. She was no expert, though. She only had her few and far between observations.

"Do you remember the babies who were born on Christmas morning?" Callum asked.

"Everybody remembers the babies who are born each Christmas. I remember the ones who were born on New Year's Eve, too." She seemed exceedingly proud of her memory reserves.

"Do you remember a sick baby that day?" Callum asked.

Hazel heard the careful anticipation in his tone. He had high hopes this woman would have something for him.

Her eyebrows lifted. "Oh, yes. I haven't thought of that in such a long time, but the Colton baby boy needed special care. It was quite a memorable time. One of the nurses who worked there gave birth to a healthy baby that same day. Her name was…" The nurse stopped as she searched for a name.

Hazel saw Callum stiffen as though this was a huge piece of information.

"Luella something. I can't remember her last name. But I do remember she left the hospital later that day, the same day she gave birth. I thought that was odd. And the other reason that morning stands out is there was the fire. I'm sure you can imagine the chaos."

"I can," Hazel said. No wonder she remembered that day so vividly after forty years.

"All of the maternity records were destroyed. They were kept in those paper boxes back then." Nancy shook her head and made a *humph* sound.

"I can see why you remember that day so well," Callum said. "Are you sure you can't recall Luella's last name?"

Nancy thought for several seconds. "No, I'm sorry, I can't." Then she asked, "Who did you say you were?"

"Callum Colton and Hazel Hart," Callum said.

"Colton. That was one of the babies born that night." She at first seemed thrilled and then not so much. "Why are you asking about that night?"

"We really appreciate all of your help, Nancy." Callum took Hazel's hand and started to turn them away. "Have a good night."

In the rental, Callum seemed edgy and tense. Hazel waited a few seconds.

"What does all that mean?" she asked.

"We have a name," he said. "A first name, but it's more than my family has gotten on Ace's being switched at birth." He turned his head and twisted in the driver's seat as though looking for anything unusual. "We have to be very careful now. If whoever shot my dad knows we came here, we are a target of another killer. I have to get you somewhere safe and work with the police…or not."

As a SEAL? A human weapon? Hazel thought he was taking this to the extreme and she knew why.

"Callum, you don't have to hold yourself responsible for my safety. If the person who shot your father finds out what we learned today, then we are in this together. The same is true for the killer Evie saw. I'm glad you're our bodyguard but if the killer succeeds and Evie and I die, it won't be your fault. It will be the killer's."

He glanced at her sharply, as though he hadn't even realized where his reaction had come from—his penchant to bear all the weight of her well-being.

"I wouldn't want you to feel guilty if anything happens to me, and I'm pretty sure Annabel would have told you the same thing."

His cell phone rang, interrupting what Hazel had hoped would turn into a meaningful conversation.

"Hi, Marlowe," he said.

Hazel waited while he listened.

"All right. We'll stop by now." Then he said to her, "Marlowe asked if I'd stop by the office so she can talk to me."

"About what?"

"She said Payne's assistant found something that might be another clue." He called Kerry next, asking her to meet them at Colton Oil. Then he called Rafe and asked him to gather up everyone in the family and meet them in Marlowe's office.

He was quiet the rest of the way and Hazel wondered if what she had said occupied his mind.

CALLUM COULD THINK of nothing other than what Hazel had said just before Marlowe called. He hadn't even realized his fear was so great that he might not be able to keep Hazel safe. That meant he already felt at least as much for her as he had for Annabel. Even as that thought came, he had a terrible feeling that what he had with Hazel went far deeper. That only terrified him more.

Hazel was right. He couldn't blame himself if someone else killed her. But he could blame himself if he didn't do his job and protect both her and Evie.

Arriving at Colton Oil, he was happy to have other things to keep him focused. They headed right for Marlowe's office.

"That didn't take you long," Marlowe said, standing.

"We weren't far." Callum pulled out one of the desk chairs for Hazel.

She took it and he sat beside her in the other one, facing Marlowe, who dressed like the CEO she was in a black fitted blazer and skirt outfit.

"Dee Walton rushed into my office about an hour ago," Marlowe said.

Dee was his father's assistant. She'd worked part-time since he had gone into the coma, helping Marlowe whenever needed.

"She was in Dad's office getting some files for me. When she dropped them and went to pick them up, she found a pin underneath the air conditioning unit. It's an Arizona State Sun Devils pin, the kind you can get at the university games."

That seemed odd. "Dad isn't an Arizona State Sun Devils fan."

"He does watch football," Marlowe said. "But he has no affiliation with that university."

"Do you think the person who shot him lost it there?" Callum asked.

"Dee thinks that's what happened."

Callum had to agree there was a strong possibility. But how would they ever know?

"This could be the first good clue other than the unhelpful camera footage," Callum said. "Do you agree with Dee?"

"I don't know. I haven't decided. She's been getting into a self-help organization called Affirmation Alliance Group. She can't praise the founder enough. Apparently, Micheline Anderson is gifted at boosting morale and giving healing talks to corporations and individuals. A while back, she asked if we could use them here at Colton Oil, to help people deal with what happened to Dad. She claims they helped her when her husband died last year. I don't know what that group is doing to her state of mind. I hope they're helping her but she may be distracted."

"Do you think they're legit?" Callum asked.

"I'm leery of anything with the word *group* in it. Makes it seem like a cult."

Callum smiled. "Some people go for that sort of thing. The self-help organizations."

Rafe stepped into the office with Ainsley. They both worked at the company, Rafe as CFO and Ainsley as a corporate attorney. Rafe had on an impeccable suit, Ainsley a flowing pantsuit.

"Grayson said he wasn't going to make it," Rafe said. "He also said Asher wouldn't either."

Owner of a first responder agency, Grayson didn't involve himself in Colton Oil matters. Neither did Asher, who was foreman at Rattlesnake Ridge Ranch.

"I'll make sure they know what we discussed today," Marlowe said. "Let's sit over here." She stood and moved everyone to the two sofas that faced each other across a long coffee table.

"Why did you want us all here, Callum?" Rafe asked.

Callum looked behind him and, through the window beside the office door, saw Kerry approaching.

"Ah. Just in time."

Marlowe's assistant, Karen, let the detective in. Her long auburn hair was up in a clip today and her blue eyes found Callum.

"What have you got? Something hot?" she asked, sitting beside him.

Yes, Hazel. Of course, he kept that unbidden thought in his head.

"I found the Mustang Valley General nurse who also gave birth at the hospital the same day as Ace was born," he said. "She quit the same day."

"What? That's huge, Callum," Marlowe said.

"Tell me you have more."

He told her about the nurse who had given birth that Christmas morning and who had left the hospital with the sickly Colton baby rather than her own.

"Her name is Luella," Callum said. "Nancy couldn't recall her last name."

Kerry finished writing on her notepad. "That makes it more difficult."

"But it's a name."

"More than we have so far," Marlowe said.

"Marlowe has some news, as well," Hazel said, joining in the conversation.

Marlowe explained about the pin. Rafe and Ainsley agreed there was a good chance it might have been accidentally left by their father's would-be killer.

"But aren't there Arizona State Sun Devils fans who work here?" Kerry asked, adding her detective insight.

"Yes," Marlowe said. "There are."

"Any one of them could have gone into Payne's office and lost their pin. We will run prints," Kerry said.

"True, but not very many workers other than janitors would have a reason to go in there," Marlowe said.

Not very good janitors, if they'd missed the pin.

"I agree. Finding a connection between the pin and the shooter isn't going to be easy," Callum said. "But it's something to go on."

"Definitely something that needs to be checked out," Kerry said. "Well, thank you for your help, Callum." Kerry nodded to Marlowe. In times like this, Callum was glad to have his family around him.

BACK AT THE inn, Hazel noticed Callum was in a better mood after that meeting. Progress had been made on his father's case but they were still no closer to capturing the killer that Evie had witnessed bashing Nate Blurge over the head. She sensed Callum would be eager to work finding the threat to her and Evie, especially after she'd forced him to face his fear of loving another woman—especially one with a child.

Right now, she just wanted to enjoy a peaceful evening. She missed her daughter terribly. She had already prepared a delicious dinner. Cooking always relaxed her.

She found an action movie that was funny and not too violent and Callum sat beside her. Their talk over dinner had been about what he and his sister had uncovered about their father's shooting. He had also called the hospital to check on Payne. Still no change. Hazel had deliberately avoided any talk about his fears.

Toward the end of the movie, when the hero and heroine acknowledged their mutual attraction, Callum put his arm up and around her.

"Come here," he said.

Warmed that he must be enjoying this quiet evening with just the two of them, she moved closer and rested her head on his muscular chest, in the crook of his arm.

Because she was in her nightgown, only a soft, thin layer separated her bare breasts from his torso. Long, sleeveless and dark green, it covered her well enough and wasn't sexy by any stretch, but she still felt intimate this close to Callum.

Her phone rang. She had been waiting for Evie to call. Her brother had said they had plans to go to an amusement park for kids.

She sat forward and picked up her phone from the coffee table. "Hi, honey, how was your day?"

"Hi, Mommy," Evie said in a loud, excited voice. "I'm having a blast here. I like Uncle Owen and Aunt Jessica."

"That's great."

"We went to a park today. It had rides. I rode in a teacup with Jessica and a train and a roller coaster!"

"Wow, you did a lot. My brave girl." Hazel knew the roller coaster was a miniature version of those that adults rode.

"And we're having pizza!"

Her brother was going to have corrupted her daughter by the time she went to go get her. "That sounds good."

"I still like your food, Mommy. You're the best cook ever."

"Aw, thanks Evie."

"When are you coming to get me?"

Hazel wished she could say *right now, right this minute.* "I don't know yet. I'll call you as soon as I do, okay?"

"Okay." Evie's tone dimmed considerably.

Hazel felt both loved by her daughter and sad, which put a damper on her mood.

"What are you doing right now?" Evie asked.

"I was watching a movie with Callum."

"What movie?"

"None that you would like. An adult movie."

"Can we watch *Brave* when I get home?"

"Of course." She heard Owen say in the background that they had that movie there. Hazel was going to start to get jealous.

"Can I talk to Cal-em?" Evie asked.

Hazel was surprised by the request. Why did she want to talk to Callum?

"Sure." She put the phone on speaker—she wasn't about to miss a single second of this. "Evie wants to say hi," she said to Callum.

"Hi, Cal-em."

"Hi, Evie. You having fun?" He sounded as though he was a good sport but Hazel wondered if this would be difficult for him.

"Yes! I like my uncle and aunt's house. They're fun."

"That's good."

"Did you catch the bad guy yet?" she asked.

"I'm not a policeman. Kerry is the one who will catch him," Callum said.

"Did Mommy tell you I'm gonna be a police girl when I grow up?"

"No, she didn't. Why do you want to do that?"

"So I can get a badge and catch bad people," she said. "Why didn't you be a policeman?"

Callum looked at Hazel with a grin. Evie was full of questions today.

"I suppose I wanted to protect people instead of catch the ones who hurt them."

A few seconds passed as Evie absorbed that. "I want to protect people, too. That's what Kerry does."

"Yes, she's one of the good guys."

"She's a girl."

Callum chuckled. "Yes, she is."

A few more seconds passed and Hazel thought her daughter had run out of steam at last.

"Cal-em?"

"Yes?"

"Are you going to come with Mommy to pick me up?"

Callum glanced at Hazel. When the time came to go get Evie, all the danger would have passed. What would Callum do? Would he run?

"Of course, I'll be there," he said.

Hazel felt a surge of warmth and hope. Maybe there was a chance for them, after all.

Did she want that? It didn't take much thinking to know what her heart desired. Yes, she did. She wanted a chance to be a couple with him, maybe more.

"Are you going to come live with us?" Evie asked.

"I already have a place to live."

He lived in a mansion.

"But you like Mommy, don't you?"

"Yes, I do like her very much."

"And you like me?" she asked in a singsong voice.

"Yes, even more."

Evie laughed, a lighthearted giggle. "Nuh-uh. You like Mommy more."

Callum chuckled again, seeming to really enjoy the banter with the girl.

"I see you with her," Evie said. "You like her a lot."

"I said I did."

"Then you should come live with us, then."

Evie was so fond of him. Hazel would worry about her state of mind if he left them, but Evie was working her kid-charmed magic on him.

"Pizza's here," Hazel heard Owen say in the background.

"You better go get pizza while it's hot," Callum said.

"Okay. See you soon."

"See you soon."

Evie must have disconnected herself. Owen or Jessica didn't come back on. Hazel leaned back against the sofa with a sigh.

"I miss her so much," she said.

Callum put his arm back around her. "She is something else. Adorable."

She tipped her head up and over to see him. "Yes, she's a heart melter."

He smiled softly, meeting her eyes.

"She likes you a lot," Hazel said.

"How does a man who leaves a pregnant woman create such a gem?" he asked.

"That's easy. She got most of her good traits from me." Hazel smiled up teasingly.

"I'd say."

And there they went again, falling into this sexual energy. They looked into each other's eyes, which ended with him lowering his mouth to hers. Basking in the aftermath of his affectionate words, she grew hot all over.

She touched his face as the kiss deepened. When that didn't satisfy her raging desire, she climbed onto him.

"Uh." He grunted and then slid his hands to her rear to move her over his jean-clad erection.

She was lost at that point. All that mattered was him and how he made her feel.

He pulled up the hem of her long nightgown. She kept kissing him as his hands traveled slowly up her thighs to her bare butt.

Pulling back from the kiss, he met her eyes.

She smiled from pleasure in his heated response. Lifting his T-shirt to get it out of the way, she unbuttoned his jeans and then unzipped them as much as she could. He helped her by raising his hips, which incited her more because of the pressure. He pushed his jeans and underwear down.

Hazel resumed kissing him and moved back on top of him. His hands returned to her rear and their breathing became more ragged. She ran her hands along his hard chest, brushing her thumbs over his stiff nipples.

Callum lifted her nightgown and she raised her hands so he could take it off. He let it fall onto the sofa beside them. Then he gripped the back of her head and pressed an urgent kiss to her lips. She reciprocated with equal verve, moving over his erection.

With a gruff sound, he set her down over him. She

was so wet and ready for him. Shivers of sensation numbed her to all else. She had to stay still for a moment, lest the pleasure end too soon.

She planted a kiss on his mouth. "I've never felt like this before." Her voice came out as a breathless whisper.

"Neither have I," he answered in kind.

That he'd confessed such a thing stimulated her passion even more. She kissed him long and deep, needing to soak every part of him into her.

He pumped his hips. Evidently his patience had run out. Bracing her hands on his shoulders, she did the same in rhythm with him. And just a few strokes later she came with such intensity she cried out.

He groaned his own release and she continued to move on him, not wanting this to end.

At last she put her forehead against his. He moved until he found her mouth for a gentle kiss. The tender, sweet action captured her heart. She was beyond backing off. She could not without suffering pain. Losing Callum would be the biggest heartbreak of her life.

Chapter Fourteen

The next day, Callum stood in front of the bathroom mirror and admitted to himself that he would have difficulty leaving Hazel. But he would have more difficulty losing her permanently. At a loss for what to do, how to preserve himself if the worst happened, he fell into silent contemplation. Hazel had studied him more than once but never confronted him. That made him fall in love with her even more. She gave him the space he needed without judging.

Wait…

Had he just thought that he had fallen in love with her?

He finished getting into his biker disguise, wig and glasses in place. He left the bathroom to find Hazel waiting, way too sexy for his confused state. He would rather take all her clothes off and stay home.

"You ready?" They were headed to Joe's Bar to conduct another stakeout.

Her white-toothed smile and animated manner warmed a nonsexual part of him. This was Hazel. Positive. Loving. Strong in so many ways.

A mother…

"Yes."

He offered his hand, more of an obligatory gesture. He was so out of sorts.

She didn't take it. Instead, she studied him before saying, "Last night was beautiful."

Beautiful.

He had other words come to mind. Scorching hot. Heart-wrenching, in a really good way.

"I am happy with just that, Callum," she said. "Don't feel pressured. I know you have been through a lot. I'll be all right no matter what happens. Evie will be, too, because she has me."

The truth of what she said penetrated deep into him. Hazel would never push him. She wanted him for who he was and nothing less. She cared about him, his happiness above all else. He wanted to give that to her, as well. All of him. But he still felt so broken. So injured. A woman like her deserved the whole man.

He slid his hand behind her head, gently, then stepped close. Kissing her, he hoped she understood the unspoken message, how amazing and charitable she was.

When he drew back she put her forefinger over his lips as though sealing the kiss. "Let's go catch that bad guy."

"Hazel…"

"Shh." She lowered her hand. "None of that now. Let's go."

He took a moment to enjoy how beautiful she was and how sexy in that biker-woman disguise. "I must be a fool."

She put her pointer finger on his upper chest and ran it down to the waist of his pants. Then her striking eyes looked up at him. "You could never be a fool, Callum

Colton. You just need to let go of past pain. I only hope I'm still in your life when you do."

She looked into his eyes, angling her head and assessing him. After she must have learned what she needed to from peering into his eyes, she turned and headed for the suite's entrance.

Rather than take a hired car, Callum called a cab. That would be less conspicuous. On the way, Callum phoned Kerry to let her know about their visit. She wasn't happy with their planning something like that on their own and on such short notice, but she said she'd assemble a team to wait in unmarked cars in the parking lot. She'd also send a plainclothes cop inside in case anything went wrong.

A short drive later, they reached the bar. Callum made sure no one saw them as they left the cab.

He guided Hazel into Joe's. After being seated they settled in to have an evening together, covertly surveying everyone there.

It was much the same as the last time they were there. Dim and dirty.

And the same biker crowd was at the pool table.

All appeared calm, until Callum noticed a redheaded waitress who kept looking behind her and all around the bar.

"Did you see that redhead last time we were here?" he asked Hazel.

She looked around the bar and zeroed in on the other woman. "No."

Hazel moved closer to him. "Might as well look the part."

"Careful."

"Of what?" She leaned in, her breast pressing against his side.

"Of more." He could have elaborated but he didn't.

"You should give in. You have no control over this. I realized that after last night."

She was sure being bold. Yes, last night had been earth-shattering. He couldn't face that right now.

"Let's get rid of this killer and then deal with that, okay?"

She smiled wide and bright. "Okay." Then she turned to survey the bar, covertly watching the redhead serve beers to a table of raucous men.

"She's wearing a wedding ring," Callum said. He looked at the other female workers. There were only two and neither wore a ring. If the killer had murdered Nate Blurge for flirting with his wife, he might have shown up tonight to keep an eye on her.

"The woman who served us last time didn't have one," Hazel said.

"And the redhead wasn't working that night, so if she is his wife, the killer probably wasn't here."

"Nope." She looked around the bar and he saw her stop short when she spotted a table with a lone man sitting there.

He was the same height and build as the man who kept showing up at the inn and following them and shooting at them. He had no hat on and no sunglasses. In a holey pair of faded jeans and a black *Deadwood* T-shirt, he had a day or two's worth of facial stubble. His longish brown hair convinced Callum he was their man.

"He's watching the redhead," Hazel said.

Yes, he was. And very intently. The killer's face turned stormy, his brows lowered. He had all the mannerisms of an insanely jealous man, a power tripper. He looked the type to need absolute control over his woman. He was so involved with policing the redhead that he didn't notice Callum and Hazel watching him.

Callum looked back at the waitress and saw her smiling at one of the men drinking at a table. The man didn't seem drunk. He was clean-cut and dressed in dark jeans with no holes in them and a nice polo. Callum watched him after the redhead left the table. He wasn't drinking fast and when the others ordered another round, he declined. He made the redhead smile and this time laugh as he talked with her.

"Oh boy," Hazel said.

Callum looked over at the killer. He had gotten up and marched across the bar toward the man at the table.

Standing up, Callum heard the killer say in a loud, angry tone, "Why are you flirting with my wife?"

Looking startled, the man looked up. "I didn't know she was married."

"She's wearing a ring, you idiot!"

"I didn't look, sorry, man. All I did was thank her for the beer and tell her she was too pretty to be working in a place like this."

"Why did she laugh like you said something funny?"

The other man stood. "Dude, calm down. Nothing happened. Just casual talk. You should be flattered I think you have a beautiful wife."

A woman who deserved better than a killer as a husband. Callum watched that man shove the other.

"Do you always hit on other men's wives?"

"Hey. What's your problem?" The man shoved him back.

The killer took a swing, hitting the other man. Callum stalked to them, planting his hand on the murderer's chest and getting between them.

"That's enough." Callum pushed the killer back, forcing him to step farther away from him and the clean-cut man.

The man behind him tried to get around Callum to go after the killer. Callum lost some balance and the killer took a swing at him and clipped his jaw. Callum's glasses went flying. The man behind him had grabbed hold of his wig, pulling it off his head. The man had meant to pull him out of the way but the wig stopped him.

Callum gave him a shove and growled, "Back off!"

"You!" the killer snarled, recognizing Callum.

Callum ducked as the killer made another swing at him and the punch caught the man behind him. Callum swiped his opponent's leg out from under him, sending him down. But the killer lunged for him, plowing into him and driving them both back into the table of drinking men. Callum landed on his back, spilling beer glasses and scattering the seated men.

Using his feet, Callum kicked the killer, sending him flying backward and sliding on his back through the broken and spilled glasses of beer. He bumped into another table.

Going toward him, he saw the killer get to his feet and look around, finding Hazel standing near their table. The other man sprinted toward her, causing an instant flash of fear in Callum.

He ran to Hazel as the killer drew a pistol and she pivoted and started to head for the exit. But the killer was on her too fast. He grabbed her, spun her around and put the pistol to her temple.

Callum stopped short, just a couple of feet from them. He looked at Hazel's terrified eyes. She must be thinking of her daughter. Callum had failed her.

He stood frozen for a few seconds, before anger took over. No way would he lose another woman like this!

With a lightning-fast gesture, he knocked the gun upward. It went off but the bullet shot toward the ceiling. Callum kicked the man and sent him back and away from Hazel. As Kerry and other officers, including the plainclothes cop, burst in, Hazel ran to the bar and huddled with some other people, and Callum drew his own gun and aimed it at the killer's head.

"I've got you now," Callum said to the man on the floor. Finally.

Kerry approached.

"That's him," Callum said. "That's the man Evie saw hit Nate Blurge over the head."

Kerry glanced at him sharply. "You're certain?"

"As certain as I can be. He's the same build and his hair is the same."

She nodded to two officers, who knelt down and searched the man, procuring a driver's license and handing it to Kerry.

"Billy Jansen," she said. "Run this by Motor Vehicle."

One of the officers left with the license.

Moments later the officer returned with the license and announced the plate number was a match.

"Take him to the station," Kerry said to the other officer.

The officer helped Billy to his feet and cuffed him, reading him his rights.

"The redhead over there is his wife," Callum said,

pointing to the woman next to Hazel who watched Billy with no small amount of apprehension.

"We'll need to talk to her."

"I'll tell her."

Callum walked over to Hazel and the redhead.

"Are you all right?" he asked Hazel.

"Yes, thanks to you." She rose up on her toes and kissed him, quick and grateful.

"You're welcome." Nothing felt better than that.

Facing the redhead, he said, "The police are going to want to talk to you."

"Why? They're doing me a favor taking him away."

"You're his wife. You can provide information they'll need to prosecute him and testify against him if you want to."

"How long will he be in jail?"

She was obviously worried he'd get out and come after her.

"If he gets convicted of murder, he'll be in prison for the rest of his life. What's your name?"

"Tina Jansen."

"What can you tell police about Nate Blurge's murder?"

"Plenty. He flirted with me the same way that nice man tonight did and ended up dead. Billy wasn't home when Nate was killed and Billy bragged about getting rid of him. He even threatened me that he'd kill every man I flirted with."

"Your testimony will only help. I can assure you he'll be put away for a long time." Callum couldn't believe that some killers talked about what they had done.

Tina smiled big. "Good riddance. I can finally divorce him without worrying he'll kill me, too."

Callum didn't doubt that. He was glad the man would be off the streets, but he still had one more problem to take care of before he could be assured of Hazel's safety.

MOST OF THE police had gone and the bar had returned to its usual business. Hazel couldn't wait to get out of her disguise. She went to the bathroom before she and Callum would go home. Finishing up, she washed her hands at the sink. They could retrieve Evie soon. When she lifted her head, she saw Carolyn's reflection in the mirror and she had a gun.

Seriously? Hazel's disbelief buffered the slight gasp of shock and fear.

The same night? "How did you know we were here?"

"Easy. I knew you were looking for that Blurge man's killer and Patsy told me you were going to be here one of these nights."

Damn that assistant.

"If you don't come quietly, I'll shoot you. It's what I've dreamed of doing ever since you left my restaurant. I knew I could never make it without a chef like you and I knew I'd have a hard time replacing you."

"Carolyn, you don't have to do this. I told you I was sorry. I never meant for any of that to happen."

"It's too late for all of that. I thought I could forgive you but I can't. Now get moving."

Hazel hesitated. If she went with this crazy woman, she would probably end up dead before morning. She had to find a way to alert Callum.

Callum.

What would this do to him? And what about Evie?

More determined than ever, Hazel started toward the bathroom exit. Carolyn jabbed her gun against Hazel's ribs, concealing the gun with the oversized sweat-shirt she wore.

Would anyone find an oversized sweatshirt odd? Arizona was hot, but it was early spring and nighttime, when it got colder.

Outside the bathroom, Hazel stalled. Just as she suspected, Callum stood where he could see the bathroom. And he spotted her right away.

"Get going!" Carolyn jabbed her and forced her to hurry to the back door, which had been propped open to allow airflow.

They passed the kitchen entrance, where heat poured out through the narrow doorway along with the sounds of frying food and workers having a lighthearted night.

Hazel dared not look back to see where Callum was. Carolyn forced her through the back door, and to Hazel's horror, she had her SUV parked right outside and the driver's side door was open. Carolyn had planned to make Hazel drive, presumably with a gun pointed at her in case she tried to escape or attract attention.

Did a dive bar like this have cameras? Not likely.

Hazel knew she had to do something. She could not get in that vehicle before Callum caught up to them.

Relying—desperately—on what she had heard about self-defense, she dropped all her weight straight down. Carolyn wasn't a big woman. Hazel felt her former boss stumble and rake at her clothes, to no avail. She stepped back to maintain her balance. It was enough for Hazel to scramble away, looking for cover.

She didn't have to panic long. Callum emerged from the back door, smacking Carolyn's head with the butt of his pistol, and she fell like a rag doll. He kicked her gun away and rushed over to Hazel.

"Are you all right?" He was breathless and his eyes were wild with fear.

She just grabbed his face with both hands and kissed him hard once. "Yes. I am, Callum. I love you." She kissed him hard again and then stopped herself.

What had she said? The words had tumbled out.

Heat hardened his eyes from frantic concern. Was the tension sexual—or maybe loving? But it appeared only for an instant.

"Go inside and get the police," he said.

She did as he asked. But as she ran into the bar and to the front, the glow of warmth she had seen in him crept into her in a different way. He'd caught the feeling and shut it off.

He wasn't ready for this, for her to have blurted out words of love.

Outside, she found the officers and told them about Carolyn. They instructed her to wait. She'd have to give a statement and so would Callum.

She would rather call a cab and go get Evie, go home and forget any of this ever happened. She needed Evie more than ever. But she'd have to wait.

Chapter Fifteen

Callum woke late the next morning. Having to give statements on two criminal incidents had taken time. He reached over to feel for Hazel and then remembered she had insisted on sleeping in her own room. He'd had a bad feeling about that the previous night, but the hour had been so late and both of them so tired he hadn't argued.

Now, with a clear head, he realized all of the adrenaline and his baggage with Annabel had taken their toll.

Hoping against hope, he flung the covers off and went across the hall. The room was immaculate. No trace of Hazel. The bed was made and all her things, and Evie's, were gone.

He ran his hand through his hair. He needed his sister.

After quickly showering, he raced to Marlowe's office, pacing outside until the worker she had a meeting with left. Then he went inside and closed the door.

"I heard you captured two criminals in one night. Nice going, brother."

"I need to tell you something." He could not believe he was going to do this.

He paced her office, one side to the other, three times.

"Okay, you're worrying me," Marlowe said.

He stopped and put his hands on the back of one of the chairs facing her desk and looked at her, still struggling with how to begin.

She angled her head. "This whole..." she twirled her pen a few times "...weak man thing isn't the twin I grew up with."

Callum lowered his head with a sigh. She had a way of reaching him he could never explain to anyone. He lifted his head. "There's something I haven't told almost anyone."

Marlowe lifted her eyebrows. "Go on. Don't stop now."

She knew him so well. He would have stopped, in this fragile state. Pushing off the chair, he straightened. "Annabel and I didn't break up."

Marlowe didn't move or blink. She just waited.

"She died."

His sister's mouth formed an O on an indrawn breath. "You lied?"

"I'm sorry." He opened his arms. "I'm so sorry."

"Stop being so weak. What happened?" she demanded.

Lowering his arms and taking a chair, he explained everything, the witness and Annabel's pregnancy—and her death.

"We knew all of that, Callum. What *happened*?"

"I was protecting a witness and was in court a lot. The drug cartel must have had me followed and the leader sent someone to assassinate her. I wasn't there to protect her."

Marlowe took several seconds to absorb that and, Callum knew, piece together what he hadn't said.

"Oh, Cal." She shook her head gently, full of empathy. And then she grew stern. "And you didn't tell *me*?"

"I didn't tell anyone. I couldn't." He had no way of explaining.

As it turned out, he didn't have to. His sister knew him like no other. "You blamed yourself but because you met Hazel, you can face it now."

Well, that he hadn't expected. His sister knew how to get to the point, but that was…he would have thought harsh but he checked himself. Her honesty, like Hazel's, showed him not only the brutality of the truth but also the healing power of facing it.

"Tell you what." Marlowe leaned back in her big leather executive chair. "I'll tell the family, and you go get this woman who's done you so much good."

Callum felt his insides twist with warning. "What? No. It's not like that."

Marlowe picked up a pen from the desk and dropped it in exasperation. "It's not? Look at you. Listen to yourself. You just told me that meeting Hazel has brought you here, confessing something huge that you kept from your own family."

He hadn't thought how his inability to deal with Annabel's death would affect his siblings. He hadn't cared about his parents all that much. They were always too involved with Colton Oil. And other than with Marlowe, he wasn't the type of brother to bleed out his soul to everyone. But Marlowe…

"I should have told you," he said. "You're right." He ran his fingers through his hair, disconcerted.

"Stop," Marlowe said. "Just stop."

He looked at her, not sure of her meaning.

"You should have told me, but I understand why you didn't. I know you like you know me. We are tough emotionally, and smart and strong. But we can be stubborn, Cal."

"I know, but—"

"What I want you to hear from me—and you better listen—is you have met a beautiful and wonderful woman who won't put up with your baggage if you can't handle it."

Nothing like putting it bluntly. He also liked the handling connotation. Baggage. Handles.

He laughed, deeply and from his core. "Marlowe, I love you."

"Go get that girl, you fool." She smiled and laughed softly in return. "There's no escaping it. Take it from one who knows."

She'd gotten involved with Bowie Robertson, the president of Robertson Renewable Energy Company, Colton Oil's rival. She'd gotten pregnant and ended up falling in love. Callum still couldn't tell she was pregnant. She looked great.

Resigned to the fact that she was probably right, he stood from the chair.

"Hey," Marlowe said.

He met her teasing eyes.

"Do you love her?"

He recalled Hazel blurting she loved him and how that had made him feel. Confused. Scared. Weak, as his sister would say.

"Yes."

BOTH LET DOWN by Callum's brusque attitude and exceedingly excited to see Evie again, Hazel walked up to her brother's house. Owen opened the door before she got there and Evie bounded out.

"Mommy!"

Immense joy burst in Hazel. She crouched as Evie ran to her and took her into her arms. "Hi, Evie. I missed you so much."

"I missed you, too, Mommy."

Hazel kissed her cheek several times, making Evie laugh. Then she stood up.

Evie looked toward the street. "Where's Cal-em?"

"He couldn't make it." Seeing Evie's crestfallen face, Hazel felt a pang of guilt for not bringing Callum with her. She'd figured a clean break would be best for her daughter.

"But he said he would."

"I know, honey." She took her daughter's hand and walked to her brother.

"She's a great kid. Whatever you're doing, keep doing it."

She hugged Owen. "Where's Jessica?"

"She went to work. She said to tell you hello and thanks for convincing her to have kids. I'd like to thank you, too."

Hazel smiled, loving Evie's effect on them. "I didn't know you wanted them."

"I wasn't sure until now." He messed up the top of Evie's hair, which she wore down today. "You come back anytime, okay?"

"Okay!"

"Thank you so much, Owen. I owe you big for watching her."

"I'm just glad you caught that killer. We were scared for you. And your ex-boss." He shook his head with raised eyebrows. "That's so wild."

"Yeah. I still can't believe it. She was always so friendly."

"I guess everybody has their breaking point."

Even if Hazel ran into hard times like that, she didn't think she would ever break to the point of attempted murder. "I think I'd have to be on my deathbed before I broke."

"Yes, and normal people wouldn't murder anybody."

"No." She looked down at Evie. "Well, what do you think, kiddo? Should we go home?"

"Okay. Will Cal-em be there?"

"I don't think so."

Her brother eyed her in question. "I thought you two had something going."

She had to be careful what she said in front of Evie. She couldn't be sure what Callum would do, now that she was safe.

"It's still too early to tell."

"That's not how it looked to me," Owen said. "I've never seen you glow like you did with him nearby."

She'd been glowing? She had not been aware of that.

"Why didn't he come with you today?" Owen asked.

"I left early. I didn't wake him," she said neutrally. "We better get going. I've got a lot of meals to cook."

"Don't let a good man go because of what Ed did to you," Owen said. "And don't hold it against Callum for being rich. He isn't the same as Ed."

"I know, Owen." She might as well tell him all of it, Evie, too. "He has issues of his own. His pregnant girlfriend died in an accident. A drug dealer did it to get revenge on Callum for him protecting a witness during his trial. He hasn't gotten over her yet."

"All he needs is someone like you to know he has a soft place to land."

She was a soft place to land? Not if being with Evie all the time made him think of the baby he had lost. And not if he held back with Hazel and never let his feelings grow with her. She wanted more than that and Evie deserved more than that.

When Hazel arrived back at her little apartment above the bakery, she did not expect to see Callum's rental parked in the back.

"Cal-em's here!" Evie exclaimed.

Hazel parked and walked around to get Evie out of her car seat. She fidgeted and swung her tiny feet, anxious to get out of the SUV. Since she had been riding in Callum's vehicles, the Mercedes' mirror had been repaired.

She freed Evie, who climbed out of the SUV and ran toward the stairs. Hazel followed, wondering why Callum was here. She saw him get out of the truck as they approached. Evie veered away from the stairs.

"Evie!" Callum crouched and wrapped his arms around her as she crashed into him.

"You said you were gonna come get me," Evie said, small arms looping around his neck as she leaned back to look at his face.

"I'm sorry. That's why I'm here now." He looked at Hazel.

She saw pure adoration for Evie's sweet charm.

"And I also came to have a word with your mother." Evie glanced back at Hazel.

"Let's go inside." Hazel walked to the stairs and Callum carried Evie up them. Inside, she felt she no longer belonged in this tiny place. She still wasn't sure she would be comfortable living in a mansion with all of Callum's family, or if she would get used to having so much money—that was, if he did love her.

He put Evie down and told her to go find them a good movie. She trotted to the living room.

Hazel faced Callum, prepared for anything. He was gentleman enough to make sure he talked to her personally about any decisions he had made.

He took her hands in his. "This last month with you has been more than eye-opening, Hazel."

"For me, as well."

"First I want to start off by saying I am nothing like Evie's father. I don't run from difficult situations or circumstances."

"I know that about you." He would face her and break things off ethically and with integrity.

"I'm rich like he was, probably richer, because of my family."

She nodded, lowering her eyes.

"But I have never lied to you, nor will I ever."

She returned her gaze to him. This was beginning to sound like he had no intention of breaking things off between them. Hope flared and her heart began to pound with responding emotion.

"You helped me through dealing with Annabel's death. And talking to my sister today made me realize that even though it's only been a month, I've fallen in love with you."

She couldn't believe her ears.

"That's why…" He got down on one knee and then let go of her hands to dig into his pocket.

No way. He wasn't…

He pulled out a ring box. "Now, I don't want you to feel rushed." He looked up at her and opened the box to reveal a sapphire and diamond ring. The sapphires were about a karat between them and surrounded by smaller diamonds. A man with his money could have gotten her something gaudy and blatantly expensive. But he knew her. He knew she wouldn't have appreciated anything like that.

"You pick the date, but will you marry me?"

Tears stung her eyes. This was the happiest day of her life! "When did you…"

"I stopped at the jewelry store on the way here. I knew you were going to get Evie so I had plenty of time. I guessed on the size."

She stared at the ring, loving it enormously.

"You haven't answered my question," he said.

She glanced at Evie, who was oblivious to this monumental moment. Hazel didn't have to worry she wouldn't approve. She was already treating Callum like her stepfather.

Then she looked at Callum. "Yes, I will marry you. I don't care when. It can be tomorrow or next spring. I'll still want to marry you as much as I do right now, because I have fallen in love with you, too."

Smiling, he stood and removed the ring from the box. She offered her hand and he slipped it on her finger. It fit perfectly.

Chapter Sixteen

Marlowe had arranged for a family gathering at the mansion to allow Hazel to get to know everyone better. Over the last few days, he had relished in living with Hazel and Evie as a family. They had decided to stay at the inn a while longer to enjoy some downtime. Callum thought a get-together would be a perfect opportunity to show Hazel his home and let her decide if it was somewhere she wanted to live. They didn't have to live in the mansion. They could build something on the ranch. It was Sunday afternoon on a sunny, clear day.

"You all live here?" Hazel asked when the sprawling mansion appeared. Made of rock and wood to match the rugged landscape and the Mustang Valley Mountains in the distance, the multiple gables of the roofline and three stories of windows and balconies gave evidence to its size.

"Yes. My mom and dad live on the first floor in one wing. There are guest quarters in the other wing. Ace, Grayson and Ainsley have the three wings on the second floor, and Asher, Marlowe and I have the third floor wings. Then there are several spaces we share, like the living areas and the library."

He parked and got out, waiting for Hazel to get Evie out of the back. She had slept the whole way there. Now she groggily walked beside Hazel to the entrance. There were other cars here, but most were likely in the huge garage.

Inside the grand entry, Hazel took in the luxurious, floor-to-ceiling windows and exposed beam ceiling of the open living room. Callum saw most everyone was already here. The only ones missing were Grayson and Asher.

"Callum." Marlowe came to greet them, leaving Bowie standing with a glass of wine near the rock pillars at the entrance of the large dining room.

Kerry was there with Rafe, seated on the sofa with Ainsley.

"I sent someone to get Grayson and Asher. They should be here soon." She turned to Hazel. "So happy to see you. Looks like I talked some sense into my brother after all."

"Thanks for that." Hazel showed her the ring.

"Oh, that's beautiful!" Marlowe gaped at Callum. "Everybody, Callum is getting married!" She held Hazel's hand out for all to see.

"He's gonna be my new daddy," Evie said. Then, seeing the huge television, she meandered over. Ainsley changed the channel to a kid friendly show.

Hazel mouthed, *Thank you.*

Just then Grayson and Asher entered. All the siblings were together, a few of them attached to significant others.

Callum rarely saw Grayson. He doubted any of the others did, either.

"This is Hazel, Callum's fiancée." Marlowe introduced her to the two. "And her daughter, Evie."

Grayson reached over and shook her hand. "Fianceé?"

"Hey, it's about time."

"And that is Asher," Marlowe said. "He's Rattlesnake Ridge Ranch's foreman and a bit of a lone wolf."

"A pleasure to meet you both. You look like a real cowboy, Asher," Hazel said. "With the longish hair and that face, you must make all the women swoon."

Grayson chuckled. "He's a lone wolf. He doesn't date."

Asher shook his head. "Thank you for the compliment, Hazel, and it's nice to meet you, too. Callum needs a good woman in his life. And a good daughter!"

"Thanks. What do you do, Grayson?"

"I run a first responder management agency."

"That sounds exciting. Do you like rescuing people?"

"He likes the adrenaline rush," Callum said.

"Yes," Grayson said to Hazel, "Helping people is the most rewarding part." Then he turned a disgruntled look to Callum.

"I've been trying to get a hold of both of you to update you on the whole situation with Dad," Marlowe said.

She hadn't told them yet?

"We found the woman who gave birth on the Christmas morning the babies were switched." Callum explained about the fire and the woman who'd left that same day with what everyone thought was her baby but must have been their biological brother.

"Her name is Luella. We don't have a last name yet," Marlowe said.

"Well, that's good news, I mean that you have at least

a first name. Is she the one who switched Ace with our biological brother?" Asher asked.

"Yes, it is possible," Callum said.

"What kind of sicko does that?" Asher asked. "We need to catch her and find out, brother. Is he still alive?"

"I want to help," Grayson said. "What can I do?"

Callum found his brother's concern odd. He believed that Grayson did like helping people but this was different. "You haven't even gone to see Dad in the hospital. Why are you so gung-ho now to step up? You don't even hang out with your family. It's like putting a house fire out to get you to come to any of these."

"Somebody switched our oldest brother. That nurse has to pay. We have to get justice for Ace. He may not be our blood brother but he's still our sibling."

"Isn't that the truth," Ainsley said.

"We can't stop until we do find this Luella and bring her to justice," Rafe said from the sofa.

"I just want to know why you care all of a sudden," Callum said. The fact that he wasn't close to his brothers and sisters and never went to see their dad in the hospital didn't support Grayson's assertions.

"My relationship was always complicated with Dad. I'm sure you've had your ups and downs with him. I haven't resolved anything with him. I'm not sure he'd want to see me."

"Dad's in a coma. You should go for yourself, not him."

Grayson didn't respond right away. "It's not that simple, Callum."

"It can be. Just go see him. Talk to him. He might be in a coma but he can still hear."

"That's true," Marlowe said. "His brain will still hear you."

"You'd side with Callum anyway," Grayson said. "You're his twin."

Marlowe put her hands up. "I think it would be good for you to go see him. It has nothing to do with agreeing with Cal."

"Anyway, the real problem here is finding whoever switched Ace," Grayson said. "I want to find our real brother. He's out there somewhere and probably has no idea where he really came from."

"I feel so bad for Ace," Ainsley said. "Why isn't he here?"

"He's laying low for now," Callum said. "Until we can find out who shot Dad."

"Yeah, but he's all alone," Ainsley said. "And what he must be going through, dealing with the discovery that he isn't a Colton by blood. Does he think we all consider him an outsider?"

"I don't think so," Callum said. "At least, not everyone."

"Dad?" Marlowe put in. "Kicking him out of Colton Oil?"

"It's not enough to make Ace try to kill him," Grayson said.

"I think all of us want to believe that," Ainsley said.

"Yeah," Rafe said.

"Of course," Asher said. He walked into the kitchen, lone wolf that he was.

"Let's start with finding Luella," Callum said.

"Hey," Marlowe said. "Let's turn this into a celebration for Callum and Hazel—and Evie, too."

"Hear, hear." Ainsley lifted her glass.

Callum turned to Hazel and slipped his arm around her waist. "Hear, hear, for sure."

THE SIBLINGS BEGAN talking of other things, leaving Callum and Hazel with a moment to themselves.

"Let me show you my wing," Callum said. "You can tell me what you think."

He took her to the third level. It took some time to get there, the home was so large. Then he arrived at a door and opened it. She stepped inside an expansive seating area with a high ceiling, a fireplace and a balcony. There was a bar, as well, and a dining table and kitchenette. That she didn't like. He showed her the master suite. It was magnificent, with a huge bathroom. No room for Evie.

"It doesn't seem suitable for a family," she said.

"I thought the same. I didn't expect you to want to live here. We can build a house here on the ranch or somewhere else."

She would probably like his family but living so close to them seemed too much for her. She preferred to have her privacy. They could come see his family as often as he liked.

"I'm not sure I want to wait that long to move into a house," she said.

"All right." He smiled. "We'll look somewhere in town." He kissed her and, as always, their chemistry heated. With a bed so close, taking this further was tempting, but with his siblings and her daughter downstairs, they should be getting back.

Hazel drew away and just looked at Callum, into his

loving and incredible blue eyes. She had to be one of the luckiest women in the world.

HAZEL AND CALLUM opted for staying at the Dales Inn until they could find a house. They were headed there now, with Callum driving. But then she noticed he wasn't heading in the direction of town.

"Where are we going?"

"I have a surprise for you," he said with a wily grin.

"Callum Colton, what are you up to?"

"Yeah. Whatcha up to?" Evie asked from the back seat.

"You'll see. If I tell you it will ruin the surprise." He drove into a rural area outside Mustang Valley city limits, into an affluent neighborhood with large homes but not mansions. The houses were all stone with big windows and each measured about five thousand square feet.

She had a pretty good idea what his surprise was going to be. She turned to him.

"If you don't like it, we can look for another one," Callum said, having read her glance.

What was there not to like?

He pulled to a stop in front of a beautiful gray stone house with white trim. There was a veranda next to the front portico and a turret on the other side.

"My family already owns this house," Callum said. "It's technically a Colton family property but my mom, as my dad's representative, said she could transfer the title to us once we're married."

"It's beautiful." She helped Evie out of the truck and walked toward the front entrance. Inside, a two-story foyer soared above a spiral staircase going to the second level. The formal living room to the left had a fireplace and was open to the dining room, where double doors led to the veranda. A groin-vaulted ceiling over a short hallway opened to the living room and kitchen area.

The kitchen.

It was obviously professional grade, but without an overwhelming amount of stainless steel, with white walls and recessed lighting. The perimeter cabinets were white and the countertops soft green granite. The kitchen island drew her like a magnet. It had a green hood with a pan holder where several pots and pans already hung. There was a five-burner stove set in dark brown and tan granite that had a counter-mounted pot filler, which allowed a cook to fill big pots with water. The stainless steel refrigerator was twice the size of the one in her apartment. There were two ovens and a microwave was mounted into a cabinet. It was a dream kitchen.

"It was designed for hired cooks to entertain guests who stay here," Callum said.

Overwhelmed, Hazel turned in a circle and just admired it. She felt like she was in a dream. "I don't need to see the rest of the house."

"Can I pick out my room?" Evie asked.

Callum chuckled. "Sure." He showed them two master suites and two other bedrooms on the second level. There was also a theater room. He took them to a room done in pale blue, light gray and white that had a built-in oversized bunk bed, the top more like a mini balcony. There was a seating area, built-in bookshelf and an antique trunk.

"Wow!" Evie ran to the bunk bed and climbed up the white ladder to her tower, peering down at them with a big smile.

"There's toys in the trunk," Callum said. "Marlowe had it filled."

"Come on," he said to Hazel, "You need to pick out our room."

The two master suites were similar except one was decorated in darker colors and the one she fell in love with was more like a beach-house bedroom. The closet was big enough to be another bedroom.

"Oh, Callum. I can't believe this." She faced him. How could she have gotten so lucky?

"I take it you're willing to live here?" he asked.

"More than willing. This is wonderful."

"Good, then we'll get help bringing our things here in the morning."

"Oh, my…" She turned in another circle. "Are you sure?" Did he really want *her*?

He walked to her. "You deserve it." Sliding his hand around to her back, he pulled her to him.

"How will I ever match all this extravagance? I can never give you anything like this."

"You gave me your love, that's enough for me."

"But…"

"Shh. What is mine is yours. Never feel otherwise."

That would take some time. She'd have to get accustomed to having money. But she would never take it for granted. She appreciated him getting them a reasonably sized house. And for thinking of her profession. She would have to pinch herself every day to make sure it was real.

"I love you," she said.

"I love you, too." He kissed her.

"I want to have your baby." She kissed him.

"Let's get started right away."

She smiled against his lips. As soon as Evie was asleep, she'd like nothing more.

* * * * *

COMING SOON!

We really hope you enjoyed reading this book. If you're looking for more romance, be sure to head to the shops when new books are available on

Thursday 6th March

To see which titles are coming soon, please visit

millsandboon.co.uk/nextmonth

LET'S TALK

Romance

For exclusive extracts, competitions
and special offers, find us online:

f facebook.com/millsandboon

🐦 @MillsandBoon

📷 @MillsandBoonUK

Get in touch on 01413 063232

For all the latest titles coming soon, visit

millsandboon.co.uk/nextmonth